Strays of Rio

Edith Parzefall

MuseItUp Publishing
www.museituppublishing.com

Strays of Rio © 2013 by Edith Parzefall

MuseItUp Publishing
14878 James, Pierrefonds, Quebec, Canada, H9H 1P5

Cover Art © 2012 by Nika Dixon
Edited by Tanja Cilia
Copyedited by Les Tucker
Layout and Book Production by Lea Schizas

Print ISBN: 978-1-77127-313-8
eBook ISBN: 978-1-77127-149-3
Production by MuseItUp Publishing

Acknowledgements

I'm most grateful to RUA e.V. and Grupo Ruas e Praças, who helped me gain first hand experience with the situation of street kids in Brazil, and to Monika Weiß, my travel companion and interpreter when my limited knowledge of Portuguese failed me. Amnesty International and Brazzil.com provided an invaluable source of background information. A special thanks goes to Thomas Rölz, my weapons advisor, and Todd Ferguson for giving me the chance to shoot real firearms. Any errors and shortcomings of this book are my own fault.

And a big thank you to the members of the Internet Writing Workshop, who helped me forge this novel in the heat of their critiques, and to my untiring alpha and beta readers, Rebecca and Antje.

For Todd Ferguson.
J'll never forget that day
in the Oregon woods and
many other great experiences.

Edith Parzefall

Prologue

Lisa Kerry lay on the roof of an abandoned factory. She watched the curved bridge through the scope of her sniper rifle. Only the fading daylight worried her. No choice though. Vitor Fraga still worked the night shifts. He hadn't changed his ways.

She waited and scanned the cars for his old silver Ford. She'd fantasized about this moment for years, the scenarios ever-changing, the outcome always the same: Vitor Fraga taking his last breath.

The monotony of commuter traffic affected her alertness, but her aching elbows and hipbones kept her focused. Through the sights she scrutinized every silver car. Her eyes burned. Blinking, she swept her gaze over the shoe-box houses of the *favela*, decrepit factories, and warehouses, before she returned to the inspection of a never-ending procession of cars, buses, and trucks.

There. A Ford. Plate matched. Lisa tensed, shifted position, and adjusted the rifle's barrel on the sandbag. The car came straight toward her. Reflections danced over the windshield. She could only make out the silhouette of a human being. Except that he hardly fit the definition of human. Rage filled her. She concentrated on her breathing. Only the one chance. Captain Hook must die.

Crosshairs on the right front tire, she waited for the car to approach the curve. Now. Lisa pulled the trigger. Despite the silencer, the shot reverberated around her. The tire burst. The vehicle swerved, went off the bridge, and dropped thirty meters, hitting the rocky ground engine-first.

Lisa pointed the scope at the busted driver-side window and searched for a sign of life. His head rested on the steering wheel. Surprisingly, macho-man had worn the seat belt. Was he unconscious or dead? A flame licked the side of the car.

When the fire reached his body, he still didn't move. She closed her eyes and lowered the weapon. She felt elation, relief, satisfaction. Little girls would sleep untroubled in their cells. If only she could tell them they'd be safe tonight. Memories rose, and Lisa smelled the rancid odor of greasy hair and unwashed bodies huddled together in a futile attempt to protect one another.

She opened her eyes and concentrated on the here and now. Cars stopped, and people clambered out to gawk. A woman flipped open a cellphone. Two men, one carrying a small fire extinguisher, half ran, half slid down the slope toward the burning car.

Lisa lifted the rifle and focused on the blackening figure in the driver's seat. With his face charred and hair seared, Vitor Fraga was beyond help.

Time to go, time to forget him. Lisa collected the spent shell. Better not to leave pixie dust, Tinker Bell. She grabbed the sandbag and her bottle of water, even though it was unlikely anyone would come looking for evidence. Accidents happened. People died. Particularly in Rio de Janeiro.

Chapter One

Screams jerked Luiz awake. Black palm leaves swayed against the dark sky. The beach, right. He jumped to his feet. Sound asleep, his friends sprawled on the sand. Tatu rolled over and muttered something. Music blared from the Copacabana bars on the other side of the street. Yelling and drunken arguments wafted over but he caught no sign of trouble.

Calming down, Luiz strolled toward the street. At a far corner, a group of tourists negotiated with a *traficante*. A crowd spilled out of one bar and moved on to the next. Two prostitutes approached them, hips swinging.

A hunched man and a young boy drew Luiz's attention. They didn't fit. The grownup pushed the boy down the stairs to the public toilets.

Luiz's heart hammered. He took a deep breath and decided to check. He ran over the cool sand, jumped the low wall, and silently crept down the concrete stairs, which felt even colder under his bare feet. Recoiling at the stench of piss, he stepped through the door.

A whimper from one of the stalls. Luiz's heart thumped against his ribs. What now? The boy might just be earning himself a meal.

"No, stop! Don't."

Luiz's stomach cramped. He thrust his shoulder into the only closed door and bounced back.

A man's voice snarled, "Fuck off."

Luiz kicked the door in, pushing the occupants against the toilet bowl and wall behind. The man cried out, his arms reaching for a hold. Luiz wanted to kick his bare ass, but he might squash the boy. He grabbed the man by the neck of his shirt and yanked him out of the stall. With his pants around his ankles, the guy stumbled and fell in front of the wash basins, swearing. Luiz kicked him in the stomach. He wanted to give the bastard the beating of his life while he was down.

Behind him, the boy sobbed. Luiz reined in his scorn and squatted in front of the kid, who'd pulled up his shorts and sat on the toilet, hiding his face in his hands. Luiz hadn't seen him in Copacabana before. Probably new to living in the streets, and its dangers. Luiz knew better than to touch him. "Hey, it's okay. He'll leave you alone now."

"I should fuck both of you," the man yelled. Luiz guessed he felt a lot braver back in his pants. He looked over his shoulder and watched him take two more steps. Luiz scowled. The man hadn't lost his craving. No use fighting fair against a bulk like his. He had to hurt him bad. All his muscles tensed. In the toilet stall he could hardly move. He needed to let him get nearer.

The guy took another step. Close enough. Luiz jumped to his feet. Spinning, he hit the man in the face with his elbow. A roar of pain. Blood shot from the guy's nose. Facing the big man, Luiz kneed him in the groin and shoved the whimpering bastard against the opposite wall between two basins. He patted him down, took his money from the wallet, and slipped it back into the man's pocket. Satisfied, Luiz pushed him toward the door and watched him shuffle away, blood dripping from his nose.

Luiz crouched next to the boy, who stared at his feet. "You got any friends here?"

The boy wiped at his eyes and shook his head. He was at least two years younger than Luiz, twelve at most.

"You want to stay with us? We're a tough gang. No one messes with us."

Eyes still filled with tears, the boy nodded.

"Okay, good. I'm Luiz. What's your name?"

"Ubaldo," he mumbled.

"Let's go."

Ubaldo trailed after Luiz. "He said he'd give me money."

"He might have."

The boy heaved a shuddering breath. "It hurt. I begged. But he wouldn't stop."

"I know. Forget it. Here, this is yours." Luiz slapped the bills in his hand.

Ubaldo stared at them. "Eighty *reais*?"

Outside, Luiz sucked in the cool, salty air. Much better. They walked to a copse of palm trees. Tatu stepped from the shadows and waved. "Thought you might bring back something." He grinned.

"This is Ubaldo. He'll stay with us, at least for a while."

7

Tatu slapped the boy on the back. "Hope you know how to earn your food."

Ubaldo flinched and darted Luiz a worried look.

Chapter Two

Lisa stepped through the gate of her run-down apartment building in Copacabana and let the latch fall into the lock. Walking down the street, she gazed up the hill and the *favela* hugging it. The shantytowns kept growing. More of the wooden shacks had been replaced with small brick houses over the years. Built on the slopes, they cascaded upon each other. White satellite dishes on many rooftops reflected the morning light.

Rounding the corner, she saw the pharmacist in a white lab coat chase off street kids. Drowsy and frozen looking, they shuffled away. No sign of Ubaldo. A loner, the boy had slept in the doorway of her bookstore for the last two weeks or so. She scanned the street. What if the police picked him up and threw him into a detention center? They didn't need a reason. Nausea curdled her stomach, as buried memories crawled up on her.

Shivering, she pulled the key from her jeans pocket and unlocked the shop. The familiar smell—a combination of old books, ancient carpet, and dust—welcomed her. In the front room, floor-to-ceiling shelves overflowed with books. She set her shoulder bag on a chair behind the counter and strode to the back room to fetch the cash locked in a safe overnight. The door bells tinkled. Ubaldo entered, followed by four more kids, one of them a girl with brown matted curls and a shy smile.

Her relief at seeing Ubaldo unharmed turned to wariness. Lisa pushed the cashbox under the counter. "*Oi*, Ubaldo. Everything okay?"

The boy fidgeted, his eyes darting around. She put her hand on her hip, close to the belt holster hidden beneath her wide shirt. Her fingers slipped under the fabric and touched the cold metal.

"*Tudo bem*, Lisa. They are friends. They wanted to see where I work."

The tallest boy looked around at the other kids. Then his gaze traveled over the bookshelves and settled on the counter, under which she'd shoved the money. Lisa's fingers slipped over the pistol's grip.

His T-shirt was torn but fairly clean. Sand stuck to his dreadlocks on one side; he and his friends must have slept at the beach and washed their bodies and clothes in the sea. They'd be hungry now.

The tall boy shrugged then met her gaze. "Ubaldo really works for you?" His incredulous voice and the frank look eased her tension.

Picking up no violent vibes, Lisa relaxed her grip on the gun and nodded. "Yeah, why not? Earns him a meal a day."

A pretty boy, with chocolate-colored skin and dimples in his cheeks, laughed and slapped the taller one on the back. "Hey, Luiz, we'll call him Professor."

The others smirked or giggled, while Ubaldo stared at his feet.

She decided to rescue him. "All right, we've got work to do. What about you guys?"

Luiz snorted. "No, Senhora, we lead a life of leisure."

She laughed. He'd likely learned that phrase from a soap opera on TV. He sure had a sense of humor. She dropped her hand and relaxed her shoulder muscles. "Too bad. I could use some help clearing out the backyard. It's full of junk. Maybe you could sell some of it. But of course I wouldn't ask your highness to do such a menial job."

Luiz tilted his head, as if deciding whether to trust her. A smile lit up his eyes. "Show us."

Lisa led them through the back room out to the yard, where the odds and ends left by the previous tenants lay scattered about. She had no clue why she wanted to get rid of it now, but her doubts vanished when she looked into the kids' awed faces, while they scanned her treasures. "Tell me your names," she said.

"I'm Luiz and this is Tatu." He pointed his thumb to the cute boy with the dimples.

She couldn't help smiling. "Tatu?"

"Yeah, cause I'm tough like an armadillo." Tatu grinned.

Luiz slapped a chubby boy on the back. "Gordinho." Then he bowed to the pretty girl. "And Princess Rena."

The boys smiled, but Rena scowled at Luiz. She reminded Lisa a lot of her younger self when she had to fend for herself—before things went seriously wrong. How did Rena end up on the streets? "I'm Lisa. So, you want the job?"

Luiz grinned. "How much?"

She scratched her head and looked at the collection. A toilet seat, an old mattress, lumps of old clothes, some boards that might have been a shelf once, broken plant pots, and more fragments of other people's lives. Between the four of them, it should be cleaned up in two hours, she guessed. "Ten *reais* for each of you. And you can keep or sell whatever you want."

Luiz's grin broadened. "Deal."

Lisa nodded and strolled back into the store. Ubaldo followed her. "What do you want me to do?"

"Make us some coffee. Have you eaten anything?"

Ubaldo shook his head while he jumped to his first task.

Lisa pulled a twenty-*reais* bill from the back pocket of her jeans and tossed it on the counter. "Get us some bread and cheese. Enough for everyone."

She smiled at Ubaldo's wide-eyed stare, aware that she might never get rid of the lot if she started feeding them. Like cats, they'd just keep coming back for more.

So what? She had more in common with these kids than with her own family.

After sorting the coins and bills into the cash register, she shoved fifty *reais* into her pocket to give to the kids. Ubaldo switched on the coffee maker and dashed outside.

Lisa dusted off the guidebooks in the window, wondering how Rena had survived so far. She was well-developed—probably around thirteen years old. Did the boys in the gang take advantage of her?

Lisa straightened and stared out the window. The street had come alive with locals on their way to work. Most tourists would still be recovering from last night's partying, but around ten o'clock business should pick up. Ubaldo sprinted across the street, his arms clutching paper bags. Lisa opened the door for him. "That was quick."

"I'm hungry!"

Lisa ruffled his greasy hair. "Take the food outside and eat with your friends." She followed him to the back door but stopped short to observe the kids, unnoticed. Luiz and Tatu had collected pieces of metal and piled them in a heap. Watching them shuffle through the trash, Lisa realized how lucky she'd been. Thanks to Jango.

Ubaldo yelled, "Food."

"Huh? For us?" Luiz stared at him. Tatu sprinted across the yard, chased by the others. They sat in a circle on the concrete near their treasure and dug in.

"Is she a bit crazy?" Tatu asked.

Lisa stepped back, smiling to herself. *Just a bit*. The door bells jingled.

* * * *

Lisa did her best to keep three customers happy at the same time and prayed her assistant would recover quickly from the flu. One woman finally decided which Paulo Coelho novel she wanted to buy, and her friend chose *The House of Spirits*. Lisa moved on to the guy lurking in the used books section. A foreigner, definitely. Red shirt, checkered shorts, and Ray-Ban sunglasses. She addressed him in English. "May I help you, sir?"

He turned and flashed a wide smile. "I hope so. You do city tours?"

"Yes, but I'm a bit short-staffed at the moment."

He grinned. "Sorry, already got a job."

Lisa laughed. "Too bad. I'm desperate enough to hire you."

"You sound American."

"I spent some time in the U.S."

"Where?"

The door bells tinkled once again and drew her attention. Two young women entered. Instead of browsing the shelves, they stood waiting for assistance. She turned back to the American. "How long are you in town?"

His cellphone rang. "Sorry." The muscles in his jaws twitched as he looked at the display. "Might take awhile."

Lisa showed the newcomers several Rio guidebooks and explained the strengths of each. She noticed the American leaving the shop, cellphone still pressed against his ear.

Around noon the bookstore emptied and Lisa collapsed onto a chair. Only a few minutes later, Luiz walked in from the back. "We're done."

"Let's take a look, then." Lisa followed him outside.

A wooden pushcart stood loaded with scrap metal. A bike with a huge metal basket between mismatched wheels spilled over with rags. Tatu balanced on the saddle, hands and feet in the air. Rena poked him in the side. He yelped and almost fell. The girl giggled and jumped out of his reach. Lisa's heart warmed. Rena wouldn't dare tease them if they treated her badly.

Ubaldo stood by, as if afraid they'd leave him behind. "Can I come along?"

Gordinho pushed him toward Lisa. "Better stay with her, Professor. That's safer for a baby like you."

Tears welled up in Ubaldo's eyes. Lisa wanted to pull him into her arms, but he'd better learn to take care of himself.

"Leave him alone," Luiz barked.

Lisa hoped they'd take care of him. The boy had grown on her.

Luiz turned to her. "Looks okay?"

Smiling, she pulled the bills out of her back pocket and handed him four ten-*reais* notes. "Yeah, nice work."

Luiz took the money and pointed at the old workshop. "That yours?"

No one had used the shed in years, and she hadn't looked inside since the last renter moved out. "Why?"

Luiz stared at her for several seconds then shook his head. "Just curious."

* * * *

Lisa locked the door and rolled down the iron shutters. She wondered if she'd find Ubaldo waiting for her in the morning. She never expected to care, but he'd brought long-buried memories and instincts back. And Rena, even more so.

The entrance to the apartments above the store lay just around the corner, but her grumbling stomach caused Lisa to make a detour along a street lined with restaurants and snack bars. She watched her step as roots of large trees skewed the pavement slabs. A wooden cage hung from a thick branch, entrapping a bird, its song reserved for those walking under the tree.

The low sun blinded her. While she tried to decide what she wanted, a hand grabbed her left arm from behind. She spun around, heart pounding. Her hand flew to the gun.

"Sorry, didn't mean to scare you. I called, but you didn't..." The American stepped back and pushed his sunglasses up in his short blond hair. "Whoa, don't shoot." He stared at her gun.

Lisa pulled her shirt over the compact pistol and took slow deep breaths, relaxing her muscles the way she'd learned. She'd almost shot him. Calm settled over her as she focused on his sparkling blue eyes. He might be a few years older than her, mid-thirties.

She cleared her throat. "Sorry about that." She hadn't overreacted like this in years.

"I saw you lock up and wondered if you'd like to have dinner with me."

Lisa narrowed her eyes. "Why don't you go to one of the bars on Avenida Atlantica and wait until a pretty girl chats you up? Shouldn't take long." She turned and marched off.

"Hey, wait a minute. Jango sent me."

She stopped and turned. "You work with Jango?"

"Yes, he recommended you as a tour guide."

With the adrenaline draining, she managed a smile. "Let's talk about it tomorrow, over dinner. What's your name?"

"Tony Norton."

"Lisa Kerry."

He tilted his head. "Are you okay?"

Lisa followed his gaze to her shaking hands.

Chapter Three

The air conditioning in the car chilled the sweat on Félix's skin. He glanced over at the American slumped in the passenger seat. Wet spots marked his blue shirt.

Félix pointed ahead. "The Sugar Loaf. Have you been up there?"

Norton straightened in his seat. "No, not yet."

"You should go." Félix had no clue where the fame of this particular rock originated, but the view from the top was stunning. "I can drop you off at the cable car station if you want." Would save him a few kilometers drive. He should have put Norton in a cab instead of offering a ride.

"No thanks, I'll take a city tour."

Félix smirked. Maybe he was one of the timid guys who didn't dare to set a foot outside the hotel on his own, calling in the hookers, drinking at the hotel bar. Of course, Norton had buckled up as soon as he got in the car. Félix never wore a seat belt.

He was not afraid to die—and he loved to make money off the fear of weaker men. His customers called themselves the elite, because they had money and power, but they wouldn't survive one night out, alone in the city. Without his security installations, they'd be scared shitless in their luxury apartments and villas. Even the fortresses built for the rich wouldn't be obstacles, without the alarm systems, cameras, electric fences, and armed guards.

They entered the tunnel leading to Copacabana.

"How did you get into this line of work?" Norton asked.

"It gives me a deep sense of satisfaction to work for the good of the community, to help protect people and businesses." What he hated about his job was acting as if he actually cared about their safety. "We can't let the scum take what honest people have worked so hard for." He glanced sideways at the American. Norton stiffened. He probably thought that was a bit extreme, but what did he know?

The car in front of him slowed. Félix slammed the brakes and honked. "Kind of ironic," he continued. "In the sixties your government sent security specialists to this country, now the roles are reversed. I'm advising you."

"Not sure what you're talking about."

"Specialists teaching police procedures..."

"You mean torture and intimidation? No need to put it so politely. We screwed up the major part of South America. Nothing to be proud of."

"No, this country would have gone to hell if it hadn't been for the support from the U.S. against communism. My uncle received some training in interrogation techniques." Félix could feel Norton's stare and decided to back off. "I grew up with some pretty gross stories."

"You mean he was one of the torturers under the military regime? Your uncle?"

"Fortunately those days are over. Now it's all about business. And, once again, security." Back on track, Félix smiled at Norton, who seemed to relax.

"What's the actual risk of burglary to a company like ours—or maybe even armed robbery?"

Félix stopped at a red light and revved the engine. He grinned. "If you go with our full surveillance system, you and your company will never find out."

Norton laughed. "I sure hope not. Almost got shot yesterday evening. That's enough excitement for me."

Always the same with the stupid *gringos*, stumbling into places they shouldn't go. "Already? How did it feel?"

"What?"

"To have a gun pointed at you. How did it feel to be at the mercy of a criminal?" Félix asked with growing excitement.

Tony snorted. "Rather the mercy of a pretty girl. I asked her out for dinner and she reached for her gun. Didn't fit my picture of Brazilian women."

Félix laughed until the image took on shape in his head, her gun pointing at him instead of the *gringo*. "Must have been quite an experience. Who was she?"

Tony chuckled. "You'll never believe me. She sells books and does city tours."

Excitement coursed through his body. "Books and guns. Fascinating." Why did something like that never happen to him?

"Do you know where the Copacabana Palace Hotel is?" Norton asked.

"Of course." Only the best for the *gringo*. Hopefully he'd also buy the best security system. His. He turned into Avenida Atlantica and saw the large colonial building. Just a little longer and he'd head back north to find a playmate.

Norton looked at his watch. "Actually, do you mind taking me a few blocks farther and turn right?"

"Not at all. Tell me when."

"At the next light."

And the light turned red. *Merda!* Félix stopped the car. They sat in silence until it changed to green. He gunned the engine. From the corner of his eye he saw Norton grab the overhead handle. Félix smiled.

"Nice little car," Norton said.

What an idiot. The low growl of the two-liter engine agreed with him. "A Mazda MX-5."

"Turn left here, please."

He did so, grudgingly.

"Okay, kick me out wherever you can stop."

Félix pulled into a driveway. "I'll see you tomorrow," he said and held out his hand.

Norton shook it. "*Obrigado*."

"*De nada*."

Félix winced when Norton slammed the door shut. What piece-of-shit car did he drive back home? He waited and watched the *gringo* cross the street and walk straight up to a woman pulling down the shutter of a bookstore. He jerked up in his seat.

The girl with the gun? He released his grip on the steering wheel and studied her: tall, slender, dark blond hair. The color of her skin showed a trace of slave blood.

She smiled when the gringo materialized by her side. As she turned, something bulged above her right hip.

They walked down the street, not in the direction of Norton's hotel but towards the beach. Félix felt tempted to follow them, get a better look at her. Maybe she'd make a challenging playmate. A woman who'd fight back.

They rounded the next corner. He eased the sports car back into traffic and drove past the bookstore. A gang of street kids slipped through the gate between two buildings. Just like rats. He turned into the side street. Ahead he spotted Norton—and the woman carrying a gun.

Chapter Four

Lisa and Tony reached Avenida Atlantica, the main street along Copacabana beach. "Something typical Brazilian?" she asked, her stomach grumbling with anticipation.

"What?" Tony gave her a blank stare.

She tilted her head toward a *churrascaria*. "Food. This is a pretty nice place."

"Sure."

She led him inside and asked for a table at the window. The delicious smell of roasted meat wafted through the air-conditioned room. "You seem a little preoccupied."

Tony flopped onto a chair, rested his elbow on the table, and placed his chin in his hand. "I met this weird security adviser today." He shook his head. "And I thought Americans were racist."

Lisa burst out laughing. "You guys are a bunch of amateurs when it comes to racism."

The hint of a smile played around the corners of his mouth. Then he craned his neck. The smile vanished. "I think I just saw him walk past."

Lisa turned in her chair. "Where?"

"He's gone," Tony murmured. "Strange. He'd sounded in a hurry to get somewhere."

The waiter ambled toward their table, offering beef. Lisa nodded and he slid a piece off the spit for each of them. She ordered *caipirinha*, Tony likewise.

"You can get salads, vegetables, and other side dishes at the buffet."

Tony followed her. While they filled their plates, he asked, "Do you always carry a gun?"

"Yes, but usually I'm more in control." They walked back to their table, where the cocktails already waited for them. She took a big gulp. "You shouldn't have grabbed me."

"Sorry, I…"

"Not your fault, really."

Tony gave her a rueful smile. "Something to tell my grandchildren."

"You look a bit young for a granddad."

"So far, I haven't found the right grandma." His smile creased the corners of his eyes. Lisa didn't believe he had difficulties picking up women, especially in Rio. Blond hair and blue eyes, tall and broad-shouldered, a bit of a sun tan, and a charming smile. Tempting.

No. She had come a long way but knew her limits.

He tasted the beef. "Mmh. Excellent." He chewed with his eyes half closed then gazed at her. "So, you gonna give me a tour?"

Lisa leaned back in her chair. "Let me guess, the most picturesque spots of Rio. A sunset on the Sugar Loaf and then off to a samba rehearsal, and party all night."

He nodded with a hint of mischief in his eyes. "Sounds great, except I'm not much of a dancer. Maybe you can teach me."

The waiter stopped by their table again, offering more meat. Tony nodded, Lisa declined.

"Three hundred and no party," she said.

He cocked an eyebrow. "Dollars?"

Well, she'd meant *reais*, but if he insisted on paying twice as much... "And that's for the tour, not for me," she added.

"Of course. Ah, that's a bit expensive, isn't it?"

"Yes, because I'm trying to discourage you."

"No way."

She couldn't deny a little excitement sneaking up on her. "Sunday, then?"

"Deal."

Tony pushed the veggies around on his plate. "How about a walk on the beach?"

"Sure, it's not that late." Lisa's gaze swept over the esplanade. Most vendors were packing up for the night.

Tony frowned at her. "Is it dangerous at night?"

Lisa shrugged. "Let's say it gets a bit more interesting." She winked. Rio couldn't scare her anymore.

* * * *

Lisa and Tony strolled along the broad sidewalk, patterned with waves of black and white limestone mosaic. By nightfall, the strip of sand cleared of the sunbathers, though small groups still lingered. Someone played a guitar.

"Sounds like 'Hey Jude', doesn't it?" Tony said.

They reached three backpackers sitting on the steps to the beach. Tony stopped and listened to the twang of the guitar. Lisa would have walked on, but one of the guys patted the spot next to him, inviting them to sit. Tony didn't hesitate.

"Hey, mate," the guitarist greeted Tony and waved at Lisa. "Don't be shy, guys."

She sat cross-legged in the cooling sand, facing them.

"You mind?" Tony nodded toward the guitar.

"Go ahead, man."

Tony took the instrument, played a few chords then pitched into Steve Earle's 'Copperhead Road'. Lisa stretched out her legs and leaned back on her elbows. He was good. Irony rang in his voice, mischief played on his face. His eyes met hers. A smile spread over Lisa's face.

The charm ended with the song's hook-line warning to stay away from Copperhead Road. Lisa sat up. The backpackers cheered him, but Tony looked only at her.

The red-haired fellow held out a bottle of wine. She shook her head. Tony handed the guitar back and accepted the bottle. He took a swig and waved it at her.

"Let's go," she mouthed.

He jumped up, held out a hand, and pulled her to her feet. She turned to the backpackers. "Better be careful on the beach at night. Don't even think about sleeping here."

"No worries."

"Let's go to the waterfront," Tony said.

Lisa slipped out of her flip-flops and carried them in one hand. Tony's arm brushed against hers. The sensation of his skin rubbing against hers sent a jolt through her. She inched away. What the hell was she doing here? A wave washed over her naked feet. She gasped.

"Want to go for a swim?" he asked.

"I don't have a bikini with me."

"It's dark." He looked up into the starry southern sky blurred by the blazing lights of Rio.

If only she could. "You don't want to get arrested for nude bathing."

He grinned. "If we can share a cell, I wouldn't mind."

Images of moldy mattresses on a concrete floor hit her. The dank smell. Sweat. Trying to shake off the memories, Lisa stared at the dark ocean and the white waves rolling toward the coastline. "I hate to destroy your illusions…"

"Then don't." He ran his fingers through her tresses.

She couldn't bear his touch. Vitor Fraga had liked to play with her hair. Or yank it, if she didn't obey. Her heart hammered. She brushed off Tony's hand. "You wouldn't enjoy my company, or the room service." Her voice sounded flat and cold. Like a stranger's. "Go back to your hotel."

She spun around and sprinted toward the street, fighting back tears. Vitor Fraga laughed and rattled the closet doors. Didn't matter that he was long dead; he lived on in the dark recesses of her mind.

Chapter Five

Max sat across from Luiz and Tatu at the large table in the *boca*, his headquarters. He dismantled his new Colt, a gift from the commando's lawyer, while the boys poured cocaine into small plastic bags and put them on the scales. Soon they'd finish the batch.

So much for Max's plan to keep the boys away from him by giving them dull jobs whenever they showed up. The brats seemed to enjoy it, concentrating so hard they'd even stopped babbling.

Max stood and walked over to the glassless window. Last night five of his people died when a rival gang tried to take over his *favela*. If only he could find a way to keep his little brother and Luiz safe. He turned around to face the boys.

Luiz nudged Tatu. "Don't sneeze." They both cracked up.

Max shook his head, smiling. He'd taught them to survive on the streets, but they were still children.

Fireworks went off. "Ah fuck! Police. Get outta here. Now!" Max grabbed his assault rifle and ran up the stairs to the roof. The first gunshots echoed through the air.

Four of his men crouched at the edge of the roof, their assault rifles searching for targets. Átila spoke into his walkie-talkie, giving instructions and collecting information. "Nothing moves uphill, boss. They can't be serious."

Max scanned the main routes leading up to the *boca* and spotted small troops of military police storming toward them, shooting more for show than anything else. A minor raid, only five squad cars parked on the border road. The cops yelled, warning people to stay in their houses. Always a great joke. "Fucking bastards," Max hissed.

His gaze swept uphill, where he saw Luiz and Tatu running up a set of stairs before they disappeared between the houses. They knew where to hide.

"Okay, let's go." Max jumped from one flat roof to the next, his soldiers close behind him, then dropped into an alley. He ran over a wooden bridge crossing the stinking garbage stream and headed further uphill. He turned a corner and burst through the door of their weapons depot, startling his soldiers, who loaded assault rifles and attached hand grenades to their belts.

"Easy on the artillery. Only five cars."

"What'd they want then?" Beda asked.

Max snorted. "More money, I guess. We'll teach them a lesson. Nobody gets hurt and we'll be doing business again in a few hours. They're just flexing their muscles."

Lana pouted. "I wanted to try the grenade launchers."

Max grinned back at her. She'd only been with the gang for a year but was more reckless than any of the boys. "Sorry, not today, baby."

They spread out and occupied the four main lookout points, staying in contact via walkie-talkie. Max and Átila dashed up the stairs to the roof of a four-story house and found Mussolini perched on the edge with his binoculars. He looked up at the sound of their footsteps. "Nassar leads the raid," he reported.

Max nodded and took the binoculars. He scanned the narrow lanes and found Nassar edging along a wall, followed by one of his men. The bastard got greedier every day. There could be only one reason for the raid. Nassar wanted to catch Max, hoping he'd pay him off big time.

Max had to put an end to it. Now. "Hey, Mussolini, keep watching the fuckers and let me know what Nassar is doing. I'll get him." He waved Átila along and handed Mussolini the binoculars.

From two different directions, Max and Átila snuck up on the sergeant. Hiding around a corner, Max waited for the cops. It seemed to take forever. About to ask Mussolini if they had changed direction, Max glimpsed the steel-gray sleeve of the military police uniform. He trained his pistol at the face of Nassar. The bulletproof vest wouldn't help him much.

They looked at each other, Max grinning, the sergeant narrowing his eyes to slits.

"Drop your guns," Max said when the second cop stumbled around the corner, with Átila close behind, poking a gun in his back.

Nassar scowled. "What the hell you think you're doing?"

"Can't you tell? I'm teaching you manners. So you don't come storming in here bothering innocent people anymore." Max took the man's submachine gun, slung it over his shoulder, and prized the pistol from his hands.

Nassar snorted. "Listen man, we got a new captain."

"And he wants more money?" Max frowned.

"Worse." Nassar sneered. "He wants to clean up."

Confused, Max stared at the police sergeant. "Clean up?"

"With the drug gangs and police corruption." Nassar smirked. "I don't think he'll live long."

Max handed the pistol back and scratched his head. "He seriously thinks he can fight the biggest business in the country? His own men live off the drugs."

Nassar shrugged. "Of course he can't do it, but the fucker will try. He's good friends with some BOPE big shots. You don't want to have the special forces of the military police on your heels, do you?"

"Damned Skulls. The arrogant bastards won't even take a bribe. Still, your raids sure make our customers nervous." Max shook his head. "The boss won't like this."

"No one likes it. So I thought we'd create a little fuss to keep up appearances. Hey, your playboy customers might even get a thrill out of the sense of danger."

"Just don't shoot anyone. What's the captain's name?"

"Emilio Costa Branca."

"I'll remember."

* * * *

When Nassar and his men retreated, Max returned to the *boca*, where a crowd of *favelados* stood grumbling and bitching. A woman had caught a stray bullet in her shoulder. As Max pushed his way through the throng, the voices died. The woman pressed a bloody towel against the wound. Two young kids were holding on to her skirt.

"Don't worry, you'll be fine." Max pulled out his walkie-talkie. "I need a car." He turned to Capone. "You take her to the hospital."

"But my children?" the woman protested.

"They can stay here. Won't take long to get the wound cleaned and dressed." He slapped a wad of money in Capone's hand. "Make sure she won't have to wait."

Max picked up the girl and grabbed the boy's hand. The mother darted him an anxious look. He smiled. "I don't eat little children, okay?"

Capone pulled her away, while the *favela* residents watched Max's every move. He studied the girl's face. About two years old, she showed no sign of anxiety while she watched her mother leave.

"We'll play until your *mamãe's* back," Max said. Inside the *boca*, he released his grip on the boy's hand and set the girl down. The cocaine and his disassembled pistol were gone. He lifted the loose floor board covering the closest hiding place, and found the stash and his gun there. His silly brother and Luiz must have hidden both before running away. As if a bit of coke was worth risking their lives for.

The girl started to cry. Max walked into the kitchen, squatted in front of the cabinets and pulled a pot and lid out, found a wooden spoon and started to drum. Attracted by the noise, the girl wobbled in, her brother following right behind her. He looked much like Tatu. His brother had been even younger when Max ran away with him, away from their crazy mother. Max handed him the pot and spoon and sat on the floor, his back resting against the wall.

He watched the kids ransack the kitchen, crawl into the cabinets, and turn them into their houses. The police raid had unnerved him, but there was nothing more relaxing than seeing children claim their space, acting as if the world was all theirs to grasp. That would change as they grew up, but for now he envied their freedom and innocence.

Átila strutted in and announced that the father of the kids was here. Max rose. "Okay, time to go home." They ignored him. Max grinned. Just like Tatu and Luiz. He walked into the main room and saw a skinny man in overalls shifting from foot to foot. "The kids are playing in the kitchen."

The man nodded and pushed past him. When he returned with the children in tow, Max held out two hundred *reais*. "I'm really sorry your wife got injured."

The man glanced at his daughter then looked up. "Can I have cocaine instead?"

Max felt like beating the shit out of him. Instead, he shoved the money back in his pocket. "I'll give this to your woman. Get the fuck out of here."

* * * *

Still mad at a father who'd rather sniff cocaine than feed his children, Max climbed up the stairs to the patio, poured himself a shot of *cachaça* at the makeshift bar, and gulped it down. He walked to the edge of the terrace and looked down at his territory. Light after light came on in the crooked houses, illuminating the hill through glassless windows. The *favela* couldn't compete with the glitter of Copacabana or Ipanema. But it was his. As long as he lasted. And no insane, honest cop would take that away from him.

Steps behind him drew closer. Soft breasts squeezed against his back. Hands slipped under his T-shirt. "Ain't you afraid I'll push you off the roof and take over the gang?" Lana asked.

Chapter Six

Lisa climbed into her car, started the engine, and set the air conditioning on full blast before she merged into the clogged-up traffic.

On Sundays, the bookstore remained closed. Usually that was her only day off—now she'd spend it working. And Tony might still expect more than a city tour. She remembered the way he looked when he played the guitar on the beach and sang. He'd called her the next day to make sure the tour was still on. Of course she couldn't blame him for the shadows skulking wherever she went. On any other Sunday, she'd go jogging along the beach. Or she'd flop down in the sand and read. She loved it when everyone was out for a walk, a bike ride, a swim. On Sundays the main streets along the beaches belonged to people, not cars, which turned into a major hassle for her now. Unable to drive down Avenida Atlantica, she had to crawl along clogged-up Avenida Copacabana to get to Tony's hotel.

She called and asked him to wait for her at the back entrance, where she could pick him up easily. She arrived five minutes late. Tony stood chatting to the doorman on duty. Wearing jeans and a white cotton shirt, Tony did not look like a hotel guest. If he lurked too long, the police might pick him up. Grinning at the silly notion, she stopped the car. Tony waved to the security guard and hopped in.

"All right, what do you want to see?" Lisa asked, easing back into the sluggish traffic.

"I don't know, you're the expert."

"Are you a soccer fan?"

Tony frowned at her. "I'm American."

"Right. So the Maracanã Stadium might not be that exciting for you. We'll start with the statue of Christ then."

"Sounds good." Tony leaned back. "Why is everyone honking all the time?" he asked.

"The most important means of communication, right after cellphones. You honk to warn someone. When you want to change lanes, you honk, begging them to let you cut in. Of course, you honk thanks afterward.

Sometimes you honk an apology after cutting someone off without honking first."

Tony chuckled. "No wonder there's so much noise."

She drove through Santa Theresa, the Bohemian, artsy part of the city. Old villas painted pink or blue with stuccoed facades lined the road. High fences safeguarded the properties.

"Everyone seems to live behind bars in this country," Tony said.

"Except in the *favelas*. But you're right. Pretty sad, isn't it?"

"Is it necessary?"

"I guess so." When she first returned to Rio, those bars had given her a sense of safety. Now she knew people locked themselves in, out of fear. But fear only grew stronger in safe places. "So, are you going to move here?"

"No, I'm just the scout, looking for a suitable office building, getting the hiring process started, and talking to suppliers, like that weird security guy. Your friend Jango is a great help, though. What does he call himself again?"

"A *despachante*—a professional agent. He helps international companies like yours set up business in Brazil and arranges passports for ordinary people who can't afford to wait in line for hours only to be sent away empty-handed. He knows how things work in Brazilian bureaucracy and greases a system where personal relationships overrule complicated laws and norms." Her mind raced. *And sometimes he finds little girls locked away in detention centers without a trial.*

Lisa parked the car. "Jango is amazing. His name opens doors." *Even prison gates.* She led Tony to the shuttle buses taking visitors up to the Statue. "Hope you brought your camera."

He tapped his temple. "Nah, I rather look and soak up the atmosphere."

They took the elevator to the lookout at Cristo Redentor's feet and gazed at Rio de Janeiro below. Little shacks made of brick spilled down the hill and met the white towers of the *centro*.

"See the *centro* with its high-rises? We'll skip that. It's deserted on Sundays."

"Really? It's been crazy during the week. People everywhere."

"Oh, right, you've been there. Even better." She pointed down the slope. "And here you see a *favela* right next to it."

"Shantytown?"

"Yep. Though many *favelados* are quite proud of their community."

"Rio is beautiful. So much green between the concrete. The hills, the white beaches, and the blue sea."

"That's why *Cariocas*, poor and rich, love their city."

"*Cariocas*?"

"The people living in Rio."

He rested his hands on the low wall and peered down. "Drug gangs rule the *favelas*, right?"

"Yes, they keep law and order. Their own laws and their own kind of order."

"And the police…"

"…have arrangements with them."

"Really? I'd never dare to offer a bribe. American cops look pretty impressive, but your military police guys make them appear like park rangers. They carry machine guns and wear bulletproof vests all day. In this heat."

Lisa turned to him. "You'd better steer clear of them."

He darted her a sideways glance. "Yeah, I've read some nasty articles."

"Most of them are probably decent guys, risking their lives for a ridiculously low salary, but that makes them dangerous. You never know what might happen when the pressure valve blows."

Tony straightened. "Do you always carry a gun?"

"You've asked me that already over dinner. Yes, always." She waited for the next question.

He faced her. "Why?"

She took a deep breath and released it. "To protect myself. I hope I'll never have to use it. I mean shoot someone." Just in time, she stopped herself from adding 'again'. "I don't carry it to scare people. I carry it for the worst-case scenario."

He looked at her intently. "Like what?"

"To save my life. Or to end it, if the alternative becomes unbearable."

Tony opened his mouth, but no words came.

She grabbed his shoulder for support and boosted herself up to stand on the low wall.

Tony grasped her wrist. "What the hell are you doing?"

Learning about Brazil's history of violence and abuse had helped her put her own suffering into perspective. "After the military coup in 1964, the witch hunt for all political enemies began. That included basically everyone with a social conscience, or anyone desperate enough to demand higher wages. Some of the prisoners were brought up here, after they'd been beaten and tortured."

"I know, by people like Félix Borges's uncle. Get down, Lisa. You're making me nervous." He tugged her arm.

"Wait. They had to stand on this wall, like I am now. Soldiers prodded them with their guns, laughing. Those who survived were brought back to their cells to suffer even more."

Tony slung his arms around her waist. "You're crazy."

For a chilling moment, a sensation of falling overcame Lisa. She relaxed into his arms as he lifted her down. His chest, pressed against her back, felt reassuring. She leaned her head against his shoulder and gazed up at his face. "If I'd been one of those prisoners, I'd have jumped."

He loosened his grip around her, his right hand lingering for a moment over the gun on her belt. "That's ancient history."

Lisa pulled away from him. "It's not. There will always be people who enjoy hurting others. And in Brazil these guys lead a pretty untroubled life." She stopped herself and looked up at the gray, simplistic figure of Cristo Redentor standing on a concrete platform, arms spread out in a never-ending blessing. Time for the tour guide spiel. "The statue's about forty meters tall —a hundred thirty feet—and weighs seven hundred tons. Built from reinforced concrete. The outer layers are soapstone. It was finished in 1931, after only nine years."

"Impressive," Tony said with little enthusiasm. He peered down the deep plunge, maybe wondering how many bodies had shattered on those rocks.

Lisa touched his back. "I'm sorry. I shouldn't have told you."

"No, it's fine. Hard to imagine, though."

"How about a hike through the rain forest?"

"Anything, as long as we get off this damned rock."

* * * *

Lisa parked the car close to the entrance gates to the Parque Nacional, grabbed her shoulder bag from the backseat, and clambered out. "We've got two options, the long or the short trail."

Tony leaned his arms on the roof of the car. "How long's the long one?"

"Three hours or so."

He smiled. "Let's do the short one."

"Wimp." She winked.

A tall, slightly hunched man with reddish hair radiating in all directions approached, grunting unintelligible sounds. He formed circles with his fingers and thumbs and held them up to his eyes, obviously used to not being understood. Tony darted a confused look at her.

She walked around the car to stand beside him. The man splayed his hands at the surrounding houses, now staring at her with an urgency that chilled her. He placed a hand on her shoulder and tried to force more words.

"Hey, buddy, keep your fingers off her." Tony pushed him back.

The man didn't look at him. His gaze fixed on Lisa. He seemed to wait for a sign of understanding.

Lisa spoke quietly, "I think he says they are watching us. He seems a bit deranged." Her gaze swept over their surroundings. "Where?"

The man shook his arm in the general direction of the hill. Lisa traced the road cutting though the forest. A flash of red caught her eye. Likely a car parked at a lookout point. Harmless enough.

Tony took her arm. "Let's go."

The man looked desperate, imitating binoculars again. Lisa nodded at him. "We'll watch out. Thanks, my friend." She patted his arm. *Poor guy.*

The trail led through thick vegetation. Lisa pointed out a pink orchid. Tony smiled and walked on. Only the large banana plants with their meaty leaves, huge purple blooms, and tiny yellow fruit appeared to impress him. "I always thought bananas grew in grocery stores."

A fluorescent blue butterfly flitted ahead of them. A rustling sound in the bushes drew her attention. A black lizard, at least an arm long, with tiny white spots, emerged and stopped. Motionless, the creature stared at them with one skeptical eye.

"Wow, that's a big one. What's it called?"

"*Teiú*. They are very docile, but shy."

"Why is its tail dirty brown?" he asked.

"Shedding its skin. See the ragged white edge? It just hasn't scrubbed off all the old tissue, yet."

Tony squatted. "Amazing." Animals obviously interested him more than plants. In that case, she knew just the place for their late lunch.

She took him to a restaurant right in the *tijuca* forest. The wind rustled the leaves of the large trees that shaded the wooden tables. Nearby a small creek glittered in the patches of sunlight. Valentim, the owner, greeted her with a kiss on each cheek, then noticed Tony. He bowed slightly and rushed to get menus.

Tony made up his mind quickly, ordered steak with mashed potatoes, and leaned back in his chair, looking up into the trees. "A beautiful place. I could hang out here all day."

Lisa ordered fish with rice in lemon sauce; then she looked at Tony's relaxed figure, so much at ease with himself and the world. Why couldn't she be like that?

"I like reptiles," he said. "Once I got to snake-sit an anaconda for three weeks."

"What? Oh. Okay." Lisa laughed. "Did you play with it a lot?"

"No, I think it never stopped regarding me as a big chunk of meat."

"Well, you are."

Tony grinned. "Fortunately too big to swallow."

After their meal, Lisa waved over the owner. "Valentim, would you mind calling the monkeys?" she asked.

His smile broadened. "Anything for you, Lisa." Valentim grabbed a bunch of bananas and whistled. He peeled the fruits and put them on a wooden tray set in the fork of a tree. Seconds later, Lisa saw the first capuchin monkeys rushing toward them.

Tony stood by her side. "This is incredible. Look there's a mother with her baby. Two babies. They are totally entangled in her fur."

* * * *

Smiling, Félix watched the woman grab a banana from the tray and hand-feed one of the sharp-toothed monkeys. As she stretched out her arm, he saw the belt holster. Tony hadn't told him a cock and bull story.

33

The two strolled toward the parking lot, and Félix leaned back in his chair to hide behind the trunk of a tree. No need for Norton to spot him.

He remembered the jolt that ran through him when she stared right at him from the other end of his binoculars. How the heck did the fellow in the parking lot notice him?

He finished his meal without hurry. He knew where to find her again. Unless, of course, she spent the night with Tony Norton.

* * * *

About an hour before sunset they arrived at the cable car station. Lisa had timed it perfectly. Only the clouds worried her. They took the cable car up to Morro da Urca, the rock next to the Sugar Loaf.

Lisa pointed out the helicopter pad several meters below the station. "Wanna go airborne?" she asked. "It's quite expensive, though."

He stared at the sign advertising the scenic flights. "Ten minutes for a hundred dollars? Makes you look cheap."

"What?" Lisa couldn't believe she'd heard right.

"The rate you charge?" He grinned.

She pursed her lips, tilted her head, and locked her eyes on his. "Keep it up, dude, and you can forget about the discount."

Tony laughed. "Sorry, couldn't resist."

She smiled. "All right, let's go up on the Pão de Açúcar."

As they mounted the cable car, more clouds moved in. "I hope we'll be able to see the sunset," Lisa said.

"If not, you've got to bring me back another time."

"That's what I want to avoid." She grinned, admitting to herself that she enjoyed Tony's company far too much.

When they disembarked, the strong wind had blown away the clouds. They walked a short trail, and Tony spotted another monkey in the trees. While they watched the animal's antics, dense fog crawled closer and enveloped them.

"This is spooky," Tony said. "Have you seen the movie *The Fog*?"

"Thanks for reminding me. But it looks cool." All around them, dense mist grayed out tall trees with lush foliage. Within minutes the clouds dissolved. Blue sky again. They left the trail and walked to the bistro at the main lookout point. Lisa bought two cans of *Guaraná*.

"What's this?" Tony asked.

"A sweet, refreshing caffeine drink made from an Amazon plant. You gotta try it."

Tony took a sip. "Good stuff. Reminds me of ginger ale."

They stood at the railing. Below them, sailing boats bobbed in the Botafogo bay. Far above, Cristo Redentor still blessed the city. To the left they saw the arched beaches of Copacabana and Ipanema rimmed by white high-rises. To the right the less fashionable *zona norte* stretched to the horizon. The thirteen-kilometer-long Ponte Rio-Niterói crossed the Guanabara Bay and connected the two cities. In between, green, rocky islands poked out of the sea.

Fluffy clouds moved in from the ocean and compacted against the mountain range as the sun started to go down, painting the most beautiful sunset Lisa had ever experienced on the Sugar Loaf. The thick blanket of clouds below and above reflected the dying sunlight, yellow then pink and finally red.

Tony smiled at her. "*Muito maravilhosa*. Like you."

The urge to run away spiked. Lisa closed her eyes and concentrated on her breathing. Tony was cute and fun. The total lack of machismo made her feel safe with him. In many ways, he reminded her of Jango. A caretaker. "So, when do you leave?" she asked.

His smile faded. "Next Saturday."

She nodded slowly. "I still owe you the ugly side of Rio."

"How about dinner first?" he asked.

She turned her back on the city and leaned against the railing. "Sure."

Tony beamed. "Great."

"Wednesday. Meet me at the bookstore at four."

He hung his head. "Wednesday?"

Lisa smiled at his beaten puppy look. His bright blue eyes and the stubble on his unshaven face attracted her. Most of all, he made her feel safe. She avoided his gaze. "Have you ever been in love, Tony?"

"What?" He cleared his throat. "Sure."

She looked at him. "What's it like?"

His smile faltered. "You mean you've never been crazy about someone, never felt as smart as a cauliflower, unable to think about anything but the one person?"

She shook her head, wondering if she could ever allow herself to feel like that.

He reached out to her then dropped his hands. Now he avoided her gaze. "The first woman I really loved died in my arms."

Surprised, she stared into his glistening eyes.

"I took her for a spin on my brand new motorbike. A car cut us off. She was twenty-three and died there on the road." He swallowed. "I took a sledgehammer to the wrecked bike and never rode one again. I still wonder if I could have saved her if I had reacted differently."

Puzzled, she touched his arm. He always appeared so untroubled, balanced. She'd never have expected he might have lived through something like that. "I'm sorry. Can't imagine how you..."

He cleared his throat. "Why did you run away at the beach? I didn't mean to scare you." He ran the back of his curled fingers over her cheek.

She looked him in the eye. "You didn't scare me. I did."

He slipped his hand around her neck and kissed her. Her skin tingled under his touch. His lips felt soft and warm on hers. A wave of emotions surged through her body. She wanted to press against him, wanted to run, scream, respond. She longed for more, but knew it would end in disaster once he'd...

She threw back her head. "Slow down, cowboy."

He chuckled, but still held her close, rubbing his stubbly chin against her soft skin, sending shivers through her. She pushed him away. "Enough."

With a rueful smile he stepped back, lifting his hands as if to show her he wasn't armed. "Don't shoot me."

"I'm tempted."

"It was worth the risk."

"Let's go. Watching sunsets with you is too dangerous."

Chapter Seven

Félix watched the Nissan pull into the parking garage. With little hope that she'd return home alone and early in the evening, he'd waited for her anyway, anticipating, fantasizing about their future encounter.

Now that reality had caught up with him, adrenaline pumped in his bloodstream. He heaved himself out of his low sports car. No one had occupied her passenger seat. Too bad for Norton, lucky for him.

Félix walked down the street running parallel to hers, rounded the corner, and increased his pace. If he timed it right, he'd pass her close to the gate to her apartment building. He turned the next corner and slowed. No trace of her. A tourist couple ambled past him. Ahead, a man with a briefcase walked in the opposite direction.

A black kid slouched in the doorway of a closed post office. Alves and his minions might enjoy bashing his head in. Félix wanted more. A challenge. A worthy adversary.

She rounded the corner. Félix shivered. She looked tall, proud, and strong. Unyielding. Unaware. Untouched. He picked up his pace. She'd reach the gate before him.

She looked straight at him. Their eyes met once more, only this time she saw him too. Her body language revealed no fear. Because of her gun? She wouldn't be able to draw it fast enough. Getting closer, he slipped his right hand into his pocket. His fist clasped the switchblade. The sound of footsteps caught his attention. A gang of kids crossed the street behind her. They wouldn't interfere. Why should they care?

As she pulled open the gate with her left hand, she glanced over her shoulder at him and slipped her right hand under her shirt. Gripping her gun? Ahead, the tallest boy stopped and peered in their direction. Damn.

Félix lowered his head and walked past her. It physically hurt not to touch her. A rubber band seemed to pull him back to her. Scowling at the kid, Félix suppressed a groan. The black boy hurried after his friends. What the fuck! Did they plan to mug him? They'd regret it.

A new surge of adrenaline flooded his system as he followed the kids around the corner, but they had slipped away. Félix stopped in front of the quaint bookstore and stared at the display without seeing. His mind trailed after the woman, up the stairs to her apartment, into her bedroom. Did she have plush carpets, red sheets? A favorite stuffed animal sitting on the pillow? His face relaxed into a smile. Another day. Something to look forward to. First, he'd find out who she was.

* * * *

Luiz caught up with Tatu waiting for him in the shadows of the corridor between the two buildings.

"What's up?" Tatu asked.

"A strange guy checking out Lisa."

"Did he do anything?"

Luiz shook his head. "Only stared at her. Like a hungry animal. Then she slipped into the house."

They reached the backyard where Ubaldo waited with Rena and Gordinho. In one of the surrounding buildings a light flared up on the second floor. Lisa's apartment? He whispered, "I think she lives up there."

Tired of sleeping on the beach, or rather dozing and jerking awake at every human sound, he'd suggested they check out the workshop behind the bookstore. Nobody seemed to use the place anyway, and it was well-hidden from the street. Ubaldo nudged him. "We could just ask her if we can stay."

Luiz shook his head. She'd never agree to let them sleep here. Why should she?

"I like her," Gordinho whispered. "She reminds me of my mother."

Tatu already worked on the padlock of the shed. "Every woman between twenty and fifty reminds you of your mother."

"Maybe, but she's got that same tough look that makes you cringe when you screw up." He chuckled.

Rena pouted. "I don't want to sleep in that stinky workshop. It's much nicer outside."

Luiz shrugged. "Whatever. As long as we're out of sight. Let's camp close to the wall, so nobody can see us from the apartments."

They picked the darkest corner and settled on the ground. It was a warm night for October. Luiz lay on his back and gazed at the few stars.

Max had once told him that outside the city you could see stars all over the sky. Hard to imagine.

Maybe he should tell Lisa about the strange guy.

"I'll ask her if we can sleep here." Ubaldo propped himself up on one elbow.

Luiz snorted. "She might not let you work for her anymore. Get a grip, Ubaldo. She's a nice lady but why should she care about us? You're just a cheap worker for her."

In the dark, he couldn't read the boy's face, but he curled up with his back to Luiz. Ubaldo was far too trusting.

Gordinho murmured, "Maybe I can work for her, too."

Luiz sighed. Every street kid missed a mother more than anything else, except perhaps Rena. Her mother beat her and tried to sell her to generous men who bought drugs for her.

Chapter Eight

Lisa stood in front of the closet, her hair still wet from the shower. She pulled on her oldest jeans, threaded the leather belt through the loops, and attached the holster with her compact Firestar. A loose-fitting blue shirt hid the gun.

The alarm clock read 16:05. She opened the window and looked down. Tony paced in front of the bookstore. For a moment, she wondered why she wanted to spend her birthday with him. Well, thirty was a landmark, and who else could she celebrate with? Jango had to attend an important business dinner. She checked her cellphone. No missed call from her father. Maybe later, likely as not.

She skipped down the stairs and strolled around the corner toward the bookstore. "Hey, Ranger. You ready?"

Tony's eyebrows shot up. "Ready for what?"

She smiled at him. "I'm going to show you the ugly side of Rio."

"You said we'd have dinner."

"First we go to the *favela*."

Tony frowned. "Is it safe?"

"Usually, yes."

He showed off a cocky grin. "I'll protect ya."

"I knew there was some macho lurking in you." Lisa grinned.

Tony burst out laughing. "Yeah, right."

They walked toward the foot of the hill and reached the street that marked the border to the *favela*. Two police cars were parked on one side. On the other, young men armed with assault rifles patrolled along rooftops.

Tony stopped. "Um, you sure about this?"

"See the woman with the baby?"

Tony nodded. "You trying to say if she's safe, we are, too?"

"Something like that, except you can't rely on it. C'mon, let's go," she said. "It's just a poor neighborhood."

"Yeah, guarded by an army."

"Drug gangs." She remembered her own unease the first few times she set foot into a *favela,* years ago, after she returned to Rio. Later she'd walked down this street lined with armed drug dealers and police every day. Desensitization, her shrink called it.

"And that's supposed to make me feel better?" Tony asked.

"No, you better stay alert."

"Just checking." His gaze swiped the roofs again.

Lisa took his arm. "We don't have to do this. I thought you might want to see how the other half lives. Okay, a much smaller half, but still."

He locked his eyes on hers. "I'd follow you anywhere."

Lisa crossed the street with Tony close behind her and slipped into a narrow alley. Out of sight of gangsters and police, she relaxed. Unplastered brick houses stood squeezed together. One shoe box on top of another. The lanes felt claustrophobic, as if she might get stuck trying to pass someone. She hadn't roamed the *favela* for years but still knew her way. They reached a small square, and she breathed more easily. She glanced at Tony, who slowly turned, taking in the drastic change of scenery.

"They're selling live chickens," he said.

She smiled. So much to see, but the living chicken for sale fascinated him most. Not really surprising for someone used to chicken nuggets. "Very convenient if you don't have a fridge."

He squinted at her. "Are you making fun of me?"

"Me? Never." Lisa smiled.

Boys on cross-country motorbikes hung around the square, chatting. "See the bikers?" she asked. "If you are too tired or maybe too drunk, they'll take you up the hill to your house for a small fee."

"Great business idea."

They took the steps, though. The stench of rotting food and excrement hit Lisa as they crossed over a garbage-clogged stream on a narrow wooden bridge. Tony covered his mouth and nose with his hand. "That's bad," he mumbled.

They came to a fountain where women washed clothes, and kids showered in the cool water. Everything was tiny: the houses, the alleys, but not the guns. Turning a corner, they faced three youngsters no older than fifteen, wearing shorts and flip-flops and clutching assault rifles. All three trained their weapons on them. *Merda!* Lisa froze, her heart raced, her mind went blank. Her body screamed to draw her gun and fight.

One of the boys yelled, "Fuck off."

She pulled her gaze from the guns and jerked Tony's arm. He spun around and stumbled after her. Of course, they wouldn't just shoot people. Not without a reason, but a trivial one would do. Lisa's hands sweated as they turned into the street they had come from.

Out of sight, Tony took a deep breath. "Fuck!"

Lisa stopped to look at him. The sense of danger faced and overcome made her fingertips tingle. "I feel like such a fool. Sorry about that. The gang must have moved their headquarters since my day."

He stared at her. "Since your days with the drug gang?"

She laughed. "No, I've never been associated with drug gangs in any way, and I never will be."

Tony tilted his head and glanced at her sideways. "Nothing would surprise me."

"Don't challenge me."

Tony managed a half-smile. "I've never looked into the muzzle of a Kalashnikov before. You think I can get one, too?"

"Could be arranged."

"Might make me feel a lot safer on our next date."

They burst into laughter and attracted curious looks from the women doing their laundry. "Maybe we should move on," he suggested.

"Yep." Lisa led him down another alley, stopped in front of a three-story house, and clapped her hands. Nobody had doorbells in the *favela*. A pot of geraniums sat in the glassless window, like it always had. Maria, the old school mistress, opened the door and looked at her with wide, incredulous eyes. "*Olá* Lisa. *Tudo bem*? It's been such a long time." Maria hugged her tight and kissed her.

"*Olá* Maria. I'm sorry it's taken me so long to come back. I've been quite busy. And now I feel ashamed. This is a friend. Tony. I wondered if I could show him the school."

"Of course you can." Maria shook Tony's hand and stepped aside. "Come on in."

"You speak excellent English," Tony said.

Maria smiled. "Lisa taught me. She's a good teacher."

Tony gave her a surprised look.

"What?" she asked.

"Hard to picture you as a teacher."

She huffed. "I guess I need to teach you a few things."

The old classroom filled her with heartwarming memories of fun times, before she had turned her back on it all. In the afternoons she'd taught the children of the community and, in the evenings, adults who wanted to increase their chances for one of the good jobs in the tourist business.

A slow sigh eased from her chest. She'd grown really fond of a boy, her best student. One day he hadn't shown up anymore. A few days later she'd seen him selling drugs. A few months later someone shot him dead. Police? Members of another gang? They never found out. And Lisa threw in the job, simply gave up. Better not to get involved when you couldn't change anything.

Hearing Maria's praise and enthusiastic explanations, Lisa felt like a traitor, a failure. Why had she come back here? To find a safe harbor from the drug gangs? What a joke.

Chapter Nine

Max stepped onto the roof terrace, lured by samba rhythms. Time to join his party, get drunk, stoned, and laid. He squeezed through the hot bodies and dancers, brushing against skin. Átila shoved a *caipirinha* in his hand, rocking to the music.

Max scanned the crowd for his Colombian suppliers. Two of them were chatting up girls, the third sniffed cocaine from a silver tray. Time to relax after the negotiations.

"Everything's taken care of," Átila shouted over the noise.

"Who's on duty?"

"Beda's taking care of the night watch. Lana's with him," Átila said.

Max sat on the short wall surrounding the edge of the roof and rolled himself a joint. The perfect night. Lovely Lana was fun but far too possessive. Not that she loved him. The alpha woman simply claimed the alpha male. He lit up and inhaled. Watching the dancers, he finished the cocktail. His muscles relaxed, his neck tingled, the grass kicked in.

His eyes met Átila's. Max grinned. The guy had taken Max under his wing when he'd moved up from street dealer to soldier. The only man he really trusted. Without him, he'd be long dead.

Tatu had just been old enough that Max could leave him with Luiz while he went after the big money. Now, Max led the gang, but Átila still watched over him. Tall, broad, and black as the night, he looked like he'd just escaped from a slave ship. Max would have made him his general, but the guy showed no interest in taking command. One of the reasons why he trusted him with his life.

Max rolled another joint. A girl caught his eye. A pretty *mulatta* in a short skirt and bikini top, swinging her ample hips to the samba rhythms, pressing against one of his soldiers, who couldn't be much older than Luiz. When the band stopped, the soldier kissed and groped the girl. As the music piped up again, they separated.

Max caught the boy's gaze and summoned him with a nod. What the hell was his name again? Didn't matter. The soldier dropped his grin, walked a little too slowly. His eyes darted around. Max smiled. A smart one.

"What?"

"Send her over," Max said.

"But she's my girl."

Brave, too. "Really?" Max laughed. "What makes her your girl?"

"She loves me."

He snorted. "Then you don't have anything to worry about, do you?"

"But..."

Was he crazy, too? "Yeah?"

"Nothing." The soldier walked back to the girl and whispered something in her ear. She studied Max, while the soldier kissed her neck. She left him standing and walked up to Max with an air of reluctance. She stood in front of him, her hands on her hips, and waited. He held the joint out to her. She set the tip aglow with one long draw and exhaled, throwing back her head, before she looked down on him. "What d'you want?"

"You."

"What if I'm not interested?"

Max grinned. He loved arrogant girls. "Well, go back to your boy then."

"Okay." With a reckless smile, she stalked up to the soldier, slung her arms around his neck, and kissed him. The boy embraced her and moved his body into Max's line of vision, but the girl glanced over his shoulder.

Still grinning, Max took a last draw from the joint, dropped it, and stood. He strolled toward the door, giving her time to decide, but he knew she'd come. Girls like her never settled for a soldier when they could have the commander. Max leaned in the door frame, waiting. She bent close to the boy's ear, her lips moving. An uncertain smile on her face, she sashayed toward Max.

For a brief moment the vision of an angry Lana flared up in Max's hazy mind, but he dismissed it. Lana was a soldier; she had to respect him. Though he loved it when she didn't. Max chuckled.

He pulled his gaze from the girl and checked on the soldier. He was calling someone, maybe he'd learned the lesson and invited a replacement.

The girl stopped before him. "What if I am interested?"

"It's never too late." He took her hand and led her inside.

45

In the small room, a single bed stood against the wall. Handcuffs hung around the bars of the headboard. The girl frowned at him. "You a control freak?"

"Nope." He rubbed his jaws but couldn't stop grinning. He pulled his T-shirt over his head and stretched out on the narrow bed. "You're the boss, babe. Come on, chain me."

She hesitated. Then a smile crept onto her face. "You got the keys?"

Max's grin grew even broader. He looked up the wall where a pair of keys hung on a nail. She strode toward the bed, quickly getting used to the idea of taking a drug lord prisoner. Pulling up her short skirt, she straddled him, pushed his arms up, and closed the metal cuffs around his wrists. Max loved the mischievous look on her face, as she put her elbows on his chest and rested her chin on her hands. "What if I'm going back to the party now?"

"You'll miss the ride of your life." He pushed up his hips for emphasis.

She laughed, sat up, and pulled off her bikini top. Max groaned and gripped the bars. She bent down to him and hovered, her breasts gliding over his naked chest. Her lips touched his, but she drew away again before he could kiss her. She slid off him and unbuttoned his fly. Rather violently she tore off his jeans and boxers then dropped her skirt and g-string. She crawled over him on all fours. Max writhed, pulled hard against the restraints. She lowered herself onto him.

The door flung open and banged against the wall. Lana? Bullets hit the walls. The girl jerked up. *No, don't!* His heart pounding, Max pressed the quick release buttons on the handcuffs, clutched the girl, and rolled off the bed with her. He grabbed his gun from beneath the pillow and shot Lana in the chest. She stared at him wildly. The second bullet hit her in the forehead. The Kalashnikov dropped from her hands. She sank to the floor. Max waited for another human shape to show in the door frame. His senses heightened, his heart racing, he noticed the band had stopped playing.

The girl. No sound from her. No screams. He swung around and stared at her. She lay on her back, blood seeping from under her. A bullet had exited her chest, leaving a large red wound right between her breasts. "Shit," he hissed. Max felt for her pulse, but couldn't find it. She coughed up blood. Her eyelids flitted.

"Hey, babe. It's okay. You'll be okay." What else could he tell her? She was dying. He stroked the hair out of her face. Her lips quivered, her eyes hazed over. She lay still. He'd killed her. His fault, not Lana's.

He didn't even know her name.

Shots outside. Max jumped up, grabbed Lana's assault rifle and stepped over her dead body. Naked, he stormed onto the terrace, where his general ended a little speech with: "Max's dead, Beda rules!"

Max pulled the trigger and sent three shots into the air. The shock registered in Beda's face. His mouth dropped open. People moved away from him. Beda swung his rifle around. Max pulled the trigger. A line of red fountains popped up across Beda's chest. He tumbled back and slumped to the ground.

Max relaxed his grip on Lana's beloved AK-47. He scanned the guests and found the soldier. The boy stood trembling, eyes wide, mouth agape. Max tossed the assault rifle, walked up to him, and choked him by the neck of his T-shirt. "You called Lana, didn't you?" He dragged him to the edge of the roof. "She's dead. Because of you. Your girl, too. Congratulations, asshole." Max grabbed his belt with the other hand and flung him over the wall. A short scream, a thud.

Max leaned over. No more than a four meter drop and, of course, the bastard was still alive and struggling to his feet. Átila held out a revolver. The boy hobbled away, clutching his left arm. Max shook his head. It was all his fault anyway.

"You can't let him get away with it." Átila pressed the gun in his hand.

"Ah fuck!" Max aimed at the center of the boy's back and fired. He collapsed. Max turned around and scowled at his friends, business partners, and soldiers. "Party's over," he announced. No one moved. He walked up to the dead body of his general. He could trust nobody. Beda had been his number one for half a year. They'd fought quite a few battles together. Mussolini handed Max a towel.

He slung it around his hips. "Get rid of him and the two bodies in my fucking bedroom."

* * * *

47

Luiz strolled along Copacabana beach, leaving prints in the wet sand. Breaking waves splashed his bare feet. He carried a soccer ball squeezed between his left arm and hip. Maybe later they'd actually play. With falling dusk, the beach emptied. Soon they wouldn't be able to pick up more money.

While Gordinho covered Luiz's back, Tatu and Rena walked parallel to him, closer to the street and the snack bars lining the beach. Tatu beat his drum and Rena sang love songs for the tourists and locals sitting at the tables. With her twelve years, Rena was changing too fast. Her growing boobs and widening hips became harder to ignore. Kind of disturbing. For two years, she'd been like a little sister. He wondered how much longer she'd want to hang out with them. He dreaded the day she'd walk off with some rich sucker to make a lot more money.

Luiz had given up begging or selling peanuts when people got reluctant to pull out their wallets in front of a black, fourteen-year-old street kid. And right they were. Now he'd snatch the money and run with it.

He loved the beaches of Rio's *zona sul*. Young men played volleyball, kids built sand sculptures, and street vendors sold sunscreen, peanuts, cold beverages, or beach towels. People lay scattered enjoying the sun, the easy rhythm of the city. The blue half-pipe shapes of the *policia militar* tents put tourists and locals at ease, while Luiz kept a watchful eye on the cops. His skin crawled as he strolled past. Two fit-looking young officers. He'd much prefer the fat guys who were on patrol the other day.

Luiz spotted a wallet sticking from a sports bag. No, too close to the cops for a grab and run. Silently cursing, he strolled on. Despite the haze, he could make out container ships on the horizon. Ahead, the white walls of the old fort loomed; to his right, high rises lined Avenida Atlantica.

A lobster-tanned guy had taken off his watch—to make sure his skin got evenly singed—and left it beside him in the sand. Luiz picked it up with his toes.

A shrill voice. "Stop! Thief! Stop him!"

Luiz jerked around, his heart beating frantically. Had someone noticed? Gordinho, clutching a duffel bag, dashed toward him, chased by a fit-looking guy in his twenties—catching up. *Merda.*

Tatu and Rena stared at the scene from across the beach. Too far for them to do anything. Luiz spun the ball on the fingers of his left hand. Tatu nodded and ran along the beach, waving at him. "C'mon!"

Luiz dropped the ball and kicked, hitting Gordinho's angry pursuer in the temple. A perfect shot. The guy screamed. Luiz squatted, picked up the watch, and slipped it into the pocket of his shorts. He jogged over to the swearing man. "Sorry, hope I didn't break your nose."

"Get out of my way." He pushed Luiz back and scanned the beach.

Tatu ran toward them, clutching the ball. "Problems?" He winked at Luiz. Gordinho had slipped away.

That was far too close. Someday, one of them would get caught.

Chapter Ten

After the *favela* tour, Lisa took Tony to her favorite restaurant, a rustic trattoria in Bairro Peixoto. Red and white checkered cloths covered the tables. Red candles and long thin vases, each holding a red rose, made it the perfect place for her first date in a decade. Lisa introduced Tony to Fabrizio, the Sicilian chef, who flashed his most charming smile and persuaded them to try the special of the day, his grandmother's recipe.

She asked for a bottle of his finest white wine. Tony ordered beer.

Eyebrows raised, Fabrizio looked from one to the other. Lisa laughed.

Tony blushed. "Did I say something wrong?"

"I already ordered wine. A whole bottle. But if you'd rather have beer, no problem. I'll drink the wine myself."

"You sure?" He grinned. "I'll have the beer."

Lisa nodded at the chef then smiled at Tony. "You're up to something."

His grin widened. "Yep, I'll get you drunk and seduce you."

Lisa pursed her lips and faked a grave expression. "Then we should get started with *cachaça*." She flagged down the waiter and ordered a little extra courage.

"What kind would you like, Senhora?"

"*Mineiro, por favor*."

The waiter nodded his approval. Maybe he was from Minas Gerais.

"What's *cachaça*?" Tony asked.

"The sugarcane rum they put in *caipirinha*."

"Sounds good." Still smiling, Tony leaned back. "I had a great time today."

"Glad to hear it."

"What do you do for fun?" he asked.

"You mean when I don't get drunk with strange Americans?"

"Uh-huh."

Lisa's mind traveled back a few weeks. When did she last have fun before she ran into Tony? "Not much. I lead a pretty boring life."

He shook his head. "Hard to believe."

"It's true, though." She put her right elbow on the table and rested her chin in her hand. "I read, I jog. Once in a while I do some target practice at a shooting range."

He smiled. "Doesn't sound that boring. What's your favorite book?"

"Peter Pan." Ever since she was ten and struggling to survive on the streets of Rio.

"What?" He stared at her. A frown wrinkled his forehead. "But that's a children's book."

"So?" Many times she'd told the story to her friends, huddled in dark back streets, trying to find comfort in Neverland, like Wendy, before Lisa turned into Tinker Bell.

The waiter set the beer and two shot glasses of *cachaça* on the table. Then he poured wine for Lisa.

"*Obrigada*." Lisa smiled at the man, took the shot glass, and clinked it against Tony's. Slowly, she let the rum roll over her tongue and down her throat, savoring the fruity taste and its burning warmth. She gazed into Tony's sparkling blue eyes.

"You're making this pretty easy," he said. His glass was still half-full.

Lisa granted him a crooked smile. "Maybe I need it more than you."

"I'm not so sure about that." He knocked back the rest of the rum and cleared his throat. "Do you like running the bookstore?"

"Most of the time. I love books. When I decided to settle down, a bookstore seemed perfect, and I was right."

"What did you do before?"

"This and that. You know how it goes." She'd never tell him. Unless she wanted to scare him away for good.

"Um, no, I don't."

"I traveled, lived in the States for a while, went to Europe, finally came back to the place where I belong. Running away doesn't make things better." Lisa fell silent. Why had she told him all that? He was a stranger. A nice one, okay, but still. And now he gave her this understanding look.

"Tell me about yourself," she said to distract him.

"Originally, I'm from Salem, Oregon. The place got too small for me. I never felt like returning. Not after my mother died."

So he knew about running away. "Is your father still alive?" she asked, wondering about her own. When had they last talked on the phone? Three years ago, on his sixtieth birthday. She'd called. His turn now.

"Yeah, but we never were very close, not since my parents got divorced. Anyway, let's talk about something more pleasant."

The parallels of their family history touched her, made her feel connected to this stranger. But she didn't want the past to overshadow the evening. "Right, let's keep the ghosts buried. When are you leaving again?"

Tony put both arms on the table and leaned close, squinting at her. "So that's a more pleasant topic for you?"

Lisa grinned.

"Saturday. And on Friday there's an official dinner with some business partners. I'd much rather spend my last evening with you."

She raised her wine glass. They toasted and fell silent for a moment while the waiter served red snapper with fettucini in pesto sauce.

"I hope you like fish. Sorry, he always does this to me, just cooks what he feels like, no chance to select from the menu."

"Fish is fine. I like an adventurous dinner. And obviously you like what he rustles up for you or you wouldn't keep coming back."

"Pretty much always." Lisa laughed. "Except that one time when I got squid. I hate the stuff. And another time it was liver." She shuddered. "So, we're lucky today."

He grinned. "I see. You're in for the kick."

Lisa laughed. "Yeah, I'm an adrenaline junkie." Maybe she'd miss him when he was gone. Someone to laugh with, someone who didn't know her past.

By the time they finished their meal, Lisa had drained her third glass of wine and poured her fourth. She hadn't felt so relaxed in a man's company for a long time. Except for Jango, of course. But he was more like a father than her real one, and he knew her darkest secrets.

The waiter brought Tony his third beer and Lisa seized the chance to order espresso *correto* for both of them.

"I don't really like espresso. What's the *correto* part?"

"*Grappa*."

Tony's face scrunched up. "That's the Italian liquor made from grapes?"

Lisa nodded and smiled.

The chef himself brought two tiny cups on a little silver tray. "Everything okay?" he asked.

Lisa beamed at him. "It was delicious, Fabrizio." Giggling, she raised her cup to her lips. "Try the brew from hell."

As soon as Tony tasted the mixture of espresso and *grappa*, he knocked it down quickly, scrunching up his face. "Are you trying to kill me?"

Lisa took an elegant sip. "It'll revive you after the big dinner. Think of it as pure medicine."

"That's what it tastes like."

She put her hands flat on the table. "Let's go to my place and start with the dessert."

Tony stared at her for a second then turned toward the bar. "Check please!" He gazed back at her. "Dessert? I better use the bathroom first."

* * * *

Arm in arm, they walked toward her apartment. Not that she needed him to steady her. Only when one of the tree roots tore up the sidewalk and grasped her foot. Vicious things. She giggled again. Tony let go of her. She swayed a little, but his arm caught her shoulders, holding her in a firm grip. She reached around his waist and pushed her thumb inside the waistband of his jeans. He felt warm and strong against her. She looked up into his face. She'd never noticed the cute dimple in his cheek before.

He smiled. "I think you may have had a bit too much to drink."

"Nah, I'm fine. The espresso will kick in soon."

They reached the gate.

"You live behind bars, too," he said.

She unlocked and pushed it open. "Yeah, my personal little prison. Come on in." She had trouble finding the right key for the door and tried two before she inserted the one that fit. "Here we go."

"Maybe I should just let you sleep it off."

An easy way out. No, Lisa couldn't run. She needed to fight her fear and win. She pouted and shook her head. "You promised."

He laughed. "I did?"

She nodded. "C'mon. Don't be a coward now."

"If you insist."

Lisa climbed the one flight of stairs ahead of him, holding on to the handrail. Inside her apartment, she took his hand and led him straight to the bedroom, where she sat at the foot of the bed and stretched out one leg to him. Tony knelt and slipped off one sandal and then the other.

"It's my birthday, Tony."

He sagged and groaned. "That's not fair. You should have told me. I'd have gotten you something."

"You are my present." She pulled off her belt and holster containing the small 9 mm.

Tony's eyes locked on her gun. He reached for it. She let him take it out. "It looks like a toy, but it's heavy."

"It's Spanish. Franco gave it to me."

Tony stared at her. "General Franco?"

Lisa giggled and fell back on the mattress. "No, Franco Oliveira, a gun dealer."

Tony chuckled and put the compact back in the holster before he crawled over her and kissed her. His hand slipped under her shirt, warm and soft against her skin. His erection pressed against her thigh. She fought back the surge of panic. The fug of alcohol would protect her.

Tony unbuttoned her shirt and kissed his way from her lips to her breasts, setting her skin on fire. Might just work, she thought. He slipped her arms out of the sleeves, reached under her and undid her bra. She closed her eyes, felt his hands and mouth all over her. Yes, more. When he stopped, her lids flew open. He pulled his shirt over his head. Scars covered his right upper arm. She reached out, touched the healed skin. "The motorbike accident?"

He nodded. "Pretty ugly, I know." His eyes looked darker, pained. "I gave Silvia my leather jacket. Didn't do her much good."

He too knew pain, physical and emotional. "The scar's part of you," she whispered and pulled him down to her.

Something cold touched her stomach. She shrieked.

"What?"

"Your belt buckle. It's cold."

"Sorry." He rolled off her. Kneeling, he pulled the belt from his jeans and flung it across the room.

Lisa flinched. She saw Vitor Fraga swing his belt, felt the burning pain. Memories spun in her head. Not now! She couldn't let him ruin this moment. She pulled Tony down to her and kissed him again. His skin against hers wrapped her in a blanket of warmth and safety. A tear rolled down her cheek. She wiped it away. His hand cupped her right breast, played with her nipple. She wanted him. Desperately. Wanted to be able to enjoy the act that once meant torture. And kill Captain Hook for good. Tony unbuttoned her jeans and pulled down the zipper. His warm hand explored her gently. So different. She lifted her hips and he stripped off her jeans and undies.

"Don't go away." He rolled off her, struggled out of his jeans, fished a plastic square from his front pocket and shed his boxers. Don't look, she told herself, growing more nervous.

"Don't think I always carry condoms. Fortunately, the restaurant had a vending machine in the bathroom."

Lisa chuckled. "Ah, that explains the sudden urge."

Tony buried his face in her hair, kissing her neck. She ran her hands over his muscular back and then down his scarred arm. His lips found hers again. His hand slipped between her legs. She forced herself to relax, enjoy the sensation. He slid on top of her. "Tony," she whispered and latched onto his mouth, a safety rope. He moaned as he penetrated her.

Lisa heard Vitor Fraga's throaty groans, felt the wave of pain crash over her. Total helplessness. She was ten again.

Chapter Eleven

Tony felt her body tense. She moaned and arched under him. Perfect timing. He couldn't have held back much longer. Her arms pushed against his shoulders. He pressed his lips on hers as he came in pulsing waves. Her body went limp under his. Confused, he propped himself up on his elbows. Lisa stared at him, eyes unseeing, unblinking, tears rolling down her temples. She trembled, whimpered. What the hell? He slipped off her. "Hey! Lisa." He stroked her face, wiping the tears away. "Lisa, look at me." Panic seized him. "Please. Lisa!"

She blinked.

"Come back, Lisa. I won't hurt you. C'mon, baby." How could he have mistaken her pain for pleasure? Her face contorted into a grimace. Tony shook her shoulders. Finally her eyes focused on him. She blinked the tears away and broke into sobs.

He stroked her face, her hair. "I'm so sorry."

"No." She sniffed. "I should have..." She closed her eyes. "I shouldn't have..." She rubbed her cheek against his hand. He ran his fingers over her lips, kissed her forehead.

"It's not fair," she whispered.

"No." Unsure whether he should leave her alone or hold her, he searched her face. She still seemed far away. "Want me to leave?"

She shook her head and closed her eyes. More tears spilled over.

"Okay." He rolled on his back, giving her space. Nausea welled in his stomach. What had happened to her? What had he done? Ashamed of his own pleasure, he sat up, disposed of the condom, and reached for his boxers. But Lisa's hand pulled him back. She curled up against his side, rested her head on his shoulder, her arm on his chest. "I'm sorry," she said.

"Hey, it's not your fault." He stroked her back and felt a crude scar. He traced it from her shoulder blade to her lower back. Goosebumps rose up on his skin. Whatever happened to her must have been worse than he'd thought. "Did they ever get him?"

"Eventually," she said.

"Want to talk about it?"

"No," she whispered.

Minutes passed while his mind tortured him with possible scenarios. Lisa's breath brushed over his chest in regular intervals. Tony couldn't believe she lay snuggled up against him, sleeping. She hadn't kicked him out after he'd been such an ass. He felt like he'd raped her.

What an end to a great day. She'd seemed so relaxed, enjoying herself. Sure, she wasn't like the girls who chatted him up in the bars close to the beach, but he'd never have suspected she'd been raped and hurt.

The scars on her back weren't from a knife. Too uneven. Another wave of nausea washed over him.

Looking back, it all made sense. The gun. Her strange speech on the Corcovado, that she'd rather have jumped from the wall than faced torture if she'd been one of the political prisoners. That she ran away from him whenever he got too close, until today. He'd been such an idiot.

Lisa stirred. Her hand slid down to his stomach. How could she sleep, feel safe in his arms after what she'd just gone through?

* * * *

Lisa lay curled up against the girl next to her. Their only comfort after Vitor Fraga took one of them. As she woke, an iron band clamped around her throbbing head. A clean, soft mattress under her. The scent of lavender. She was home. Her eyes fluttered open. Her arm lay across Tony's chest.

A turmoil of conflicting emotions raged inside her. The memory of his hands on her body mixed with those of Vitor Fraga's belt, the pain, the crushing weight of his body. The digital alarm clock behind Tony on the nightstand read 6:07. He breathed regularly. Careful not to wake him, she slipped out of bed, grabbed clean clothes, and rushed into the bathroom.

Lisa bent over the toilet, retching. How could she have been so stupid? She should have known it wouldn't work. Her third attempt. The first time, she'd been seventeen and in love. They got drunk and stoned. She didn't feel anything. The revulsion came later when he wanted to sleep with her again, totally sober. The second time was a disaster, but she suffered through it. And now, the complete meltdown. Damn!

Naked and shivering, she sat on the floor and leaned against the wall. She fought to bury the memories, forget the smells, the grunts, and the helpless fear. She had to lock all that away.

Her gaze wandered to the window. She stretched her wings, jumped through and flew with Peter Pan. High up into the sky over Rio. The ocean glittered in the sun, the palm trees swayed in the wind. Joy filled her. She was safe and free—Tinker Bell, with a body too small to hold more than one emotion.

Chapter Twelve

Like a thief, Lisa stole out of her own apartment, checking all directions before she stepped through the gate. Rage boiled inside her. At herself and the world. Her own fault. First she let the old man lure her away from her mother with a stuffed crocodile, now, when she should have known better, she had invited a stranger into her place. She'd deserved every bit of pain. Because of her, her mother had died alone in a mental hospital and her father had turned into a self-righteous prick.

Relief washed over her when she saw no sign of Ubaldo waiting for her at the bookstore, looking at her as if she were the Virgin Mary come to save him. This morning she'd have blown up at him. A clang. She swung around, hand on her gun. Nothing out of order. Damn, she needed to break the pattern before she took a full spin down into old habits. How she'd love a cigarette now. She stopped and went through her breathing exercises, relaxed her clenched fists then her arms, shoulders, neck...

Her gaze fell on the gate to the backyard. It stood ajar. Strange. She walked down the short corridor and peered around the corner. A bunch of kids lay huddled against the far wall. She swallowed the residual anger still burning inside her. The kids had invaded her space. Like Tony. And she'd shown them the way in. With a sigh, she turned away. It wasn't their fault she couldn't cope.

Lisa sorted the books on the shelves. People always put them back in the wrong places. Usually she enjoyed the task. Spotting a misplaced one she hadn't read yet, she'd scan the blurb and the first page. If it sounded interesting, she'd put it on the stack of books to read. Now she couldn't be bothered. She simply sorted them in alphabetical order, while she fought the rage bubbling up again. This wasn't her, but Tinker Bell, the angry fairy.

A knock at the roll-down gate made her jump. Her heart raced. She knew it was Tony. Bad timing. She'd hoped he'd silently disappear, embarrassed by last night's disaster. But he was a nice guy. Nice guys didn't just run away when things got rough. She opened the door.

Head lowered, shoulders sagging, he looked like a beaten puppy. She wouldn't be surprised if he blamed himself.

She forced a smile. "Hey."

He leaned in the door frame. "How are you?"

"Okay."

"You couldn't sleep anymore?"

"Woke up too early and couldn't bear the thought of having breakfast with you and pretending everything was all right."

He pulled her into a bear hug. She couldn't resist, pressed against him, her arms wrapped around his back, her cheek against his. Just a good-bye hug, she told herself. For a moment she felt safe and comforted.

"Can I see you tonight?" he asked, his voice scratchy.

She pulled away from him, fighting back tears. "No. You go home. I'll cope."

"C'mon, give us a chance, Lisa."

She shook her head. "It won't work, Tony. Please, go away and don't come back."

His eyes grew darker. "If that's what you want. But I'll never forget the night you slept in my arms."

No words squeezed through her knotted throat.

He brushed a strand of hair out of her face. "I'll call you later."

She watched him stroll down the street. Battling the urge to run after him, she slammed the door shut.

* * * *

Tony sat at his desk in the luxurious suite. Pressing the phone against his ear, he tried to listen to Frank, his manager, and Carlos, the new general manager for South America. All he saw was Lisa's pain-stricken face. He shouldn't have left, but she wanted him to stay away from her. No wonder. He cleared his throat and unmuted the conference phone. "Carlos, do you think you'll need me down here for the hiring, the job interviews?"

His boss cut in, "I planned to send you to China, Tony. But of course, if Carlos needs you in Brazil..."

Frank sounded reluctant to give up control over one of his scouts. This was the first Tony had heard about an assignment in China.

"Actually," Carlos said, "I could use someone who knows the place and the business."

Office politics, locking of horns, Tony thought. Well, he'd sit back and wait.

"But you can work with the agent we've got down there," his boss said.

"Are we that tight on money that I can't have the best start possible? Frank, you know it'll be your fault as much as mine if the Brazil office doesn't kick off."

Tony smiled. *Good one, Carlos.*

"Well, yes, of course. I mean, no, we're not that tight," Frank babbled. "I'm just wondering if Tony's time couldn't be spent more efficiently, doing something other than holding your hand."

Tony jerked up in his seat. That was way out of line. Icy silence followed. He wished he could see the faces, convinced his boss had just made a new enemy.

Frank cleared his throat. "Let's talk about it on Monday, when you're back in the office, Tony."

His boss was caving in. He'd let him return to Rio. With extra time in Brazil, maybe he could earn himself a second chance with Lisa. And get to know Carlos. Maybe he'd want Tony to stay long-term. Settling down didn't sound bad after years traveling all over the world. Always searching, never staying to enjoy what he found.

* * * *

Tony met Félix Borges in a conference room of the hotel. The slick guy, wearing a tight-fitting suit, smiled widely as he stood and shook Tony's hand. No wonder. Tony had told him on the phone they were ready to sign the contract.

"Mr. Norton, you've made the right decision."

They sat on opposite sides of the large desk. Borges riffled through papers then placed several pages in front of him and led Tony through the main items.

Reaching the end of the last page, Tony nodded. "Looks good. Thanks for your time and effort, Senhor Borges."

Borges bowed his head with a mocking smile. "Thanks for your business. I hope you had a great time in Rio and will come back someday."

"A great city with interesting people." Some of them weirder than most.

"How was the tour?"

"Fantastic."

Borges grinned. "No more guns pointed at you?"

"Only a few AK-47s in the *favela*."

"You went to a *favela*? Well, I guess you had your bodyguard with you."

Puzzled, he stared at the man. "My what?"

Borges's left eye twitched. "The hot, gun-wielding lady? No?"

Tony remembered telling him about Lisa and regretted it. He stood.

Borges sorted his papers into his briefcase then looked up. "How do you like Brazilian women? You think they live up to their fame?"

Trying to cool the anger bubbling up inside him, Tony placed his hands on the desk and leaned toward him. "Keep your nose out of my personal life."

"Okay." Smirking, the man stood and held out his hand. "All the best to you, Mr. Norton."

After a second's hesitation, Tony shook it. He'd still have to do business with the man. "And to you."

Teeth clenched, Tony marched to the elevators. *What a jerk.* Fortunately, he wouldn't have much to do with him from now on.

Back in his room, he flopped down on the bed and stared up at the ceiling. Lisa... With a sigh he sat up, pulled out his cellphone, and searched for her number. His hands felt damp, his heart picked up a beat. He pushed the dial button. An unknown female voice answered.

Surprised, he cleared his throat. "Hi, this is Tony Norton. May I talk to Lisa Kerry?"

"One moment, please."

Tony imagined the woman telling Lisa his name. He saw her shake her head violently.

"Yes?" Her voice sounded hard and uninviting.

"Have you changed your mind about tonight?"

"No."

"Listen, I'm really sorry. I was an idiot. I should have realized. It won't happen again. I'll…"

"You're right." Her voice sounded husky.

"What?"

She cleared her throat. "It won't happen again." She disconnected.

Tony flopped back on his bed. He couldn't simply give up on her. How could he forget last night? He needed a drink. *Make that a double*.

Chapter Thirteen

Max parked his inconspicuous brown Chevy in a dirt lot for commuters. He wore cut-off jeans, a soccer shirt, and a baseball cap. A good disguise for a drug lord sneaking out of the *favela*.

A hundred meters down the road sprawled the boys' favorite entertainment center. Like many times before, Max wondered if he was doing the right thing for Tatu and Luiz. Was he really helping them or getting them into more trouble? He couldn't see an alternative. Car theft was far less dangerous than the drug business.

Tired, he heaved himself out of the Chevy and strode along the road. Luiz and Tatu sat on a low concrete wall. They chatted, hands in the air, feet swinging. Just like any other kids. Tatu noticed Max first, jumped off the wall and came running, a bright smile on his face. For years, Max's main responsibility had been to keep that smile there, but now it was time for Tatu to grow up.

Luiz was different. Max watched him slide down the wall and saunter after his friend. Being responsible for the other kids had toughened him. Max felt like he was looking at himself in a mirror that reflected the past.

Acting as a role model for Tatu and Luiz scared the shit out of him. As if Tatu could read his mind, he slowed and assumed a cocky grin and a swagger. The boy trying to act like a man. Max was proud of his little brother. If something ever happened to that kid, he'd shoot himself.

Max shook off his doubts and worries, luxuries none of them could afford. The boys stood before him, the excitement at the prospect of some action shining through their solemn expressions. "Okay, guys, time to take your driving test. This is fucking serious. If you fool around, you're on your own."

Luiz and Tatu nodded, staring at him intently.

"What do you do if the police pull you over?"

"We stop the car and run," Luiz said.

"What do you not do?"

"Try to shake them off," Tatu replied.

"Right. And why not?"

Luiz said, "They are better drivers."

Tatu added, "For now."

Max couldn't suppress a grin. "What do you do if you wreck the car?"

They yelled in unison, "Steal another one."

Max burst into laughter.

* * * *

Luiz felt the thrill of his first real car theft. He wiped his sweaty palms on his T-shirt as they walked down the aisle in the parking lot.

Max sounded casual. "You go first, Luiz. Pick one."

Luiz scanned the rows quickly. "The blue BMW."

He was about to point, but Max caught his arm. "No pointing. It's supposed to be ours, right?"

"Right," Luiz whispered, cowed by his mistake.

When they reached the car, Max lit a cigarette and watched the entrance. They had gone through this many times. Luiz knew he could do it. He bumped against the car. No alarm. He marched to the driver's door and slid the thin bar between window and rubber lining. The lock opened. He eased behind the wheel and unlocked the doors for Max and Tatu. He removed the plastic covers below the steering column and tried to hot-wire the engine. Nothing happened. A knock on the roof. Luiz jumped out.

Max grinned. "Electronic immobilizer. Too new."

"You could have told me," Luiz protested.

Max shrugged then smirked.

Yeah, right. According to him, even failure served as a lesson. Luiz looked around. Nobody had noticed. He moved on and saw an older Toyota SUV. That should work. Again, he tested for an alarm. Then he opened the lock and set to work on the ignition. The engine came alive. The signal for Tatu and Max to get in.

"Well done," Max said. "Now, stay calm and get moving."

Luiz put the car in reverse and released the clutch. The engine stalled. *"Puta merda!"*

Max groaned. Frantic, Luiz restarted the engine, carefully backed into the aisle, and drove from the parking lot.

Relaxing now, Luiz steered the SUV through the hectic Rio de Janeiro traffic with ease until Tatu yelled from the backseat, "Fuck, police!"

Luiz battled his panic. A squad car passed them in the left lane. The cop in the passenger seat looked at him then signaled to pull over and stop the car.

"Okay, do it, Luiz," Max commanded in his no-bullshit voice.

Luiz pulled onto the shoulder, but left the engine running. The police car stopped in front of them. Max took a wad of money out of the front pocket of his jeans. "You stay," he said and stepped out.

Two cops walked toward him, hands resting on their guns. They slowed down, took in Max's appearance, and let their gazes settle on the money in his hand. Luiz watched him count out bills, hearing his voice through the rolled-down windows.

"Driving without a license," Max said. "Forgot the papers for the car." His fingers separated more bills. "Speeding, bribing police officers." Max held out five hundred *reais*.

They took the money without a word and strolled back to their car. Max watched them drive off. Then he swung around. Grinning, he slipped onto the passenger seat. "What are you waiting for? Just remember," he added, "without me around, you stop the car and run. You don't have the money to pay them off, but you're young and fast."

Ten minutes later, they reached the used car dealer on Avenida Dutra. Luiz pulled into the lot and parked near the little cubicle office. An older fellow ambled outside and greeted Max with a slap on the back. "Hey, nice to see you back in the biz, Max."

"No way, Renato. I'm training the boys. We'll be back with another one in an hour."

Renato scrutinized the car. "Great, I'll be waiting."

Luiz and Tatu took everything from the car that wasn't strictly part of it until Renato yelled, "Hey, leave the radio, I'll pay for it." He laughed out loud. "Must be your bad influence."

Max sneered at the man. "If you ever try to rip them off, you'll be dealing with me."

The laughter died in Renato's throat. "Me? Never!"

"Good."

Luiz grinned at Tatu. Everything was easy with a friend like Max.

Chapter Fourteen

Friday morning, Lisa was about to leave her apartment when her phone rang. Jango's voice sounded cheerful. "Hey Lisa, how's it going?"

Tony must have talked to him. "Jango, what's up? You're not calling to find out how I'm doing."

"All right, let's skip the pleasantries. What's with you and Tony Norton?"

"Why? Did he complain?"

"No, he looks like a junkie in withdrawal, shot and left on the street to bleed to death."

Lisa couldn't help smiling at his pathos. "And he didn't even get a last fix."

"Don't mock me. The look on his face, I've seen that before. When I looked in the mirror after Wanda gave me the boot."

Jango's ex-wife. He'd adored Wanda, but she'd run off with a rally driver. When she came crawling back, tired of her lover's cocaine excesses, Jango slammed the door in her face. Lisa pressed her right hand over her eyes and rubbed them. "I'm sorry, but it's not my fault if he can't take a no. He'll get over it."

"All right, you're a big girl, you know what you're doing. Lunch tomorrow?"

She knew he wouldn't accept a no. He'd keep bugging her until she agreed. "Okay, but don't even think about bringing Tony."

"By noon tomorrow he'll be on a plane back to New York."

"Good." Lisa hung up and sighed.

* * * *

She dreaded the evening, convinced Tony would contact her again, one way or another. When he hadn't by the time she closed the bookstore, she went out to the backyard. No sign of the kids. She opened the double doors to the workshop. The ancient smell of metal works hit her. It wasn't exactly a nice place. She tried the light switch. Neon tubes flickered alive. She took in the grimy windows, the oil stains on the concrete floor, the dust, and the cobwebbed lamps. She knew what it felt like to sleep in the open, being vulnerable to anyone and everyone. But this place looked like a prison.

She returned to the bookstore and called Jango. "Hey, my friend. Remember the workshop in my backyard? It's not likely that I'll be able to lease it again, right?"

"Yes, with the apartment buildings around, it's hopeless. You can't make too much noise. Why do you ask?"

"Maybe I'll have some use for it." Next she rang the handyman who did all the repair and remodeling work for her.

Shortly before eleven Tony called. She answered and listened to his drunken apology. She sighed. "Tony, I wanted you to sleep with me, okay? It's my fault it didn't work out. Have a safe trip home." She pushed the red button, switched the phone off, and tossed it on her desk. He'd be out of her life in a couple more hours.

Chapter Fifteen

At noon the next day, Lisa met Jango at their usual place, the restaurant across the street from her bookstore. Despite the lunch crowd, Jango had managed to secure their favorite table in the corner. She arrived two minutes early, but he'd still beaten her. Unlike most Brazilians, he was never late. Somewhere in his fifties, he still looked like a man in his best years. His dark hair showed silver streaks. His dark eyes sparkled when they saw her.

Jango rose to kiss her on both cheeks. "Lisa, it's good to see you. I'm worried about you."

They sat. Lisa leaned back and studied her friend. "There's nothing to worry about." Of course, he wouldn't believe her so she'd better distract him. "Are you going soft with old age?"

As she'd hoped, he flashed an indignant scowl. "I'm not old." Then he narrowed his eyes and smiled. "Nice try, Lisa. But I won't make it that easy for you to derail me." His face clouded over. "I'm so sorry, Lisa. If I could turn back time, I'd–"

"What the hell is going on in that thick head of yours?" Lisa growled, still hoping to discourage him. "It wasn't your fault. None of it." She leaned over the table. "Without you, I'd have rotted away in that prison."

She hadn't seen the military cop standing at the corner when she'd snatched Jango's wallet. Two decades ago.

Instinctively, Jango had grabbed her hand. She'd tried to struggle free. He retrieved his wallet, let go of her, and held out the sandwich he'd bought. Lisa stood transfixed until a big paw grabbed her neck and squeezed hard. Jango argued with the policeman, but he dragged her away.

Lisa shook her head to clear it. "Who knows what might have happened if you hadn't found me. I doubt I'd still be alive."

"So, what's been going on with Norton?" Jango asked.

Lisa sighed. "You can't solve all my problems."

"I can try."

She gave up. "Okay, I made a mistake. I thought it might work out. It didn't. That's all. I won't do it again. And certainly not with one of your clients."

"How can a clever girl like you be so stupid?"

"Says the man who changes girlfriends on a weekly basis."

"That's different. I'm too old to find a new wife."

"Bullshit. You're afraid to fall in love again."

He leaned back in his chair and crossed his arms. "Touché."

"No, you're right, I've been stupid."

"Feel like going to the shooting range with me tonight?"

She smiled. He knew how to cheer her up, how to make her feel in charge of her life; ever since he first placed a rifle in her hands.

* * * *

Félix drove along Avenida Vieira Souto. Like every Saturday, a crowd of people milled about the Ipanema beach promenade. With the roof of his convertible down, he drew a few lazy gazes from the girls, pretty and proud but attracted by his shiny red sports car. Every woman had a price, but he wasn't willing to pay.

Tony Norton sat on a plane now on his way back to the States. Out of his way. Félix grinned. And the girl with the gun would be his.

When he reached Copacabana, the streets bustled with shoppers.

He found the bookstore, but no parking space. Crawling past, he saw no sign of her behind the window. Maybe he should walk in and have a look around. No, he didn't want to meet the bookseller, but the girl with the gun.

He drove off and found a parking garage. Savoring his growing anticipation, he strolled back and turned into her street. There she stood, at the curb. She scanned the traffic and then weaved through the slow-moving cars. She disappeared into a restaurant.

Félix walked past the windows, but only saw his own reflection. He smiled at himself before he followed her inside. His eyes found her immediately. She sat at a table with an older guy, mixed race. Damn, the *despachante* who worked for Tony. Would he recognize him? Félix picked a table that offered him a good view of her, but was out of Jango's direct line of vision. So what if they saw him? Why shouldn't he sit in a restaurant in Copacabana?

Speaking rapidly, she looked agitated, maybe even angry. Under her wide T-shirt something bulged. A small gun? Definitely too big for a cellphone.

Félix leaned back in his chair, legs sprawled out. She wouldn't just scream and cry and let him do whatever he wanted. She'd fight, defend herself, and maybe even succeed? What a thought.

The waiter blocked his view. "What would you like, Senhor?"

"A glass of pineapple juice," he said without looking up. The white shirt and black pants disappeared.

What if he walked over and greeted Jango? He would introduce him to the woman. Maybe they'd ask him to join them at their table. No, he didn't want to have lunch with her, making small talk. He wanted her to get to know his real self and watch her fear grow. He wanted to smell and taste her despair. At the end.

A glass appeared on the table with a slight thump. Félix smirked. He'd pissed off the waiter by simply ignoring him. Why should he acknowledge a servant?

The woman leaned closer to Jango. He sat back crossing his arms. No, she wouldn't serve anyone. The defiant look on her face aroused him even more than her gun.

Chapter Sixteen

Luiz and Tatu got off the bus and approached the train station, where they'd arranged to meet with the rest of the gang.

"Fuck! I can't believe it," Tatu said.

Luiz glanced at him sideways. "What?"

"That's Rena, trying to turn on the old fart." Tatu nodded straight ahead toward the stairs leading up to the entrance of the old building. Now Luiz saw her too. She was talking to a man in a dark suit, carrying a suitcase in one hand and a briefcase strapped over the opposite shoulder.

Luiz shook his head. "I didn't know she started hooking."

Tatu sighed. "Me either. Just look at her."

Rena threw her head back and laughed at the man, hips shifted to one side, small breasts pushed out. The man bent and put his suitcase down. When he straightened up again, he stood askew, with the briefcase pulling on his left shoulder.

Tatu turned away. "Sorry, I can't bear it."

He put his right arm on Tatu's shoulder. "We better watch out for her, though."

"Yeah you watch, and tell me if he gives us a reason to beat him up." Tatu kicked an empty can.

Luiz kept his eyes on the ill-fitted pair. The man smiled at Rena and put the briefcase down between his feet. She made a step toward him while he pulled out his wallet. Luiz grabbed Tatu's arm and pulled him around. "Watch this."

Rena clutched the briefcase, snatched the wallet, and ran. The man gaped for two seconds before he chased after her, pushing through the crowd around him. Then he stopped and swiveled around, obviously remembering his suitcase. Too late. Ubaldo had dragged it away. Luiz and Tatu burst out in laughter.

"You think they still need us?" Tatu wondered.

Luiz shook his head. "Not anymore."

* * * *

72

When they arrived at their usual meeting point behind the central station, Ubaldo wore a far-too-big, pin-striped suit jacket, and silk boxer shorts over his cut-off jeans. Rena had slipped into a white shirt that reached below her knees. The suitcase lay open with clothes scattered around. Gordinho scavenged their booty.

"That was excellent. Risky but excellent," Luiz said.

Rena's eyes sparkled with excitement. "You saw us?"

Tatu laughed and ruffled her hair. "You're crazy, Rena."

She beamed at Ubaldo and kissed him on the mouth. Tatu and Luiz looked at each other and then back at the girl.

"He's my boyfriend," she announced.

"Ah, okay," Tatu said darting Ubaldo a sideways glance.

"Have you checked what's in the briefcase?" Luiz asked.

"No, not yet. It's heavy though," Rena told him.

Luiz squatted and opened it. "Wow, a laptop. That should be worth something. And the wallet?"

Rena grinned. "A bit more than five hundred."

"Cool," Tatu said. "Enough to pay off a cop."

Luiz laughed at the idea. "Fantastic. So, are you going to take us out for dinner, Princess?"

"Yes."

"Okay, take the silly clothes off."

They abandoned the suitcase and marched off to their favorite hamburger joint, Luiz carrying the laptop. He had no idea what it was worth, but even the elegant case drew attention from people passing them. They should get rid of it quickly. Self-conscious, he kept watching out for cops and saw the gang too late. Five boys crossed the street and headed toward them. Shit. Luiz stared at the guy walking three steps ahead, flanked by a fat boy, tall and broad.

"Watch out," Tatu whispered. "I've seen those guys beat up someone pretty bad."

The leader smirked at Luiz. Then he grabbed Rena while the fat boy pulled the case from Luiz's shoulder and pushed him back. "What you got, baby-face?"

Luiz held on to the strap and yanked hard. The boy stumbled toward him, and Luiz slammed a fist in his stomach. Fatty doubled over. Luiz brought up his knee in the guy's face. He screamed but Rena's outraged cries rang louder. Luiz swung around. She struggled with the leader, while two of his boys had Tatu down on the ground, kicking and punching him. Another had his arm around Gordinho's neck. Ubaldo stood in the center of the fight not knowing what to do. Luiz kicked the fat boy a last time; then he ran toward Tatu.

"Let her go!" Ubaldo yelled.

Luiz saw the shock on the leaders face and spun around. Ubaldo pointed a gun at the boy and Rena. Dammit. Where'd he get that? Luiz's heart pounded. "Don't shoot."

Rena shook off the hands clasping her.

"Hey, it was just a joke," the leader cried.

Ubaldo's hands shook, but he kept the gun trained on the guy. Luiz walked toward him. "It's okay. Let them go."

Ubaldo kept aiming at them as they retreated. Rena slung her arms around him and pushed the pistol aside. It pointed at Luiz.

"Fucking hell!" He grabbed the barrel and pried the gun from Ubaldo's fingers.

"Hey, it's mine," he protested.

"Idiot! You could have killed someone." Luiz checked the little Taurus. Loaded but on safety. He released the breath he'd held. "Where the hell did you get it?"

"It was in the suitcase."

Luiz glared at Rena. She should have had more sense than to let him keep it. She pressed her lips together and hung her head.

"Leave her alone." Ubaldo kicked his shin.

Luiz slapped him.

Scowling, the boy rubbed his cheek. "It saved us."

"From what?" Luiz stared at him.

Ubaldo looked confused. "From getting beaten and robbed. And...and the guy was touching Rena."

"And you'd have shot them if they hadn't run away?" Luiz saw tears well up in the boy's eyes. "You don't pull a gun if you're not willing to kill someone." Max's words when he and Tatu had asked him for guns two years ago. Tatu sat cross-legged on the sidewalk, with a bloody face but grinning anyway. He probably remembered Max's lecture well. Luiz struggled to keep a straight face while he shoved the pistol in the waistband of his shorts and pulled the T-shirt over it.

Chapter Seventeen

Luiz felt a foot gently pushing him in the side. Feet were never gentle. He opened his eyes and saw Lisa standing over him. Shit. Sooner or later she had to catch them. But she didn't look pissed off, only a bit spooky in the early morning light.

"You've got to be outta here in twenty minutes."

"Okay, sorry. It just..."

"You can come back tonight." She turned and walked away.

Luiz couldn't believe he'd heard right. He shook Tatu awake. Why had nobody noticed her? She could have killed them all. Well, maybe not her. But someone could have.

* * * *

After a long day working with Tatu at the recycling site, sorting other people's trash, Luiz felt more than ready for a little fun. They heard the music before they saw the party. Everyone living in the *favela* was out dancing, drinking, chatting. The bands played for free—for some, their first public gig. Samba, funk, and hip-hop dominated. Beer and cocktails were cheap. Women sold hot dogs, pastries, and corn sticks while men roasted meat on barbecue pits. The girls were dressed up for their *favela* party, the second biggest event of the year after *carnaval*. The boys wore their coolest rapper outfits. Couples danced to the samba rhythms as if they were making love. Luiz bought two bottles of Brahma and handed Tatu one. "Have you seen Max yet?"

Tatu shook his head. "No, but his men are everywhere."

Luiz shrugged. "Maybe he's found himself a girl."

"Don't think he has to search."

"Look at those guys." Luiz nodded toward three men standing close together, wearing jeans and ironed shirts. "They look like cops."

"Stiff and scared."

"What the hell are they doing here?" Luiz asked. Normally the police would stay far away from a *favela* party.

"Let's check if there are more."

"Okay." Luiz slipped through the throng, watching out for anyone who looked like they weren't having the time of their life. The crowd grew denser. He squeezed through and saw some of Max's soldiers push an older man with a white beard and nice suit toward Max, who stood chatting with a pretty girl selling beer. Max turned and gave his soldiers a puzzled look. Luiz ventured closer.

"What's up?" Max asked Mussolini.

"He was snooping around, asking people strange questions. Maybe a cop."

Max frowned at the man. "You a cop?"

The man shook his head. "I'm a journalist writing about drug trafficking and the parallel society with its own laws." He reached into his jacket.

Mussolini pressed his revolver against the man's temple. Unfazed, the journalist flashed a press ID.

"Nice to meet you, Jimmy Duraz." He held out his hand. "I'm Max."

The reporter's hand hung suspended in midair. "Shit," he breathed.

Max smirked. A second later Jimmy grasped his hand and shook it. "The big man himself. More than I could've hoped for."

Luiz couldn't wait any longer and squeezed through the bystanders. "Max, there are cops around."

Max arched his eyebrows. "Cops?" He looked at the journalist. "You brought cops?"

The man's eyes widened. "Maybe they heard about my project? But why should they care?"

"Just kidding, man." Max turned back to the girl.

"Wait, can I do an interview with you?

Grinning, Max looked over his shoulder. "First, I'll get you a beer."

The journalist smiled at Luiz. "I always imagined drug lords to be a lot rougher."

Luiz laughed.

"What?"

He shook his head at the strange man. "You don't want to meet Max when things get rough."

"You work for him?"

"No, I'm a friend. Gotta run." Luiz dove back into the crowd, afraid of more dangerous questions.

* * * *

The Copacabana streets felt too quiet after the party, and Luiz wanted nothing more than sleep.

"You think we can camp in her backyard again?" Tatu asked.

"She said we could come back. I bet the others are already there." Luiz liked the place. He felt safer in that backyard than he had anywhere else, except the few times Max had let them sleep at the *boca*. As a rule he didn't want to have them near. Too dangerous, he kept saying, but Luiz couldn't see why.

They strolled past the bookshop and sneaked through the gate. Something was wrong. A dim light illuminated the backyard and the double door to the workshop stood open. As they ventured closer, they heard subdued voices. Luiz looked at Tatu, but his friend only shrugged and moved on. When they reached the door, Luiz didn't trust his eyes. The floor was covered with tiles in all kinds of colors. Along one wall, real mattresses were lined up, covered with linen. And pillows. Rena, Ubaldo and Gordinho lay scattered on them, giggling, talking.

"Hey, what's going on?" Luiz asked.

Ubaldo sat up. "Lisa did it. I helped."

"For us?" Luiz felt his voice crack. Tears burned in his eyes. Nobody did stuff like this for street kids.

"I like it," Rena said. "It's much prettier."

Luiz let his gaze wander. A large table stood at the other side of the room with chairs around it. He sank onto a mattress. "Wow."

Despite his exhaustion, he couldn't fall asleep for a long time after the excited voices of his friends had died down. Not used to pillows and mattresses, he lay awake wondering about Lisa, unable to make any sense of her behavior. When he did fall asleep, he dreamed of his mother. She was holding him in her arms, singing a song. Her voice was the only thing he remembered.

* * * *

78

Luiz woke to the rustling of paper. When he opened his eyes, he saw Lisa pouring a bag of bread rolls into a large bowl on the table. A basket held fresh fruit. She placed butter, jam, and cheese next to the bread, and a stack of plastic plates. Then she tiptoed toward the door.

"Hey," Luiz whispered.

Lisa flinched. Her head whipped around to look over her shoulder. She stared at him for a moment before she relaxed her pose.

Luiz scrambled to his feet and walked outside with her. "Why are you doing all this?" he asked.

She smiled. "A simple thank you will do."

"Thanks, but I need to know anyway."

"Need to? You don't have to come here." Her eyebrows drew together and her lips formed a thin line.

"How do I know I can trust you?"

"You don't. Never trust anybody. You should have learned that lesson on the streets."

What an arrogant bitch. "You don't know anything about living on the streets. Trusting your friends is the most important thing."

"Your friends can't always help you." Her face softened. She looked away.

His anger turned into frustration. He'd never be able to figure her out. Just then, she fixed her gaze on him. "I know what it's like, Luiz. I used to be one of you, one of the lost and forgotten children of Rio."

Luiz stared at her. Lisa a street kid? "No way." He looked her up and down then spread out his arms. "You own all this and I bet you didn't make the money with drugs or bank robberies."

She laughed. "No, my father bought the apartment building for me. I guess he felt guilty." She fell silent and turned away.

Luiz snorted. "How can a street kid have a rich father?"

"Anything's possible, Luiz." She strode toward the back entrance to the bookstore.

Luiz shook his head and returned to the hall.

Tatu stood in the doorway looking at him. "What were you talking about?"

"I'm not sure."

Chapter Eighteen

Lisa leaned against the back door to the bookshop and watched the painters file in. Staying busy helped to keep the past locked away.

She couldn't change the world, so she had ignored it for the last three years. And she'd been happy. Lisa grunted at her lie. She had buried herself. Now she'd grown roots and sprouted to new life. She cared about something other than books that allowed her to escape reality. But caring was dangerous. Got you hurt.

All the kids helped with the remodeling work. They carried buckets for the painters, cleaned brushes, and handed them their tools. Luiz and Tatu painted the outside wall, while Rena stuck adhesive tape along the window frames.

Every morning, Lisa rose early to buy breakfast for the kids and drink her coffee with them. They were fun, smart, independent children. Now she repaid what she owed other street kids. She shook off the memories of her wandering alone through the streets of Rio, at the age of ten, and entered the bookstore. Rejane had already opened up, but there were no customers yet. "Morning, Lisa. What's up with those kids in the back?"

With her dark hair tied back and her lips pressed into a thin line, Rejane looked much older than her twenty-four years. Lisa ignored the disapproving look on the shop assistant's face. It was none of her business. "They're going to stay in the old workshop."

"People won't like it. They are criminals."

Lisa stared at her in disbelief and felt twenty-year-old rage boil up inside her. Rejane lived in the *favela*. She knew how easy it was to end up in the streets. If one of Lisa's tenants complained, she could forgive them. They were part of the thin middle class, fending for themselves, never getting very far, suppressed by the rich, and threatened by the poor.

"You telling me all poor people are criminals?" Lisa asked and heard the irritation seep from her voice. She clenched her hands. Get a grip.

"No, but street kids have to beg or steal to survive." Rejane pouted.

"They have to eat and sleep, just like you and me. They'll stay. If you don't like it, you can quit."

"Don't be so self-righteous. I don't mind the little guy doing odd jobs for you. He wants to earn his keep. But this lot is different." Rejane turned away with a huff.

Lisa unclenched her hands and jaws with a conscious effort. She was overreacting. "I won't send them away."

Rejane swung around to face her. "You're the boss—but you'll land yourself in big trouble."

"I guess that's my problem, then." Lisa couldn't stand Rejane's company right now. "Sorry, I need some fresh air."

Rejane's mouth dropped open, her eyes went wide. She reached out a hand, but Lisa brushed past her. She couldn't afford to lose control now. Whatever the girl had seen in her face needed to be contained.

She marched down the street to work off her anger. When she passed the pharmacy, the owner stepped outside and called to her. "Senhora Kerry! What's with those street kids hanging around your bookstore?"

She ignored him and walked on. Rejane's words rang in her ears.

* * * *

That evening Lisa returned to the backyard and took Luiz aside. They sat on a makeshift bench of spare wooden planks and bricks. She asked him to keep a low profile.

"Trouble?"

She nodded. "People are noticing."

"And they don't like it."

"No, they don't."

"Did you really live on the streets?"

Lisa smiled. He wouldn't give up. Why not drag her memories out into the light? She trusted Luiz would understand better than any of the mental health professionals her father had asked to fix her. "My father was American. He held some important position at a gold mine in Minas Gerais. My mother worked as a waitress in a restaurant or bar. They fell in love, *Mamãe* got pregnant, they married."

Luiz's eyebrows shot up. "He married her?"

"Yeah, and they lived happily for many years. For my tenth birthday, *Mamãe* took me to Rio. My father couldn't come because of an emergency at the mine. On the train, she read my favorite book to me. *Peter Pan*. The Rio train station bustled with people. I wanted to see and hear and smell everything. *Mamãe* looked at handbags on a rack outside a shop next to a toy store. She let me go inside on my own. There was this nice old man smiling and asking me questions. He let me pick a stuffed animal. I wanted the crocodile, and he bought it for me. I have only vague memories of him taking me to an ice cream booth. Then he said my mother was waiting for us. I followed him into a dark alley, clutching my crocodile and happily licking my ice cream, when I realized he wouldn't know where *Mamãe* was. I ran away. He tried to catch me, but I escaped. There were people everywhere. I asked for directions to the train station, hoping to find *Mamãe,* but she wasn't there. Scared, I searched until it got dark. A man in a uniform chased me away. Hungry and thirsty I stumbled through the streets and asked for food. Most folks turned away. Too tired to go on, I crashed behind a restaurant where I managed to find some leftovers in the trash."

She swallowed and met his gaze. His mouth hung open, lips moving, but no words came.

"The second day I met other children. They helped me. And now I help you. Does that make sense?"

"Wow," he said. "But how did your parents find you?"

Lisa's eyes filled with tears. "During the next couple of months, my friends taught me to steal. At first, food from the market stands, then I learned to pick pockets, and became pretty good at it. When I went for the wallet of this rich-looking young man, I screwed up and got arrested."

"Shit! Don't tell me you were in the detention center?" He stared at her.

"I was. Three days at the police station, then off to the detention center without formal paperwork. You ever been arrested?"

Luiz nodded. "It was hell. I was tough enough to fight off the older boys, but the things they did to the younger kids..." Luiz made a throwing up gesture.

"No boys at ours, but two male guards for the night shift. One of them liked to have fun with the little girls." She couldn't go on. Her throat tightened.

Luiz pressed his lips together, his eyes moistened. She wondered how a tale like hers could still shock him. She had to wipe that expression off his face. "I killed him many years later when I returned from the U.S."

His lips parted. He blinked. "You didn't."

"I did. And I'm proud of it. Just because you've been a victim once doesn't mean you'll always be one." She scrutinized his face. "But you know that, don't you? You're smart."

Again, his puzzled stare.

"What?" she asked.

He shook his head. "Nobody's ever called me smart."

Lisa laughed and ruffled his greasy hair. "The important thing is that you know what you can do."

"How did you get to America? How did you manage to kill him? What —"

"Too many questions for one day." She rose, but he grabbed her arm, a silent plea in his eyes.

"Do you have family?"

Luiz nodded. "An aunt. My father died in a gang fight and *Mamãe* got sick."

Lisa sat down again. "Okay, here comes the fairy-tale part. The guy whose wallet I tried to steal, Jango, he felt really bad about the police taking me. He went to the station and asked to see me. They claimed I'd never been there. Later he told me I called for Peter Pan when the police dragged me away, but I don't remember that. He wondered if I was English or American. So he checked with the U.S. and British embassy, and when he learned about a missing ten-year-old girl fitting my description he contacted my father. It took them several weeks to find me in the labyrinth of justice and get me out of that hell-hole."

"This Jango really exists?"

"Yeah, he does. He's a *despachante*. Maybe you'll meet him someday. You know what's funny? When they came to get me, I only remember Jango being there, not my father. Maybe I blamed him for not keeping me and my mother safe. I kept staring at Jango. He'd turned into a grown up Peter Pan for me."

"Who is this Peter Pan you keep talking about?"

She smiled. "The hero in a children's story. Maybe I'll tell it to you someday." Her smile faded. "My father blamed my mother, even though he had put his job before his family. I remember some screaming fights ending with my mother in tears. Then he took me to the States and broke her heart.

83

He wouldn't allow her any contact with me." She remembered those sad birthdays when she waited for the mailman to bring a card, or maybe even a present, from her mother.

"I returned to Rio when I was twenty-one, to face the demons of my past, and to find my mother. But by then she'd killed herself—in a mental hospital. I never meant to stay, but couldn't leave. For whatever reason, I feel at home here. The very place where I'd spent the worst time of my life. A couple years later I tracked down Captain Hook."

"Who?"

"Vitor Fraga, the guard who liked to beat and rape little girls."

* * * *

Lisa lay awake for a long time that night. Glad she'd told Luiz, she allowed images of her past to spin in her head and chase each other. Only when memories of Tony seeped in and got entangled with images of Vitor Fraga did she curl up and cry. She hadn't wanted much, just a sliver of happiness. At least for one night. Maybe even more? What if she hadn't sent Tony away? Could she build a normal life with him? No more dreaming, Tinker Bell. You're trapped in Neverland.

This time, Lisa didn't allow anger to take over. She hugged herself and let the tears flow. If only her mother were still alive.

Chapter Nineteen

Max sat at the large table in the otherwise bare main room of the *boca*, reading Jimmy Duraz's article on police corruption and the law of the drug traffickers when his cellphone rang. He answered and flinched at the outburst. When his boss had vented his anger and fell silent, Max pressed the phone against his ear again. "You done congratulating me?"

"Fucking idiot. Shouldn't have let you take over the gang."

Max spoke rapidly while he had a chance. "The bastards got their asses kicked and I didn't even have to move a finger. I don't think we'll see Nassar storming in again just to prove to the new *capitão* that he's a good doggy." Silence on the other end. "How did you like the part about the good tyrant?"

Max groaned while he half-listened to the scratchy outburst. Prison life didn't become the man, but from his cell he could safely do business. All the big shots pulled the strings from inside.

The door flew open. Tatu and Luiz stormed in. Max held up a hand to them. "Yes, boss, I know what irony is." Max rolled his eyes. "Sorry, gotta run, delivery's coming in. Talk to you later." Max disconnected.

"Hey, Max, what's up?" Tatu sat next to him.

"I'm in the newspaper. Luiz, you coward, why didn't you tell Jimmy anything?"

"Me? No way." Luiz put his hands up as if to keep the devil away.

Max laughed and pushed the paper to Tatu.

His brother pushed it back. "You know I can't read."

"Course you can, lazy bastard."

Tatu crossed his arms. "I forgot everything."

Luiz put a shoulder bag on the table.

"What's that?" Max asked.

"A computer," Luiz said. "We thought you might want it."

Max unzipped the bag and took out the laptop. Carefully, he opened the lid and pushed the power button.

Tatu sneered. "With your education and all."

Max slapped him over the head. Tatu sprang up and swung his fist at him. Max caught it, twisted his arm, and forced him back down on the bench.

"You sit down, too," he told Luiz. "You're going to learn how to read and write. Now. And don't you fucking dare say it's my fault you dropped out of school."

They remembered the alphabet pretty quickly. Max kept them typing words and sentences into the computer for over an hour. Then he made them read the newspaper article aloud. The first half Tatu, the second Luiz. They stumbled over complicated words but fought their way through the jungle of letters. "All right, that wasn't too bad. Now get outta here."

They jumped up and made for the door.

"Hey," Max yelled after them.

They stopped.

"Tomorrow, same time. Bring the newspaper."

They nodded. Max nodded. They ran; he grinned.

* * * *

Luiz and Tatu strolled down the narrow alleys and stopped to buy sandwiches. "How much money do we have left?" Tatu asked.

"Twenty-seven *reais*. We need to get more, but not today."

"Getting breakfast makes us lazy."

Luiz grinned. "I don't mind though."

Tatu nudged him. "You're getting fat."

Luiz punched him in the arm. "I got more muscles than you, baby boy."

They arrived at the workshop just before dusk to find a new surprise. A toilet and a shower had been installed during the day. Luiz struggled to understand why Lisa would spend so much money on them. He shook his head. A hand touched his shoulder.

Lisa stood behind him. "You like it?" she asked. "The pipes were already in place."

"I haven't had a shower in years, I think."

"Yeah, I can smell that." She winked at him.

"You are crazy."

"Maybe."

* * * *

The next day Luiz bought a newspaper at the little kiosk across from the bookstore, something he'd never done before. He felt...educated.

He hit Tatu over the head with the paper. "Don't look like that, it's all your fault."

Tatu snorted and glared.

"Stop sulking. You provoked Max. I think we got a pretty fair deal."

"Gimme the damn paper." Tatu snatched and opened it. "Hey, is that the guy Max told all the stuff about corrupt cops?"

Luiz peered over Tatu's shoulder at the picture of Jimmy Duraz. "Yeah, that's him."

They bent over it and worked through the headline: SHOT DEAD: JOURNALIST ACCUSING POLICE OF CORRUPTION.

"Shit," Tatu said.

"Max's gonna be pissed off."

They climbed the narrow stairs behind a hunched old woman carrying two plastic bags of groceries. They couldn't pass her. Luiz sighed.

"*Olá*, senhora, you need a hand?"

She looked surprised, then smiled. "I live all the way up the hill. Best view, but too many stairs."

"We'll carry your stuff," Luiz said.

"I'll do it." Tatu grabbed the bags and stepped aside. "You take Max the paper."

Luiz nodded and squeezed past them.

The old lady said, "If you rob me, I'll tell the drug gang. They'll give you a good hiding."

Grinning, Luiz didn't wait for Tatu's reply. He ran to the *boca*. The door stood ajar. Luiz pushed past Mussolini.

"Where's my dear little brother?" Max asked looking up from his coffee cup.

Luiz threw the paper on the table. "Carrying an old lady's grocery bags," he said, trying to catch his breath. "Be here soon. Read." He stabbed his finger at Jimmy's picture.

Max slammed his fist down on the paper. "The fucking bastards." He kept reading and swearing. When he reached the end, he flung the paper across the room. "I bet that roach Nassar killed him. He'll pay for that."

Chapter Twenty

Lisa locked the bookstore at seven in the evening and pulled down the iron shutters. One of her renters passed. She greeted the middle-aged bureaucrat, who was wearing the same suit as every workday.

He glowered at her. "What are those brats doing in the back? You shouldn't let them stay there."

She battled the onslaught of anger and managed to keep a calm voice. "That's none of your business, Senhor Mahler."

"They're dangerous. If they break into the house and rob us, you'll be responsible."

"They won't. There isn't even access to the apartments from the backyard. So get a grip."

"Me? I should get a grip?" He grasped her arm and shook her. The shock of the physical contact froze her blood, and her right hand clutched the butt of her gun.

"If those kids don't disappear, I'll call the pest control." With that, Mahler flung her arm away and stormed off. Lisa trembled. *How dare he?* She willed herself to calm down, taking deep breaths. After a moment she managed to release the grip on her pistol under the denim jacket. She'd kick the bastard out of the apartment. Pest control? What an asshole. Others would feel the same way.

She pushed through the gate, marched to the backyard, and stepped into the workshop—now shelter. The kids lay sprawled on the mattresses. Luiz, Tatu and Gordinho played cards, all three with burning cigarettes dangling from the corners of their mouths. Ubaldo and Rena lay on their stomachs close to each other, whispering. How could anyone mind having them around?

"Hey, have you ever been up on the Pão de Açúcar?" she asked.

Luiz looked up, took the cigarette between two fingers, and blew a cloud of smoke in her direction. "Are you kidding?"

Rena and Ubaldo both turned. Tatu threw a pillow at her. Lisa caught it.

"Meet me at the corner in five minutes if you want to see the most beautiful sunset." She hit a gaping Luiz full in the face with the pillow and ran.

Lisa jogged down the street to the parking garage and got the van she used for larger tour groups. The five kids squeezed in. The short drive to Urca might have ended in a war on the backseats with Rena teasing Tatu and Gordinho taking away Ubaldo's ball cap, if she hadn't started to sing "Wheels on the Bus", making up additional lyrics in Portuguese. Tears threatened as she remembered her parents singing to her, taking turns, and switching languages. She looked in the rear view mirror. Not exactly the right age level for a group of teens, but it worked like magic. They fell silent, listened, giggled; then they fell in with the refrain and started to make up new lines.

"Little fingers go snatch, snatch, snatch," Rena sang.

Gordinho piped up. "Lisa takes us round, round, round."

Tatu chimed in. "Kalashnikov goes bang, bang, bang."

"Good boys don't shoot, shoot, shoot." Rena cracked up laughing and they all joined in.

At the parking lot in front of the station, they spilled out of the van and gaped at a departing cable car.

Gordinho looked at her, a frown wrinkling his forehead. "You'll take us up there in one of those glass boxes?"

"Yeah, if you are not too afraid." She locked the van.

The boy chuckled. "I don't care if I shit myself, I want to go."

Rena tugged on her shirtsleeve. "Will they let us get on?"

Lisa smiled. "Of course. If you can afford it, nothing's off limits in Brazil."

"Even when you're black?"

"Yeah. Money makes you as good as white." She sighed and stroked the girl's hair.

"What are we waiting for?" Tatu said. "Let's go."

They strolled over to the ticket counter. She paid with her credit card and ushered them past the souvenir shop up to the departure platform. Luiz murmured, "Are you crazy?"

"Why do you keep asking?"

"I'd have to steal a car to afford that."

"Well, I don't, which is good. I never learned how to do that. And I wasn't a very skilled pickpocket either."

Luiz chortled.

In the cable car, the kids stuck close to her. Lisa's most appreciative tour group. They laughed with excitement and asked her many questions, their curiosity insatiable. She had to identify the beaches they saw and where the *centro* lay. They'd never seen a map of Rio and had no idea of the city's outline.

Maybe for the first time in their lives, they realized how big their home town was. They couldn't get enough of the view. On the second leg up to the Pão de Açúcar, they saw a plane dip toward Santos Dumont Airport in the bay.

"It's going to fall into the sea," Rena yelled, her face and hands pressed against the glass window of the cabin.

"Don't worry, the pilot knows what he's doing." After the plane landed safely, Rena smiled at her. The cable car came to a wobbly stop.

The sunset wasn't as spectacular as on the evening she brought Tony up here, but her charges stared awestruck at the rose-colored mountains, the city lights flashing on, and the reflections in the sea at the illuminated boat harbor.

"I never thought Rio was so bright," Gordinho whispered and slipped his warm soft hand in hers.

And dangerous, Lisa thought. The dark and evil lurked among all those lights.

Rena leaned into her. "Thank you, Lisa."

* * * *

Driving home, Lisa realized she'd just had the most fun since she took Tony up there. Tony again. She had to put him out of her mind. She dropped the kids off at the gate and pulled the van into the parking garage. Walking back, she saw the kids still loitering in front of the gate, waiting for her. Not good. She feared more complaints, but spotted no familiar faces in the street ahead.

Looking over her shoulder, she saw a black car approach, slow down, then pass. The BMW stopped near the kids in a no-parking zone. Why?

Simply to drop someone off? Lisa's stomach cramped with a surge of panic. The passenger door opened. A black-clad arm reached out. A flickering bottle smashed on the ground and burst into flames. Among the kids.

Lisa drew her gun. Her heart raced. She fired several shots at the car. The back window shattered, the door closed, and the engine roared.

"Fucking cowards!" Lisa yelled. She emptied the magazine into the moving car. High-pitched screams. She swung around. Luiz and Tatu tried to extinguish the flames eating at Gordinho's legs and torso. She ran toward them, pulling off her jacket.

Luiz and Tatu jumped back as she wrapped the denim around the burning boy and pushed it down toward his legs, suffocating the flames. The acrid smell of melting plastic and burning flesh stung her nose. Beside her, Luiz retched. She pulled her shirtsleeves over her hands and peeled off the black ooze the polyester T-shirt had turned into. Her stomach cramped. The wounds looked nasty. Her gaze traveled down to his charred legs. She wanted to throw up, like Luiz.

Gordinho drew quick flat breaths, his eyes staring into the sky. Shaking, Lisa stood. She swallowed hard before she found her voice. "Stay with him. I'll...get the van." Lisa ran back to the parking garage. The guards flanking the driveway must have heard the shots and tried to stop her. "A child's been injured. Get out of my way." She pushed past the men, hopped in her van, sped down the ramp, and stopped with screeching brakes next to the motionless Gordinho. She pulled open the sliding door. Luiz grabbed him by the charcoaled shoes and Tatu reached under the boy's arms. They lifted him onto the first row of seats and jumped in behind him.

Chapter Twenty-One

Félix leaned back in the driver's seat and closed his eyes. His heart still raced. Three hours of waiting had paid off. He hadn't dared to hope she'd actually witness the attack. But she'd seen everything and shot at the idiots. He'd just meant to get the brats out of his way, but this was much better. Maybe she killed Cortez. The thought aroused Félix even more.

When he'd told the fool about the gang of street kids in Copacabana, Cortez had acted all disgusted but his eyes sparked with the possibility of a more public action. Cortez and his cronies thought him a coward, because he didn't enjoy shooting street kids and bums, or burning them alive. Not that he had qualms about it, but where was the fun in that? Just like his uncle's disgusting tales of torturing helpless, tied up people. Where was the challenge if they stood no chance? He played a different game, needed the fight, the possibility that things could go wrong. He rubbed his groin. He wanted her.

What now? She was gone, likely taking the boy to a hospital. Félix snorted. How could she? But her caring made the game much more interesting. She was so different. His obsession and his enemy. Snorting, he started the engine.

Heading toward quaint Bairro Peixoto, he passed the popular square, where families ate a picnic dinner, and children kicked balls and roamed the playground, oblivious of what he'd done. He reached the Túnel Velho. A man slept on the sidewalk in the dark, stinky tube. What a miserable existence. Cortez and his buddies might kill the lowlife. But right now they were probably too shocked, because they had been on the receiving end for once. Félix chuckled. Served them right.

The image of Lisa flared up in his mind again. The professional stance she took, the way she held the pistol firmly in both hands and shot to kill, without a second's hesitation. He tugged at his pants, trying to make room for his erection.

He reached Botafogo and turned into a small street where prostitutes of all shapes, colors, and ages lined the sidewalk. Félix slowed the car, scanning them. Adrenaline pumped through his body. None of them resembled the woman. Fuck it, he thought, and stopped in front of a tall black girl. She looked strong and healthy. Félix pushed the passenger door open.

"*Olá, gato*," she purred, folding her long bare legs into the car. Félix noticed the high heels on her blue shoes. Not that tall, but maybe she'd put up a good fight anyway. He gazed into her black eyes and smiled. "*Olá, querida.*"

Chapter Twenty-Two

Lisa followed the emergency admittance signs and blew the horn twice when she stopped. Two men in white came running with a stretcher. Relief flooded her. Help was close. Luiz and Tatu pulled back the sliding door and jumped out. The medics picked up the boy and transferred him onto a gurney. One of the men told her to move the car. She parked the van and walked back. No sign of Luiz or Tatu. The smell of disinfectant hit her as she entered the neon-lit hallway. Lisa spotted them in the busy waiting area. Luiz talked into the public phone.

She settled next to Tatu and noticed his burned hands. "Hey, what's up?"

"Luiz's calling a friend."

Lisa nodded. Of course they'd have friends, and possibly family.

Luiz hung up and gave Tatu the thumbs up. When he met Lisa's gaze, he blinked a few times. Gazing at the ground, he ambled over.

"You need some care too," Lisa told Tatu.

He snorted. "First they need to fix Gordinho."

"True, but maybe another doctor has time. The sooner the better." Lisa stood and flagged down a nurse.

After a quick glance at the boy's hands, the woman sighed. "He'll survive."

Lisa slipped her fifty *reais* and sent Tatu with her.

While she waited with Luiz, she listened to the crying of a mother. From the fragments she understood, her fourteen-year-old boy had been shot in a gang war. Luiz's age. Worried faces lined the wall opposite her, the faces of people frozen in fear.

The words 'pest control' kept popping up in her head, and the image of the black car had burned itself into her memory. She clearly remembered the registration number. There were different kinds of pests and this one she needed to weed out.

Luiz sat next to her, head in his hands. He didn't cry. Maybe he was too furious—like her. Why kill children in such a horrible way? Just because they didn't want to have street kids in their neighborhood? Burning a twelve-year-old alive to drive the rest away? She couldn't wrap her brain around it.

Luiz hit his head against the wall behind their bench. She took his hand. He did it again.

"You okay?" she asked

"No, I'm not okay. They had an assault rifle, they'd have shot us all, but first they wanted to watch Gordinho burn and die." Luiz sniffed. She put her arm around him.

That moment, Tatu staggered through a door, both hands bandaged, his leg cleaned up and covered in some ointment. The nurse followed.

Lisa stood. "Did you give him a sedative?"

The woman raised her eyebrows. "Those kids are tough. He'll be scarred, but nothing major."

Lisa couldn't believe she heard right. She walked up close to the nurse, kept her voice low and calm. "The boy watched his friend burn, got badly injured himself, and you didn't even give him something for the shock and pain?"

"It's okay," Tatu whispered and swayed. Luiz jumped up to steady him, but a tall black man caught him before he fell. Lisa stared at the apparition for a moment. He looked familiar. Maybe she'd seen him in the *favela*. He smelled of drug money and not just because of the gun stuck in the waistband of his jeans, and the gold chain around his neck. She met his gaze. His black eyes sparked. With scorn, fear, or recognition?

Lisa tore away from his intense stare. "Put him down. Feet up." She looked over her shoulder at the nurse. "And you, get him something strong."

"I'll take care of him." The force of the man's voice made her shiver.

"I know you," she whispered.

"Could be. Thanks. For your help." He lifted Tatu up in his arms and nodded at Luiz.

Lisa stepped back and watched him leave, carrying Tatu away.

"Your friend?" she asked.

Luiz nodded. "Max."

"He's with the drug gang, right? One of the big guys."

"The local boss since last spring."

"Why would he care about a street kid?"

"He's Tatu's brother. He taught us to survive when nobody else cared."

Lisa's jaws clenched, but she didn't say anything. She hated drugs. They destroyed lives, families, humanity, and hope. Almost sent her over the edge, too.

Torturous hours passed before a gentle squeak of rubber shoes accompanied the doctor's approach. Her heart beat faster. When she looked into his face, she knew Gordinho was dead. He slowly shook his head. Then he glanced at Luiz. His lips pressed into a thin line.

"He didn't make it," the doctor said.

Lisa squeezed Luiz's shoulder. He stared at the doctor before his gaze locked on her. Lisa slung her arm around him.

The doctor asked, "Do you know his name, address, family?"

"We called him Gordinho. No family."

Chapter Twenty-Three

Luiz rang the bell. What would he tell Tatu if he asked about Gordinho? After a long minute, the door opened. An elderly lady looked at him through squinted eyes. "What do you want?"

"Are Max and Tatu here? I'm a friend."

She nodded and buzzed the gate open. "Down the stairs."

Grabbing the handrail, he descended into a dim basement and walked down the corridor toward the open door ahead. He'd let Max down. He'd promised to keep Tatu safe. His hands shook.

He peered into the room. Tatu lay in bed, legs uncovered, and a blanket over his upper body. He slept. His arms, no longer bandaged, rested on top of the sheet. Blisters glistened on his hands. A needle stuck in his left arm, attached to a thin tube leading to a plastic bag. Luiz had one of those drip things when he got shot in the leg. He knew Tatu slept untroubled now.

Max sat in a chair next to the bed, head in his hands. After a while he looked up. He stood and put his hands on Luiz's shoulders. "He'll be fine. In a week he'll be able to use his hands again. Now, tell me what happened."

Max's jaws ground, while Luiz told him about the attack and Gordinho's death.

"And you have no clue who it was?" Max asked.

"No. Just people who hate us. Had a fancy submachine gun."

Max's jaws clenched. "I don't understand why you stayed with that woman."

"Because it's our place."

"It never was your place. Never will be." Max started pacing. "Of course, people would try to chase you away."

"Now it's all our fault? I guess none of us should have been born," Luiz yelled and stormed out of the room. He knew Max wouldn't do anything. As soon as Tatu recovered, he'd send him back on the streets with a warning not to return to their shelter. But that was exactly where Luiz headed now.

* * * *

Max slammed his fist against the wall. He'd never felt so helpless. Anyone could kill Tatu. Any day. He couldn't protect him anymore, unless he gave up the drug business and went back into car theft or robbed a bank to provide a home for his brother. He slumped down on the chair. Sleeping, Tatu looked like a child. Max had taken care of him since he was fifteen months old—when their mother went crazy and tried to kill her own baby.

Tatu's father, a white motherfucker, didn't even know he existed. Their mother had worked for his family as a maid. One day, the bastard raped her. She came home crying and hardly ever got out of bed again. Max took care of her and the baby. They named him Rigo. *Mamãe* didn't nurse him. She didn't hold him in her arms. But Rigo lived and grew. He learned to walk and followed her everywhere. She couldn't bear it. She didn't want to look at him. The first time she picked Rigo up in her arms, she threw him out of the window. Screaming with helpless rage, Max ran outside and found the toddler lying in the shrubbery with hardly a scratch after the ten-foot-plunge. From then on he called him Tatu, because he was tough like an armadillo, and he called himself Max, after *Mad Max*, still one of his favorite movies.

Max left with his baby brother and swore he'd never tell Tatu that their mother tossed him away.

Now he listened to the boy's even breathing. Always a survivor, he'd never been sick, never complained that he was hungry when Max couldn't make enough money. A real sunny boy.

Max struggled to his feet. He felt old. Killers roamed the streets of Rio, sniffing out prey. Last night they'd picked Gordinho and Tatu. And Max couldn't do anything about it. All his money and power didn't change a damned thing. And the fucking cops? Nobody called the police over a dead street kid. They'd take a look, dispose of the body, and go on protecting the rich.

What was that woman thinking when she let them stay? Miss English Teacher wasn't a fool. She knew how things worked in Rio. Damn those do-gooders.

Chapter Twenty-Four

Lisa dragged herself to the bookstore. No energy left. She wanted to sleep, but Rejane wouldn't be in until later. Relief swept over her when she saw Ubaldo lurking in the doorway. "Hey, kiddo." Lisa hugged him and the sobbing boy clung to her.

"Gordinho died this morning," she whispered in his ear and held him even tighter. She led him inside and made coffee. "Where's Rena?"

"At the beach. Couldn't stand the waiting any longer."

"Luiz will be back soon, I hope, but Tatu is with his brother."

Ubaldo nodded then looked around. "Can I do something?"

She couldn't think of anything, her mind no more active than a mushroom. "Want me to read something to you?"

A smile lit up his face. "Yes, please."

Lisa picked *The House of the Scorpion*. Not a fun read, but fitting. They settled at the little reading table. Twenty pages into the book, Rejane entered.

"*Olá*, Rejane. Can you take over for the rest of the morning?"

The salesgirl put her purse behind the counter. "I guess so, but there are cops outside. They are talking to the neighbors."

"Shit!" After all these years, police were still bad news. "I'll go talk to them."

"Can I come with you?" Ubaldo asked.

Lisa shook her head. "Better stay out of sight."

Two *Polícia Militar* cars were parked at the curb. One officer examined the glass shards and burn marks of the Molotov cocktail on the sidewalk. Three more interviewed shop owners. She guessed they simply hadn't made their way to her yet. Her hands wouldn't stop shaking. She took a deep breath. Breathe. Slow and deep. This was one of the most touristy parts of Rio. They couldn't simply let death squads burn children alive in Copacabana and then clean up after them. Bad for Rio's reputation. Maybe they would investigate.

Lisa forced her legs into action. "Can I help you?" she asked the cop squatting by the fire marks. "I know what happened last night."

He rose and stared at her with a slight frown. "You do? We got a call that street kids shot at a car. When the patrol arrived, they'd disappeared."

Damn her neighbors. She couldn't let the cops think an armed gang of kids terrorized Copacabana. They'd go arrest or kill any stray children they found in the area. "No, I shot at the car after the guy in the front passenger seat threw a Molotov at the kids. One of them died last night in the hospital. You can check."

"What were the kids doing here?"

"Nothing. Just hanging out. I've got the registration number of the car."

"The minors weren't armed?"

"No. I told you I shot at the criminals." She couldn't let them go after Luiz and his friends. They might not even see the insides of a court house but end up dead somewhere on the outskirts of Rio.

"If the kids show up again, you better chase them away or call us. This is no place for street kids."

Lisa bit back the question what better place there might be. She narrowed her eyes. "What about the killers? You want the registration number or not?"

The cop straightened and smirked. "I want your name, address, and the gun. And the registration number, of course."

She should have known they wouldn't try to catch the murderers of homeless children. Why had she bothered to tell him?

He held out his open hand. "You've got the gun on you? It's evidence."

Bastard!

* * * *

Luiz trotted toward the bookstore. First he noticed the police cars. As he drew closer, he saw Lisa talking to a cop. Not good. He slipped into a side street and walked around the block. When he reached the street from the opposite end, Lisa stood glaring after the cop car driving away.

He approached her. "Everything okay?"

"When's anything ever okay?"

Luiz swallowed.

101

"The bastard took my gun," she growled. "I bet they won't do anything."

"Lisa?" He waited until she looked at him. "You hit one of the guys."

The anger drained from her face. "Are you sure?"

Luiz nodded. "In the left shoulder or arm. He had an assault rifle aimed at us. It wasn't an AK-47. Looked more like an Uzi, but bigger and fancier."

"Right. We better be prepared." She swung around and headed for the store. Luiz followed.

Crying, Ubaldo clung to the shop girl. Luiz never liked Rejane. She darted them suspicious looks all the time, but now she sat with Ubaldo and tried to console him.

At the sound of a shotgun being loaded, Luiz swung around. Lisa stood behind the counter holding a twelve-gauge, pump action shotgun with a modified stock. He gaped. If she fired that, she'd probably land on her ass.

"None of you kids will touch this, okay?" She stored the loaded weapon under the counter.

Luiz and Ubaldo nodded.

Rejane stared. "Has that thing always been there?"

Lisa showed a crooked smile. "Yeah, but I mainly bought it for show. Like in the movies."

"You could have told me."

"Rejane, I think you should take some time off. Or maybe it's time to quit the job."

The shop girl rose and walked up to her. The women whispered. Luiz could make out "kids" and "guns" and "pest control."

Then Rejane stepped back. "I'll stay."

For some reason, he felt better.

* * * *

Late in the evening, Luiz went to the beach with Rena and Ubaldo.

"I can't sing and beg," she said. "I'd have to smile, but I can't stop thinking about Gordinho."

Luiz wasn't in the mood for stealing either. "Let's just chill out."

With the waves too high for a dip, they stood and stared out to sea.

"I can't believe Gordinho's dead," Ubaldo whispered.

Rena leaned against Luiz. "You think Max is going to let Tatu come back?"

Luiz heaved a deep breath. "If not, Tatu will find a way. That is, if we want to stay at the workshop."

"I do," Ubaldo mumbled.

Rena took Luiz's hand. "Me too."

When night fell, they ambled back. A mob of people crowded the sidewalk in front of the bookstore. Luiz stopped, taking in the scene. Rena and Ubaldo stayed close.

Lisa stood in the doorway, one step above everyone else. "Maybe it was some of you?" she called. "Are you the kind of people who burn children alive, or shoot them dead?" She put her hands on her hips. The crowd inched back.

"Hey, Senhor Mahler. Did you call the pest control? Did you pay them to do the dirty work for you?"

A man hunched and shied away, shaking his head.

"The kids haven't bothered any of you. Why can't you just leave them alone?"

A middle-aged man stepped forward, shaking his fist. "The brats steal and beg. We can't have that here."

Lisa spread her arms. "They don't have enough to eat, no place to sleep but this workshop, and you only worry about your business, José? Aren't you going to church every Sunday? What about loving your fellow human beings, sharing your meals, offering the other cheek? Suffer little children..."

The man looked at his feet.

Luiz couldn't restrain himself anymore. "Hey, if you want us to go, we will. We can survive anywhere."

The crowd shifted in his direction. Eyes scanned him and his friends. Maybe they actually saw them for the first time.

Only Lisa smiled. A proud smile.

The murmur grew. A woman walked away. The gathering broke up. Shuffling or hurrying, people left. Luiz would never understand why they feared those poorer than themselves so much. What was so horrifying about losing a digital camera or a cellphone or money when they lived in a house, slept in a bed, and had enough to eat? Maybe they'd let them stay now.

Lisa draped an arm around his shoulders. "Thanks for the help."

"I didn't do anything. You were great. Nobody ever speaks up for us."

Rena hugged her. "You think they'll leave us alone now?"

"I don't know," Lisa said.

Chapter Twenty-Five

Max sat with his most senior soldiers around the large table in the *boca*. He struggled hard to keep Tatu off his mind. The doctor had promised he'd fully recover within a few days, but he couldn't shake the thought that his brother could have died, like the other boy.

"Nassar wants to meet you," Capone said.

Max slammed his fist on the table. "I want the bastard dead."

"Killing a cop only causes a fuss." Átila squeezed his shoulder.

"He killed the journalist because he couldn't get to me. I take that personally. And he's become too greedy."

Átila grunted. "It'll teach them a lesson."

"That's insane," Mussolini protested. "They'll come storming in with the cavalry."

"Bullshit!" Capone said. "Why would they risk getting killed instead of paid?"

Right, the cops wouldn't start a war if he killed the rat. "Tell Nassar to meet me at the Rosa Vermelha club. Alone."

"But..."

"What?"

Capone stared at him. "You really think he'll come without back-up?"

* * * *

Max wore red shorts, a white T-shirt with a blue parrot printed on it, and a red Ferrari baseball cap. Most of his own soldiers wouldn't have recognized him. He sat on a stool, his back to the bar. Eighties pop crap blared from the speakers. He regretted his choice already. He'd picked the place because he knew it well from the times when it was a cheap hip-hop joint, called the Black Rose. He smiled at fond memories of long nights and hot girls.

Old-fashioned strobes stabbed his eyes as he pretended to watch the dance floor. Capone sat in a booth in the far corner.

Max's cellphone beeped. A text message from Mussolini. "4 squad cars. Trap."

Nassar really wanted to deliver him to his new captain, wrapped in silk paper and with colorful ribbons tied around.

Well into his second Vodka Orange, Max grinned.

Nassar pushed through the door. Alone. He scanned the dancers then the booths. Capone waved him over. The sergeant frowned but settled across from him.

Max slipped off the stool and sauntered toward them. "Move over."

Grinning, Nassar slid along the padded bench to the wall. Max squeezed in next to him, blocking his way out. "Why did you kill the journalist? He was a good guy. Smart, too. I liked him."

Nassar snorted. "He didn't make you look bad. All the bullshit he wrote about the gangs protecting the *favelados* from random police violence..."

"He called me a macho dictator in for the power. That's not very flattering." Max smirked. "But he was right about corrupt, incompetent cops taking drug money and selling us weapons they should be using against us. And that's what pissed you off." Under the table, he eased the knife from his belt.

"You shouldn't have talked to him. Costa Branca read the article. Guess what? He's dead-set on taking you down. Best way to prove you wrong, isn't it? You've drawn a little too much attention, amigo."

"Thanks for the warning. I'm still going to kill you, though."

Half-turning, Nassar pressed his back against the wall. "You won't kill a cop."

"Watch me." He sliced the blade into Nassar's body just below the ribs.

Nassar's mouth dropped open. A gurgling sound. Max twisted the knife, pushed down the handle, and felt the sharp steel cut upward through vital organs. Nassar fell onto the table. Rid of one asshole.

Capone gave him the thumbs up. Nobody had noticed.

Max pulled the knife from the corpse and wiped it on Nassar's pants under the table before he slipped it into the sheath on his belt. He nodded at Capone, who stood and walked toward the back entrance.

Max strolled to the main door. Outside in the cold night air, he looked up at the weak light of the stars. Blazing Rio could not quite outshine them.

A police car blocked the exit of the parking lot. Max staggered past the four cops guarding the front door. Watching out for a drug lord, they ignored the stumbling black drunk in clothes far too colorful for him to be dangerous.

Max had to force himself not to fall into his usual swagger, while a deep sense of satisfaction soared through him.

"Hey, you."

Max cringed but stumbled on. Ahead he saw a bike pull into the parking lot. Átila, or so he hoped. The tread of heavy boots drew close.

"Hey, asshole!"

Max stopped and slowly turned as if he might lose his balance.

The cop had his hand on his gun. "I know you."

The bike swerved around them and knocked the cop over. Max jumped behind Átila and held on tight as they sped off. Gun shots exploded.

Chapter Twenty-Six

Lisa sat at her kitchen table sipping coffee, staring blindly at the sink overflowing with dirty dishes. Six o'clock in the morning. Too early to call Jango. She held the slip of paper with the registration number, placed it on the table, and ran her finger over the writing. What if she found out who killed Gordinho?

The police might investigate the murder—not likely, though. Street kids died every day. Sometimes they starved, sometimes they were burned alive like Gordinho, or got raped and strangled, or were simply shot by death squads. Pest control. Quite often these *Grupos de Extermínio* consisted of cops or former cops. The police were more likely to revoke her license to carry a gun than to investigate the death of a homeless child. She'd been naive to talk to them at all. But she couldn't let them believe an armed gang of street kids fired guns in Copacabana.

She went to her bedroom and took the heavy precision rifle, a Steyr SSG 69, out of her closet. She hadn't used it for years so she carried it to the kitchen to dismantle and clean it. The combined smell of metal and oil calmed her, filled her with a strong sense of power and control. Maybe Jango would spend an hour at the shooting range with her tonight.

After her shower, dawn had turned into gentle morning light. She checked the clock. Seven. She dialed Jango's number. He sounded sleepy.

"I hope I didn't wake you."

"Not quite. What's up?"

Lisa ignored a female voice in the background. "If I give you a car registration number, will you give me a name?"

"I'll talk to some friends in the registration office. What happened? Did you have an accident?"

"Something like that. They hit my car and drove off." She could tell him the real reason when she had the name. Jango wouldn't want her to hunt the guys. If that was her plan.

Lisa strolled past the bookstore and through the gate to the backyard. She closed it and attached a heavy padlock. Walking down the narrow corridor, she noticed a dandelion growing from a crack in the wall.

The doors to the workshop always stood ajar as if the kids couldn't stand sleeping behind four walls without an opening. She peered inside. Only three sleeping figures now. Would Tatu return? Judging by the look on his brother's face, he'd never set a foot near her again.

Lisa squatted and shook Luiz's shoulder. He didn't move. The night spent waiting in the hospital must have taken a lot out of him. She decided to let him catch up on sleep, but when she rose, he grabbed her ankle.

"What?" he croaked.

"Come outside."

His eyes still half closed, he shuffled after her. She handed him two sets of keys. "I bought good locks for the gate."

"Great, thanks." He waited. Maybe he sensed she wouldn't have pulled him away from the others early in the morning just to tell him about a lock that couldn't keep out anyone determined to break in.

Lisa looked around to check if Rena or Ubaldo had followed them. All quiet. She focused on Luiz. "Do you know how to use a gun?"

He knitted his eyebrows. "Never fired one."

"Seriously?"

"What do you think? I don't belong to the drug gang. Wouldn't sleep on the streets if I made a lot of money selling drugs."

"Of course not." She rubbed her chin. "That's fine." She had hoped he'd be able to defend the kids if she wasn't around.

"Lisa what's going on? Why do you ask?"

"Don't worry."

He lifted his T-shirt. "I've got this though." A small Taurus stuck in the waistband of his shorts.

"How...?" She couldn't believe he carried a gun.

"Ubaldo found it in a suitcase. Meant to sell it, but I think I might hold onto it a while longer."

Lisa held out her hand. He slapped the pistol into her palm.

"That's the safety catch."

"I know."

She raised her eyebrows then flipped the catch. "You hold it like this and aim along the barrel. Don't play cowboy trying to shoot from the hip. Here, take it."

Luiz held the gun with both hands, just like she had, and aimed at the wall.

"Don't pull the trigger or all hell breaks loose." She put her hand on his stretched arm and he lowered the pistol. "I wish I could take you to the shooting range, but this will have to do for now."

* * * *

Lisa entered the bookstore. Behind the counter, Rejane sorted the change into the register.

"Can you take care of the shop today?" Lisa asked. "Got errands to run."

"Errands?"

Sometimes Rejane reminded her of her aunt in the States, who'd worked hard to turn her into a nice, polite girl. Except Rejane was only twenty-four. Lisa rolled her eyes then smiled.

Before Rejane could say more, Lisa's cellphone rang.

"Hey, Jango, got something for me?" Her heart raced.

"A name and address. You may want to try the polite approach, first."

"Why?" Lisa pressed the phone harder against her ear.

"The car is registered in the name of Filinto Rocha, the artist. He's a university professor. Hard to believe he'd do a hit and run. Should I call him for you?"

Shit. Not just some wretched ex-cops making a few extra bucks. "Ah, no. It's not necessary. Give me the address and I'll pay him a visit. A very polite one, of course. Thanks, Jango."

Damn, a professor and artist. She squeezed her eyes shut. No matter. She unclenched her left fist and forced herself to put the cellphone away before she wrote down the street and number. Could she simply forget about it all? She turned to Rejane. "Do you know an artist called Filinto Rocha?"

Rejane frowned. "I've read about him in the newspaper. He's pretty famous."

Lisa winced. If even Rejane knew his name, he was high-profile. Then a thought crossed her mind. What if he had a driver or bodyguard with a side business?

* * * *

At her favorite gun shop, Lisa picked up a Czech-made 9 mm, heavier and bulkier than her confiscated compact... But sometimes looks mattered. The gun dealer promised to get her a new Firestar within a couple of days.

Lisa drove to Santa Teresa. Slowing the car down, she checked out Professor Rocha's Bohemian villa. Two stories, razor wire along the top of the spiked fence. A security camera. No doorman. The rich artist would feel quite safe here.

What kind of man taught young people, took pride in his art, and killed children for a thrill? Doubts battled her urge to do something. The scenario made no sense.

Lisa drove back to Copacabana, parked the car in the garage, and walked to the bookstore. A cardboard box filled with used clothes sat on the other side of the locked gate to the backyard. Somebody must have changed his mind about the kids and thrown it over. The thought improved her mood.

Inside the shop, two customers browsed shelves while Rejane talked to a sunburned couple. She nodded at Lisa, the usual sign that she had everything under control.

Lisa strode to the back room and sat down in front of the old computer. She searched "Filinto +Rocha +artist" and found his web site advertising his upcoming exhibition at the Museu de Arte Moderna. *Perfect*.

The short bio painted him as an educated and well-traveled man. In addition to Portuguese and Spanish, he spoke English, Italian, and German. He'd spent a year in Rome, studying art, and two years in Berlin, teaching art history. A liberal-minded intellectual. The vehicle might have been stolen. Or maybe he had a son who drove the car. She'd find out soon enough.

Chapter Twenty-Seven

Lisa stepped from the gloom of the bookshop into the bright afternoon sun. Time to get ready for the big night. She blinked. Tony leaned against a steel fence across the street. For a moment she couldn't move. Panic and joy merged to confusion before her brain kicked in. What the hell was he doing here? Tony grinned and showed her his open palms. The gesture made her smile. She crossed the street. "You're back."

"Yep."

"For how long?" she asked.

"Another two weeks."

"Why were you just standing out here?"

"I was willing you to come to me. Seems to have worked."

Lisa laughed. "Pure coincidence."

"No, only a question of time. How about dinner tonight?"

Her heart sank. She couldn't whirl through an emotional maelstrom again. She had to focus on the hunt. "Sorry, got other plans."

"Tomorrow?"

"Forget it. Won't work." She turned to run, but he grabbed her arm.

"I never took you for a coward."

Lisa's hands balled into fists. She wanted to punch him, but he'd guessed right. She was scared—of the memories he'd stirred up, of falling in love with him. She controlled her breathing and forced her arms and hands to relax. "Maybe I *am* a coward."

He shook his head. "I missed you."

Lisa blinked until she could focus on his features. She saw hope in his eyes, and something else. Alertness. Maybe he expected her to throw him a blow. She tilted her head to one side then the other to stretch the tense muscles in her neck. "I'm not good for you, Tony. Since that night I feel even more like a ticking time bomb."

He spread his arms. "Then let me contain you."

Lisa looked at the capuchin monkey printed on his T-shirt. A smile stole onto her face. Then she saw the scar starting just above his right elbow.

He'd never worn a T-shirt before and now she knew why. She gazed into his blue eyes. "Would you like to come to an art exhibit? It's opening night."

His eyes sparked, his lips curled into a smile and the cute dimple in his cheek appeared. "I'd love to."

"I'll pick you up at seven. Are you staying at the Palace again?"

"Yeah. Feels like home already."

"See you there." Lisa sprinted across the busy street, dodged honking cars, and rounded the corner. She unlocked the gate to the little front yard of the apartment building, slipped through, and pushed it closed. Then she unlocked the front door, entered and made sure it was firmly shut. But no gates could shut her feelings out. She climbed the stairs, imagining Tony's steps behind her—like the other night. Damn, why had she asked him to come along to the exhibition? He'd distract her. She pulled out her cellphone and called Jango. "You could have warned me," she said without preliminaries.

"About what?" Jango sounded genuinely surprised.

"Tony Norton."

"Oh, I see. Didn't think you cared."

"I did when he showed up on my doorstep unannounced." Lisa rang off. Had Tony returned because of her? No, he was here for business and felt lonely. Who was she kidding? If that were the case, he'd stay away from her and find himself a nice girl. He knew she was anything but easy, yet he persisted. Her chest tightened. If only she could erase Vitor Fraga from her memory. Then, maybe they'd stand a chance.

She shed her clothes and stepped under the shower trying not to think, which proved impossible. Round and round in circles. Tony. Rocha. Gordinho. Vitor Fraga...Not him! She shampooed her hair. Wrong smell! Geez, she'd used the shower gel on her hair. She rinsed it out and forced herself to concentrate.

She pulled her best dress from the closet. Black, body-hugging, low cut, hem to the knees. Tony would misunderstand for sure, but no other outfit suited the occasion. Where would she put the large pistol? She rummaged through a drawer full of handbags and purses, collected and abandoned over the years. The gun fit into a large black one that didn't exactly match the elegance of her dress. So what? She stood before the mirror. Transfixed, she stared at her reflection. She looked like a different person. A woman ready to enjoy life.

* * * *

Lisa parked in the museum garage and walked with Tony to the gallery. It felt good to be near him. His presence calmed her mind and made her skin tingle. Maybe they deserved a second chance.

People in elegant clothes bustled in the foyer, even though Rocha's exhibition wouldn't open to the public for another twenty minutes. When they reached the ticket counter, Lisa's cellphone rang. Tony paid while she took the call.

"Hey, Jango, what's up?" She headed for an open door into one of the exhibition halls to get away from the crowd and noise in the foyer. Looking over her shoulder, she made sure Tony had noticed and followed.

"Just wanted to let you know that Rocha's work is on display at the Museu de Arte Moderna. This is the opening night. I'll be there. I could talk to him about the accident."

"No!" Too quick, too urgent. "I mean, I'm here with Tony. I'll talk to him myself."

"Oh."

"Don't worry about it, okay?"

"If you say so. I guess I'll see you later then." His voice dripped with suspicion.

"Jango?"

"Yes?"

"Please don't say anything to him."

"Understood."

She'd have to do some explaining later. "Thanks, Jango." She slipped the phone back into her purse and tapped the cold barrel of the pistol.

"Problems?" Tony asked.

"No. Jango is going to show up later." Impressionist paintings surrounded Lisa. The colors and light soothed her. A lady in an old-fashioned white dress holding up a parasol against a cloudy but bright sky drew her closer. In the far background stood a boy. Or was it a man?

Tony's voice whispered behind her. "Monet. Isn't it beautiful?"

"It is." She moved on to the next painting. The famous *Lilies in the Lake*. She knew this one well. A cheap print hung in her dentist's waiting room.

A resonating gong reminded her of her purpose. "Shall we?"

Tony took her arm and they joined the crowd streaming into the room for contemporary exhibitions. She gazed at the walls. After the pleasing colors, the lightness, the elegance, and harmony of the impressionists, Rocha felt like a fist to the eye: harsh contrasts, sharp contours...a style that reminded her of Nazi propaganda art. She studied the nearest canvases. A Gaucho on horseback, radiating machismo, watched over his grazing cattle. A Spanish lady in a red dress smiled at her baby being nursed by an African woman in a white dress. A World War II battle scene: three white Brazilian soldiers heroically marching through enemy fire. A self-portrait: Rocha sitting in an old-fashioned leather armchair reading a leather-bound book, his angular face softened by candle light that added a strange glow to his short salt and pepper hair. Again the perfect image of the intellectual. She had to find out who drove his car the night Gordinho burned.

Tony offered her a glass of champagne. "He's a megalomaniacal fascist," he murmured close to her ear.

Lisa raised her glass to him. "If not something far worse."

Chapter Twenty-Eight

Félix blinked a few times when he saw Lisa Kerry staring at the paintings, distaste etched into her face. How had she found Rocha? Of course, the registration number. Smart and cool-headed in the moment of danger.

Where was Cortez, the fool? He craned his neck and spotted him chatting up a woman. Always the same, a dick for brains. Might spice things up...

Félix weaved through the forest of people. Reaching Cortez, he mumbled an excuse and pulled him away. "You should sophisticate your tastes, Salvador."

"What's wrong with her?"

Félix chuckled. "She's boring."

Cortez yanked his arm out of Félix's grip. "How would you know?"

"I don't, but I'll show you someone far more exciting."

Cortez nudged him. "Keep talking."

He nodded toward Lisa. "See the woman in the black dress standing close to the entrance?" Shit, what was Tony Norton doing here?

"What's so exciting about her?" Cortez asked.

Félix swallowed. No turning back now. Norton didn't matter. "She shares some of your proclivities."

Cortez frowned. "What do you mean?"

"She's a slut and she hates street kids."

Cortez stared at him for a moment before he gave Lisa a once over. "You sure?"

"Absolutely. Why don't you go talk to her? Maybe mention the bullet you caught in your arm." He smirked. "Play it cool. She doesn't know me, or I'd make the introductions."

"Thanks, man." He tapped Félix's arm.

"She's got a guy with her. He's a wimp, don't worry about him. She'll forget him as soon as you dangle more interesting bait in front of her."

Cortez's grin broadened. Félix watched him strut toward her. The fool didn't even wonder why Félix left the girl to him. He never understood why

Rocha and Alves risked taking such a dimwit on the hunt. Someday they'd have to kill him and shut his big mouth. And now Lisa might take care of that.

Félix bristled with excitement. He recalled the outrage on her face when she shot at Rocha's car. She'd definitely go after Cortez.

Lisa. What a girly name for a woman like her.

Didn't take much to find out who owned the bookstore. Obviously it didn't belong to the young black girl working there. He knew where Lisa Kerry lived, knew everything on public record, about her mother's death, even her time in the detention center. No wonder she was so tough. Félix chewed his lower lip.

His longing for her was almost unbearable. At the same time he wanted to savor the anticipation, hold back a while longer, and enjoy the show he'd staged, see her in action before he took her.

* * * *

"Lisa."

She flinched, feeling caught, until she realized it was Jango's voice. She turned and looked into his smiling face. Next to him stood a stunning beauty. Maybe in her early forties.

"This is Ana. Ana, I've told you about Lisa."

Ana granted her a shy smile. Not a society woman. Lisa immediately liked her. Maybe Jango had finally found a woman to keep.

"You look beautiful," Jango said. "You should dress up more often." He kissed her on both cheeks then greeted Tony. "So, what do you think?" Jango asked, waving his arm at the paintings.

"It's pretty horrible," Tony said.

Lisa spotted Rocha near a small podium talking to excited fans. The artist wore black pants and a black, tight-fitting T-shirt.

"Want me to introduce you?" Jango asked.

Lisa shook her head. "No, I don't want to speak to him. I'll just forget about it."

"Forget about what?" Tony asked.

The hall grew more crowded. "Let's get out of here." Lisa turned and bumped into a man. His jacket slipped from his shoulders. Lisa caught it and held it out to him. "Sorry."

He carried his bandaged left arm in a sling.

"Oh." Embarrassed, she stared into his smiling face. The man was slightly shorter than she was, the dark hair slicked back, and his skin tanned.

"Do you mind giving me a hand?" he asked.

"Of course not." Lisa draped the jacket over his shoulders and noticed his paunch. "What happened to your arm?"

"Caught a bullet. Nothing serious."

"Wow." The left arm, Luiz had said. She swallowed, reminded herself to keep breathing while she stared into the stranger's grinning face, and watched his gaze wander down to her cleavage.

Could he have been the second man in the car, the actual killer? She blinked twice. "A bullet? How did that happen?"

"Oh, that's a long story. Maybe I can tell you over dinner?"

Her heart hammered against her ribs, her hands tingled. She definitely wanted to hear more. "Sorry, I'm with someone. Maybe another time?" She held out her hand, hoping it wouldn't tremble. "My name is Sandra." If he was Gordinho's killer, the less he knew about her the better.

He grasped her hand and bowed. "Salvador Cortez."

"Pleased to meet you." Lisa leaned closer to him. "I'm afraid my fiancé is a bit jealous."

He produced a business card. "Give me a call if you ever need company." He winked.

She stuck the card in her purse and flashed him a bright smile. "See you."

Lisa turned and saw Tony's scowl. Taking his arm, she walked away with him in elegant little steps, swinging her hips ever so slightly, just in case the sleazebag still watched. Euphoria spread through her. What an evening. Had the killer really introduced himself to her? And she'd smiled into his face. He had no clue. Buoyed by her sense of control, she floated back to the deserted impressionist showroom. The muscles in her cheeks burned with the strain of her wide grin.

Tony stopped and turned to face her. His eyes narrowed. "What the hell was that, *Sandra*? You run away screaming when I ask you out for dinner but flirt with that slimy toad."

She laughed then realization dawned on her. "I'm sorry. Really. It's... I..." She didn't know what to say, how to explain. She simply wanted to laugh.

"Forget it. I'm making a fool of myself." He turned and marched toward the entrance.

Surprised, she stared at his retreating back. If she wanted to get rid of him, now was the moment to let him walk out of her life. If.

No! Don't go. Lisa ran after him and caught his arm. Tony shook her hand off, but waited, his eyebrows knitted together.

Lisa whispered, "I think that man killed a street kid in front of my store."

"What?" Tony stared at her in horror.

"That was the only reason I flirted with him."

"I don't get it."

"I wanted to find out if he was the guy I shot."

Tony gaped at her. "You shot the guy?"

"I know this sounds crazy, but it's the only reason I came here. The car's registered in Rocha's name. Cortez must have been the second man. He threw a Molotov at the kids."

"I can't believe this."

"I know. Please trust me. I'd rather jump off a cliff than let him touch me."

"Let me know if you need a push."

Chapter Twenty-Nine

Lisa glanced over at Tony slouching in the passenger seat. Maybe she had lost him. He hadn't said anything since they left the museum. She couldn't stand guessing what was going on in his mind any longer. "What are you thinking?"

"You're a great actor. Very convincing show."

She cringed. "I've always been honest with you, Tony."

"I know."

"Really?"

"Really. Just took me by surprise. What are you going to do about these people?"

Lisa focused on the road. "Make sure they won't do it again."

"I heard him brag about the bullet wound. In case the police won't believe you."

No way she'd drag him into this or go to the police. They'd only disarm her again, if she was lucky. "Thanks."

"Do things like that happen often?"

"Sometimes. Rarely in Copacabana."

"Back in the States, once in a while you hear about a serial killer going after bums or prostitutes. Usually such deaths wouldn't even hit the news."

"Yeah, that's the problem. Nobody cares about the poor and homeless."

When she turned into Avenida Atlantica, he said, "I'll be pretty busy the next few days."

"So this really is a business trip?"

"Let's say there were several good reasons to come back. Disappointed?"

"Relieved that you're less crazy than I suspected."

Lisa pulled into the driveway of the Copacabana Palace. "Care for a drink at the hotel bar?" She didn't want to go home to her lonely apartment. She needed Tony to ground her in reality, normalcy.

He raised an eyebrow at her then smiled. "Sounds great."

* * * *

Tony led her to the piano bar, which looked more like a lounge.

"Let's sit close to the source." Lisa climbed one of the stools at the bar.

The glass shelves in front of a mirrored wall distorted their reflections. The young mulatto barkeeper greeted them with a shy smile, the kind most poor workers in rich environments showed foreign customers.

"*Duas cachacas, por favor. Mineiro.*"

His smile broadened at her local accent.

"*E uma cerveja, por favor,*" Tony added. "*Antarctica.*"

"You've practiced that phrase a lot," she said.

Tony chuckled. The barkeeper set the two shot glasses before them and poured the beer.

They clinked their glasses. Tony drained his. "I'm getting used to this."

Lisa shook her head. "You've got to savor it." She took a sip and enjoyed the burning sensation in her mouth and throat, the fruity aftertaste.

Tony grinned. "Okay, teach me more about the pleasures of life."

"Ha, ha, very funny." If only he could teach her.

"Sorry. I like the way your face relaxes when you drink that stuff. Your eyes sparkle."

"Nonsense, I close my eyes." She emptied the glass.

"Afterward."

"You promised to behave."

"No, I didn't."

"True. I should go." But she didn't want to leave, didn't want him to behave.

"I think we should have another round."

Lisa felt the tension leave her neck and shoulders. Warmth spread from her stomach. She gazed into Tony's smiling eyes. "Okay, one more. This time, you'll get it right."

Tony grinned. "I'll do my best."

Lisa groaned at the ambiguity of her words. "That's not what I meant."

"What?"

"Don't give me that innocent look."

Two more shot glasses appeared in front of them. Tony's beer stood neglected. They raised their glasses. Lisa watched him sip, roll the liquid in his mouth, and swallow. "Much better. A bit showy perhaps."

Tony laughed. "Okay, how's this?" He put the glass to his lips, let the golden rum flow slowly into his mouth, closed his eyes for a second, then swallowed. He looked at her, one eyebrow raised.

"Very convincing." Lisa downed her glass in one go.

"Hey, you can't just gulp the stuff down."

She grinned at him. "Course I can, if I feel like it."

Tony raised two fingers at the barkeeper.

"Not a good idea," Lisa protested.

"Don't be a wimp."

"Grandma, why are your ears so big?"

"What?"

"You're the big, bad wolf."

"Took you a while to figure out."

Lisa lifted the glass and drank. The last one for sure. She had to get out of here before she did something stupid. Again. Except, she wanted to feel his arms around her, his skin against hers. Why couldn't she enjoy a man's closeness, like any other woman? Lisa crossed her arms on the bar and rested her head on them. "You're making my life complicated. Before you showed up, I had everything under control."

"And now?"

She mumbled into her arms. "Now I've got a bunch of street kids hidden in my backyard and I'm hunting killers."

"What?"

She turned her face to him. "Everything was easier for Sleeping Beauty. She didn't know what she was missing."

"You're getting your fairy tales all mixed up." Tony stroked her hair. "Are you okay?"

"I think I'm drunk."

"That's fine with me."

Lisa laughed and straightened up. She reached for his beer and took a big gulp. "Need to dilute the *cachaca*." And build up courage...

"All yours."

She drank more of the beer then pushed the glass away. "I need water." She waved at the barkeeper. "*Agua, por favor.*" When he sat the glass before her, she drained half of it. "I like you, Tony."

"Are you really okay?"

Lisa giggled. "Probably not." She tried to focus on his blurred face. "Why don't you go find yourself a nice girl?"

"Nothing wrong with cutting through a few thorn bushes."

Lisa lifted the shot glass and let the last drop of liquor slide onto her tongue. "Empty."

When Tony raised two fingers, she shook her head. "No." She slid off the stool and slung her arms around his neck. "I want you." She kissed him. Tony held back. She pulled away. "What?"

"You're drunk."

"Yeah, I hope it'll help."

He drew her close, his lips warm and hungry on hers. The barkeeper set two more glasses in front of them.

"Fate," Tony said.

Lisa giggled.

* * * *

Tony pushed the elevator button, his arm around Lisa's waist. He shouldn't have ordered the last two rounds. He didn't know if she had eaten dinner.

"I'll get them, Tony," she mumbled.

"Sure. Whatever you say, my dear."

The doors opened. He steered her into the elevator and pushed the button for the fourth floor. Lisa leaned into him. He lifted her chin and kissed her. Maybe they still had a chance. She rested her head against the elevator wall. He kissed her neck, sucked on her cute little ear lobe. She moaned. Yeah, this time he'd get it right. The cabin stopped, the doors opened. He stepped back. "C'mon, babe. We're almost there."

Lisa slid down the wall. He caught her, lifted her onto his arms, and carried her down the corridor. She was heavier than she looked. Setting her down, he pressed her against his chest with one arm while fishing for the key with the other. He held the card to the sensor and pushed the door open.

Lisa rubbed her cheek against his. "You need a shave."

"Hey, you're alive."

"Mhm."

He marched her to the bed and laid her down. Now what? She pulled up one leg. Her dress slipped back. Not fair. She raised her right arm over her eyes, but her left reached out for him. Tony shed his suit and shirt and crawled over her, stroking her thigh, kissing her.

Her fingers found his scarred arm. Her eyelids fluttered. "Your chance," she whispered.

His heart raced. "What?"

"Won't hurt me now."

"Not like that, Lisa." He watched her face for a sign of understanding. "I want you to feel it, enjoy it." No reaction. So close and still beyond his reach.

Tony groaned and rolled on his back. Time for a cold shower. Lisa turned on her side and curled up against him, her arm on his chest. He doubted he'd get any sleep. And when she woke, she'd probably scratch his eyes out. Or worse. But for now she slung her naked leg over his.

He stroked her silky hair and imagined she'd wake and kiss him, slide on top of him, want him as much as he wanted her. No use torturing himself. He thought about snow storms and glaciers.

* * * *

Tony woke when Lisa rolled onto her back. His arm was numb. He eased it out from under her. She whimpered.

"It's okay, baby."

"No. Please. Not me," she whispered.

The desperate plea in her voice chilled the sweat on his skin. "Lisa."

"Don't hurt me." Her voice choked.

He stroked her face. "Lisa, wake up. You're dreaming."

Her eyes flicked open. A tear rolled down her temple. Tony kissed it away. She turned her back on him. He didn't know whether he should touch her or not. After a few seconds, he stroked her arm and inched closer.

She leaned against his chest. "I'm glad you're back."

Happiness flooded him. Tony kissed the nape of her neck and wrapped his arm around her. "I won't let anyone hurt you."

When he woke in the morning, Lisa had left. Panic seized him. Did she remember anything? What was she thinking when she woke in his arms? He checked the alarm clock. 8:37. Did she hate him? At 9:30 he had an appointment with Carlos, the new general manager for South America. How come he always woke up alone when he went to bed with her? A job interview. Tony jumped out of bed and stared at the phone on the night stand. He should call her. Less than an hour to get presentable.

Chapter Thirty

Lisa drove along Avenida Atlantica, wishing she could go for a swim. The fog in her head wouldn't lift. She didn't remember much of the previous night, only some drunken nonsense she'd babbled and the wonderful feeling of total relaxation. When she woke and found herself curled up against Tony, she'd felt safe and happy. He hadn't touched her. How much self-control did that take?

The traffic stalled in Avenida Copacabana. Walking all the way from the hotel to her bookstore would have been faster. Next to her, in the opposite lane, a powerful engine produced a low growl. She saw a black Ferrari convertible then noticed the driver staring at her. Max. Behind him Tatu waved frantically. Lisa smiled and lowered the window. "Hey Tatu, you okay?"

Max focused on the traffic that didn't move.

"I'm great. Tell Luiz I'll be around later."

"Will do. He missed you."

"You look pretty," the boy yelled and flashed a charming smile.

Lisa laughed. "Thanks."

Max's glance brushed over her low neckline and settled on her face. "Gotta go."

"Me too." She waved a hand.

Max tipped his forehead with two fingers and revved the engine.

* * * *

Lisa parked the car and strode straight to the backyard. Ubaldo and Rena lay on one mattress, limbs entangled. Luiz sat cross-legged on a mattress, his sneakers on. She'd have to teach them a few things, like no shoes or smoking in bed. And it was about time to introduce them to the concept of tooth brushes. Her gaze traveled back to Rena. And tell them to use condoms? Oh, boy, if she had to explain sex to them, they'd be doomed.

Luiz stared at her then scrambled to his feet. They walked outside. "Where you goin' dressed like that?"

126

Lisa smiled. "I just got home. Had a rather unusual night."

The disapproving look on his face made her laugh. "Hey, you're not my father, okay?"

"Gordinho is dead and you party all night."

She hadn't thought about the boy's horrible death all morning. Her heart sank. Guilt crept in. "Sorry, Luiz. But I think I found the killers."

His face brightened. "What are we gonna do?"

"First I need to make sure we've got the right guys. Then we'll see."

"Let me come with you."

"I've got to work this morning." She gazed up to the windows of her apartment. "Need to hop in the shower and open the bookstore."

"And then?"

"I'll let you know when I know. I saw Tatu on the way here."

"Really? Why didn't you bring him?"

"He was with Max."

Luiz chewed on his lip. "Did he say something?"

"Yeah, he'll be around later."

"And Max?"

"Hardly looked at me. Why?"

"He doesn't like us to stay here. He thinks it's dangerous."

She ran her fingers through his hair. "Maybe he's right."

"You want us to leave?"

"No, I want you to stay and be safe."

* * * *

Max wandered aimlessly through the *favela* with his little brother. He'd picked him up from the doc this morning. Tatu's hands had healed, but now that he was off the medication, he steamed with rage over Gordinho's death.

"You can't let them get away with it."

"What do you want me to do?" Max asked.

"Kill them."

"How do I find them?"

"I don't know."

"There's nothing I can do. Happened before, gonna happen again."

"But you never take shit from anyone."

Max groaned. The boy still thought his big brother ruled the world. "I'm in the fucking drug business. I've got enough problems. I don't know who these people are and I don't have the time to find out and go hunt them."

"But..."

"What?" Max stopped.

Tears glistened in Tatu's eyes. "I don't know." He sighed. "They can't just kill us. They burned Gordinho alive. And they had a submachine gun. They'd have shot me if Lisa hadn't scared them off."

"What?"

"She shot at them."

Wow, Luiz hadn't told him that part of the story. Miss English Teacher shooting those bastards? The bitch had refused to teach gang members and kicked him out of her class when she caught him dealing. Max suppressed a smile. "Want to stay with me? Not in the *boca*, though. I'll find you a safe place."

Tatu's chest heaved. "I'll stay with my friends. I can't just hide and leave them on their own. I'm no coward."

"I know that. And it's not like you'd be much safer with me. Where's Luiz?"

"Protecting the kids."

"How?"

"He's got a gun."

Max frowned. Tatu put up his hand. "Don't say it. Some of your soldiers are younger than us and they have guns."

"You're right. Maybe it's time for you to get one, too."

Tatu's eyes widened. "Really?"

"What else can I do?" Max pulled out his pistol and gave it to him. "Fuck, I hate doing this." He looked around then dragged Tatu down a narrow lane until they reached the edge of the *favela*. They followed a path through the wild undergrowth into the rain forest for ten minutes until they reached a clearing. Max picked up an empty beer can and put it on a rock then pulled Tatu away. "Try hitting that."

Tatu stretched out his gun arm, aimed at the can and missed by a few meters.

Max burst into laughter. "That looked really cool, but cool gets you killed. Use both hands." He showed him how to hold the pistol, how to stand, and how to aim. Tatu sent the can flying.

"Much better." Max slapped him on the back. "See the red piece of plastic?"

"That's far."

"Give it a try."

Tatu emptied the magazine, every other shot a hit. Good enough. Max still hoped he'd never use the gun. "And now I'll show you how to clean it."

Max watched the excitement drain from his brother's face. Always the same. He might as well have told him to wash the dishes. "Listen, Tatu. If you carry a gun, you'll use it. After you use it, you clean it, because you'll need it again."

Tatu nodded. "Gotcha."

"And someday another gun might kill you. And me too."

Chapter Thirty-One

Lisa opened the shop late. Ubaldo awaited her and jumped to his usual chores. The boy brewed coffee before he swept the sidewalk. Lisa didn't have time to give him more jobs. Her stomach and head felt worse as the morning wore on. The shop bustled with customers and Rejane had the morning off. While Lisa presented various Rio guidebooks to a French couple who only spoke a little English, the phone rang. "Excuse me." She picked up the receiver. "Kerry Books."

"Hey! It's Tony."

Lisa looked over her shoulder at the French folks smiling at her. "Sorry, can't talk right now."

"You mad at me?"

She lowered her voice. "Of course not. I've got customers waiting."

"How about tonight?"

She thought for a moment. "No."

"Hey, I'm sorry. I didn't mean to knock you out like that."

"Friday. I need to take care of a few things."

Half an hour later the phone rang again. Jango summoned her to another lunchtime confession session.

* * * *

Lisa entered the restaurant across the street just in time, but for once Jango was five minutes late. "Sorry, Lisa." He kissed her on both cheeks. "Tony kept me busy. Did he tell you he wants to stay in Rio?" Jango lowered himself on a chair.

"What? He told me he was leaving in two weeks."

"He is, but he wants to take on a job here when his company opens the office in January."

"Why would they keep the boy scout here when everything is scouted out?"

"The what?"

Lisa smiled. "That's how he described his job."

Jango laughed. "I guess that's accurate."

"Tell me about Ana."

He smiled. "She's gorgeous, isn't she?"

Lisa nodded and grinned. "Looks like the right woman finally found you."

A master of deflection himself, Jango put both hands on the table and leaned toward her. "So what's the story with Rocha? No more lies now."

Lisa took a deep breath before she told him everything: about the kids living in the old workshop, the trip to Pão de Açúcar, the Molotov, the dash to the hospital, the registration number, Luiz having seen the guy with the submachine gun catch a bullet in his left arm. She spilled it all.

Jango put on his 'Spanish Inquisitor' look. "What are you planning to do?"

Lisa didn't have a plan yet. She looked into his dark eyes and held his gaze. He should know how she felt.

Pursing his lips, Jango nodded. "Things like that happen. *Grupos de Extermínio* killing children like vermin. Hired by the rich to clean the streets. Protected by the rich who make sure the killers won't be troubled by the law. You know all that." Jango kneaded his hands. "They are above the law. Believe me, I know what I'm talking about. Some things haven't changed since the military regime."

"I have to do something," Lisa said. "They're children. They're smart. Survivors, but helpless against machine guns and Molotovs cocktails."

He took her hand. "I know, Lisa. I know. But it's highly unusual for someone like Rocha or Cortez to do the dirty work themselves. Rocha is a famous artist and professor. Cortez dabbles in local politics. Ran for mayor once. There's only one explanation."

Her eyes locked on his. "They do it for fun. Sadists. Even more disgusting. But that means they are amateurs."

"No, Lisa. They are dangerous people. Untouchables."

"You mean the *police* can't touch them."

131

Chapter Thirty-Two

With the afternoon off, Lisa decided to do some reconnaissance. She drove past Rocha's villa and parked in a side street further up the hill. She scanned the neighborhood and spotted a house with broken windows and a flat roof on the border between the rich neighborhood and a *favela*. She trod along an overgrown path to the deserted house. No sign of inhabitants. She sneaked around the building. A huge, untended garden. Easy to slip away afterward.

She pushed open the back door. Empty bottles and mud carried in by squatters littered the floor. She tiptoed upstairs and checked each room. She stepped out on the balcony facing the garden, climbed onto the railing and heaved herself up to the flat roof. Smiling to herself, she walked over to the other side. An unobstructed view of Rocha's place. Her heart beat faster when she saw the black BMW backing out of the garage. Lisa crouched.

Could she kill him? If not, next time he might kill Luiz, Tatu, or Rena. Or Ubaldo. She remembered Gordinho's moans in the back of her car. Of course she could do it. The only question was when and how.

Time to take a closer look at Cortez. The sleazebag had a small office in the *centro*. According to Jango, his main occupation was a back-bench on the city council, taking money to vote in the interest of the highest bidder. She drove home and changed into a short skirt and tight tank top. Standing before the mirror, she went through her breathing exercises.

He wouldn't do anything in his office, a safe enough environment. And she had to confirm her suspicions. She grabbed the handbag holding her pistol.

Lisa took the underground to the *centro*. Much faster than by car. She merged into the stream of people meandering down the street lined with shops and offices while she searched for the right address.

When she found it, she took several deep breaths, telling herself she had to stop the killers. Nobody else would. She checked her watch. Six thirty. *Perfect*. In the foyer of the office building, she scanned the index board, found Cortez, and took the elevator four stories up.

Entering the office, Lisa smiled at a bored secretary. "I would like to see Senhor Cortez. I'm Sandra Oliveira. We met at Professor Rocha's exhibition." She'd picked the most common last name in Brazil.

The woman looked up, raising an eyebrow before she picked up the phone and punched a button. Lisa could hear the ring tone through the closed door. She wiped her sweaty palms on her skirt and willed her heartbeat to slow. Finally the ringing stopped.

"Sandra Oliveira would like to see you." The secretary put the phone down. "You may go in."

Cortez met her at the door. "What a pleasant surprise," he purred. "I didn't really expect to see you again."

"Your name rang a bell. You are a rather interesting man."

Her directness didn't seem to put him off. He offered her a seat beside his desk and pulled his chair close up, their knees almost touching. Lisa crossed her legs.

"And your fiancé?"

"He's buying a house right now. I can't bear the wedding preparations anymore. My mother is going berserk. So I thought I'd escape for a while and relax."

He smacked his fat lips. "And so you came to me."

"For dinner," she replied with a teasing smile.

"And dinner it will be." He stood and grabbed his suit jacket, then opened the door for her.

"How's your arm?" she asked.

"Fine." He turned to his secretary. "Tell the driver we'll be down in a minute."

A driver? And maybe bodyguard, too? Rocha might be innocent after all. In the elevator, she felt trapped and struggled against her panic. Cortez put his right hand up against the wall behind her. "I really like your style. A woman who knows what she wants."

"And I usually get it." She licked her upper lip and hid her clenched fist behind her back. Under the long sleeve of his shirt she could make out the white stripe of the bandage. "I hope I won't hurt you."

He leaned in closer as if to kiss her.

Lisa faked a giggle. "Rein in your horses, gaucho."

He burst into laughter and backed off. The elevator wobbled to a stop, the doors opened. Lisa relaxed.

Cortez walked one step ahead of her toward a black Mercedes. When the driver climbed out, she knew for sure he also served as his bodyguard. Big, broad-shouldered, maybe even dumb enough to throw himself between a bullet and his boss.

* * * *

At the beach-side restaurant, Cortez picked a table under a yellow awning that intensified the golden evening light. She welcomed the salty scent of the sea after breathing the polluted air in the *centro*.

The bodyguard sat out of earshot, drinking water. What an absurd scenario. Why would someone like Cortez need permanent protection? She relaxed in the public space and held back a laugh.

Cortez smiled like a victorious conquistador while he ordered steak. Lisa opted for a salad. She had no appetite at all, and no definite plan as yet. She just wanted to get him talking. But how? Instead, she babbled her cover story. "Officially, I'm at the university right now, studying in the library. I still want to get my degree."

"An educated beauty."

"My parents thought I needed a good education to marry well. I didn't think so." Lisa leaned forward and gave him a chance to glance down her low-cut top. "Men don't necessarily care for brains in a woman."

Cortez chortled. "Well, it's nice to have a witty conversation with a girl who's both beautiful and smart like you."

Lisa leaned back and granted him a satisfied smile. "Now that I'm about to be married, my parents don't care if I get my degree. But I want to graduate more than ever."

"And right you are. No woman should depend on a man. They are far too unreliable." He laughed as if he'd made a great joke.

While she forced a smile, an idea formed in her head. "Sorry, but you'll have to buy me dinner. This morning one of those little brats stole my purse and I don't have a new bank card yet."

He waved a hand. "Of course I'll pay." The sudden turn of the conversation sank in and put a frown on his face. "These little rats are pests."

"Yeah, one of them bumped into me, the other pulled my purse from my shoulder and ran. If I'd caught him, I'd have tortured him to death. Very slowly."

Cortez laughed raucously, attracting curious looks from other guests. Lowering his voice, he said, "Unfortunately our laws forbid murder."

Lisa scowled. "And how does the law protect us from these criminals? One of my fellow students had her car stolen last week."

The amusement drained from Cortez's face. He leaned closer. "The brats should be put in concentration camps."

Resisting the urge to slap him, Lisa tilted her head and narrowed her eyes. "Like the Nazis did with the Jews?"

"Exactly like that." He seemed to study her face for a reaction.

She opened her eyes wider, parted her lips, and held his gaze. Then she spoke, "Rio would be so much nicer without them. But I suppose you can't just do that either. Can you imagine, our maid caught a bullet a few weeks ago during a drug-gang shootout in the *favela* where she lives. Sometimes I think I should get a gun and learn to use it."

Cortez smirked. "And shoot them one by one?"

She pursed her lips and nodded. "Yeah. Still illegal, but would anyone care?"

"Someone like you and me could get away with it. All people care about is the mess left behind."

Lisa leaned closer to him and locked her eyes on his, forbidding them to gaze down to her breasts again. Her voice carried subdued excitement, just like she intended. "Have you killed?"

Cortez nodded, a slight grin on his face. "Can get dangerous though. Last time someone fired at us. A bullet grazed my arm."

Lisa leaned back in her chair, displaying a look of admiration. The man who burned Gordinho sat across from her and bragged about it. She felt like shooting him right here, right now. "Must have hurt."

"Hardly. Ripped off a bit of skin."

The waiter broke the spell when he brought their food. When he left, she asked, "What's it like? To kill someone, I mean."

He leaned forward, elbows on the table. "The best kick you can get, next to sex." He winked at her.

Lisa ignored the innuendo. "Will you let me shoot one, too?"

He rubbed his chin. "We'd have to hunt at night or in a place where nobody cares, even in daylight."

"Take me with you."

"Will you let me make love to you?"

She smiled. "Maybe. Afterward."

Cortez's shoulders sagged, the corners of his mouth drooped, but Lisa continued, "I've never even seen a dead person, you know."

"They aren't people. They're trash."

Lisa wanted to scream and throw the salad bowl at him. Instead she faked a happy smile. "When?"

"Tomorrow night I'll take you hunting," Cortez promised.

Chapter Thirty-Three

Max mixed himself a *caipirinha* on the roof terrace of the *boca* and stretched out on a deck chair. All he needed was a pool. He longed for a day at the beach, swimming, surfing, and kicking around the ball with Tatu and Luiz.

Átila's heavy tread sounded on the outside stairs. He'd recognize the man's heavy clomp anywhere.

"*Oi*, Max. Time for the community meeting."

"*Merda*, I completely forgot. Why don't you take care of it?"

"No way. I did it last week. How are people supposed to respect you if you don't give a fuck about their problems?"

Groaning, Max sat up. "All right." He was responsible for order in the *favela* whether he liked it or not. "But you're coming with me."

Átila chuckled. "You ain't scared, are you?"

"Who? Me? Of course. Give me a police raid or gang war anytime, but petty complaints about a blocked garbage stream or someone rewiring the electric cables terrify me."

Together they marched down the hill toward the community house. Some residents fell in behind them. A man caught up. "One of your dealers molested my daughter."

Ah shit. "You sure she didn't seduce him?"

"My daughter is a good girl."

Max stopped and turned to the indignant father. He'd seen him around but couldn't remember the name. "Which dealer?"

"He didn't introduce himself."

"When and where?"

"Yesterday evening, near Senhora da Silva's kiosk. She saw it."

With a sigh, Max nodded at Átila, who pulled out his walkie-talkie and instructed Mussolini to find out who the culprit was and take care of him.

The satisfied father fell behind without a thanks. Max called over his shoulder, "Next time you wait in line like everyone else."

As they approached the community house, a single gunshot thundered. A few seconds later Átila's walkie-talkie crackled. Mussolini reported the execution.

Max grabbed the transmitter. "Who was it?"

"Nico. He's always been a dog. I checked with Senhora da Silva first."

"Thanks, Mussolini." One complaint taken care of already.

At the door to the community house a small crowd had gathered. The faces showed a range of expressions—anger, fear, spite, and an occasional smile from a woman or two. A small corridor opened before him. Inside the house, three of the community council members sat at a table in the center of the main room. The smell of citrus fit in with the spotlessly clean floor and furniture. Kitchen cabinets lined one wall, bookshelves another.

"Olá Max. Átila." Jaime, the chairman, shook hands with them. "There's quite a line of people wanting to talk to you. So we'll make this quick. We need more money for the school."

"Why's that? Didn't we just donate a large sum?"

"That was last year." Jaime nodded at the school mistress sitting next to him.

"More children are attending, but they can't afford to buy books," Maria said. "And we need more school T-shirts."

"T-shirts? What the fuck?" As if they didn't have more serious problems.

"It's the best marketing," Jaime said. "If the kids are proud of their school, more will attend. And..." The man looked away. His Adam's apple bobbed as he swallowed a few times.

The man's unease irritated Max. They'd known each other for years and he'd always respected him. "Spit it out, Jaime."

"The kids don't get hassled by the police so much if they wear school T-shirts. Sets them off from your soldiers."

Max snorted. "I see."

Jaime stared at him. "I didn't make the rules."

Max nodded. "How much money do you need?"

Átila's walkie-talkie crackled. "We've got visitors. Police. Five men. One of them in captain's uniform."

Max stared at Átila, who shrugged.

"What are they doing?" Átila asked.

"Sitting at the fountain as if they belong here."

"Let's go," Max said. "Sorry, Jaime." He turned to Maria. "You'll get the money."

The chairman nodded. Max stormed outside, expecting a series of complaints from the waiting *faveldos*, but the news must have spread already. People jumped out of his way and followed at a distance.

"You think it's the new *capitão*?" Átila asked.

"I bet. Who else would have the balls to walk in here?"

"Maybe he wants to make a deal."

"We'll find out. Maybe he's pissed because I killed Nassar."

Átila slid his assault rifle from his shoulder.

Max touched he pistol in his waistband and wished he'd brought his AK-47. "Just look at the arrogant motherfuckers." The four men in military police uniforms sat on the short wall around the fountain drinking from cans, smiling at the gaping *favelados* and Max's soldiers on the roofs around the little square. The *capitão* stood with his hands on his hips. The murmurs died with Max's approach.

"What's his name again?"

"Emilio Costa Branca."

The *capitão* spotted them and placed his foot on the wall. First he glared at Átila; then he focused on Max with intense gray eyes. "The mighty leader of the gang himself. Gives me a chance to tell you personally that I'm going to arrest you and throw away the keys at the first chance."

Max marched up to him and grinned. "You're not going to kill me?"

"Unfortunately, that's against the law. Though for a cop-killer I'm tempted to forget the law for a minute."

"Nassar was a murderous, greedy roach."

A frown appeared on the *capitão*'s forehead.

"What's your price, man?" Átila asked.

Costa Branca cast his icy gaze on him. "I've got more respect for a hired killer than for a drug pusher."

For a moment Max thought the *capitão* would spit on Átila, but instead a slow smile crept on his face. "We'll clean up this crime-infested city and kick you scum out. The days are over when your dirty money could buy you impunity."

"And you came all the way here to warn me?" Max said. "How considerate of you."

The man blinked twice. "We can go anywhere we want, even into gang territory."

Max grinned. "This time, yes, because I allowed it. You'd better not show your face here again. And now, leave before my hospitality wears out."

Costa Branca grunted. "Maybe we'll turn your *boca* into a backpacker hostel when we're done cleaning this dump."

"Don't forget to build a pool on the roof."

The *capitão's* eyebrows drew together. Then he swung around and motioned to his men.

"Hey!" Max called.

Costa Branca turned and bared his teeth. "What?"

"Watch your back."

The cop's face reddened and contorted into a grimace of scorn. He glared at Max. "You little shithead of a drug peddler. Are you threatening me?"

Max looked him in the eye. "Just saying. Your men will still take our bribes and sell us back our weapons after they confiscate them. And they won't like that you interfere with their side business."

"I'll personally lock up anyone on your payroll."

Max grinned. "That's why I told you to watch your back."

Another frown wrinkled across the cop's forehead. "What the hell?"

"Quite refreshing to meet an honest cop. I'd hate to see them feed your head and fingers to the sharks and bury your rotting carcass in the woods."

Costa Branca snorted, shook his head and stormed off, shoving an old man out of his way.

Átila grunted. "What a stubborn *filho da puta*."

"I think he means it."

"Shoot him. Now, while you've got the chance."

"No fucking way. I'm not going to kill the first honest cop I've met in years. That'd feel like raping a virgin."

"Max, you're full of crap."

Chapter Thirty-Four

Unable to sleep, Lisa lay in bed, staring at the shadows dancing across the ceiling. She couldn't believe Cortez had been stupid enough to tell her about his favorite sport. Now she even had a confession. Every judge in the world would convict him, every jury, too. Except in Brazil. She hadn't thought it through before she asked him to take her on the hunt, but she wouldn't get a better chance. They'd be driving into poor neighborhoods, alone. She'd encourage him to park somewhere then stab him, make it look like a car robbery. Her heart raced at the thought. She'd never killed close up. Could she pull it off? She had to. For the kids and for herself. No way could she turn a blind eye and allow them to continue. She'd waited too long to take down Vitor Fraga. But she had been only a child then.

How many girls could have been saved if her father had cared, caused a fuss, pressed charges against Fraga? He only cared about getting her back as a precious possession misplaced by his wife. Tears stung her eyes as she tried to imagine her mother's suffering, her self-blame probably tormenting her more than her father's accusations. Lisa never really forgave him.

Rubbing her eyes, she concentrated on the task at hand. Before she killed Cortez, she had to get him talking about the second man. If he confirmed Rocha's involvement, she'd shoot the professor/artist the next morning when he drove off to the university, before he had a chance to learn about Cortez's death. Seemed so easy. Why, then, did she feel so scared? Too much could go wrong. What if Cortez brought the bodyguard? No, he had him sit out of earshot, didn't want him to know what they were talking about. She'd be alone with the killer. Why didn't that make her feel better?

* * * *

Lisa woke to the soft patter of rain against her windowpanes. Always a welcome change. Rain put her at ease. She thought of Luiz and the kids, happy they had a clean, dry place to sleep.

The early shift in the bookstore didn't offer much distraction. Ubaldo handled his usual chores before he ran off with his friends. Tourists seemed to retreat to museums, and locals hurried through the light rain to their destinations. Few people lingered in front of the shop window or strolled in for a browse. Far too much time for Lisa to think about the evening ahead and get nervous.

Rejane came in shortly before noon carrying a large pizza box. "I thought you might prefer to have your lunch break here."

Lisa smiled. "Thanks, Mom."

"The sky is brightening up. Only light drizzle now."

"I love the rain."

They sat at the table in the back room. Lisa forced herself to eat a slice of pizza.

"You okay?" Rejane asked.

"Sure. Just not very hungry."

"Who was that guy waiting for you the other day?"

Lisa looked at her, baffled. Rejane had never met Tony. "What guy?"

"Outside on the street. You talked to him. He's cute."

"Yeah, isn't he?"

* * * *

Restless, Lisa took another shower. Five hours. She stood in front of her closet, wondering what to wear for the kill. She slipped into a red bikini top, in case she got blood on her, and picked an innocent white blouse, cut low enough to reveal the top of her breasts. She ran her hand along the short skirts and grabbed a red one. It would go well with the boots. Lisa smiled and slipped it on.

She picked up a large cardboard box from the bottom of the closet and lifted the lid. Her red cowboy boots. She hadn't worn them since she'd returned to tropical Brazil, but they'd given her confidence back in the U.S. She took the right one, felt inside, and pulled the knife out. She touched the blade with her thumb and drew blood. Still sharp. No wonder, it had never been used. What would it feel like to cut into a human body? A killer of children wasn't human, she tried to convince herself.

* * * *

As arranged, Cortez had parked in front of the Hotel Praia Ipanema. Too late to walk away, Lisa realized he had company. His bodyguard served as driver, even tonight. Cortez climbed out of the Mercedes, took in her appearance, smiled in appreciation, and kissed her on the mouth, his hands taking advance liberties. Fighting her revulsion, Lisa forced a girlish giggle and pushed him away.

Laughing, he opened the rear door. Lisa slipped in and scooted over when Cortez bent to get into the back with her. She gasped inaudibly when he ran his hand over her thigh. The gentle whir of the engine made her feel even more trapped. She battled her panic by conjuring up images of the wide, open sea. Had Cortez simply borrowed Rocha's car and his bodyguard drove it? She hoped so. Then she could end it all tonight.

Cortez kissed her and slipped his hot moist hand in her blouse. She wanted to bite him, press her thumb in his eye, but managed to restrain herself and keep a clear head. When he shoved his hand under her skirt, she pushed it away. "Hey, you don't want to have the dessert before the main course, do you?"

He sighed and leaned back in his seat. "Why don't we go to a hotel right away, darling?"

"Later. You promised. I'm too excited about the hunt."

He lifted her right leg over his knee. Her heart raced when she saw the tip of the knife handle clearly visible inside the boot. What if he slipped his hand all the way down and touched it? With the adrenaline rush, she hardly felt his fingers on her skin. Stroking her upper thigh, Cortez spoke of hunting lowlifes. "You know, a lot of people would never have the guts to kill a human being, no matter how depraved. It's a gift, a strength. Gives you power. You think you can do it?"

"Honestly..." She paused for effect. "I don't know, but I want to."

The bodyguard turned into the deserted parking lot of a supermarket and pulled in next to a black Corolla.

"What are we doing here?"

Cortez smiled. "Some friends are coming along."

"Oh." Lisa's heart pounded; she broke out in a sweat. Her throat tightened. Concentrating on her breathing, she put down her leg and noticed the goosebumps on her skin.

Cortez climbed out, Lisa followed. She walked around the Mercedes and memorized the number on the Corolla's plate. Two men sat in the front. He'd led her to more killers, but now she had to deal with four guys instead of one. She'd take down as many as possible before they killed her.

She grabbed Cortez's arm and clung to it. Best way to stop her hands from trembling. Her heart hammered against her ribcage. The driver of the Corolla scowled at her, opened the door, and stepped out. The man stood a few inches taller than Cortez. He pulled back his broad shoulders and raised an eyebrow. His tailored suit must have cost a fortune and his neat haircut probably needed a weekly trim. The man's mustache twitched. "What's she doing here?"

Lisa swore silently, bounced on her feet, and tried to look stupid and hyper. She hadn't even brought a gun, relying on Cortez to provide her one.

"I promised her a kill," Cortez said in a firm voice.

Lisa heard the passenger door open. Rocha's angular salt and pepper head popped up on the other side of the Corolla. He folded his arms on the roof of the car and studied her. Damn, what a stupid plan.

The driver flashed Rocha a quick glance before he focused on Cortez again. "Stop thinking with your dick, Cortez. Fuck you, and your little whore. You are not coming with us tonight." With a last contemptuous scowl at Lisa, he climbed back in his car and slammed the door. Rocha followed suit, a smile playing around his lips. The Corolla pulled out of the parking lot.

Lisa took a deep breath. "What an asshole," she said, relieved they had simply left. For a moment she considered calling it off, but then what? She tightened her lips and gazed at Cortez. "You promised."

The man cringed but nodded. "We'll go on our own." He opened the trunk and took a submachine gun from its case.

"Oh, wow."

"An Ingram Mac-10. There isn't a better one on the market." He ran his fingers over the weapon.

Lisa reached for it. Instinctively he turned away from her. "You'll shoot a pistol," he said. "That's more lady-like." He pulled his gun from the shoulder holster and handed it to her. Lisa took the pistol and smiled. Why not shoot him right now, right here? She scanned her surroundings. The driver still sat behind the wheel. No one around. What was that? A dark shape moved in a red sports car parked three bays down. Man or shadow?

Cortez put the Mac-10 in the foot space of the passenger seat and took the pistol from her. Too late. Damn.

"I'll show you how to use this piece," he said.

She hardly watched as he flicked the safety catch and pulled back the slide, released it and slapped the gun into her hand with a grin. Impatient now, he climbed into the front passenger seat.

Lisa settled in the rear and leaned forward. "Were those rude guys friends of yours?"

"You're better off not knowing anything about them."

"Of course I know Filinto Rocha, but the other one...I mean, he called me a whore."

"I'm sorry about that, darling. He is not a nice man. He shouldn't have treated you like that."

"Maybe he's gay." Lisa giggled.

Cortez laughed. "No, he's not, but he is more interested in making money and hunting."

"Is he very rich?"

"Yes, and he is smart."

"What does he do?"

"Enough questions."

Lisa leaned back and fell silent, frustrated that she couldn't find out more about the man with the scowl. At least she had her confirmation on Rocha and remembered the car's registration number.

They cruised the poorer neighborhoods of *zona norte*. Lisa needed a plan. Could she take on both of them? She had the knife and Cortez's pistol. She'd been naive to expect a coward like Cortez to go hunting without the bodyguard. He wasn't ashamed of his hobby. Why hide anything from the man hired to protect him? She studied the bulk of the driver. Squeezed behind the wheel, he'd need time to react.

At that moment, Cortez signaled to the driver, who switched off the lights, killed the engine, and stopped the rolling car. A group of children slept in the entrance of a run-down shop. Lisa's heart raced. No choice anymore. She couldn't let him kill the kids. Her heart beat in her throat. Fuck.

Cortez turned around to her. "All right, my love, you shoot first. When they panic and start running away, I'll finish them. Of course, you can keep shooting if you want."

A flash of red passed on the road and disappeared. No help there. Shit! What now? She told herself to stay calm, keep her breathing under control. She checked on the impassive driver, who watched the rear view mirror and the street ahead.

Lisa's hand slid down and pulled the knife from her boot. The noiseless weapon would give her extra seconds. She couldn't save Vitor Fraga's victims, but she could save these children. She lifted the blade to the headrest. Cortez opened the door. *Now!* She rammed the knife into the right side of his neck. He slumped sideways and fell out of the car, releasing a gurgling sound.

The driver stared at him. "Hey, what…"

Lisa raised the gun and shot him in the head. Bone, blood, and brain exploded around her. Her ears rang. The man's head flopped against the side window then fell forward. Lisa felt like throwing up. She pushed the door open and scrambled out. Trying hard to keep herself from retching, she stumbled away from the car. The kids stared at her. She wanted to tell them that everything was okay. No time. The Mac-10. She tore the submachine gun from Cortez's grasp. The knife still stuck in his throat with her fingerprints on the handle. She squatted and slowly pulled. Blood pumped from the wound and drenched her arm. Not dead yet but soon. His eyes stared, unfocused. Lisa wiped the blade clean on his shirt, shoved the knife back in her boot, and ran.

Chapter Thirty-Five

Félix passed Cortez's car and parked around the next corner. Nervous now, he wondered if he'd taken too big a risk. What if Cortez killed her? If Alves and Rocha had agreed to take her along, the game would have come to a premature end. No, Cortez didn't stand a chance against Lisa, bodyguard or not.

A gun shot. Félix flinched. No. Couldn't be her. He crept to the corner of a multistory apartment building, pressed his back against the wall, and peered around. A body sprawled beside the car. They couldn't have shot her. Impossible! He had to find out. On trembling legs he inched toward the Mercedes. Nothing moved, only the kids stirred. Lisa. No. Please. You can't be dead. You killed Cortez. Come on. Show yourself. He leaned against a fence unable to walk on. Despair suffocated him.

The rear door pushed open. Lisa stepped from the car. Alive. Relief surged through him. He slipped into the shadow of a tree and watched her pick up Cortez's Mac-10. A magnificent view—Lisa cradling the submachine gun as she dashed down the street.

Félix sprinted back to his car.

* * * *

Lisa couldn't hear her own footsteps. Her ears buzzed. But she didn't need to hear. She'd gotten one of them and survived. She entered a poorly-lit tunnel under one of the major roads. A dark figure came her way on the other side. She'd never felt less threatened. Light-footed, she ran past. The man's stare fixed on the Mac-10 in her right hand. At the end of the short tunnel, more street lamps illuminated the road. She stopped and looked down at herself. The front of her white blouse was spattered with blood. She ripped the fabric off and wiped her arms and face, wearing only the red bikini top with the miniskirt now.

How would she get home? If she threw away the guns, she could call a taxi and tell the driver she got attacked. But she didn't want to give up the submachine gun. Staring into the eyes of the man with the Corolla, she'd seen cold-blooded malice. She needed the Mac-10. He might come looking for her.

She sat down on the curb. The noises of the night filtered through her numbed ears. For a moment, she listened to the sounds of cars, far-off music, and little nocturnal insects and mammals.

The *rodoviária* wasn't far. She could catch a local bus or taxi there, but not while packing a submachine gun. One or the other. The gun or getting home. She picked up her blouse, wrapped the Mac-10 in it, walked back to the middle of the tunnel, and laid it down close to the wall. Nobody would stop here to check out some trash left behind. She wiped the pistol and threw it into the next trash bin.

Never more aware of her outfit, she marched into the main bus station. Half-naked, she only had the knife to defend herself. And she couldn't reach it fast. She told herself to calm down. Ignoring shouts and grunts, she crossed to the other side of the station. She was just a hooker who'd had a rough day. The scars on her back added credibility to her disguise. She left through the back where taxis waited, jumped into the first one, and gave the driver her address.

"You got money?" he asked with a suspicious sideways glance.

She pulled several fifty *reais* bills from the small pocket in her skirt and waved them in front of his face. "Should be more than enough."

"Sorry, you don't look like you had a very successful night."

Lisa smiled at him, while he started the engine. "Quite successful. Just a little rough."

He cackled and pulled onto the road. "Good for you then."

Lisa leaned back and relaxed. The drive took half an hour. The cabbie dropped her off and asked if she wanted to pay him with some overtime work. Lisa declined and gave him a good tip on top of the fare. "Better get the money home to your wife and kids."

"Hey, I don't have any," he protested.

"Yeah, right."

She fumbled with the lock and ran up the stairs. Her pale and blood-sprinkled face in the mirror shocked her. She stepped under the cool shower and longed for scalding heat.

Chapter Thirty-Six

Luiz jerked awake in the dark. Somebody stabbed his shoulder with a finger. Lisa squatted next to him. He scrambled to his feet and followed her outside. Her wet hair glistened in the moonlight. She wore shorts and a sweater.

"I need your help."

"Anything, Lisa."

She flashed him a ghastly smile. When they reached the street, the light from the lamps softened her pale face.

"Where are we going?" he asked.

"We need to pick up something. I'm sorry I had to wake you. The pickup will be a lot easier with your help."

"No problem." He walked next to her into the parking garage, greeted the guard, who would have shooed him away if he'd shown up alone, and climbed into the passenger seat.

"Buckle up," she told him. Luiz smiled. When he stole a car, he didn't have time to put on the seat belt. And it would slow him down if he had to abandon the car and run from the police.

"We are going north," he said after a while just to break the silence.

"Yeah, you know this part of town?"

"We used to hang out here. You're not going to make me buy drugs, are you?"

Lisa laughed, a bit too loud, too hysterical.

"Everything okay?"

"Yeah, I just had a hard day."

They passed the bus terminal. Luiz and the kids had spent many nights under overpasses in the area. Some people even built little shacks down there. And the cars drove over them, their owners unaware.

Lisa slowed in a tunnel. "See the white bundle ahead? I'll stop and you get it for me. Be quick, I don't want to draw attention."

"Okay." Luiz took off the seat belt. Lisa stopped and he jumped out. The thing was heavier than it looked. The red and white cloth slipped a little and he saw the barrel of a gun. He uncovered it completely and stared at Lisa.

"Get in," she yelled.

Luiz did. The weapon rested on his lap. He gripped it with both hands. "I've seen this one before." The night Gordinho died. He'd only caught a glimpse, but no doubt, it was the same make. "What did you do?"

She clutched the wheel so hard, her knuckles turned white. "I shouldn't have brought you. What was I thinking?"

"Lisa. Tell me."

Her head whipped around. "You want to know? They were about to kill again, Luiz. But I didn't let them. You understand? Gordinho's murderers are dead. No, only one of them and his bodyguard. The second man will live to see another day, but only the one." Lisa gunned the engine.

Luiz let her words sink in. Why had she done this? Not even Max had cared enough. How could she? The night streets seemed full of threatening shadows until they reached Copacabana bustling with life.

Side by side, they walked from the garage to the bookstore, Lisa carrying the gun in a duffel bag. At the gate, she stopped and turned to him. "I'm sorry. I really shouldn't have taken you along. I...I was losing it. Needed someone to..."

Luiz studied her. She'd never looked so shaken before, not even when Gordinho died. Or maybe he hadn't noticed then. "I don't think you should be alone tonight. You want me to sleep at your place?"

A smile spread over her face. "Thanks, Luiz. I really don't want to be alone right now." She put her left arm around his shoulders and pulled him along.

Her apartment looked much plainer than he'd expected. Wood floors covered by a few rugs, a red sofa in the living room, shelves with books, and a dining table and chairs. She shoved away a coffee table and pulled out a mattress from under the sofa and turned it into a bed.

"Hope you'll be comfortable," she said.

"Hey, you forget who you're talking to."

Lisa smiled. "Sorry, I really did for a moment." She tossed him a pillow. "Bathroom is right there." She pointed at a door off the hallway.

"Okay, I'll be fine." He flopped down.

"Good night."

Luiz listened to her fading steps. He knew he wouldn't sleep. Too much going on in his mind. He still found it hard to believe Lisa had killed one of the murderers.

The fuckers had burned Gordinho. They'd enjoyed seeing him suffer, hearing him scream. A human torch. Nausea crawled up from his stomach. He stumbled to the bathroom, clung to the bowl, and threw up, kept retching. His stomach wanted to turn itself inside out. Shaking, he flushed then washed his face and rinsed his mouth.

When he returned to the living room, Lisa sat on the sofa bed. "I can't sleep either," she said. "I don't feel bad about killing them, but I can't get the pictures out of my mind."

Luiz settled next to her. "Tell me."

"One I stabbed in the neck. Then I shot the bodyguard. In the head. Have you ever seen someone getting shot in the head?"

Luiz nodded. "Max shot a traitor."

"Max? Your drug lord friend?"

"Yeah."

"I knew a kid who worked for the gang. He was a good guy. Sixteen. I gave him English lessons. He was smart, too. Could have made something of his life, but he joined the gang and was shot. I hate drug gangs."

"That's why Max doesn't want to have us around."

"You're kidding." She got up and went to the kitchen. She returned with a bottle of wine and two glasses, smiling at him. "You're not legally allowed to drink alcohol unless in the company of a responsible adult. Or something like that. Want a glass?"

Luiz smiled. He hadn't drunk much alcohol in his life. He'd sniffed glue for a while until Max beat that out of him. He smoked pot, which Max gave him for free. At parties he drank beer. This was the first time he'd have wine.

"Sure," Luiz said. "Thanks. Did you ever sniff glue?"

Lisa laughed. Her normal, amused laugh without the hysterical note. "Yeah, I tried and liked it. Nothing mattered, hunger and fear didn't exist. You don't sniff that shit, do you?"

"Not anymore. Destroys your lungs and your brain too."

"Smart boy."

"Max told me that."

"Max again."

"All I know I learned from him." He sipped the wine and cringed at the sour taste. Another sip and he could feel the stuff relax the muscles in his neck. "Would you read a book to me?" he asked.

"I don't think I've got a book here you might like, but I could tell you the story of Peter Pan and Captain Hook."

Luiz stretched out and listened. He could see the bored rich kids flying off with Peter and Tinker Bell. He felt like Peter Pan himself, picking up the stray kids of Rio. When she ended the story, neither of them spoke. Lisa stretched out next to him.

Chapter Thirty-Seven

The next morning, Lisa set two coffee mugs on the table. Looking at Luiz's brooding face, she sensed what would happen next and blamed herself.

"You going to kill the other guy today?"

"Yes."

"Take me with you."

"No."

Luiz gripped his mug with both hands and pressed his lips into a thin line.

"Listen, Luiz, I feel pretty good about killing these people, but I don't want you to watch me."

"I'll know it anyway."

"You should know. That Gordinho's killers are dead, I mean. That there is justice even for people like Cortez and Rocha. But I don't want you to be there."

"Gordinho was my friend. I watched him burn. Do you really think it's bad for me if I see you shoot his killer?"

He was right, of course. If he watched children die and drug lords shoot traitors, he could cope with her shooting a killer of street kids from a distance. But risking her life was one thing, dragging the boy into it something completely different. "Too dangerous for you to come along."

"If you take the risk, I do too. You hardly knew Gordinho. Please, Lisa." His eyes pleaded with her. His hands lay flat on the table now, palms up.

Maybe he needed it as much as she did. Or more. "Okay."

Luiz's features relaxed.

She walked over to the small desk in the corner and rummaged in the drawers for her old prepaid cellphone. When she found the mobile, she gave it to Luiz together with the charger. "You better take this. Should still have some air time, but not much."

* * * *

153

Lisa drove past Rocha's house and pointed it out to Luiz. She'd hoped to catch him early in the morning on his way to work. Almost noon now, they'd have to get him when he returned home. She parked the car in a side street, a straight line down from the deserted house, through the rain forest. "You sure you want to come along?"

"Positive."

"Okay." Lisa climbed out of the car and marched to the back. She took her rifle from the trunk and handed Luiz a small sand bag. "Now, listen to me carefully. You don't shoot. You wouldn't hit him at that distance with your little Taurus. You only use it in case something goes seriously wrong. Understood?"

"Understood."

"*Vamos.*"

* * * *

Kneeling at the edge of the roof, Lisa loaded the five round clip of the Steyr, a wonderful piece of Austrian craftsmanship designed to kill. One of these bullets would penetrate Rocha's body. Maybe two. She'd play it safe. While attaching the clip to the rifle, she noticed Luiz's gaze on her every move. "It's extremely accurate up to eight hundred meters," she said.

"How far away do you think we are?"

"A bit less than four hundred."

Lying on their stomachs, they watched the house and street with nothing to do but think about killing a man and listen to the squeaks of monkeys, chirps of birds, and the rustle of lizards. If she'd forced herself to get up early enough to catch him on his way to the university, she could have spared them the long wait in the baking sun.

Killing Captain Hook all over again. The Steyr in her hands, waiting for Vitor Fraga's car. Her first kill had changed her in many ways. Most of all, his death had empowered her to take her life in her own hands. She didn't know it then. Not right away. Spending her teenage years in the States, she'd felt like he couldn't reach her, but he had always been there, in her nightmares and in the sessions with her shrink. When she returned to Rio, an overwhelming dread suffocated her. She couldn't walk through the streets without looking over her shoulder. But she didn't want to run any longer and learned to fight instead.

She looked at Luiz staring at the street. He noticed and glanced back at her. "*Tudo bem?*"

"*Tudo bem.*" She wouldn't let these kids live through the same fear.

The black BMW crawled up the hill. Lisa's distracted mind sprang into action, her heart shifted gears. She gave Luiz the thumbs-up and rested the barrel of the rifle on the sandbag.

The car eased into the driveway. Lisa thought of Gordinho and the pain he'd suffered. Of future victims whose lives she'd save now. Looking through the scope, she could clearly make out Rocha's angular face as he climbed out of the car. A man who killed children for fun. She searched for a trace of his secret passion in his features but found none. Darkly good-looking, in good physical shape, he was a man who could have had a great life, yet had forfeited it. Time for Tinker Bell to act. Complete calm settled over her. Captain Hook must die.

As Rocha walked toward the door, Lisa took a deep breath, held it and squeezed the trigger. The bullet penetrated his back. He jerked and slumped against the car. Lisa chambered a new round and shot him in the head. He collapsed. She released the air in her lungs and pulled herself up. Her eyes locked on Luiz's. He nodded gravely.

Two down. A smile tugged at the corners of her mouth as she picked up the spent shells. Luiz grabbed the sandbag. They jumped onto the balcony, dashed down the stairs, out the back, and ran toward the rain forest. Damp shadows enveloped them. A deep sense of satisfaction filled her. Precious lives saved.

Chapter Thirty-Eight

Luiz left the garage with Lisa, but took a detour around the block before he slipped through the gate to the backyard behind the bookstore. He didn't want the neighbors to see him with her and get them all upset again. Someone donating clothes and a crate of food didn't mean everyone liked their presence.

This early in the afternoon Luiz didn't expect the kids to hang around, but Tatu and Rena were already sitting in the shade of the apartment building.

"Hey, what's up?" he asked.

Rena looked at him through red eyes. She must have been crying. "Ubaldo didn't come back last night after he visited his sister."

"Maybe he slept at her place." Luiz wasn't worried. Kids often disappeared for a while.

"He's too afraid of her husband," Rena said. "That's why he ran away. The bastard gets drunk every night and beats her and the children."

"Maybe the guy is dead?" Luiz grinned. "Maybe the shithead had an accident."

"Ubaldo would have come back anyway. He's my boyfriend."

Great, now he had to go look for the boy. "All right, you stay here in case he shows up. Tatu, you come with me."

Tatu jumped to his feet. "Better than waiting."

* * * *

When they reached the *favela* squeezed between the rich areas of *zona sul*, people were protesting in the streets. Military police kept them at bay with machine guns. Luiz's heart sank. He addressed an enraged woman. "Senhora, what happened?"

She darted him a fiery glance, and Luiz backed away. Her features softened when she took a closer look at him. "The police. They came in yesterday evening and shot at everything moving, but they didn't get the drug gang. So they grabbed two random boys, beat them up, and took them away."

Luiz swallowed. "You know the boys?"

"Sure, the older one, Enrique, he's sixteen and training to become a carpenter. He's no drug dealer."

Luiz asked, "What did they arrest him for then?"

The woman snorted with disgust. "Drug trafficking, of course. Doesn't matter if you have anything to do with it or not. It's enough to live in a *favela*." She paused and glared at the cops. "If I had a grenade, I'd blow them up."

Luiz followed her hateful glare. The police in heavy armor had barred the streets. They chased away tourists on one side of the barrier and fought off the angry mob on the other.

"We're dirt to them," the woman stated coldly. "I wonder why they don't bomb the *favela*s."

"Don't give them ideas," Tatu warned.

Luiz asked, "What did the other boy look like?"

"Black and poor, of course. He was younger though."

Luiz grabbed Tatu's arm and pulled him away. "This is fucked up. We need to find someone who knows the other kid."

They worked their way toward the center of the crowd, catching snippets of curses, then the name Ubaldo. Luiz stopped in his tracks and turned toward the man who'd uttered it. "Ubaldo? Did the police take him?"

The man shook a fist at him. "Yeah, the cowards took Mirella's little brother and another boy. We can't let this go on. They just do with us what they want. We have rights, too."

"We've got to do something," Tatu said. "But what?"

"We, nothing. Maybe Max?" Actually he'd thought of Lisa first, but he didn't want her to take it up with the police, too.

Tatu sighed and looked down at his feet. "He won't do anything. He'll say this happens all the time."

"Let's try anyway. Come on."

They ran to the next bus stop.

* * * *

Luiz and Tatu stormed up the hill, taking two steps at a time.

"Hope he's there," Luiz said. They turned the last corner and saw the guards. A good sign. If they were here, Max was, too.

One of them barred their way with his Uzi. "Hold it."

"Hey, we need to see him," Tatu protested.

"Not now, he's busy."

"Fuck!" Luiz hissed.

"Please, it's important," Tatu begged.

"Get lost, I don't wanna get in trouble."

Luiz snatched the walkie-talkie from the guard's hand and ran, ignoring the shouted curses. He knew the guy couldn't leave his post.

Tatu dashed after him. "You're crazy."

Luiz stopped and pushed the button. "Max, we need your help. A matter of life and death."

He stared down the street. The guard still stood at the door, waving his hands and shouting for them to come back.

"Luiz?" Max's voice crackled through the speaker.

"Yeah, don't be mad, it's really important."

"Two minutes. On the roof."

Luiz exhaled with relief.

"He's gonna rip off your head and play soccer with it," Tatu said.

"Yeah, probably." Luiz swallowed. No, Max wouldn't be happy.

They jogged back. He tossed the walkie-talkie at the guard and raced up the outside stairs to the roof.

Tatu followed at a slower pace. "He's gonna be mad as hell."

"Shit." Footsteps sounded on the inside stairs. Luiz stared at the door with anticipation. It flew open.

Max, muscles tense, jaws grinding, marched towards them. "Hey, what's up?"

Luiz swallowed. "The cops arrested Ubaldo. You've got to help him."

Max's forehead furrowed. "Who's Ubaldo?"

"One of us," Tatu said.

"A street kid? You want me to bail out a street kid?"

"I'm a street kid," Tatu countered.

Max glared at him. "You're my fucking brother."

"I'm a street kid," Luiz said.

Max's eyes narrowed. "What the..." He exhaled, looked from one boy to the other. "Okay, what happened?"

"A police raid," Luiz explained, trying to calm down. "They arrested him. He's got nothing to do with drugs. They just took him and another boy."

"So what?" Max shouted, spreading his arms. "Happens all the time. Right here in my *favela,* and there's nothing I can do about it. They'll beat him up and let him go. Or throw him in prison. I don't give a fuck."

Tatu turned away from his brother, the corners of his mouth pulled down in disgust, but Luiz couldn't give up yet. "Ubaldo's got a job and all. It's not fair."

Max swore and stared at the back of his younger brother. "Fucking cops." He sighed. "Okay, I'll talk to the lawyer. Maybe he can pull some strings."

Tatu spun around, his eyes sparkling with tears. "I know the lawyer can get him out."

"Thanks, Max. We owe you. Anything you need, just let us know," Luiz said.

Max chuckled. "Sure, Luiz. Someday I'm gonna call in the favor. Now give me the boy's name. Which *favela* was it?"

Chapter Thirty-Nine

Lisa sat at the reading table, sipping hot bitter coffee. She set the chipped mug down and watched Rejane dust the shelves. Although off duty, she'd spent the afternoon in the bookstore, reluctant to face the solitude of her apartment.

Soon Tony would drop by, but she'd failed to resolve her problems. She'd killed Cortez and Rocha, but she couldn't forget the cold stare of the Corolla's driver. His whole demeanor showed he was in charge.

And he'd seen her with Cortez on the night he died. Even if he'd taken her for one of Cortez's lovers, he might have second thoughts now. She'd taken too many risks. So what? She'd succeeded, and she'd deal with the third man too.

But first she deserved a break. Tonight she'd see Tony. Nothing else mattered.

"I'll go take a shower," she told Rejane. "If someone asks for me, send him over to the apartment."

Rejane gave her a quizzical look. "The cute guy?"

Lisa smiled. "Maybe." She rose and walked outside. In the bright afternoon sunshine and heat, the past two days seemed more unreal than ever. She headed for the entrance to the apartments and bumped into Tony at the corner.

"Hey," he said. "Am I too early? Couldn't stand it in the office anymore."

"No, I'm glad you're here."

For an awkward moment they just looked at each other then she reached out to him. Tony took her in his arms and held her tight. She rubbed her face against his. He kissed her cheek. They separated and Lisa took his hand.

"You want a coffee or something?" she asked.

"I don't even have to buy you dinner?"

Lisa smiled. "I thought we might watch a movie."

"I can do a movie. You got popcorn?"

"Nope. Sorry."

Lisa led him through the gate, the front door, and up the flight of stairs to her apartment. "I've got a nice selection of Brazilian films."

"Sounds exciting."

"Save your sarcasm, I'm immune. Do you know *Central do Brasil*?"

"Don't think so."

"Okay, it's a cute one and I think the DVD has an English sound track."

Lisa made lattes for them, put on the movie, and settled on the sofa with Tony. She grabbed his wrist and slung his arm around her shoulders. She leaned her head against his chest. Pure animal comfort.

As always, she cried at the bitter-sweet end of the movie. One child saved from a life on the streets.

Tony smiled and stroked her hair. "Hey, all is well."

She blinked. The movie scenes faded. No happy ending for her and the kids yet. One more to take down. The man with the Corolla. She untangled herself from Tony and got up. "Beer?"

"Sure."

Nervousness settled in her stomach. Images of Cortez bleeding on the ground and the bodyguard's bloody head wormed into her mind. She squashed them, couldn't allow any of these memories to surface in Tony's presence. No room for Tinker Bell now.

* * * *

Still worried about Ubaldo's fate, Luiz and Tatu kicked the ball around Lisa's backyard. Rena sat in a shady corner staring at her bare feet. Luiz hadn't told her they'd asked Max for help. He didn't want to get her hopes up. Every now and then, he or Tatu would look toward the small corridor between the buildings. They'd exchange glances. Time dragged. Tatu had never been in a detention center, but Luiz's mind replayed terrible images and memories. Ubaldo featured in the most horrifying scenes Luiz had witnessed or experienced.

"Ubaldo!" Rena screamed.

Luiz's heart jolted. He swung around and saw the boy, a bit the worse for wear, but in one piece. He laughed. Everyone cheered and crowded Ubaldo.

"Hey, what happened?" Rena asked.

"You won't believe it." Ubaldo shook his head. "The police arrested me. They beat me up and threw me in a cell with some pretty rough guys. Drug dealers. They laughed at me, the bastards. Made fun of me and asked how many battles I'd fought with the police. I told them I'm with Max's gang. That shut them up and they left me alone." Ubaldo beamed with pride. "I'm just glad they didn't ask me what commando Max worked for. I couldn't remember."

Tatu gave him the thumbs up. "Smart, professor. And you haven't even met Max."

Ubaldo grinned. "But you and Luiz keep going on about him."

"But how did you get out?" Rena asked.

"I have no clue. This afternoon they pushed us all into a police van and took us to the prison. I thought I was gonna rot there, but then this cop walks up to me and tells me to go home. I couldn't believe it. For a second. Then I ran for my life. Took me a while to find my way back."

They all laughed, slapped his back, and ruffled his hair.

Luiz grinned at Tatu.

* * * *

The credits ended. Tony turned off the DVD player, and the television screen switched to the news. A familiar face appeared. Where had he seen the man? Then realization hit him. The guy Lisa had flirted with at the art gallery. The camera angle-panned to a car. Through the shattered driver-side window he saw a bloody mess slumped over the steering wheel. The camera moved around the car. Another body lay in a pool of blood beside the Merc. Tony swallowed. The newscaster returned. The background picture switched to Filinto Rocha, the artist.

Tony flopped back in the sofa, remembering the paintings, Lisa's scowl, her flirting, and her hyper behavior afterward. No way. Lisa wasn't a cold-blooded killer. He remembered her speech on the Corcovado, that she hoped she'd never have to use the gun, use it to kill. But still…Too much of a coincidence after she'd told him these men killed children. She'd cried over the orphan in the movie. What would she do for real kids?

A gasp. Lisa stood staring at the screen, two beers and a pack of peanuts in her trembling hands.

No, he still couldn't believe it. "What happened?" he asked, but she didn't react. Tony rose and walked toward her.

She turned to face him. "What?"

"The fascist artist and the guy who chatted you up. Both dead?"

Lisa brushed past him and set the bottles and nuts down on the table. "I don't know what you're talking about." She avoided his eyes.

Tony grasped her arm. "Look at me!"

She shook him off and strode over to the window, staring outside. As good as a confession? Tony felt sick. She'd killed them and he'd watched her set the trap. She'd fooled him. But he couldn't just leave. He had to hear it from her.

Tony stepped behind her and rested his hands on her shoulders. In the glass he saw their reflections. "You did it, right?" No response. He turned her around. Her face was a pale mask. "Lisa?"

She looked at him through narrowed eyes. Her nostrils widened. The muscles in her jaws twitched.

He shook her. "Tell me."

She pushed his arms away and drew back a clenched fist. "Go away."

Surprised by her reaction, he fought the impulse to retreat. "Come on, hit me if that's what you want."

She tilted her head. Her wild stare glazed over. Her arm relaxed and dropped to her side. "I'm sorry."

"For what exactly?"

Tears glistened in her eyes. "Please go."

"Tell me what you did."

Lisa shook her head and stepped closer to the window as if she wanted to jump.

Tony stared at the woman who'd killed two people. No, she wouldn't talk to him, explain why. Hopeless. He turned to leave.

Chapter Forty

When the door clicked shut, Lisa's tears flowed unrestrained. She collapsed on the sofa and cried. What the hell had she done? Why did she want to hit the only man she ever cared for? She'd lost Tony. She didn't deserve him. He was much better off without her. She sobbed. No love for her.

The news filtered through to her. The anchorman speculated whether the deaths of two prominent public figures were connected, despite the different mode of killing.

Lisa took a shuddering breath.

"Maybe two murderers," he continued, "but acting for the same reason?" He explained how Cortez and Rocha went back a long time, had been friends since university. Involved together in a drunk hit-and-run eleven years ago. A boy had died. A three-year sentence on probation for Cortez, who'd been driving, one year for Rocha for keeping quiet instead of helping the victim. They showed a photo of the boy, a fifteen-year-old black kid.

Lisa's thoughts raged. Of course nothing had happened to them. Maybe that time they'd developed a taste for killing and learned they could get away with it even if caught.

A sense of satisfaction spread through her. She had punished them. They would not kill again. Lisa startled at the sound of her phone. Jango. She cleared her throat before she answered.

"Lunch, tomorrow," he said.

"Tony talked to you?" she asked.

"No. I saw the news."

Of course, he'd made the connection. Just like Tony. "Come to my place, okay?"

"Okay."

Lisa opened one of the beers and clinked the bottle against the second one. "Cheers, Tony." She drank, then picked up her cellphone and selected his number. He answered after the second ring.

"I'm sorry I couldn't talk to you. I'm sorry I wanted to hurt you. I'm sorry I'm so screwed up."

"Okay." He sounded distant and cold. Or was it her imagination? She hung up and tossed the cell next to her on the sofa. She couldn't blame him for hating her. Would he go to the police? No. He'd never do anything to hurt her. She curled up on the sofa, hugging a pillow, wishing Tony were there to hold her. No, she was a cold-blooded killer. He could never love her. Maybe if she felt a sliver of remorse…but she didn't.

Lisa sat up. The image of the man with the Corolla popped up in her mind. One more to take down. He had acted like the boss, the man in command. He'd treated Cortez like a schoolboy. And rightly so. He'd been such a stupid bastard. Lisa smiled to herself and reached for the phone. "Jango, can you get me another name and address if I give you another registration number?"

Jango exploded and cursed into the phone. Lisa let the wave wash over her until he'd exhausted himself. Then she asked, "You got something to write with? Bring the name and address tomorrow. After we've talked, you decide if you'll give me the info."

He exhaled audibly. "All right, tell me."

Chapter Forty-One

Jango rang the doorbell three times. A sure sign he was still mad at Lisa. On the camera screen, she saw him shift from foot to foot. She buzzed him through the gate and door. Lisa stood waiting for him in the door frame to her apartment and listened to his slow steps on the stairway. When he looked up at her, he smiled. "Smells lovely."

Lisa grinned. "I made your favorite dish to appease you."

"Clever girl."

She stepped into the small kitchen, grabbed the two plates with large homemade cheeseburgers and curly fries from her favorite American diner. She carried them into the living room. A stack of napkins and a jug of water already sat on the dining table.

"Mean trick," Jango mumbled as he sat down. He picked up the burger with both hands and took a huge bite. He closed his eyes while he chewed. "Ah, yours are simply the best."

Lisa smiled. It always worked. She'd only eaten half of her burger by the time he devoured the last of his fries.

"You did it, right?" he asked, wiping his hands on a napkin.

Lisa nodded, her mouth too full to speak.

"You're crazy. Do you really think you can get away with it?"

Lisa swallowed. "Getting away isn't at the top of my priority list."

"But on mine. I haven't taken care of you all these years so you can get yourself killed in an insane rampage."

Lisa put down the burger. "My dear Jango, you gave me the shooting lessons. You bought me the Firestar and the Steyr, and now you're getting upset because I used my training and the weapons?"

Jango rolled his eyes. "That was for self-defense."

"A sniper rifle?"

After a five-second staring contest, they burst out laughing.

Finally, Jango sighed. "Circumstances were different with Vitor Fraga. He more than deserved to die, and he had no friends with influence to protect him. Now you're messing with the wrong kind of people. Powerful people."

Lisa raised an eyebrow. Cortez and Rocha powerful? They wished. "Who is the third man, Jango? The Corolla driver? C'mon, spit it out. You know his favorite sport. Don't tell me he doesn't deserve to die."

"Just so you realize what you're up against. The car is registered in the name of a retired judge. Diego Alves. A highly respected man."

"That doesn't sound like the driver. He was forty at most."

"Maybe a relative, but if he drives the judge's car..." Jango took her hand. "Please, Lisa. Forget about him. You had your revenge."

"And let him go on killing children like vermin?"

Jango leaned back and closed his eyes. After a few seconds he straightened and pulled a piece of paper from his jacket. "The judge lives in Alto da Boa Vista. Probably in a high-security home. And I don't believe he's killing anyone."

"Can you find out something about his family background?"

The doorbell rang. Lisa stared at Jango. Could be Luiz, but he'd never before come to her place uninvited. Jango slipped the paper with Alves's address back in his jacket pocket and nodded. She rose, walked to the door, and checked the camera. "Cops." Her pulse raced. She broke out in a sweat. Get the gun? No, they'd shoot her. Not the worst-case scenario. Stay calm.

Jango's steps behind her. He put a hand on her shoulder. "Can they possibly know?"

The bell rang again. Lisa shook her head. "I can't imagine how."

"Better talk to them."

Her hands trembled as she buzzed the gate. Breathing hard, she opened the door. Heavy boots on the stairs. Moving fast. Two policemen, their faces a mask of indifference. One stopped at the bottom of the last flight of stairs, the other ascended slowly, keeping his eyes on her. "Lisa Kerry?"

She nodded. The young cop looked familiar. Shit. The guy who'd taken her gun, the one she'd given Rocha's registration number to. Damn. She'd completely forgotten about that. He peered past her into the apartment. His gaze brushed over Jango before it settled on her again.

"You're under arrest," he announced with authority.

Jango pulled her back. "On what charge?"

"Murder."

No. They couldn't...How? The house crumbled. Walls of concrete and iron bars rose around her.

Never. Lisa shook off Jango's hands, elbowed the cop out of the way, and dashed past him. She wouldn't go to prison. Not again. Jango called her name. Steps behind her. A hand clutched her arm. Below, the second cop drew his gun and aimed at her. Better dead then locked up. Lisa kicked at the gun hand. A boot at the back of her knee. She buckled, slid down two steps. Hands grasped her. Blurred faces. Curses.

Handcuffs snapped around her wrists. Lisa choked.

"You come with us." Hands pulled her up. A sneering face. Too close. They dragged her down the stairs.

Tears streaked her cheeks. Game over. She sniffed, had to calm down, control her frantic breathing. Think! They couldn't have anything on her, except that she reported the registration number.

"I'll get you a lawyer," Jango shouted, likely more a warning for the cops than a consolation to her. Could they hear the fear in his voice?

Think. It's not over yet. If they compared her fingerprints with those found in the car, they'd know she'd been riding in the backseat, but that didn't mean she killed Cortez. And no evidence connected her with Rocha's death. His secretary might remember that she went out for lunch with him. Oh God. They only needed to search her apartment to find the murder weapon in her closet. Would the lack of a search warrant keep them out long enough that Jango could get rid of it? They didn't show her an arrest warrant either.

The cops dragged her out into the sun. A neighbor stopped next to the squad car and stared. Lisa managed a faint smile. They had nothing, and Jango would hide the rifle. With more confidence now, she shook off the arms clutching her. "I'm coming. I just panicked. You guys don't have the best reputation."

The cop who'd drawn the gun on her laughed. The one behind her growled, "For a good reason."

"Who do you think I've killed?"

"You'll find out." He shoved her into the back of the squad car. She fought hard to stay focused and keep the memories of her first stay at a police station locked away. She wasn't a street kid anymore. They'd treat her with more respect this time. They couldn't just let an almost-white middle-class woman disappear.

Lisa stared out the window, telling herself over and over again that they had no evidence. Like a mantra. After a short drive, the car pulled into a parking lot. A different police station.

They dragged her out of the car and pushed her toward the entrance. She wanted to run, but that would only give them a reason to shoot her. The cop grabbed her arm as if he'd read her mind. They'd have to let her go for lack of evidence.

An officer at the reception desk raised his eyebrows. The second cop stopped to talk to him. This wasn't an official arrest or they'd check her in. The cop who'd taken her Firestar pushed her into an interrogation room. Just like in the movies, mirror on one side, a table, three chairs.

She raised her cuffed hands. "Will you take these off now?"

"No." He smirked. "You killed Rocha. First you shot at his car, a few days later you shot him with a rifle."

"I didn't and you won't find any evidence pointing my way."

"Your confession will do."

Lisa leaned over the table and glared at him. "I have nothing to confess."

He slapped her hard. Stunned, she stared at him. Her cheek stung. The pain egged her on. "Forget it."

He tilted his head and smiled. "You're tough. Let's find out just how tough." He grabbed her arm and dragged her out of the room, down a dark corridor. Lisa stumbled. Just a bluff, she told herself. A familiar smell crept in her nose. Sweat, excrement. Voices shouted. The cells. Lisa balked but he pulled her along. No!

Chapter Forty-Two

Luiz and Tatu ran up the stairs to Max's headquarters, panting in the early afternoon heat. The guard greeted them with a salvo of curses, but this time didn't block their way. They pushed past.

Max stood with one foot up on the bench, forearm resting on his thigh. Three of his soldiers sat at the table, which was littered with guns and coffee mugs. Another leaned against the wall, while Mussolini, Max's new general, paced the room.

Luiz hesitated, but Max glanced over his shoulder and waved them in before he continued. "That was the second time our couriers got arrested. The cops weren't just lucky. They've got ears and eyes in my *favela*. Watch out, guys. I want the mole. I trust you. You'll be the only ones to know when the big deliveries come in." Max straightened and put his foot down. "Of course, that means if something goes wrong again, I'll know I've made a bad choice today." He looked from one to the other. Each man held his gaze, unblinking.

Luiz glanced at Tatu, wondering if they should leave. Tatu shrugged slightly.

Mussolini said, "Costa Branca is crazy. He makes our dealers nervous. We've got to kill him."

Max shook his head. "We can't get to him, and I'm pretty sure someone's going to take care of him. Likely a cop."

The soldiers filed out. Capone slapped Max's shoulder. "I'll keep my eyes open. Can smell a rat from afar."

"Thanks, man." Max sat down on the bench with his back to the table, legs stretched out. He seemed relaxed. "Hey guys, what's up?"

"Ubaldo is out," Tatu said, giving his brother a high five.

Luiz's gaze fell on the newspaper. The front page showed the picture of the man who'd aimed the submachine gun at them. He picked it up and stared at the letters, unable to decipher them. His heart pounded. His fingers left sweat marks. "Hey, can I have that?"

Max raised his eyebrows and smiled. "Of course. I'm glad you've changed your attitude toward reading."

"It's kinda useful." Luiz carefully folded the paper like a precious trophy. A small plastic bag slipped from the table. Grass. Luiz grabbed it and grinned. "Can I have this, too?" Just what he needed right now.

Max laughed. "Sure, man."

* * * *

Luiz and Tatu sprawled in the shade of a palm tree at Copacabana beach, sharing a joint and a coconut, while they read yesterday's paper.

"I can't believe she did that." Tatu slurped the last water from the green nut and took out his knife.

"Man, she told me. And I was with her when she shot the other one. Like they were roaches. Squish." Luiz buried the stub of the joint in the sand.

Tatu cut the green nut in four pieces. "I'd have killed them if I got a chance."

"Yeah." Luiz took one of the pieces and nibbled at the thin layer of fruit. "I don't think we should tell anyone."

"She's like a mother for Ubaldo and Rena. They might get upset."

They looked at each other and laughed.

"Maybe we should tell Max," Luiz suggested.

"Nah, he doesn't like her. He thinks she's crazy."

Luiz snorted and Tatu burst out in more laughter.

"Man, that was pretty good shit," Luiz said.

"I haven't laughed so much in a long time."

"And we've still got a bit left."

"Maybe Lisa could use a smoke."

"Are you going to ask her?"

Another giggling fit shook them.

Chapter Forty-Three

A short man with a large key ring waited at the end of the hallway.

"Open that one," the cop commanded.

"But Chicão, that's..."

Lisa looked into the scrunched up face of the jailor then at the cell. Several men of different ages and skin color were crammed in there, cheering now, shouting obscenities. No! They couldn't possibly lock her in with this lot.

"Do it," Chicão said.

Lisa tried to wriggle free. He pushed her against the bars. Leering faces stared at her. No doubt what would happen if he locked her in with them. "If you do this, I'll kill you." Her voice trembled, betraying her panic. She closed her eyes. No, she couldn't give up yet.

Chicão pulled her around and slammed her back against the bars. "Did I just hear a confession?"

The foul breath of someone right behind her crawled into her nose. "No, a promise. I haven't killed anyone, but for you I'll make an exception." A hand reached under her T-shirt from behind and cupped her breast. Her whole body went stiff. A voice groaned in her ear. She couldn't allow herself to break. Panting, she struggled to blank out the hand, the smells. She stared at the grinning cop. He looked over her shoulder then back at her. "They have a pretty dull life in here."

"Listen, asshole. If you make me confess now, I'll retract in court and tell them what happened here, about the dead boy and that you didn't give a fuck. I'll talk to the press. They'll love it."

Chicão clenched his jaws and glared at the guard. "Open that fucking door."

Like a tentacle, a second hand groped her. She couldn't ignore the calloused fingers stroking her skin. Strangely gentle.

"Mmh, you feel nice," the voice rasped in her ear.

Waiting for the familiar panic, she closed her eyes. But he wasn't hurting her, he caressed her. Another tortured human being. "Thanks," she whispered.

"No way, not during my shift," the jailor shouted. "You're more fucked up than I thought. Put her in with the women or get out of here."

A glimmer of hope. Strength seeped into Lisa's body.

Chicão stared at the jailor; then he snatched the keys from his hand. "I won't forget this, man."

Lisa twisted her neck to look at the man behind her, his hands still stroking her. "Let go," she whispered.

Black teeth showed between his grinning lips as he squeezed his face through the bars next to her. She winked and managed a smile. His hands slithered away.

Lisa brought up her cuffed hands and lashed out at Chicão. He jumped back. She missed but lunged at him again. His fist slammed against her cheekbone. The prisoners cheered her on. She blocked his next blow with her arms.

The coward pulled his gun. "Step back."

Lisa couldn't move. Murmurs and grunts from the cell. At least she'd won their respect. Chicão grabbed her arm and pushed her toward the door. She stumbled, lost her balance, but the jailer grabbed her other arm and steadied her.

Sneering, the cop unlocked the cell door. "C'mon boys, get her."

Nobody moved. Someone grumbled a curse.

"Don't be shy," the bastard coaxed. The shadows moved.

Someone laughed. "I'll take her." Strong arms reached around her waist. She struggled while Chicão stepped back and smiled. "Let me know when you've had enough and we can talk."

"Noooo," she screamed, kicking at her captor. Not again. She lashed out and writhed. If she hurt him bad enough he might kill her.

"Hey, Chicão. Stop this shit." The cop who'd helped arrest her strode down the corridor. "Her lawyer's here."

Chapter Forty-Four

Lisa lurked in the second floor photo gallery featuring famous residents of the Copacabana Palace Hotel. Leaning on the banister rail, she watched the reception desk below. Her thoughts circled around the cop and the staged arrest. He didn't have any evidence, or he'd have checked her in, and taken her fingerprints and a mugshot. No, he wanted to find out if she had anything to do with Rocha's murder in a clandestine manner. Who gave him his orders? The third man? Alves?

Tony stepped from the revolving doors, dragging his feet, shoulders drooping. Maybe he hadn't slept too well after the disastrous evening. He talked to the receptionist, a pretty girl who smiled at him and laughed. When he moved on with a wave, Lisa walked over to the elevator and waited until the display showed the cabin had reached the ground floor before she pushed the button. Moments later, the door slid open.

"Hi Ranger." Lisa slipped in.

Tony gaped at her. "Lisa, what the...?"

She fought the temptation to shut him up with a kiss. Instead she put a finger on his lips. "You want to know the truth?"

He nodded.

She withdrew her finger. "Which floor?" She couldn't remember. Last time she'd been too drunk on the way up and too confused on the way down.

He reached around her and pushed a button.

* * * *

Lisa flopped down on his bed. "You sure about this? You could just go home, avoid moral conflicts and possible danger. Run for your life now."

He leaned against the door, hands in his pockets. "Tell me what you did."

"I killed them both. First Cortez then Rocha."

"Why did you have to kill them?"

"They burned a child to death. They meant to shoot the rest of the bunch. But I scared them away. Cortez was about to kill other children. I saved their lives. But I would have done it anyway." Lisa sat up, crossed her legs, and rested her elbows on her knees. She searched his stony face for a reaction—in vain.

"How can you take justice in your own hands? Why didn't you talk to the police?"

Lisa looked at him for a long time, wondering how she could make him understand. "Because the police won't do anything. I told them. They couldn't care less about rich men killing poor children."

He took his hands out of the pockets. "Maybe I'm too naive, but can't they be forced to act?" He paced the room.

Lisa attempted a smile. "Of course, by the rich." She paused. "The cop I told about the killers arrested me today."

"What?" Tony swung around and stared at her.

"He tried to make me confess to killing Rocha. He probably couldn't imagine that I took it up with Cortez and his bodyguard. Maybe he wanted to speed up the investigation. Maybe someone else put pressure on him. Someone important pulling the strings." Possibly a retired judge.

Tony squatted in front of her, his hands on her knees. "What did he do?"

"Not much, but he was dead set on getting a confession. Jango showed up just in time with a high-profile lawyer." She smiled at the vision of the two stern faces awaiting her and her captors.

"How did you become like this? So tough, so fearless."

Lisa ran her fingers through his hair. "I'm scared shitless. That's why I constantly have to prove that I'm brave, that nobody can hurt me." She gazed into his sad blue eyes. "That's why I wanted to sleep with you."

He stroked her thigh. "And I was such an idiot."

She shook her head. "No, you weren't."

"What happened to you? Back then, I mean."

"If I tell you the story of my messed up life, you'll go all cowboy on me and get tangled up in this mess. You've got to stay away from me. You understand?"

"Bullshit." Tony stood. "If you wanted me to leave you alone, you wouldn't have come here today."

"When they released me, I kept thinking that you'd never have known what happened if they'd actually found evidence. You'd have thought of me as a psychotic killer who suddenly disappeared."

"Then tell me everything."

Her chest tightened. She held his gaze and saw determination in his eyes. With a sigh, she nodded. "Okay, you asked for it." She struggled to her feet. He took a step back to give her more space.

"My mother took me to Rio for my tenth birthday. A grandfatherly man bought me a stuffed crocodile and lured me away from her. I escaped him and lived on the streets for half a year or so, begging and stealing. When I tried to steal Jango's wallet, I got arrested and thrown into the juvenile detention center. One of the guards there raped me. I wasn't the only one. The younger the better. And when we didn't do what he wanted, he'd beat us with his belt." She'd meant to keep her story as simple and clinical as possible, but rage took over. She pulled off her T-shirt. Tony stepped further away as if she'd lashed out at him. She spun around to show him the scars on her back.

He touched the healed skin, stroked her. She remembered his fingers tracing the scars their first night, but she knew how ugly they looked in daylight. Then she remembered he had his own scars to hide. "Once I bit him and he used the buckle end of his belt."

Tony gasped.

She continued before her courage failed her. "It was one long nightmare. I never knew when my turn would come again. If he pulled out one of the other girls, I was so relieved. Then I cried for her and imagined her suffering. For the rest of my life I felt guilty, because Jango found me and my father got me out, but I didn't do anything to help the others."

Tony's hands reached around her waist and pressed her against his chest.

Lisa slipped her fingers under the sleeve of his shirt and touched his scar as if it might ensure his understanding. She took a deep breath. "Several years ago I shot him. I felt exhilarated, knowing he was dead and couldn't hurt anyone else."

Tony's arms tightened around her. "You need to stop killing and start living." He rubbed his chin against her cheek.

His soft lips against her ear sent a pleasant shiver through her. "I can't. Not yet."

He released her, turned her around, and grabbed her shoulders. "You're crazy. They've arrested you once already."

"That's why I can't see you anymore."

He stared at her. "Is that really what you want?"

"No. I don't want to give you up. I want you to understand why..."

"Why what?"

"I have to finish this. And you need to stay far away from me."

"I can't. I want to be with you, get to know the real Lisa, build a future with you."

She blinked. "Future?" Gazing into his bright blue eyes, she felt tears welling up in hers. "With me? Despite everything I told you?"

He nodded. "Give us a chance, Lisa."

If she'd sink into his arms, maybe he'd chase away the nightmares, but she couldn't ignore reality. "You have no idea how much I long to do that. But you won't be able to live with me if I can't live with myself."

"I don't want to lose you, Lisa."

Chapter Forty-Five

Tony ordered two beers at the bar and took them up the stairs to the roof terrace of the small *bodega*. After a long day talking to suppliers in an office with chilling air conditioning, he enjoyed the sun on his skin. Jango had shed his jacket and tie, and sat staring at the wooden surface of the table.

"Trouble?" Tony asked.

He smiled. "Lisa."

Tony nodded and lowered himself onto the chair. He raised his glass, not knowing what to say. No matter what he'd done all day, he could never stop thinking about her confessions.

"She told you what she's done?"

Tony took a big gulp. "Yeah, yesterday. After you got her out of prison." So far they'd mostly avoided talking about Lisa.

"Yeah. She's..." Jango's voice cracked. "I just want you to know that you're the first guy she's shown any interest in. I don't know what's been going on between you two, but don't give up on her."

Surprised, Tony glanced at him. He'd expected a warning to leave her alone. "I screwed up. And since then she's kept me at arm's length." Except that she'd slept in his arms twice. He lowered his voice. "And now she's killing people. Sometimes I wonder if it's all my fault. Like I brought all the rage back."

Jango shook his head. "No, if it's anybody's fault, then it's mine. I taught her to shoot. I bought her the first pistol. When she came back to Rio, she didn't dare leave the hotel on her own. She saw him everywhere, called him Captain Hook." Jango took his glass and wiped off the condensation with his thumb before he drank.

Tony couldn't picture her as a timid girl, but then he remembered her whimpers in her sleep, her pleas not to be hurt. Nightmares still dragged her back to that place. Tony shivered despite the heat.

Jango continued, "She was twenty-one then, only planning to stay for a few weeks to find her mother. Naturally, she turned to me. I found out her mother had died in a mental hospital a few years before. Despite her disappointment and grief, I convinced Lisa to stay longer, get reacquainted with Rio, and maybe learn to live with her demons. When I showed her the pretty side of Rio, she remained fully alert, always scanning her surroundings. Then I took her to the shooting range. I thought it might make her feel safer."

"Did it work?"

"I'm convinced she decided to stay when she'd made up her mind to kill her abuser, Vitor Fraga."

"You couldn't get him arrested?"

Jango sighed and took another sip from his beer. "It was too long ago, and she refused to talk about it, said she'd already used up three shrinks on her past. When I first visited her in the detention center, she crouched in a corner, as far away from me as possible. She didn't talk, just stared ahead, but she was well aware of my presence. I talked to her for ten minutes or so, told her I would get her out. She showed no reaction. When I rose from my chair, she darted me a wary glance. Then she focused on that invisible spot on the wall again, watching me from the corner of her eye. I made a step toward her and she squeezed deeper between the walls. When I turned to the door, I heard her voice for the first time. She whispered, 'Get me out, Peter Pan.' I complained to the director about her mental and physical state. Nothing changed. Vitor Fraga kept the night shift. Of course back then I didn't know what he was doing to her."

Tony cleared his throat. If only he could clear his head of the images of raped and beaten girls the same way.

"You know she got arrested because of me?"

Tony nodded. "Lisa told me. How come you cared so much about a girl you'd never seen before?"

"She was the cutest thing. Filthy and smelly, but the way she stared at me with wide, incredulous eyes when I offered her my sandwich touched my heart. That was the last time I saw her smile until she returned to Rio ten years later. And even then it took her a few days." Jango paused, his eyes likely staring into the past. Then he focused on Tony again. "When I accompanied her father to pick her up at the detention center, she hardly looked at him, but kept staring at me. She whispered 'Peter Pan' again. I think her father never really reconnected with her afterward. He took her away from her mother and home, but at least he sent her to therapy."

Tony remembered Lisa's question as to what love was like. No wonder she never learned to love. "And that's why you became more of a father to her than her own."

Jango heaved a deep breath and nodded. "I guess Joseph Kerry didn't think much beyond keeping her safe and sane. If the man knew what she's doing now, he'd probably try to get her committed." He sighed. "Maybe that's not such a bad idea. I almost had a heart attack when they arrested her yesterday."

"You think she's doing the right thing?"

Jango shook his head. "I'd do anything to stop her. It's dangerous."

"You're avoiding the question."

Jango's eyes locked on his. "What she does is justified. If more people cared, fewer people would die."

Tony drained his glass then nodded. "How the hell can we stop her?"

Jango looked at him for a long time before he answered. "I think you're the only person who can."

Surprised, Tony stared at him. "Why me?"

"Lisa loves you."

Tony closed his eyes. He wished Jango were right. Then the massive responsibility hit him.

Chapter Forty-Six

Félix stood at the back of the crowd Rocha's death had drawn to the cemetery. His gaze swept over the solemn faces gathered to see Rocha off, or to be seen by the cameras. No one suspected his true killer stood among them. Though he hadn't pulled the trigger, he'd caused Rocha's and Cortez's deaths and didn't regret it one bit. Cowards and fools both of them. They'd deserved Lisa's wrath.

He smiled, thinking of his avenging angel. So compassionate when it came to protecting the weak—and a cold-blooded killer at the same time. He only wished he could have watched her in action.

If his uncle, the torture master, were still alive, Félix would feel tempted to point Lisa in his direction and tell her some stories about the monster of his childhood. A shiver ran down his spine as he remembered those dreadful summer holidays at his uncle's farm. Everyone had to kiss the man's feet and bow to his every whim, or face humiliation and worse. Once Félix talked back and got the beating of his life. A few years later he fought back, but his uncle was still too strong and too mean.

Félix's hand touched his throat, where his uncle's grip had squeezed his windpipe. "Never, ever, fight back," he'd whispered, his face an ugly grimace of rage. He said it over and over again until Félix nodded, on the verge of passing out. He'd never become like the old bastard, a man who liked to inflict pain without taking any risk himself. A coward protected by his money and vicious temper. Félix grew up among people groveling in front of his uncle. Even his mother did. When Félix turned sixteen, dear uncle had an accident, fell on a pitchfork. It hadn't been difficult to arrange. No one asked questions, but his mother smiled at him more often. She inherited her brother's farm and money, and he started to enjoy the summer breaks in the countryside.

Félix looked around. People drifted away. He'd missed most of the ceremony. So what? Rocha wasn't any better than his uncle. And neither was Alves. He craned his neck, trying to spot the man. A nudge at his arm.

Alves, dressed in a black suit and tie, had sneaked up on him. "We need to find the woman."

Félix raised his eyebrows. "What woman?"

"The one Cortez brought along for the hunt."

The man wasn't quite as stupid as his friends. Félix smiled. "You think she killed him?"

Alves snorted. "Of course not. But she played bait and lured him into a trap. How could a little slut like her take down Cortez and his bodyguard?"

He laughed. It was so easy to overrate Alves when he was just a worm drawing self-esteem from his power over others, without a fiber of fairness in him. "Want me to look for her?"

Alves smirked. "I'd be forever grateful."

"Grateful friends within the justice system, what more can a man ask for?"

Alves slapped him on the back. "You can always count on me when one of your adventures goes wrong."

"One condition. You'll leave her to me."

"Sure, when I'm done with her, she's all yours."

Oh Lisa, where are you? Have you picked up this trash-scavenging coati's scent yet?

Chapter Forty-Seven

Lisa drove past Alves's colonial mansion. Its white facade glowed in the morning light. Three-meter-high walls encircled the premises; razor wire coiled on top. A burgundy-colored Mercedes sat behind the gate. No Corolla.

Only the finest for the judge. Alto da Boa Vista, set in the Tijuca Forest, was one of the best neighborhoods in Rio, except it didn't have a beach. Of course, the judge wouldn't care. He represented old money and ancient power. Not his style to mingle with common people on public beaches.

Afraid to attract attention, Lisa moved on. Nothing she could do right now. Last night she'd watched the news coverage of Rocha's funeral, a big event for the city. Lots of politicians, artists, and famous people had attended. She'd scanned the faces on TV for the third man. Without luck.

Today Cortez would be buried. She decided to attend the service. The sleazebag surely wouldn't attract such a big crowd as the artist. But the Corolla driver might show.

The cemetery lay in the *centro*. Lisa still had enough time to get there, even in bad traffic. She arrived an hour early and strolled through the old part of the graveyard. Marble headstones, memorials with sculptures of angels, the Madonna, Jesus, and the saints held watch over the dead.

One day, her body would be rotting in the earth. Nobody would take the trouble to mount an angel over her grave, and that was fine by her. She didn't believe in resurrection of any flavor. How she lived now was all that mattered. Tony's words echoed in her mind: *"You need to stop killing and start living."* But she hadn't lived before she killed Vitor Fraga. She'd been trapped in a bubble of fear and nightmares. It burst when the car swerved and broke through the guard rail, hauling her abuser down the ridge.

Tony would never understand. He lived in a different world. A bright world of fun, not a war zone. Maybe one day she could join him. But would she ever feel satisfied with such a life while there were still killers, rapists, and sadists out there?

A woman in black clothes passed by, carrying a bunch of flowers. A relative or friend of Cortez? Lisa shivered. She had killed men who abused, tortured and murdered for fun, but she had also caused grief for people who loved these men.

Lisa jumped when her cellphone vibrated in her pocket. Jango. A friendly voice was just what she needed. "Hey, Jango."

"I've dug up some information about Alves. The judge has a daughter who lives in the States, but there's a nephew living in São Conrado. A lawyer. Maybe the judge has been something like a mentor to him?"

"And there's no one else in the picture?"

"Doesn't look like it. The judge's brother died of a heart attack last year."

"Can you send me the address as a text message?"

Lisa decided not to wait for the funeral service after all. She'd rather check out the place where Alves junior lived.

More mourners arrived while she made her way out of the cemetery. She crossed the busy four-lane street. A black Corolla sped toward her. Lisa froze, heart hammering. The world blurred. Brakes screeched. She sprinted to the sidewalk and swung around. The number plate matched. The driver stared at her as he slowly passed, ignoring the honking cars behind him.

Merda! Did he recognize her? Lisa sprinted down a side street, turned right at the first intersection, and zigzagged her way toward the parking garage, looking over her shoulder at every bend. What now?

She reached the safety of her car, locked all doors, and leaned back. Her body shook. *Breathe, think*!

He didn't know who she was, even if he recognized her. How stupid to come to the cemetery and expose herself.

She calmed down, relaxing her tense muscles. Then she checked her cellphone. Jango had sent the address. The urge to complete her mission rose inside her. *Let Tinker Bell take over*. Lisa looked in the rear view mirror. *Captain Hook must die*.

Driving to São Conrado, she hardly noticed her surroundings until she reached the rich neighborhood and started searching for his street and number. Alves junior rented an apartment in one of the high-rise condominiums, five hundred meters from the beach and a kilometer from *favela* Rocinha. Maybe he usually found his prey there. No, a man like him wouldn't dare enter a *favela*. He'd prowl the borders.

A security guard sat in the shade between the gate and the entrance to the building. How could anyone stand the boredom of such a job? A camera mounted over the door filmed her while she walked past the building, but Alves wouldn't come home and ask to see the tape, would he? No use getting paranoid.

Damn, she wasn't paranoid enough. She pulled out her cellphone and deleted Jango's message. Better not to leave any trails leading to him.

She reached the back of the building. Two men guarded the driveway to the parking garage below the apartments. She couldn't make out a camera, but there had to be one. Anyone attempting to carry out a robbery in the building would enter this way.

Lisa returned to her car parked in the street behind the building, where she had a good view of all vehicles driving in or out. If the Corolla pulled in, she'd know who the third killer was. The nephew of a judge.

Chapter Forty-Eight

For two hours, Lisa sat in the car, waiting for Alves to return home, sweating while the sun heated up her bubble of air. She cursed herself for not bringing water. Maybe she should buy some at the nearby beach, but Alves might return home the moment she left. What if he returned late at night? What if Alves junior didn't drive the Corolla himself, but lent it to a friend? He might be home already, watching his favorite soap. Without water, she might turn into a mummy before he showed his face.

Lisa started the engine and switched on the air conditioning at full blast before she pulled away from the curb. Hot air blew from the vents. At the next intersection she turned toward the waterfront. A black Corolla headed toward her. Damn. She slid down in the seat and accelerated.

She stopped at the promenade, bought two bottles of water from a street vendor and drove back to Alves's place. This time she parked on the other side of the road, further away and in the shade. She lowered the front windows and drank. The cold liquid refreshed her body and spirit. She'd wait a couple more hours, now that she'd picked up his scent. What else could she do? She had to catch him. Kill him.

Slowly, the sun slipped toward the mountain range. Her eyelids grew heavy. With nothing to do she would soon fall asleep. Maybe she could turn on the radio? But that would attract the attention of people walking past her. She closed her eyes. Just for a moment. No way! She'd sleep for hours. Lisa sat up straight, recalled images of Gordinho burning and the shocked faces of his friends. Her heart raced. She kept her rage burning.

Half an hour later, the Corolla pulled out of the garage. She let him pass and waited a moment before she followed. He stayed below the speed limit although there wasn't much traffic. She kept her distance. Was he on the hunt, or simply being careful not to attract the attention of the police?

He headed up into the mountains toward Alto da Boa Vista. To visit his uncle? Concerned that he might notice her car and maybe even memorize her license plate number, she decided to play it safe. She turned into a side street, let other cars pass, and backed out. If he drove to the judge, she would find him there. If not, she could track him again tomorrow, learn his routine and vulnerabilities.

When Lisa drove by the Alves mansion, she spotted the Corolla parked in the driveway. No sign of the burgundy-colored Mercedes. What did junior want here if his uncle wasn't home? Or did he swap cars to shake her off?

She circled the block and parked at the curb between other cars, yet close enough to keep the gate in view. With the AC off, the car heated up again. She lowered both front windows and leaned back. Not sure what she was waiting for, she still couldn't give up. She needed to get closer to him, sniff him out. She scanned her surroundings. All the stately houses were set back from the street. Her presence shouldn't draw attention.

Footsteps sounded behind. She checked the outside mirror. A man in a suit with a white poodle on a leash. She relaxed. Just a neighbor walking the dog. He passed her car, stepped into the gap between her and the next vehicle, and looked both ways as if about to cross to the other side. His gaze brushed over her. Smiling, he stepped closer. Neighborhood watch? What could she tell him? Damn.

He bent down to her window. "Don't move."

Lisa looked into the muzzle of a gun. Shit! "Hey, no problem. You can have my money." A mugger with a poodle? He'd fooled her completely.

She reached for her bag on the front passenger seat. The guy pressed the gun against her temple. "I said don't move."

"Okay." Definitely no robbery.

"Hands on the steering wheel."

She obeyed, trying to figure out what he wanted. From the corner of her eye, she studied his face. Didn't look familiar.

He stepped back and opened the door. "Get out."

Not good at all. "What do you want?"

"You. Move your ass."

She eased out of the car, thinking of the pistol in her bag. If only she had the Firestar on her. But it was just one guy. If he intended to kill her, he'd have shot her in the car.

"Turn around, hands on the roof." He patted her down with one hand, the other pressing the gun against her neck. Okay, she wouldn't have kept the Firestar for long either. Very professional. He could be a security guard working for the judge. Maybe his duties included walking the dog. "Listen, I was just taking a break, because I couldn't keep my eyes open anymore. I might have heatstroke."

The sound of a car engine approached. Had he called the police, mistaking her for a burglar on reconnaissance? The motor died. A door opened. She turned her head and saw a man in plain clothes stepping from a station wagon. To help her?

"Get in the car." The first man nodded toward the station wagon.

If she did, she was doomed. *Merda!* But what choice did she have? Scream for help and get shot? The gun prodded her back. She let the guy shove her across the street. The second man opened the rear door for her. She eased into the backseat. Who were these men?

"Scoot over." The poodle walker climbed in beside her. Where was the dog? The other guy slipped behind the wheel and threw her handbag on the passenger seat. He started the engine and pulled away from the curb. The poodle sat panting beside Lisa's car, one front leg in the air. She blinked. What did she care about an abandoned dog? If it weren't for the damned poodle, she'd have been more careful.

The man beside her kept the gun aimed at her, while he pulled out a cellphone. "We've got her."

Lisa's heart raced. Her palms felt sweaty, her mouth parched. She wouldn't survive the night. They'd picked her up in front of Alves's mansion, didn't want her money…and now this phone call. He must have talked to Alves junior. Lisa looked over her shoulder. Time to stop acting like a victim. The two-lane road was busy with traffic. Close behind them drove a red car. She could only hope the guy would pay attention. The driver hit the brake as the cars ahead slowed down. Now or never.

Lisa wrenched open the door and jumped. She hit the street hard and rolled onto the shoulder. Tires squealed, leaving black rubber tracks on the asphalt. A car stopped right next to Lisa. Her face was level with the front tire. She scrambled to her feet, dizzy and bruised. The smell of burnt rubber stung her nose. She looked around for the station wagon. It had moved on. Obviously they didn't want to draw any more attention than her jump already had.

Relief spread through her while cars honked as if they cheered her escape. Grinning, she opened the passenger door and bent down to the driver, who stared at her. "Hello, sorry to scare you. Would you mind giving me a lift?"

The young man in a fawn-colored linen suit and dark blue tie nodded at her, his gray-green eyes wide open. He looked like a playboy far out of his depth. Only a faint scar on his cheek gave him an adventurous flair. Still grinning, she folded herself into the sports car.

He found his voice. "Are you okay?"

"Just a bruise here and there." She laughed with the exhilaration of her escape.

"You're bleeding."

Lisa looked down. Blood seeped through the torn sleeve of her blouse. "It's nothing."

"Nothing?" He snorted. A smile played around the corners of his mouth.

"All things considered," she added. With his fine clothes and expensive aftershave he didn't look the kind of man used to women bleeding in his car.

"Where do you want me to take you?"

"Just somewhere I can get a taxi." Lisa still grinned. She'd beaten them. She was still alive and kicking. Bastards. Next time they wouldn't catch her so easily. Her cheeks burned with the strain of grinning but she couldn't stop. She pressed her thumb and fingers into the tense muscles.

The growl of the engine soothed her. "This is a great car," she said to put her rescuer at ease.

He smiled and darted her a quick glance. "Thanks."

After five minutes, the playboy turned into a narrow street and stopped at an electric goods shop. "I need to pick up my new stereo. I'll ask them to call you a cab. Want to come inside?"

"Sure." She climbed out. The more innocent people around her the safer. With the adrenaline draining from her system, she felt the pain that stretched from shoulder to knee. She knew it'd get worse over the next days, a reminder to always stay alert.

The driver opened the door for her. She stepped into the gloom of the store and saw a bulky man.

"*Olá*, Félix." The fellow's face cracked into a grin as he pointed a gun at her. "I see you've brought us something."

Lisa stopped dead. She'd walked right back into the same trap. The playboy stood close behind her and placed his hand on her shoulder, the fingers kneading her tense muscles. "No reason to be shy now." His hand slipped to her throat and felt her racing pulse. He leaned close to her ear. "There's always a chance."

Her vision blurred. She trembled. He shoved her toward the back of the store. Lisa couldn't feel her legs. Heaving a deep breath, she fought her panic attack. Worst time to crumble. She needed to unleash her rage.

Chapter Forty-Nine

Lisa's vision cleared. She stopped swaying. Her heart pounded in a steady rhythm, like drum beats cheering her on. Alves junior, in a sharply pressed suit, sat in an armchair and smiled. "Hello, again."

The suave bastard seemed genuinely pleased to see her. Quite contrary to their first encounter. *"Merda,"* Lisa hissed. Her eyes darted around searching for a back entrance, an open window, a way to escape. All she found was a closed wooden door, possibly leading to an office. Somewhere behind her, the fat man and her false rescuer blocked the entrance. Her throat tightened. Not over yet. Her fingernails dug into her palms. She unclenched her fists. Her forearms burned.

"I hear you're in the killing business." Alves rose from the armchair and sauntered up to her. "Just like us. But, unfortunately, on the other side of the fence."

"That's right." Her thoughts stumbled over each other. Why hadn't he simply eliminated her?

He laughed and Lisa took that as a good sign. She'd cling to anything right now. Maybe she could bullshit her way out.

"You killed Cortez?" he asked.

Did he really doubt it? No, he played with her. Lisa decided to stay with the truth as much as she could afford to, without showing weakness. Come on, Tinker Bell. "Yes. He wanted me to suck his dick while he killed some children. Seemed a bit sick to me."

Alves chortled. "And Rocha?"

He'd made the connection. Why did he ask then? Simply to make sure he didn't kill an innocent? As if he'd care. "I thought why not exterminate some more vermin while I'm at it."

Squinting, Alves tilted his head and studied her. His calm riled her. Lisa arched her left eyebrow and pushed back her shoulders. "And I guess the world would be an even better place without you in it." She'd conquered her fear and managed a smile. He'd kill her, but at least she'd told Tony everything. He'd know who she was and why she had to die.

Alves did not smile any longer. "Quite entertaining. Funny that I took you for a dumb little slut when Cortez brought you along." He circled her. "Who are you? Tell me who helped you and I might even let you go."

Lisa chuckled. "Sure you will."

"How did you find out about Rocha, Cortez, myself, and whoever else you might be after?"

"I followed the smell of burning human flesh." She took a deep breath. If only she could take him out before she died.

Alves stepped closer. His black eyes locked on hers. "I want to know who helped you."

Lisa blinked a few times under his stare. The smile faded from her face. He wouldn't just kill her. Her mind raced. Of course, he wouldn't let her live. If she told them even as little as her name, they might connect her to the kids and go after them just for the fun of it. Rocha and Cortez had likely told him about their adventure burning Gordinho. Maybe they'd also go after Rejane, just in case. They might connect her with Jango, and Jango with Tony.

No, telling them anything wouldn't help her, but would drag other people into this mess. She had nothing to gain, nothing to offer, nothing to bargain with. Fear gripped her. A shiver zigzagged down her back. Her only hope was to speed up her own death. "I'm Sandra Oliveira. Nobody helped me."

"Not good enough," Alves said and nodded at the playboy, who walked past her and opened the door she'd noticed earlier.

Lisa didn't move. Alves pulled a huge Raging Bull revolver from his shoulder holster. She'd shot one once and the recoil had almost knocked her off her feet. He trained the gun at her. "Follow the nice gentleman."

Lisa snorted but walked toward the door. Stairs led to the basement. A damp, moldy smell crept into her nose. She descended. Maybe the basement had another exit for deliveries. Alves pressed the gun between her shoulder blades.

"Nice penis enlargement," Lisa riled him, willing him to pull the trigger. Half way down, she stooped and scanned the basement. A single light bulb illuminated the windowless room. Next to it hung a strong chain.

Her stomach cramped. A pair of shackles dangled from the chain, which ran through a hook on the ceiling to a fixture on the wall, the length adjustable. No! Despair paralyzed her. A foot on her back. She yelped. Arms flailing, she fell and hit the ground hard.

Dark spots filled her vision. Footsteps faded. Then nothing.

* * * *

Cursing, Félix pushed Alves out of the way and dropped to his knees beside Lisa's slumped body. Wary, he touched her shoulder. No trick. He turned her over. Her slack jaw hung open, her eyes stared unseeing. Blood trickled from her forehead onto her pale face. "She's unconscious. Why the hell did you kick her?"

"The bitch deserved it."

"Just great," he growled. Nothing to do but wait and prepare. He unbuttoned her torn cotton blouse and pressed his hand over her heart. A slow regular beat. Sleeping Beauty would wake. He pressed his lips on hers. Seconds passed. Nothing.

Gently he pulled one arm then the other out of the long sleeves of her blouse. Finally, she was his. When she climbed into his car, he'd been tempted to drive off with her, keep her to himself, but he didn't mind a little foreplay.

Alves wanted answers, but Félix would play the end game his way. He glanced over his shoulder. Alves watched him with his cold eyes. Did he still think him a wimp? The man had begged him to find her, not knowing that he'd found her a long time ago.

Félix turned his attention back to Lisa, unbuttoned her jeans, and tore them off. He pulled out his pocket knife, cut her white thong at the hips then the straps of her bra, and gently slid the blade under the thin fabric between her breasts until it ripped. He ran his hands over her soft flesh, pushing away the remains of cloth. So beautiful, her skin so soft. He traced one nipple. It hardened.

He sat back on his haunches savoring the moment of anticipation. Even in her relaxed state, her muscles were well defined. A fighter.

Lisa's eyelids twitched. Félix picked her up in his arms. "Lower the chain."

Alves strode over to the hook in the wall and let down the shackles.

Félix hated to let him touch her, but saw no alternative. Alves grabbed her arm and snapped the metal around one wrist, then the other. He walked back to the hook and yanked the chain. Félix set her feet on the ground and watched her limp body stretch toward the ceiling. He felt dizzy letting go of her. She groaned. Félix stepped back.

For the first time, she would look in his eyes and know him.

Chapter Fifty

Lisa's wrists burned, and her head ached. She couldn't move her arms. Something wrong. She opened her eyes and blinked. A blurred face before a concrete wall. Where...? So cold. A draft brushed over her skin. Was she naked? Images flared up in her mind. Chain and shackles. A basement. Metal ground into her wrists. Her body tensed. Only her toes touched the cold floor.

The playboy leaned against the wall watching her. "She's coming around." He smiled as his gaze wandered over her body. He pushed away from the wall and circled her. Helpless, exposed, she screamed, worked up her rage to chase away the despair creeping up on her.

She stretched to get a grip on the chain and release the pressure on her aching wrists, but couldn't reach. She shivered. Her clothes lay scattered on the floor.

Her worst nightmare come true. They'd torture her before they killed her.

Alves's laconic voice bounced from the concrete walls. "Are you going to tell me the truth now, Sandra?"

A whistle behind her. Warm breath rippled over her skin. "Someone got her first." The playboy sounded disappointed. Two fingers gently traced the old scars on her back.

"You keep surprising me," Alves said. "Who did this to you?"

"None of your business. At least you can't ruin my good looks."

"We can try."

"Is this the only way you can get a hard-on?" Lisa's voice cracked with the futile attempt to fight her rising fear.

Hollow footsteps approached. Alves stood close to her face. She refused to meet his eyes, but smelled his musky aftershave. His black mustache looked like a large centipede. She watched it wriggle as he spoke.

"Right now this is merely a question of self-preservation." He gripped her chin and lifted her face. His black eyes bore into hers. "Tell me who else knows about us."

"Nobody."

"Let's find out then." He walked around her and took several echoing steps. A streak of fire scorched her back, took her breath. Lisa screamed, a little girl again, the helpless plaything of Vitor Fraga. She smelled his sour odor, heard his grunts and groans.

The next lash hurt as if it ripped off skin. She cried out, waited for the pain to fade so she could tell him she'd do anything he wanted.

Then Lisa remembered where she was, who she had become. She would not be broken again. The third strike only forced a gasp from her mouth. She saw flames. Flames eating Vitor Fraga's face. The image blurred.

The playboy leaned against the wall right in front of her. His fists clenched, he stared at her unblinking. Lisa focused on his gray-green eyes. Another lash.

She found her voice. "The last man who did this to me died a horrible death."

The playboy's left eye twitched. A smile crept onto his face. He nodded slightly as if to encourage her.

Alves's laughter echoed. "Actually, I believe you, but this time will be different."

"You will burn, you piece of shit," Lisa promised.

Another crack. Unprepared, she screamed. Closing her eyes, she concentrated and focused her mind on a layer of ice covering her body. Nothing happened. She flinched. Hands touched her hot, swelling skin, gently stroking. Her eyes flung open. The playboy no longer stood in front of her. A groan from behind. Fingers tucked a strand of hair behind her ear. "You're lovely," the playboy whispered. Lisa shuddered. His breath on her skin was worse than the pain inflicted by the whip.

Alves entered her vision. "Tell me who you are and who's helping you. In return, I'll let you die quickly."

Death, the ultimate escape, lured her. She blinked, lifted her chin. Jango. Luiz. Rejane. She had to protect them. "My name is Sandra. No one knows about you. I killed Rocha, Cortez, and his bodyguard without any help."

Alves stepped closer. The playboy circled them both, his face covered with red spots.

Alves pulled off his tie and slung it around her neck. "Sandra who?"

"Sandra da Silva." Her voice trembled. Damn, she'd used Oliveira earlier. She gazed past Alves, refused to show him her fear.

The playboy stepped into her line of vision and stared at her intently.

The strong silk tightened around her neck, pinched her skin. The playboy shook his head. Did she see pity in his eyes? Help me, Lisa thought. Her windpipe compressed. Panic seized her. She gasped for air in vain. Her lungs felt like bursting, her head throbbed.

The gray-green eyes before her blurred. "Enough!" the playboy shouted.

The cloth loosened, she sucked in molten lead. Tears burst from her eyes. She didn't want to breathe again. Not worth it. But her body forced her to inhale and punished her with more pain.

"Same question, Lisa."

She could hardly make sense of the words she heard.

"Lisa Kerry, born in Ouro Preto. Who helped you?"

What? How did he know? Slowly her vision cleared. Alves held her ID card in his hand. Behind him the playboy rummaged through her bag, found the pistol, grinned at her, and put it back. Why? Maybe she was hallucinating. Lack of oxygen.

"Who helped you?" Alves repeated.

She had to press the word through her squeezed throat. "Nobody."

He grabbed the ends of the tie again.

A raspy scream slipped from her mouth. "Nooo!"

"How did you learn about Rocha and Cortez?"

"Cortez told me. Was so full of himself, so proud. I did you a favor killing him."

"Not good enough." The cloth tightened around her sore neck. Not again. Despair shook her. Maybe he'd let her die now. Need to breathe. Her mouth opened, her lungs tried to suck in air, couldn't.

"Stop this shit," the playboy barked. "You're going to kill her." No, no, don't stop now. Finish it. The dizziness returned just before she gasped and the fire surged down her throat and chest.

The black spots cleared slowly. Alves stood with his back to her, slinging the tie around his shirt collar. Could it really be over? Tears rolled down her face.

Alves straightened the tie then nodded at the playboy. "She's all yours."

Chapter Fifty-One

The playboy dropped Lisa's bag. His eyes met hers. His warm encouraging smile soothed her, while Alves's steps echoed up the stairs. She broke out in gooseflesh all over her naked body. He'd saved her from more pain and a slow death. Why?

"I apologize for my friend's behavior." He stepped close, stroked her cheek with the tips of his fingers, let them run down her neck and stop above her left breast. "I can feel your heartbeat."

"Will you let me go?"

His gaze traveled up the chain. "What a shame to do this to a woman like you. You're tougher than any of them. Let's get the chains off."

Her heart pounded a frantic beat. The man removed his hand from her chest and stepped around her.

She listened to his footsteps, the metal scraping. Would he really...? The chain slackened. Despite the pain, she yanked down her arms with force. The chain slipped all the way through the hook in the ceiling and crashed to the floor next to her. She swayed.

The playboy laughed. "Looks like you feel pretty passionate about chains."

She turned, holding out her shackled hands to him. "Wouldn't you?" Wary, she wanted to humor him, her ticket out of this torture chamber.

Still smiling, he fished a key from his jacket pocket. "I'm Félix. Now, don't do anything rash. Armed guys are keeping watch upstairs." He unlocked the shackles and removed them. "That looks nasty."

Lisa's gaze dropped to her chafed wrists, the broken skin. "It's nothing."

He laughed. "That's what you said about your bleeding arm when you climbed in my car."

She stared at him struggling to comprehend what kind of role he played in all this. "Who are you?"

"I told you, I'm Félix. The lucky one. I'm not one of them, Lisa. I don't burn or shoot children."

An involuntary smile tugged at the corners of her mouth.

He stepped back and let his gaze travel over her. "What kind of fun would that be?" He tilted his head, studying her.

Fun? She snorted with disgust as realization dawned. What a fool she'd been to believe even for one second that he might let her go. Her fighting spirit seeped back into her. Goosebumps returned to her bare skin.

"Kneel," he commanded. His mouth twitched.

Surprised, she stared at him then shook her head. She didn't think he wanted her to obey. He'd freed her for a reason. "No."

He pulled a gun from a shoulder holster hidden under his suit jacket. "How about now?" His face betrayed no emotions.

Lisa closed her eyes for a second. If he shot her, he'd put her out of her misery. She stepped toward him. The barrel touched her skin just above her bellybutton. "Shoot."

A smile played around the corners of his mouth. He ran the gun up her chest and stopped under her chin. His left hand curled around her neck. She trembled. Too close, too intimate. The pistol clattered to the floor. His lips pressed on hers, his tongue slipped between them. Her jaws clenched. He withdrew and shoved her.

She stumbled back, her mind struggling to understand what he wanted, how she could play him. The gun lay at his feet. He backed off until they stood about the same distance from the pistol. "I believe in fair chances, Lisa."

She lunged for the gun, her route to freedom, and grasped it. His foot kicked her in the face. She fell back, raised the gun, and squeezed the trigger.

Hollow clicks echoed from the concrete walls. Félix towered over her, his mouth open, head tilted. His eyes sparkled. "You'd have shot me." He held out his left hand to her.

Certain he was right-handed, she smelled another trap. Still, her only chance to get on her feet. She grabbed his hand and yanked herself up. Félix hit her across the face before she gained her balance. She crashed into the wall and slid down, scraping her back. The surge of pain fueled her. She pulled away and took a fighting stance.

Félix stood between her and the leather bag holding her own gun. Now she knew why he'd left it there.

With this eager, almost benevolent look on his face, he took off his jacket and dropped the holster.

Lisa touched her cheek where the tip of his shoe had hit her and felt sticky moisture. More blood. "Serves me right for trusting an asshole like you." She made a step toward him, the unloaded gun her only weapon. For now. He unbuckled his belt and pulled it from the loops.

Lisa recoiled. Not the belt. She shook her head. "No."

Holding the buckle in his left, he let the leather slide through the fingers of his right hand and caught the end. He dropped the metal piece and let it swing, watching her reaction. "I've seen scars like yours. Wasn't a knife or a whip." He lashed out. The buckle swung toward her. Lisa reached out, caught the belt. The buckle hit the bones in the back of her hand. She winced at the sharp pain, but yanked and pulled him off balance. Félix stumbled toward her. She slammed the gun against his temple and brought up her knee in his groin.

He folded. She sprinted to her bag and dropped the empty gun. Félix still lay curled up on the ground, groaning. Lisa pulled out her pistol, checked that he hadn't tampered with the magazine, and flipped the safety catch.

What now? She had no clue how many guys waited upstairs. She had to kill Félix silently so as not to alert them. She scanned the room, ran to the workbench, and spotted a hammer. She snatched it and darted over to Félix. Kneeling, she rolled him on his back.

The look on his face stunned her: pure excitement. He panted, his gray-green eyes staring at her. While she aimed the gun at him, she lifted the hammer. He gasped, closed his eyes, and tilted his head, offering her his temple, the weakest point of his skull. She swallowed and braced herself. Her arm trembled. She couldn't bash his head in. His lips curled into a smile. Confused, Lisa lowered the hammer. She noticed his bulging groin. Even after she kneed him?

He opened his eyes. "You don't want to let it end like this? I know. Too unsatisfying."

What a weirdo. She had to kill him. Her grip around the wooden handle tightened. "How many are upstairs?" He'd saved her from Alves. Okay, only because he wanted to fight and likely rape her, but without his interference...

"Only Gaspar, the short, fat guy. You won't have a problem with him. Not you."

Again his freaky awed look. Lisa put the gun back on safety, dropped the hammer, and hit him across the face to wipe off that creepy smile. She rose, pulled on her jeans, and slipped into her torn and bloody shirt. She slung Félix's holster around her shoulders. Her gun fit.

She peered at Félix. He watched her intently, but didn't move. Sprawled out on his back, he seemed to enjoy himself. She should kill him, but instead she picked up the shackles and marched over to him, gun pointed at his face. "Put them on."

He sat up and fastened the cuffs around his wrists. Unfortunately, when she'd pulled the chain all the way through the hook in the ceiling, she'd destroyed the only means to fix the chain somewhere.

Lisa shrugged into his jacket to cover the holster and checked to see if he'd put the key to the shackles back. She found it in the right pocket.

Grabbing her bag, she glanced at him a last time. She should strangle him. "Don't move."

His snicker followed her up the stairs. *Go back and kill him. No, because of him I still stand a chance. So what? He's dangerous. But he doesn't go after children.* She looked over her shoulder. Félix sat cross-legged on the floor and tipped his forehead with both hands. Last chance. No. She couldn't bring herself to bash his head in, and she couldn't shoot him without bringing down the cavalry.

She reached the top of the stairs and slung the shoulder strap of her bag across her chest. Gripping the door handle, she closed her eyes and hoped it wouldn't squeak while she pressed down. No noise. Only her heartbeat disturbed the silence. She inched the door open and peeked through the narrow gap.

No sound of anyone moving around. She pushed the door further open. A creak jolted her. She stopped to listen. A grunt, shuffling of feet. Sounded like one guy. Maybe Félix spoke the truth. Lisa flung the door open and swung around aiming the gun in the direction of the showroom. The shopkeeper stood frozen. Lisa gestured for him to lift his hands. With surprising speed, he dove for cover behind the counter. Lisa fired. Three shots. At least two hit their mark. She could only see his legs. Lisa sneaked toward him. "You had your chance." No reaction. She reached the counter.

The man's eyes stared at the ceiling. Lisa squatted and felt his pulse. Still alive.

"Drop the gun."

Lisa's heart thumped against her ribs. She looked over her shoulder. The man walking the poodle at Alves's mansion trained a revolver on her. She hesitated, her gun hand trembling. He'd be faster, but she'd rather die than face more torture, or worse. A shot exploded. She flinched. Echoes bounced off the walls. No pain. Still crouching over the fat man, she tried to comprehend.

Metal crashed to the floor. Footsteps approached, accompanied by a clinking rattle. Lisa rose. The poodle walker lay on the floor, blood seeping from his chest wound. She turned toward the door to the basement, her gun hand dangling limp beside her.

Lisa gazed into the playboy's eyes then at his shackled hands pointing the gun at her. How could she've forgotten his gun? Of course he must have hidden a full mag somewhere.

"I guess I should have warned you about Plínio, but I didn't expect you to have any troubles with him. I'm a bit disappointed, Lisa. You made me kill my friend to keep you alive." His gun aimed at her chest, he came closer. "The key, Lisa. Put your gun on the counter and bring me the key."

Tempted to end it right here, her fingers grasped her gun firmly. Try to shoot him, or herself? No, not while she still had a chance. She placed the weapon on the wooden surface and slowly walked up to him, trying to read his expressionless face.

"Close enough." He pressed the muzzle of his pistol against her chest. With trembling fingers she fumbled for the key in the jacket and unlocked the cuffs. She lowered her hands, watching his sneering face for a warning sign.

The barrel brushed over her left breast, moved up to her throat, her cheek, traveled over her lips. The smell of metal and oil mixed with his spicy aftershave.

"I'll forgive you this time." He slipped his fingers inside his jacket, brushing against her left breast, and retrieved his wallet. "Go."

Did he mean it? Only one way to find out. Lisa spun around and sprinted to the door.

"Stop."

She froze.

"You forgot something."

She glanced over her shoulder.

"Take your gun."

Lisa reached for the pistol and ran.

Chapter Fifty-Two

Félix wiped his prints off the unregistered gun, squatted and curled Gaspar's fingers around the butt and trigger. The police would assume the two guys shot each other. Damn, he should have kept Lisa's gun to shove it into Plínio's hand.

Oh well, Alves could discourage any overly curious cops. Félix would have to tweak reality a little though when he told him what happened.

He rose and walked toward the door. Two old men stood peering through the shop window. He stepped outside. "Call the police and an ambulance. Somebody's been shot." Ignoring their questions, he strode toward his car. Exhausted but exhilarated, he eased into the MX-5.

Lisa was still alive out there, running from him, thinking about him. He smiled. He'd miss her after he killed her. His smile faltered. If she'd kissed him back, he might even let her live. He snorted. But the bitch hadn't.

* * * *

Lisa ran down the narrow side streets, turning left, right, and left again, looking over her shoulder at every corner. Why had he spared her? And let her go? She shivered with the memory of his gun in her face, caressing her. This guy would be back on her door step. She should have killed him when she had the chance. But if she'd done that, she'd be dead now.

Where to? Home? He'd seen her ID and knew where she lived. Panting, she stopped and leaned against the iron railing around a one-story residential house. She pulled out her cellphone. Past eight already? She pushed the quick dial for Luiz.

"Hey, Lisa. I was—"

"Get the kids out. Hide somewhere else. Tell Rejane to close the shop and not come back until I tell her."

She disconnected. Her knees trembled as she walked on. The sinking sun turned orange clouds a darker crimson. Keep going, she told herself. She had no clue where she was, wading through dense fog in her head. Her legs gave out under her. She sank down in the door frame of a closed shop and leaned her head against it.

* * * *

A hand shook her shoulder. Lisa struggled to open her eyes. Another tug. Blinking, she glimpsed a wrinkled black face. The man's lips moved. Lisa didn't understand what he said. Why didn't he just go away? Her lids drooped. Another shake and she jerked awake with a jolt. Where was she?

"Tudo bem?" he asked.

Lisa nodded. Everything was just fine. She struggled to her feet while he took her elbow and helped her up. Pain lashed across her back.

"There's blood on your jacket," he said. "You need help?"

"I'm fine." She swayed.

He pulled her gently. "Come on, it's just a short walk." Lisa stumbled along and followed him into a dark hallway.

"Sofia," he yelled.

An elderly woman appeared and ushered her into a large kitchen-living room combination. Lisa sank onto a simple wooden chair. The woman saw her wrists, put her hands over her mouth, and mumbled a prayer. Lisa rested her arms on the table. Red and swollen, her wrists looked worse than they felt. She could move them as long as she ignored the pain. The old lady wanted to send for a doctor, but Lisa convinced her she just needed something to drink and sleep.

"Take off the bloody jacket," Sofia said, while her husband shuffled from the room.

Lisa shed the fine cloth and caught a whiff of musky aftershave. Félix's scent. Very male, very macho. Images of the torture basement flared up in her head.

Sofia's eyes widened at the sight of her gun. Lisa slipped out of the holster and slung it over the backrest of the chair, feeling like she had infected their house with a lethal disease. "I'm sorry. I shouldn't have come here."

"No, you stay." Sofia brought her a glass of water.

Lisa drained it.

The woman smiled. "Take off the blouse and let me take a look."

The chafes on Lisa's back burned as she ripped off the caked blood together with the fabric.

"Who did this to you?" Sofia asked. Gently she washed the wounds and accepted Lisa's silence. "Now you need to eat."

"I can't. I have to go."

"First you eat." She put a bowl of black-bean stew in front of her.

Lisa's stomach balked at the smell. "I can't eat."

"You have to. You need your strength to heal."

Lisa smiled at her. The woman might spoon-feed her if she resisted any longer.

* * * *

Luiz watched Tatu pace the backyard. "I'm not going anywhere. What about you?" Rena shook her head. Ubaldo focused on his feet. Nobody wanted to leave.

"She sounded serious." Luiz warned. "She wants to close the bookstore, too."

Rejane stood in the frame of the back door. "I won't close the shop. If she needs to hide, I can still keep the business going."

"Maybe you better do what she said. It's just a job. Why risk your life for it?" Luiz asked.

"Will you give up the shelter?" Rejane asked.

His gaze swept over the expectant faces of his friends. "No, we'll stay."

Rejane nodded. "Me too." She went back inside.

Luiz turned to Tatu. "Should we talk to Max?"

"We don't even know what's going on yet."

"We could get more guns."

"You want to teach the kids how to shoot?" Tatu asked, pointing his thumb at Rena and Ubaldo, only a year younger than him.

"No, you're right. But we need to put a guard on the roof."

Tatu looked up. "Let's get some chairs."

They went inside, grabbed two chairs and a plastic box which they put on the second one. Perfect steps for quick access. Luiz climbed up and walked to the edge from where he could see the gate and, behind it, the street. Then he lowered himself onto his stomach and simulated Lisa's pose when she shot Rocha.

"Put a sniper up here and we can hold the fort for weeks."

Tatu laughed. "Now we just need a sniper. Maybe Max has a spare one."

The angle wasn't right though. If someone stood at the gate, Luiz would have to sit up to shoot him or move all the way to the edge and become a target himself. "Hey, Tatu, get Gordinho's mattress. We'll put a guard up here. And maybe we can get a rifle, too." Lisa's. He wanted to be like her, tough and taking no bullshit from anyone. He pulled the imaginary trigger as a woman with her dog walked past the gate. Damn, he'd better be more careful.

Chapter Fifty-Three

Lisa awoke in the dark. Groaning, she sat up. All the muscles in her back tightened. Stiff and aching, she rose from the sofa. She had to leave, shouldn't have allowed herself to fall asleep.

Hardly able to bend her swollen wrists, she took three hundred *reais* from a small pocket in her bag and spread the bills on the table. Her last fifty she'd need for a taxi. *Taxi or Tony? No. Yes.* He would understand, take her out of the city to a place where she could hide, recover, and think.

She fumbled for her cellphone. Five-thirty in the morning. Damn. Three missed calls from Luiz. She pushed the dial button. It rang once before the boy answered.

"Where are you, Lisa?"

"I'm safe. Where are you and the kids?"

"At the shelter. We are not leaving. No fucking way. This is our place. You gave it to us."

"Shit, Luiz, they might be coming after you. You don't know what you're up against."

"We've discussed it, Lisa. No one's leaving."

"Okay, I'll be there in an hour." She rang off and cursed the kids. What were they thinking?

Lisa grabbed her bag and sneaked out the door. The sky had already turned a lighter shade of black. She walked to the next intersection and read the street names before she called a taxi. Ten minutes later she was on her way to Copacabana. When they reached the gate to her apartment building, she asked the driver to wait until she was inside. All seemed quiet, but Lisa knew they'd come looking for her. But what could the cabbie possibly do, if he wanted to help?

She slipped into the house and up the stairs but didn't switch on the lights. Better not to draw attention. With aching hands and wrists she struggled to put on underwear, army surplus pants and a thin long-sleeved shirt. She packed more clothes and money in a duffel bag and threw it out the window. Then Lisa grabbed the sports bag with the Mac-10 and tossed the ammo for her pistol into it. She tied a rope through the handles and lowered the equipment through the window to the backyard, one story down.

Lisa took a hunting knife and a flashlight from the kitchen and sneaked out of her apartment. The latch clicked into the lock when she remembered the rifle. Did Jango hide it after the cops arrested her? She unlocked the door and hurried into her bedroom. The large rifle leaned in the corner of her closet. The only evidence the police would have needed. For a moment she imagined herself rotting in a prison cell. No use thinking about what-ifs now. She shouldered the Steyr and picked up the box of bullets. Fewer than fifty rounds left.

She tiptoed down the steps and opened the front door a fraction. She wished the apartment building had direct access to the backyard. Cars parked on the street. No Corolla, no red sports car, but a station wagon. With no choice, she slipped through the door and eased it shut behind her. She made a great target, but they hadn't shot at her yet. Either they weren't out there or they wanted her alive. She wouldn't let that happen again.

Maybe they watched the bookshop. She walked to the corner and peeked around. The street looked deserted. She passed the barred window and reached the gate. Damn, where was the key?

The gate swung open. "Come in," Tatu hissed.

"Glad to see you." She noticed the butt of a gun sticking out of his shorts. "Here, take the flashlight. Two flashes if something suspicious happens. Three for danger."

He gave her a solemn look and nodded. "Okay."

She crept down the narrow corridor. Rena stepped out from behind the corner.

Relieved, she hugged the girl but flinched when the small hand touched her back.

"We'll be fine," Rena whispered.

Lisa stroked the girl's hair. "At least we'll try." She straightened and crossed the backyard. Luiz sat on the bench, her bags next to him.

"Stubborn idiot. We're trapped here," she hissed.

"No, this is our fortress. We can defend it."

Lisa let her gaze sweep over the multi-story apartment buildings surrounding them. Were they putting the lives of dozens of people at risk? She focused on the narrow corridor between her building and the neighboring one; it was the only entrance to the backyard. Should be easy to defend without her tenants finding stray bullets in their Sunday roasts. And they could sneak directly into the bookstore if they had enough time. Squatting, she unzipped the duffel and pulled out the submachine gun. "The only ammo we have is in the mag. So you better think twice before shooting." She dropped the Mac-10 in his arms. "What else do we have?"

"Tatu and I have a gun each. That's it."

"Ammo?"

"Tatu has a box of fifty bullets. I have only six in the mag."

"I have more ammo for your Taurus in the bag." She slumped on the bench. "Might fit Tatu's gun as well. Did he get it from Max?"

"Yeah. What happened, Lisa?"

"They found out, Luiz. I escaped, but they won't give up. Not until they've killed me, or I've killed them. And now they know who I am."

Luiz stared at her wide-eyed. "They caught you? What...?"

"I'm fine. I've been through worse, but if they really storm in here... Shit Luiz, why don't we just load everything into the van and head out of town? This is insane." She gazed into his dark eyes and imagined the possibilities flashing through his mind.

Shaking his head, he looked up at the high-rises surrounding them. "This is our place. Please, Lisa?"

She sighed. No way could she chase them away now. "I have to sleep some more. Wake me if you need me. Tatu's got a flashlight, two flashes for something suspicious, three for danger. If they don't attack tonight, they'll probably think of a more sophisticated way to get to me."

Lisa slipped into the shelter and saw the sleeping form of Ubaldo. Carefully, she lowered herself onto one of the mattresses. Her wrists throbbed. She couldn't move a finger without hurting. Rolling onto her back, she felt the wounds and cuts burn. Worse could have happened. She embraced the pain and wrapped it around the core of herself like a protective shield.

* * * *

"Wake up, Lisa. It's a bad dream."

Her chest tight, Lisa couldn't breathe. She fought her way out of the basement to the light, to the voice. Panting, she pushed open the creaking door.

A girl's voice. "It's okay, Lisa, wake up. It's just a dream."

Lisa broke out in sobs. Rena embraced her. "Nobody is going to hurt you. You're safe with us."

Chapter Fifty-Four

Max paced the roof terrace while Átila leaned against the bar sipping spiked pineapple juice.

"Fucking Costa Branca," Max muttered. Three of his men arrested, one dead, and ten thousand *reais* down the drain. He swung around. "What are we going to do?"

Átila gulped the rest of the juice and slammed the empty glass on the bar. "Take him out."

Max stopped in front of his friend. "And how do we get to him? It's not like he's going to walk in here."

"Max?" Mussolini stood in the door, his right hand resting on the gun in his belt.

"What?"

"I think I know who blabs to the police about our deliveries."

Finally. Max marched up to him. "Who?"

"Capone."

Max slammed his fist against the wall. "I can't believe it. Capone? Are you sure?" He scrutinized his general's face.

Unfazed, Mussolini replied, "I had this hunch and kept an eye on him. When the cops arrested our couriers, he was watching through binoculars from the water tower. Then he pulled out his cellphone. 'Course I thought he was calling you."

"No, didn't hear about it until Átila told me. Dammit." Max stared at a bullet hole in the wall. "The greedy little rat. Where is he now?"

"At home."

"Tell Capone—and only him—that tonight's delivery has been rerouted to the old water tower, ten-thirty. Watch him closely. Just watch and listen."

With a curt nod, Mussolini clomped down the outside stairs. Max started pacing again.

Átila stepped in his way. "What if we set a trap for Costa Branca? Force Capone to call him and arrange a personal meeting."

Max held Átila's gaze. He didn't want to kill the *capitão*, but couldn't ignore him any longer. The man cost the syndicate too much money. "Sounds like a plan. But first we need to make sure Capone really is his man." He snorted. "Quite ironic. If the *capitão* knew Capone set the trap for Nassar when I killed him..."

Mussolini returned and stood panting at the top of the stairs. "Told him the new location and left. He made a call. Didn't know I stood right outside the window."

"What did he say?"

"Ten-thirty, water tower. Nothing else."

Max nodded. "Let's take care of him."

As they marched toward Capone's house, Átila darted a sideways glance at him. "Microwave after he's called the *capitão*?"

A groan escaped Max before he got a grip. He'd thrown up and crawled away on all fours when he'd watched a man with a tire around his chest and arms burning alive for the first time. He still couldn't stand the smell of gasoline when he filled up his car. He dreaded the spectacle, but punishing a traitor in public was the only way to keep up discipline. "Sure."

"Get Capone." Mussolini's voice.

Max swung around and stared at the man holding the walkie-talkie to his mouth. He slapped the device out of his hand. "Idiot! He must have heard that."

Átila ran down the narrow lane. Max dashed after him. On the roof tops, some of his men closed in on Capone's house. Átila pushed through the door and stormed up the stairs. Gun drawn, Max checked the ground floor. Nothing. A shadow at the window. Hunched over, Max moved toward it. Crunching noises outside. He jumped up aiming right at Mussolini's face. Max's heart hammered. He'd almost shot the fool.

Mussolini gulped. "No sign of him."

For a moment, Max felt like pulling the trigger.

Átila's heavy footsteps on the stairs. "Nothing."

Max stowed the gun and punched Mussolini in the face. "Stupid asshole."

The man stumbled backwards. "Sorry, Max."

"Find Capone."

The guy scampered away. Max's gaze swept the room. A new sofa stood against one wall, and a flat-screen TV hung on the opposite wall. How the hell had the cocksucker paid for that? Only one way. The *capitão*.

Max turned to Átila. "You were right. I should have killed Costa Branca when I had the chance."

"You've always been too soft for this job. I'm surprised you're still alive."

Max snorted. Only Átila would dare to say something like that and actually get away with it. Without his help, Max would never have survived this long. "Just promise me one thing."

Átila raised an eyebrow. "What's that?"

"Don't let him catch me alive."

His friend laughed. "Come on, a couple years in prison. Don't be such a sissy."

Max shook his head. "I'm just a gang leader, not one of the big shots. They'll throw me into a dirty hole and toss the key. The guy who taught me to steal cars got three years. After five they still hadn't released him. Nobody cared."

"Went to see him?"

"Yeah, but only once. I can't go to prison, Átila."

"That why you joined the gang?"

Max nodded. "Better dead than locked away in a dump with twenty other stinking men."

Átila slapped him on the back. "Why don't we get him first?"

"Right." He pulled out his walkie-talkie. "Catch Capone alive."

Chapter Fifty-Five

After two more hours of sleep filled with nightmares, Lisa marched across the backyard to the corner where Ubaldo stood guard, ignoring her screaming muscles and burning skin.

"Anything happened?"

He gave her a drowsy-eyed look. "All quiet."

"Good, I hope it'll stay that way." She swung around and gazed up at the roof. Tatu gave her the thumbs up. She waved at him. "I'll slip into the bookstore and check the street."

She unlocked the back door and smelled the dusty scent of books. A sense of homecoming enveloped her. She strolled to the little kitchenette and fed the coffee maker. The aroma wafted through the back room and seeped into the shop with her. The normality of coffee and books paralyzed her for a moment.

Then she grabbed the shotgun and pulled a chair up to the window. Through the rolled down shutters, she peeped out between the bars, watching for suspicious movements. People hurried past on their way to work. Some jogged in the cool morning air before the day became too hot.

And she would go kill Alves. But how? Shoot him on the road? Not good. She needed the name of his sidekick. Félix who?

Rejane walked past the window. Damn, what was she doing here? Did they catch her to get access to the store and backyard? Lisa retreated behind a bookshelf. The bars rolled up. The door opened and brushed against the bells.

When no one followed her assistant, Lisa whispered, "Rejane."

The girl jumped. "You scared me."

"Sorry, but what are you doing here? Didn't Luiz tell you to—"

"He did, but why should I keep the shop closed?" She smiled. "If you need to hide, I can still do business for you, right?"

Lisa wondered what had happened to always careful Rejane.

"You could even lease the shop to me," she added. "I'll tell everyone you left the country."

Lisa whistled through her teeth. Clever girl. Jumping to the occasion. And why not? Renting to Rejane was a lot better than closing. "Might be dangerous for you. Some people don't care who gets in their way." She stowed the shotgun behind the counter to emphasize her words.

Rejane showed no reaction. "I don't know what you've done or who is after you, but I can't give up the store. This is the first decent job I've ever had. I learned so much from you. Please, Lisa. I can do it. Don't close the bookshop."

Lisa sighed. Torn between reason and following her heart, she slowly nodded. "You have to promise me one thing."

"What?"

"Over the next days and maybe weeks, if I ever call and tell you to get out of here, you do so immediately."

"I promise."

"I get ten percent of the profits."

Rejane shrieked with delight. "No fixed rent?"

"No."

Rejane hugged her. "Thank you."

"I'll call Jango to get the paperwork done. And I might be hanging around your shop for the next few days. Hope you don't mind."

"Not at all." Rejane chuckled.

"And I'll borrow your straw hat and sunglasses."

* * * *

Feeling a little safer in her simple disguise, Lisa hopped on a bus to Ipanema. The rattle of the vehicle set her muscles and chafed skin on fire, a welcome reminder and motivation. She found a quaint hairdresser she'd never been to before.

"Hi, what can I do for you?" the girl asked. She didn't even look twenty yet.

"Chop it off and dye the rest black."

"Are you sure?" She ran her fingers through Lisa's shoulder-length, dark-blonde tresses.

Lisa nodded. Lying back to get her hair washed, her aching body focused her thoughts on Alves and Félix. She'd get them. Alves first. He'd lead her to Félix. The lucky one. Not much longer. A warm flame of anger burned inside her.

When the girl took the scissors to her hair, she couldn't watch. She kept her eyes closed throughout her metamorphosis. The girl seemed to understand that her customer was in no mood for a chat and silently cut away at her hair before she applied the tint.

While Lisa waited, she pondered and dismissed ways to catch Alves alone. She couldn't get into his house without a small army, or stop him on the road. He'd certainly have a driver and bodyguard with him now. Play bait? Lure him somewhere? But how to protect herself? Bring Luiz and Tatu along as bodyguards? Ludicrous. She might have to track him for weeks to learn his routine, find a vulnerable spot, and act without time to prepare for the moment he bared his chest to her.

The girl rinsed her hair, shampooed and massaged her head.

She should check out the parking garage at his office. The blow dryer promised the end of the session. Could she slip into his apartment building posing as a hooker? She snorted. And drop the blow dryer into his bath. Yeah, right. She'd have to do better than that.

"Okay, we're done. Brace yourself and open your eyes."

A stranger looked back from the mirror. "Excellent." She could almost pass for a boy. Now her smile destroyed the illusion. Okay, no smiling. She needed a baseball cap and large sunglasses, which she'd get at the beach. Then she'd stock up their arsenal.

Chapter Fifty-Six

Lisa entered the bookstore. Rejane greeted her as she would any customer. Lisa took off the cap and new, pink sunglasses, ignoring the pain that shot up her back as she lifted her arm.

Rejane gasped. "What have you done?"

"Pretty good, isn't it?" She handed Rejane the plastic bag containing her hat and glasses. "Did anything unusual happen? I still think we should close the store for a few days."

Rejane darted a worried look past her. Was something wrong? Lisa glanced over her shoulder. Tony sat at the reading table. She exhaled with relief.

He stared. "Lisa?"

"The very same." Content that not even Tony would have recognized her on the street, she smiled. "What do you think?"

"Um, you look very different, but I guess the new look fits your...personality."

"Thanks." Her smile faltered.

"Can we talk?"

"Okay, but it's better if we're not seen together." She beckoned him to the back room.

Tony followed her, concern etched into his face. "I wanted to see you. Make sure you're okay. But you're not."

She sat with him at the small table and gazed into his blue eyes. For a moment they seemed to turn gray-green. She blinked. "I'm okay, Tony. Really. But it's not over yet."

"I can't bear it, Lisa. I keep thinking you might end up in some ditch, tortured and killed."

Her throat and chest tightened. *If he knew...*

He covered her hand with his. "You have to stop this crusade and think of your own safety. I need you, Lisa. I want you."

She blinked away tears. "I must cut the snake's head off before it bites me."

"Then let me help you. I can't watch you risk your life any longer."

She shook her head. "No, Tony. You're on one side of the sewer I'm wading through. Maybe someday you can pull me out, but only if I don't drag you in."

"What's on the other side?"

"People who kill for fun."

His grip on her hand tightened. His gaze dropped to her chafed wrist. He gulped. "Who did this?"

She shook her head, struggling for words.

He grasped her other hand. "Let me pull you out now."

She heaved a deep breath. Alves was still out there and likely searching for her. "Too dangerous, Tony. They'll come after me."

His lips parted. He looked away then focused on her again. "I've got a job offer here in Rio. Need to decide in the next few days. If I don't accept, they'll send me to China, and I might not see you again."

She could hear the hope in his voice, see his vision of a future together. "I don't know what's gonna happen, Tony. If I'll be here..." Lisa felt tears welling up. She wanted him close, but his safety came first. China sounded like a great place to be right now. She might not survive the next few days. A tear rolled down her cheek. Damn.

Leaning over the table, Tony brushed it away with his thumb before he kissed her. He pulled her to her feet and wrapped his arms around her. The embrace set her back on fire but she didn't flinch. She lost herself in the sensation of his body pressed against hers until the growing urgency of his passion scared her.

She pulled back. "Sorry. I can't." This wasn't the time to fight a ghost in addition to her real enemies. She cleared her throat. "Not yet."

Someday, she told herself. If she lived long enough.

Tony exhaled. "I understand that you need to do this. How can I help you?"

She wanted to reach out to him, feel the warmth of his body again, his protective arms, the promise of happiness. Even the pain. "You can't. I can't...risk your life as well."

He closed his eyes. "Three days, Lisa. If I don't hear from you, I'll leave for good." He gazed at her, unblinking. After a few seconds, she whispered. "I'll call you. I promise." She couldn't lose him. He was the only man who might defeat the ghost rattling her closet door.

Tony nodded. "Three days." He veered round and marched through the bookstore. Rooted to the spot, she stared after him, desperate to call him back before he reached the door.

* * * *

Lisa hauled the sports bag up to the roof of the shelter, climbing the wobbly chairs. Tatu grabbed the bag.

Luiz held out a hand to steady her. "Boy, you look different."

"Good." They settled on the mattress under the blazing sun. "I've been shopping." She handed Luiz a cardboard box. "For the Mac-10. Five hundred bullets." Placing a smaller box between them, she said, "And these are for your Taurus. Share the ammo with Tatu. His is the same caliber. And spare magazines." She held one out to each of the boys. "Load them."

And now for the best part. She retrieved the new Firestar from the bag, stood, and slipped it into her right front pocket. The piece hardly showed. Could be a wallet or a cellphone. "Would you guess I'm armed?" Looking down she noticed the butt of the gun in her shoulder holster bulging out a little under her light denim jacket.

Tatu grinned. "Either that or your left tit is bigger than your right one."

Luiz snorted and pushed his elbow in Tatu's ribs.

"Ouch. Why did you do that?"

They both laughed. Smiling, Lisa admired their indestructible sense of humor. "I think we're good to go."

Her sniper rifle lay on the mattress ready for action. Luiz filled up the Mac-10's magazine. She let her gaze sweep the buildings again. A curtain behind a window fell back into place. If Alves and his thugs managed to get into one of the apartments, they could cut them down like ripe papayas.

"What if they don't come?" Tatu asked.

"I hope they won't. I'd rather get to them before we start a war here."

"Don't get mad at me," Luiz said, "but I think you should ask Max for help."

"Max?" A vision of Max storming into the torture basement and mowing her abductors down with an assault rifle popped up in her mind. Not a bad image at all.

"Yeah, maybe you should," Tatu said.

And owe one to a drug lord? The last thing she wanted. But could she deal with Alves alone? "You think he would help me?"

Tatu sighed. "I don't know. He wouldn't have done it a couple weeks ago, but maybe he's going soft with old age. He got Ubaldo out of prison."

"What? They caught Ubaldo and nobody told me?"

"Well, you weren't around much, hunting killers and all that." Luiz grinned.

"And Max got him out?"

"Yeah, he knows people." Tatu smiled proudly.

If the boys trusted Max, maybe she should take the risk. He was Tatu's brother after all. "I'll talk to him."

"Just be careful. He's no saint." Tatu's smile had vanished. "He deals with drugs and kills people if necessary. And he's the one who decides when it's necessary."

"Kind of like me," Lisa added cynically.

Luiz shook his head. "It's different. He kills for the money."

"Now, don't start talking me out of it." She studied Tatu's drawn face. "You'll take me to him?"

The boy looked at Luiz, who pulled a face then shrugged.

"Luiz will take you. He can get away with a lot more shit, because he's older. Max still treats me like his baby brother."

Luiz laughed. "Well, you are a baby."

Tatu punched him in the arm.

"Can we simply show up at the *boca*?" Lisa asked.

Luiz shrugged. "Let's go tomorrow. He's less busy in the mornings."

"Maybe you want to put on a short skirt?" Tatu winked at her.

Lisa winced. "Do I have to?"

The boy laughed. "No, but he likes pretty women."

"I want him to take me seriously." Which was only half the truth. She didn't want him to get ideas either.

"He will when he hears why you've come," Luiz promised.

Lisa crossed her legs, rested her arms on her knees, and hung her head. Stretching every muscle in her back, she welcomed the pain and braced herself.

Chapter Fifty-Seven

The rising sun warmed Luiz while he kept his gaze fixed on the gate, hardly registering anything. He wanted to fall over and sleep. During the cold early morning hours, he had found it much easier to stay awake. His imagination had tortured him all night, conjuring up moving shadows and glinting barrels.

At least he could see the real world now. He tried not to think about what had happened to Lisa. Her injured wrists told him more than he wanted to know. He had to protect her, allow no one to get to her again.

"Luiz! Quick," Rena called.

Alerted, he jumped down. "What?"

"Lisa passed out. She's in the shower."

Luiz ran, his heart beating frantically. In the bathroom, he found Lisa, naked and unconscious, curled up on the floor of the shower. The sight of old scars and new wounds chilled him. He stood staring when Rena tugged his arm. He fought his nausea, turned off the water and helped Rena pull her out. Then he saw the bruises and chafed skin down her right arm, hip, and leg. "Oh shit. Look what they've done to her." Tears blurred his vision. He forced a deep breath.

Rena grabbed a towel and patted her dry. "Lisa, wake up," she begged.

"She'll come around." Luiz tried to convince her as much as himself. "We should let her sleep awhile."

"Okay. Let's carry her over to the mattresses."

Awkward, he reached under her arms, trying not to touch her breasts.

Grabbing her feet, Rena giggled. "Don't be stupid, Luiz. She won't know."

His cheeks burned as they carried her. Rena covered her in as many sheets they could find, but Lisa still shivered.

"I've got to tell Rejane," Luiz said. "She can get a doctor or medicine."

"Isn't that dangerous?" Rena asked.

"We don't have a choice."

Trembling, Luiz sprinted across the backyard and entered the bookstore. The door remained unlocked now during the day. Rejane was talking to a customer, a man who didn't look like much of a reader, mainly because his jacket bulged under his left arm. He smelled of money and power. The clothes, the hair cut, his arrogant smile. Luiz pressed against the wall, removed his pistol from the waistband of his shorts, and listened.

"Do you know how I can reach her?"

"No, she calls me once a week to check in. She's traveling. But maybe I can help you? Or would you like to leave a message?"

"I heard there was an apartment for rent in this building."

"No, all apartments are occupied."

"Really? I thought maybe some people had moved out after the recent troubles in this area."

Rejane's voice rang with false cheeriness. "I have no idea what you mean."

"I heard street kids were causing problems."

Luiz tensed. This guy didn't want to rent an apartment.

"Sorry, you must have heard wrong. Now, if you'll excuse me, I have work to do." Rejane left him standing and disappeared somewhere between the shelves.

Luiz flipped the safety catch.

The man hesitated a moment then said, "Five hundred *reais*."

"What for?" Rejane's voice sounded cold.

"Tell me where she's hiding." He moved closer and pulled back his jacket.

Luiz still couldn't see Rejane, but the man's mouth curled into a triumphant smile.

Luiz willed her not to do it.

"Get out of here," Rejane yelled.

Luiz stepped into the light, aiming his gun at the man. "You heard her. And don't come back."

The guy looked over his shoulder and grinned. Luiz had never seen green eyes before.

"I'll be around," he said and left, walking slowly past the display window. Still grinning.

"Shit!" Luiz said.

"You shouldn't have shown yourself," Rejane whispered.

"He scared the shit out of me. I thought he'd kill you."

"No, I don't think so. Too risky in the middle of the day." Rejane flopped down on one of the chairs. Her trembling hands contradicted her words.

"Lisa is sick. She's unconscious."

"What!" Rejane jumped up. "I'll call a doctor. And Jango."

* * * *

By the time Luiz returned to the shelter, Lisa was sweating and murmuring, legs and arms fighting the bed sheets. He felt her forehead. Burning hot. The doctor came around noon with Jango, the man Lisa told him about. Rejane treated him like an old friend, so it was probably okay. But when he motioned Luiz outside and asked him what had happened, he didn't know how much he should tell him.

"Was there any trouble?" Jango asked. "Did someone try to get in here?"

"No."

"What's your name?"

"Luiz."

Jango dropped his big hands on Luiz's shoulders. "Listen carefully, Luiz. I know what's going on. Do you think you can take care of her here? If not, I'll take her to a safe place until she recovers."

Luiz swallowed a lump in his throat. It would be best for Lisa if this man got her out of town, but the thought horrified him. "Don't take her away."

Jango nodded, staring at him intently. "You know what she's done?"

His heart hammered. Could he trust this guy? Then he remembered more details of Lisa's story. "You're the *despachante* who got her out of the detention center?"

"Yes, but that was a long time ago."

Luiz chewed on his lip. "I know she killed two of them."

Jango looked toward the back door of the bookstore as if he expected Lisa to stand there and watch. Then his gaze fixed on Luiz again. "When she comes to, tell her to stop. I've talked to a cop. A straight one. *Capitão* Costa Branca."

Luiz stepped back. "No. You didn't." His stomach lurched. His hands tingled. Costa Branca meant trouble.

"He promised to end the impunity of private death squads, Luiz. He'll help, but first he needs to get the drug-trafficking and corruption under control. The man's under a lot of pressure to clean up Rio before the Olympic Games and the Soccer World Cup, and he has powerful friends. Things are changing."

Luiz took another step back, not sure whether he should worry more about Lisa or Max.

"Rejane knows how to reach me if there's a problem."

"Okay."

"I'll drop in again tomorrow."

Jango headed toward the bookshop but stopped and spun around. "I know how much you kids mean to her. I rely on you. Don't make me regret my decision."

Luiz stood in the blazing sun, feeling more helpless than ever.

* * * *

Lisa emptied the magazine of the Mac-10 into his chest, but he kept coming at her. His gray-green eyes piercing her. "No!" she screamed. A huge hand squeezed her neck. She struggled but couldn't slip out of his grip. He pushed her forward, slammed her against a wall. It cracked. A chain snaked around her, its head a knife. He grabbed her shoulders and shook her.

"Lisa, you're dreaming. He can't hurt you." Where did the voice come from? Just a whisper, but it promised escape.

He slipped the knife into her mouth. The blade went far inside, and blood flowed down her chin, her naked chest, and her legs.

"Lisa, look at his nose. Can you see the big black hair?"

Lisa tried, but his face blurred, the knife disappeared. She opened her eyes and saw Rena's smiling face.

"That always works." The girl giggled.

Something wasn't right. Drenched in sweat and entangled in several sheets, she tried to free her hands. Rena helped her.

Slowly, fever-dreams and reality separated. "So it did happen?"

Rena tilted her head. "What?"

"How long was I out?"

"Only one day and one night."

"I'm thirsty."

Rena put a mug with water to her lips. "I have to tell Luiz and Tatu." The girl jumped up.

"Wait. Can you find me my clothes first?"

Rena laughed and scampered over to the bathroom. Yeah right. Too late to hide anything.

* * * *

Lisa felt like an exotic zoo animal. The kids wouldn't take their eyes off her, a stupid grin on every face. Ubaldo, Rena, Tatu, and Luiz, all sitting with her at the table, eager to get her coffee, tea, food, her gun, whatever.

She had eaten a bread roll with butter and jam and chunks of pineapple. Her strength returned. Her brain kicked in. "Anything happen while I was out?"

Luiz bit his lip and stared at her.

"Spit it out," she said.

"Someone asked for you at the bookshop. He offered Rejane money and then threatened her with his gun."

Lisa's stomach wanted to expel all she'd eaten. "What did he look like?"

"He was tall, blond hair, and the strangest eyes I've ever see."

"Gray-green?" Every nerve in her body bristled.

"You know him?"

"Félix. We have to stop hiding and start hunting."

"You still want to ask Max for help?" Luiz chewed his lip like he always did when something troubled him.

"More than ever." She'd pay the price, no matter what, if Max agreed to help.

"There's something else," the boy said.

"What?"

"Jango came when you were sick. He said he talked to the new *capitão* about the death squads, and he promised to go after them."

She snorted. "That's something new. I hope Jango didn't tell him any details."

Luiz shook his head. "I don't think so. He also said Costa Branca wants to fight the drug gangs."

Lisa stared at him. "And next he's going to end hunger in the world? Listen, Luiz. The new *capitão* sounds fantastic, but I doubt we can expect any changes soon."

He leaned close and whispered, "I'm worried about Max."

"Oh, of course. I'm sorry. I didn't think. Should we still go see him? Sounds like he has enough problems already."

"Won't hurt to try, right?"

Chapter Fifty-Eight

After a morning drizzle, the city steamed in the diffused sunlight. Lisa slipped through the gate, with her baseball cap pulled low, and followed Luiz down the street. During the long walk to the *favela*, she fought her nervousness. Luiz scanned the police cars, then Max's soldiers on the roofs. Trusting his judgment, she followed the boy up several flights of stairs squeezed between walls. Halfway up the hill, they turned left and headed along a narrow lane. At the next corner, the first youths cradled assault rifles. One of them was a girl with black braids and a red bandana. Like Lisa, she wore army surplus pants.

The soldiers weren't any older than Luiz, who greeted them as he led her through the protected zone. Approaching a large one-story house with a guard on the roof and a second at the door, she paused.

Luiz didn't seem to notice. He walked up to the man at the door. "Hi, Mussolini."

Lisa suppressed a smile. She once met a guy named Hitler. Maybe his middle name was Jesus. Her tension eased and she stepped closer.

"Hey, Luiz. Max's busy."

"Have you caught Capone yet?"

Mussolini scowled. "No, the snitch got away."

Luiz darted Lisa a quick glance then asked, "He's in a bad mood?"

"You bet," Mussolini said.

A grumpy drug lord, great. Just what she needed.

Luiz sighed. "Lisa here needs to talk to him. It's urgent. Can you ask him?"

The man let his gaze wander over her body. "Doubt he's in the mood for girls."

Lisa stepped back, but Luiz grabbed her arm.

"That's not what she came for," Luiz said, his voice sharp.

Mussolini smirked while he pulled a walkie-talkie from his belt. "Max, Luiz is here with some chick. Lisa. She wants to talk to you."

Max's garbled voice ask, "Lisa who?"

Luiz grabbed the walkie-talkie. "Max, it's Lisa from the shelter. She needs your help."

"Take her to the roof and wait."

Lisa fought the impulse to run. Luiz climbed up the outside stairway ahead of her. With every step, she grew more nervous. When they reached the top, the man cradling an AK-47 turned. He was taller, broader, and older than any of the gang they met on the way. His skin, a dark shade of brown, glistened. Muscles rippled in his bare chest as he slightly adjusted the assault rifle. A far more impressive bodyguard than Cortez had employed. Lisa lifted her chin and pulled back her shoulders.

"*Oi*, Átila," Luiz said.

"*Olá*." The man's lazy gaze lingered on Lisa. "Does Max know she's armed?"

Luiz looked at her then frowned at the guard. "He should expect that."

The Hun's face cracked into a wide smile. "If you say so."

Lisa relaxed and walked toward the edge of the terrace. Below her, shoe box houses encrusted the hill and met the high-rises lining the beach. A better view than from the top suites of the Copacabana hotels. She looked around. Several deck chairs, beer bottles, towels, and clothes cluttered the roof. Max was just another human being who obviously cared about Tatu and his friends. And that made them allies.

Luiz stepped behind a makeshift wooden bar and poured drinks. She joined him. Colorful bottles lined a shelf.

A door next to the bar burst open. Max marched through. Muscles twitched in his jaws. His gaze brushed over her and fixed on Luiz. "What the...?"

"It's Lisa," Luiz said.

Of course, Max wouldn't recognize her in her disguise. She removed her sunglasses and baseball cap and ruffled her short, black hair.

"Damn, you look different." Max's voice softened. "You better have a good reason to come here, Miss English Teacher."

He remembered her from her teaching times? Shit, couldn't be fond memories if he was with the drug gang already.

"The alligator got your tongue?" His black eyes bored through her. "Don't waste my time. These brats have it in their silly heads that I'm some kind of Good Samaritan. But I'm not."

The words finally spilled from her mouth. "I need your help killing two powerful men."

The drug lord snorted, swung around, and walked to the edge of the flat roof. Luiz nudged her to follow him. Reluctantly, she did.

He looked over his shoulder at her. "I'm not an assassin."

Fighting her panic, she stepped up to him. "But I am, and I'm not asking you to kill for me. I need your help to catch one of them."

He raised one eyebrow.

She continued, "He's a rich man, living in a high security building. I bet he doesn't go anywhere without a bodyguard these days." She darted a quick glance at Átila, who'd settled on the surrounding wall, watching, rifle on his lap.

She turned back to Max. "I have to kill him. Ideally without being killed in the process, because there's the second one I have to take out."

Max laughed. Luiz strolled over to her. Definitely a good sign. She flinched when Max took her hand and raised it to her face. "The man who did this?"

Lisa looked at the colorful rims around her wrists. Underneath the red skin, her bruises had turned green and yellow. She scowled at Max. He released his grip.

Stay cool, you need him, she reminded herself and twisted her hand. "Yeah. But this is nothing. He kills street children. For fun."

Max lifted his chin and looked even taller. Again the muscles in his jaws twitch.

"How do you know?" he asked, his voice low and dangerous.

"I've been after him and his buddies for quite a while now, and I've killed two of them."

Max's eyebrows shot up. "You killed the fuckers who burned the boy and almost got Tatu?"

"And a bodyguard." This time she managed not to look at Átila.

Max stepped back and gave her a once-over, his gaze lingering on her fatigues for a moment. She didn't like the appraising look on his face.

His eyes locked on hers again. "What do you want from me then?"

Lisa focused on his chest. "Alves is too big for me." She looked up at him through her lashes. "He's well-guarded. I need your help to stop him on the road. Or maybe you can think of another way."

He grunted and took a step toward her. "And what do I get in return?"

She took a deep breath. "A city with less scum."

He sneered. "I want more."

She held his gaze. "What do you want?" Her jaws clenched.

Luiz stirred. She looked at him for help.

"Luiz, get lost," Max barked.

The boy flinched but didn't move.

"Luiz?"

Lisa squirmed inside. *Don't leave me alone with him and the Hun.*

"Shit, Max, don't do this," Luiz pleaded.

Max glared at him. "Get the fuck outta here or I'll throw you off the roof."

Luiz stared at Lisa, his lips a tight line, his eyes wide. She nodded. What else could she do? Her hands tingled. She should leave with him.

"Now," Max growled.

Dragging his feet, Luiz headed for the stairs. Max turned his attention back to Lisa. She shoved her sweaty hands in her pockets. "I'm outta here, too. Sorry for wasting your time."

Max scratched his chin. "You can't just come and go as you like. This is my fucking *boca*, not your little school. You came to me and asked for help. Now you tell me what's in it for me."

Lisa gripped the Firestar in her pocket, her index finger hugging the trigger, her thumb on the safety catch. A gun stuck in the waistband of Max's shorts, only mildly disguised by his T-shirt. She'd likely be faster. She glanced at Átila. The man stood, holding the Kalashnikov ready to fire. A grin spread over his face.

The Hun saw right through her. She shivered. How could Luiz have brought her here? Then she remembered. "Did you really save Ubaldo?"

Max smirked.

Lisa tried to relax. Luiz trusted this guy. Or had until just now. Max was pissed off. So what? She had to raise the stakes and stop acting like a fool. "You get whatever you want," she said and released her grip on the gun.

Max grinned. "I like the sound of that."

No turning back now. Whatever happened. She shed her jacket.

His face contorted into a grimace of scorn. He tore the Czech pistol from her shoulder holster. "What's this shit? Luiz lets you carry a fucking gun into my headquarters?"

For a moment, Lisa thought he might hit her. "I don't go anywhere unarmed," she said. "I've got another one in my pocket."

He gestured for her to hand it over, and Lisa pulled out the Firestar. Reluctantly, she placed the compact in his open hand. It looked so tiny in his large palm that she wanted to take her precious gun back.

"What else are you hiding?"

"Nothing."

He placed his hands on her shoulders, ran them down her arms. She flinched when he touched her bruises. He stopped. "Take off the shirt."

With trembling fingers, she slipped out of it. A whistle behind her. The Hun? Max circled her. His hands touched her waist before they slid down her legs.

She felt dizzy. A blade glinted before her. She focused. The knife she'd carried in the sheath on her belt. Damn, she'd forgotten all about it.

"You call that nothing?"

She blinked. "Sorry. Forgot."

"Looking at your scars and bruises, I'm not surprised you're armed to the teeth. Bloody hell." He stepped back and tilted his head. "I get whatever I want?"

She swallowed the lump in her throat. "You're the boss."

"Boss my ass." Max grunted. "You know a white guy who can wear a business suit like he was born in it?"

Puzzled, Lisa stared at him. "Actually, yes. He's American though."

Max nodded. "Perfect. Take him out for dinner tonight."

"I don't want to drag him into this."

Max ground his teeth. "But you have no qualms dragging me into your little crusade? I'm just a low-life drug pusher after all."

Merda. She'd insulted him, couldn't backpedal now. "Okay, I'll ask him, but I can't promise."

Max smiled. "Okay, here's the plan."

* * * *

Lisa dashed down the stairs two steps at a time. Luiz sat on the last step, resting his elbows on his knees, his head on his arms. He jumped up at the sound of her sandals and stared at her. "You okay?"

She nodded. "He's going to help us."

His face brightened, but he scrutinized her. "He didn't...?"

"He just played with me. Like a well-fed cat plays with a mouse." She put her arm around Luiz's shoulders. "Let's go. We need to steal an expensive car. Max said you can do that."

Luiz gaped. "Steal a car? Now? What for?"

"So we won't leave traces when we kidnap Alves."

They strolled down the hill. "Are you going to help me?" Luiz asked.

"With what?"

"Steal the car."

Geez, what else would she have to face today? "Of course, if you tell me what to do."

Luiz grinned.

They reached the border street, ran across, and walked toward Avenida Copacabana. "Where are we going to find an expensive one?" Luiz asked. "Must be old enough not to have an immobilizer." She considered the parking garage where she kept her van and car safe, but the guards might recognize her. Then she remembered she didn't have a car anymore. Was it still parked outside the Alves villa as bait for her?

Luiz looked over his shoulder. "São Conrado?"

"No. The last thing I want is to run into Alves unprepared. Leblon?"

"Okay."

They hopped on the bus. Lisa paid for both of them then struggled through the turnstile. The bus rattled off, and she hurried to sit down before she got thrown into someone's lap. Luiz squeezed in next to her. She leaned over and whispered in his ear, "I've never stolen a car before."

"Yeah, you told me."

"I did? Oh well. Just wanted to make sure you're aware of what to expect."

He laughed. "You just have to drive. Much less conspicuous than a black fourteen-year-old boy. Just don't kill the engine."

They got off at the last stop and strolled back in the direction of Copacabana through narrow side streets and headed toward the beach. Lisa saw an old silver Volkswagen bug. She'd pick that one for herself. She smiled as she ran her fingers lightly over the round roof. "It's a beauty," she said.

"Lisa, concentrate on the job. That's not an expensive car."

"Took a lot of time and love to keep it in such good shape."

Luiz stopped and turned to her. "What's wrong with you?"

She slowed when she saw the black convertible parked at the curb. An older model Mercedes SLK. "That's just right for Max."

Luiz whispered, "Walk away if the alarm goes off." Without a glance at her, he strode up to the passenger side, bumped against the car and ducked.

Her heart raced. After a few seconds, the door swung open. She stepped to the driver's side and peered in. Luiz's head disappeared under the steering wheel. If they caught him, they'd lock him away for a few years. What the hell was she doing?

With sweaty hands, Lisa opened the door. Luiz's head popped up, the engine purred. She lowered herself onto the seat, closed the door, and put the gearshift into drive. She'd never been happier to drive an automatic. Much harder to stall the engine. She felt like everyone was watching her, knowing she'd stolen the car. They passed one of the little military police booths scattered along the city beaches. *Calm down. How would they know?* "Excellent work, Luiz."

"Thanks. Max taught me." Luiz grinned at her. "You did pretty good, too."

"You're not going to tell anyone about this, you hear me?"

Luiz chuckled. "Of course not."

With the adrenaline subsiding, she said, "You know where this career leads, right?"

A sigh from the passenger seat. She stopped at a red light and looked over, raising an eyebrow.

Luiz shrugged. "Prison. But I won't let them catch me."

"Famous last words. I wish you'd go look for an honest job."

"Oh, I've got a few honest jobs. Like work at the junk yard, begging, stealing. Oh wait, that's not honest, is it?" He chuckled.

Lisa couldn't help smiling. She might have become like him. Except she did get caught. "Where do I park the car?"

He gave her a blank look. "I usually don't have that problem." Then he smiled. "Renato can hide it for us."

"Renato?"

"The dealer I would normally sell the car to. Max can pick it up there."

"Okay, one problem solved." Now she just needed to call Tony. Her stomach lurched. Anger at Max flared. She suspected that beyond the requirements for their trap, he wanted her to put the life of someone she cared about on the line. She could still call it off. Find a different way. Give up. Cave in. She darted Luiz a quick look. "What the hell am I doing?"

The boy grinned. "Kicking ass."

Lisa groaned.

* * * *

Tony pulled his vibrating cellphone from his suit pocket to hit 'Ignore', but saw Lisa's caller ID. He looked from Carlos to the job applicant. "I'm sorry, I have to take this one."

Carlos frowned but nodded.

He rushed out of the meeting room. "Lisa?"

"Tony. Were you serious when you said you wanted to help me?"

Tony held his breath for a few seconds. "Yes. As long as you don't expect me to kill anyone." He released a nervous chuckle.

"No, but will you help me catch a killer?" She sounded desperate.

"The snake's head?"

"Yes."

"I'll help you. Whatever it takes."

"When can you get out of work?"

He closed his eyes and tried to conjure up his schedule. His brain failed him. He only remembered they had job interviews nearly all day. "Is six o'clock early enough?"

"Excellent. Thank you, Tony."

He disconnected and noticed his hands trembling. He waited a moment to collect himself before he reentered the meeting room.

Carlos rambled on about the importance of South America, and Brazil in particular, for their company's expansion plans. He glanced at Tony. "Are you okay? You look pale."

Tony swallowed. "Just some troubling news. Personal."
Carlos nodded. "Sorry to hear that. Okay, where were we?"

Chapter Fifty-Nine

Lisa led Tony to a table in a far corner of the restaurant, with a good view of both the room and the entrance. They ordered drinks. "You don't have to do this. Actually, I don't want you to do it, but..."

"But?"

"With your help it would be so much easier."

"Go on."

"Let's wait for Max."

Tony frowned. "Who's Max?"

"A drug lord."

"Are you kidding?"

Lisa shook her head. "I'm desperate. I need help from both of you." A flash of black leather caught her eye. Max strode toward them with a grin on his face. Of course, he'd donned the full drug lord gear to leave no doubt about who they were dealing with. She closed her eyes for a second. "I'm sorry, Tony. Really." She must be mad to even consider Max's plan. First she got Luiz to steal a car, now she was involving Tony in a kidnapping.

"Max, this is Tony."

"*Olá* Tony." Max flopped onto the chair and stretched out his legs.

"Good to meet you." Tony straightened a little.

Max smiled at Lisa. "*Perfeito.*"

"Perfect for what?" Tony asked.

"Kidnapping," Max replied with a smirk.

* * * *

Tony drummed his fingers on the steering wheel of the stolen Mercedes convertible. Max tore his gaze from the exit of the parking garage and glanced at the gringo. He looked the part, but could he pull it off? "Stop that. Gets on my nerves."

"It's after seven. Where is he?"

"Alves is a busy man."

"What if I stall the car?"

"Lisa gets into trouble."

"Shit. I don't like this." Tony grasped the steering wheel so hard his knuckles turned white. "What if someone wonders why we're parked here with the engine running?"

"Can't risk losing precious time to hot-wire it when he pulls out. Stay cool, Tony. We can do it."

The gringo took a deep breath. "Here's a question for you. Why did you need me for this scheme? Lisa looks even more harmless. She could have driven the Mercedes and one of your guys the Ferrari."

Max kept a straight face. "Sorry, my English isn't very good."

"Cut the crap. Your English is excellent."

Max turned in his seat and put his arm around Tony's headrest. "Would be even better if Lisa hadn't kicked me out of her class for dealing drugs. Okay. Two reasons. You're proof that she's serious and doesn't just want me to do the dirty work for her. Now I can trust her. Second, I got plans for her and don't want her to get squashed in a car crash."

"What plans?" The gringo narrowed his eyes at him.

"None of your business."

"And you don't give a rat's ass if I get squashed."

Max turned back and focused on the garage, suppressing a grin. "Right."

Tony beat a drum roll on the wheel. "Well, at least we're in the same car."

Max laughed. He liked the guy. Mama Lisa, Daddy Tony, and a bunch of black and chocolate-colored children, maybe with some white ones sprinkled in. He sobered quickly when a black Corolla pulled out of the parking garage. "There he is."

* * * *

Tony shot across the intersection as the light turned red. He couldn't lose Alves. And Lisa. He squeezed between two cars in the left lane then cut behind the Corolla. Someone honked.

He chuckled. "Nice car." The wind dried the sweat on his skin and his heartbeat slowed.

At the next red light, Max craned his neck. "Dammit, the Ferrari's too low. Can you see her?"

Tony leaned out of the car. "Yep, Lisa's right in front of him."

"Ah, yes, I think I hear the humming of the engine. If she wrecks my car..."

Tony darted him a quick glance, but Max smiled.

Traffic flowed more smoothly as they pulled onto the arterial road. Not much further. At least Lisa wouldn't get into the car crash. If all went according to plan.

Max tapped Tony's thigh. "Just a hundred meters or so now."

"Okay." Tony checked the seat belt again. His pulse raced. He leaned his head back and tried to relax. Hopefully German engineering would live up to its reputation. He hit the accelerator and pulled up close to Alves's Corolla.

He checked the speed. Fifty kilometers per hour. About thirty-five miles? Shit. This was crazy. The Corolla's brake lights flashed. He braced himself. A metallic crunch. Tony jerked forward. The world turned white, smelled of rubber and chemicals. The airbag deflated in a swirl. Footsteps approached.

Tony looked up. Alves's driver said something in Portuguese but didn't sound too concerned. He was big. Alves obviously bought by the size.

Max grunted something in response.

"My car," Tony screamed, sticking to the script, and stumbled out of the Mercedes. He squatted and cried over the damaged hood. "Oh, man, I can't believe it. Why did you brake like an idiot?"

Max slid out of the SLK.

The bodyguard raised his hands in defense. "The car in front of me braked."

So he did understand English. Tony ran his fingers through his hair. "Ah fuck."

Max put a hand on his shoulder. "Come on, Tony, get a grip. The insurance will pay."

Tony sighed. "My wife won't let me buy another one like this. Not now that I've wrecked it."

Max talked to the bodyguard in Portuguese. He'd point out non-existing damage. And then...

Max waved at the honking traffic squeezing around them before he went down on one knee and peered under the Corolla.

Tony held his breath as he tried to understand what they said. Something about a gas leak.

As the driver squatted and bent forward, Max drew a gun and slammed the butt on the man's head. He collapsed.

Max gave him the thumbs up. "Distract Alves."

On stiff legs, Tony walked up to the driver's door. He opened it and bent low to address the passenger. "Excuse me, sir, but your driver isn't feeling well." He looked into puzzled black eyes. The man did not look like a killer at all with his foppish mustache.

Max pulled open the door behind Alves. "Don't worry." He pushed his gun against Alves's neck. "He'll be fine."

Alves growled something in Portuguese.

Max eased onto the backseat.

"Somebody wants to see you." Tony slipped behind the wheel and patted down Alves's upper body. "Look at this monstrous thing." He pulled a huge revolver from a shoulder holster and handed it to Max. He felt like he was watching himself in a movie.

Max whistled. "A Raging Bull for our baby-killer. I bet if he ever fires this thing, he'll land flat on his ass."

"Baby-killer?" Alves screeched. "What are you talking about?"

"Shuddup," Max barked.

Tony had memorized the route and drove on autopilot while his mind spun. He still couldn't quite believe he was an accomplice in a kidnapping. And he only played a role in the easy part. He dreaded the moment they'd reach the lonely old house.

"Hey, turn right," Max said.

Tony slowed down just in time to swerve into the narrow street hidden by trees swaying in the breeze.

Five minutes later he pulled onto the dirt road leading to the abandoned house. "The Ferrari's here."

"Where the hell are you taking me?" Alves asked, his voice hardly more than a whisper.

Tony parked next to the Ferrari and got out first. He walked around the car and opened the door. He pulled Alves out, shoved him against the car and frisked him more thoroughly, while Max climbed out, pointing his gun at their prisoner.

"He's clean." Tony swallowed. This man would die at Lisa's hands. He wanted to throw up.

"Move your ass, man." Max shoved Alves toward the isolated house. Taking a deep breath, Tony opened the door and stepped aside.

Chapter Sixty

Lisa watched the shock of recognition ripple across Alves's face, while she tried to control her memories of the basement, his cold eyes scrutinizing her, his tie choking her. She wondered if he would beg for his life. Mute, Alves squared his shoulders and lifted his chin in an arrogant pose.

She glanced at Max and then Tony. Her gaze lingered but she saw no resentment in his eyes. "Thanks. We'll take care of the rest."

Max frowned. "Can we watch the show?"

Did he want to make sure she kept her part of the deal? "Be my guest." Her eyes locked on Tony's. "I don't think you want to see this."

He shook his head. Lisa wished he'd leave. She closed her eyes then turned her back on him.

While Luiz trained the Mac-10 on Alves, the murderous bastard scanned the room. Lisa stepped up to him. "Remember what I promised you?"

The man stared at her, as if all this had nothing to do with him. A familiar rage bubbled up inside her, dousing her nervousness. "Strip, tough guy."

"What?" Alves gaped.

"Oh, you can talk after all. Take off your clothes." She pulled the hunting knife from her belt and twisted the blade in front of his eyes. "Want me to help you? Your guys helped me. I wouldn't mind returning the favor."

"You have no idea what you're up against." He started to unbutton his shirt. "My uncle…"

"We don't have all night to crush a cockroach like you."

"You won't get away with this," he said, his voice still confident.

"General misconception. Getting away is not my highest priority. I told you I will hold you responsible for all that happened to me. And for the children you killed."

He stepped out of his pants.

"All the way."

His eyes darted around. For the first time he looked nervous. She touched the tip of her knife to his throat. "Do it."

Luiz kept the Mac-10 aimed and within his sight. Alves complied.

Lisa pulled up a chair. "Sit," she commanded, grabbed a roll of duct tape, and fixed his arms and legs to the chair. All the while she felt Tony's gaze on her back.

"Hey, I didn't harm you, did I?" Alves said.

"You didn't harm me? You fucker." She spat the words at him and picked up his tie from the floor. Dangling it in front of his eyes, she put her foot on the chair between his legs then noosed the tie around his neck. Slowly she pulled it tight.

"You didn't hurt me, you say? Well, how does this feel?"

She watched the fear grow in his dark eyes, until his mouth opened and he struggled to suck air through his squeezed windpipe. She knew too well how he felt. She held her breath. The memory made her arms go limp. Alves gasped and coughed. She pulled away the tie, set her foot down and swung around. She couldn't show him her weakness, couldn't look at Tony either.

She picked up the knife and strode up and down the room, fighting her nausea while she waited for Alves's breathing to return to normal. Maybe he'd talk now. She waved the knife in front of his face. "You are a tough guy, but not for much longer. I promised you'd burn, didn't I?"

A cold stare in return.

"Tell me who the man in the red sports car was, and I might reconsider."

Alves snorted. "We both know you'll kill me anyway."

She shook her head. "I'll let you live as long as you don't burn more children."

His contemptuous laugh raised goose bumps along her arms. Maybe he did fear his accomplice more than her, but he deserved a last chance. Or rather, she did. "I thought you were the head of the sickos. Looks like I was wrong. You're scared of Félix." His head perked up as she mentioned the name. "He's in command, isn't he? You wouldn't be able to control someone like him. You couldn't even keep Cortez from telling half the world about your favorite sport."

She picked up a jerry can and unscrewed the top. "You'll die a martyr. Are you proud?" Gasoline splashed over his lap. "Your dick will turn into charcoal first."

Alves screamed and pulled on his bonds, frantically trying to free his hands and legs or break the chair, but he still didn't beg for mercy. Tony's eyes seemed to burn holes into her back.

"His last name?" She put the jerry can down, several meters away, and pulled a matchbox from her jeans pocket. Feet shuffled behind her, someone gasped.

"You sure you want to die in such a painful way?" She struck the match. Alves stared at the flame unblinking, shaking his head.

"Last call." Lisa waited long seconds. He wouldn't talk. She blew out the match. The smell of gasoline mixed with sulfur. "I'm not like you. I don't enjoy hurting people." She drew her Firestar. "But you've got to die anyway."

Alves's face relaxed into a sneer, looking straight into the muzzle of her gun. She could hear Tony's voice in her head. Stop killing and start living. Except he remained silent. Tears burned in her eyes.

Luiz stepped forward. "I'll shoot him."

"No." Lisa moved between Alves and the boy. Realization hit her with the force of a blow. What had she done to the boy? "No, Luiz. You don't want to be like me." Looking into Luiz's scornful eyes, she shivered. She'd passed on her hatred, taught him that guns gave power. All wrong. Her rage at Alves evaporated.

"He deserves it," Luiz said.

"Right, but you don't deserve this." A sense of power and control filled her. She didn't have to kill him. "He's nothing, Luiz. Just dirt under our feet."

Luiz frowned at her then shook his head. "Have you gone mad?"

"No, I'm coming to my senses."

A hand fell on her shoulder. Lisa twisted to see Tony's face. His eyes shone. With relief? Something more?

Max stepped up to her other side. "Get the boy out of here. I'll take the rat back."

"No, leave him. Let him find a way out or starve to death." She glanced at Alves a last time. "Just like he left me." Except there was no creep like Félix around to play with him some more.

"As you wish." Max headed toward the door.

Lisa put her arm around Luiz's shoulder. "Okay?"

"Okay." He sounded unconvinced.

Tony placed his hand on her back. "Let's get out of here."

Alves's laughter rolled in waves over them as they left the house. The fresh air cleared her nostrils of the stench of gasoline. Lisa didn't look back. A scent of lilies filled her nose. Maybe she was hallucinating. Lilies didn't grow in Brazil. The scent of satisfaction?

The four of them walked toward the Ferrari.

"Fuck that shit." Max grabbed the Mac-10 from Luiz, swung around, and marched back.

"Max, don't," Lisa called. He didn't react.

She pulled Luiz into an embrace as the staccato burst from the submachine gun. When she relaxed her grip, Luiz looked up at her. She pressed her lips together and shook her head. "I don't want you to become a killer like me or him."

"I'm glad he's dead," Luiz mumbled.

Max returned. "Sorry, but he might've killed Tatu or Luiz next time." He tossed the Mac-10 in the trunk of the Ferrari, leaned against it, and crossed his arms.

"That gun's ours," Luiz protested.

Max silenced him with a flick of his hand. "You don't need it. She's right. You don't want to become a killer. You and Tatu will go back to school and then you'll get a proper job. Not every street kid has that chance. You better grasp it—or I'll rip your head off."

Luiz looked from Max to Lisa. "Are you both going nuts?"

Max grinned. "You owe me a favor. I got your friend out of prison."

Luiz's mouth dropped open but no words came. Lisa smiled.

Max turned to her. "Now you, Miss English teacher. Whatever I want, you said. You'll make sure they go to school every day and do their homework. And I think you should go back to teaching. Why sell books when so many people in Rio can't even read? But that's up to you."

Lisa wanted to protest, but Max's grin disarmed her.

Tony wrapped his arm around her shoulders. "The man's right."

Chapter Sixty-One

Lisa stepped into her apartment. Stale air mixed with a hint of rotting trash greeted her. Her shoes stood in a neat row as if nothing had happened these past few days.

"Everything okay?" Tony asked.

She released the air in her lungs. "Yes. It just feels too normal to be back here." Félix the freak was still out there somewhere, but she didn't care. He let her escape. Now she'd let him live in return. If he came for her, she'd kill him. Now was the time to let go. And no more hiding.

She snuggled against Tony. "Will you spend the night with me?"

"Of course. I wouldn't want to be alone right now."

"Why?"

"I'd think I've been hallucinating and none of it really happened."

"I'm so sorry I dragged you into this."

His arms tightened around her. "Don't be. For the first time, I feel I really know you."

She lifted her head and gazed into his eyes. "And you still like me?"

"If you'd set him on fire, I might have shot you, like a rabid dog."

She blinked. "You wouldn't."

"Anyone who's capable of burning a human being alive deserves to die."

"You mean...?"

"He deserved to die, but I'm glad you're not like him, a monster with a heart of ice."

She leaned her head against his shoulder. "I'm not, but I might still need a little thawing."

He nestled his face in the nape of her neck. "Nothing better than body heat."

She never wanted to let go of him.

* * * *

In his office, Tony spent the last day of his assignment in Rio in a daze. Slouched in the chair, he tried to catch up with his correspondence, but his mind drifted. He found it hard to reconcile last night's experiences with normality. He'd hardly slept while Lisa lay in his arms and for once didn't whimper in her sleep. The images of Lisa the avenger had haunted him. He'd jerked out of nightmares as soon as he'd drifted off.

He'd gone through a roller coaster of emotions as he watched her interrogate the killer of children, but he didn't regret helping her. He understood now. And he loved her. Since the moment she lowered her gun, he knew it deep inside. This was much more than an infatuation with a mysterious woman.

"What are you smiling at?" Carlos asked from his desk across the rented office space.

Tony sat up straight. "I'll accept your job offer." He'd said the words before he really had time to make up his mind, but he still smiled.

Carlos stood and walked over. "Glad to hear it. Welcome aboard." They shook hands. "Fancy a drink after work? To celebrate a successful mission."

"If we leave now, I'll have time for one or two. Then I need to see someone."

"A lady?"

Tony nodded. "And what a lady."

"If she waits for you until January, I hope I'll get to meet her." He winked.

Tony laughed. He stood and grabbed his jacket. "Ready to go?"

Carlos looked around the office. "I guess. Next week we'll move into the new building. The security equipment still needs to be installed. Félix will supervise the work himself."

Tony screwed up his face at the mention of Félix Borges, the arrogant prick.

* * * *

Lisa took a shower. Less than half an hour until Tony would pick her up. Unarmed and unable to hear much above the rush of water, she felt vulnerable. Careful not to irritate the healing wounds on her back and wrists, she dried herself with a large, soft towel. She resisted the temptation to look at her back in the mirror. Alves and Félix had left marks. She felt them with every move. No need to see them.

She rifled through her closet and pulled out a denim skirt and tank top. No, she didn't want to torture Tony. She donned jeans and T-shirt and reached for her gun on the nightstand. She hesitated, then withdrew her hand. She could survive the day without firearms. Lisa smiled at her reflection, feeling strong. Without a crutch. The smile faltered. She grabbed the gun.

When Lisa entered the bookstore, Rejane greeted her with a wide smile. "*Olá*, Lisa. You've got a visitor."

Tony sat at the reading table. "Ready?"

"Yep. For your last evening in paradise."

He grinned. "Sounds scary."

They walked toward the old fort at the end of Copacabana beach and on to the Parque Garota de Ipanema. Settling on the rocks dividing the two famous beaches, they watched the surfers.

"I wish we had more time," Tony said.

"Me too." She rested her head on his shoulder, staring out at the waves rolling onto the beach, which was filled with people out to play and have fun.

"I love this city," Tony said.

"Me too. I couldn't leave." Rio had destroyed and recreated her. How could she possibly exist somewhere else?

"I don't want to go." He sighed. "I don't want to lose you just after I've found you."

Lisa smiled. "You found me? Well, maybe you did."

"Did I say something stupid?"

"No. And you're not gone yet."

She rose and held out her hand to him. Grinning, Tony took it and let her pull him to his feet.

She balanced on the rock. "You're heavier than I thought."

He put his hands on her hips and drew her into his arms.

"Lisa, I…"

She slung her arms around his neck and kissed him.

"I—"

"No promises, Tony. We'll see what happens."

He put a finger to her lips. "I accepted a job in Rio, starting in January."

A cascade of warm water seemed to douse her. "Are you sure?" After all he'd seen her do? And she hadn't even slept with him yet. Not really. Not the way it should be. Maybe she never could.

"Hundred percent."

She leaned into him. He squeezed her tight and buried his face in her hair. "I never want to let go of you again," he whispered.

"What if I get hungry?"

He sighed. "I guess I'll have to feed you."

She disentangled herself, took his hand, and pulled him up to the old cannons on the rock. "I know a great place for your last meal in Rio. Before you return, I mean."

* * * *

Félix pulled out his cellphone and dialed while his gaze swept over the buildings across Avenida Atlantica. He didn't know which roof the man had picked. After three rings Hot Shot answered. What a stupid name for a professional killer, but he was supposed to be good and available on short notice. Félix grew impatient now that Tony had led him back to Lisa. He'd never have recognized her with the short black hair. She looked even tougher now. Right, no more foreplay. Time for the showdown.

"I'm in position," the man said.

Félix peered around the tree. "See the man and the woman walking among the old cannons? He's blond, wearing jeans and a white shirt."

"Got him."

Damn, Lisa slung her arms around Norton's neck and kissed him. Félix looked away. Disgusting. "Wait 'til they're done smooching."

"Which one's the target?"

He stared at the happy couple and felt tempted to say both. No, she'd suffer for this.

"Are you there? Can't wait much longer."

"He is. Don't even scratch her. She's mine."

"Gotcha."

Félix walked away.

* * * *

"Lead on, guide. I trust you with my life," Tony said.

Lisa looked over her shoulder at his grinning face. "Fool," she teased.

He twitched, stumbled back.

A gun shot exploded. Lisa flinched, ducked behind a cannon. Tony fell. No. What? She waited for a second shot, while she stared at Tony immobile on the ground. People gathered around him.

Why couldn't she move? She had to help him. Her lungs felt like they'd burst any moment. She released the air trapped in her lungs and crawled over to him. Fear tightened her chest. She still had to force herself to breathe. She pushed between legs, ignoring the curses or comments. She saw his sneakers, his jeans-clad legs, and the white shirt with a stain of red over his heart. "No!" Her own voice echoed in her head. The dark rock beneath him was streaked with blood.

She knelt and grabbed his hand, still not daring to look at his face.

"He's alive," someone said. "Call an ambulance."

Her eyes found his face. She only saw the white of his eyes. "Don't die on me, Tony. Please." She clutched his hand hard, as if she could hold him back in a tug of war with death.

* * * *

Lisa sat in the wooden chair, leaning over Tony's unconscious body. His pale face was a mask. The doctors wouldn't say more than that his condition was critical. They'd told her to go home and come back in the morning. She couldn't. Tony was all alone here in this foreign country, fighting death's grip. She wouldn't let go of his hand until he'd made it through the night. Someone had to connect him with life, keep him going. Her aching muscles consoled her, made her hang on.

If only the images would stop swirling in her head. She saw him smile, twitch, spin. Over and over again. The shot still echoed in her ears.

The bullet must have been meant for her. What a fool she'd been to think it was over. And Tony had to pay for her idiocy. As if the world had suddenly changed.

The door opened. She jerked around. Jango peered in. Relief seeped into her. She and Tony weren't alone anymore.

He sneaked into the room. "They didn't want to let me see him."

Lisa nodded. "They tried to keep me away, too."

Jango turned the shades to let early daylight filter in. Tony had survived the night. She drew comfort and hope. Jango placed his hands on her shoulders from behind and kneaded her tense muscles. "He'll be out for several more hours. Let's drink a coffee."

She stared at Tony. There wasn't anything she could do now. Or was there? Bending over him, she kissed his lips. She whispered, "If you keep living, I'll stop killing. I promise, Tony."

Jango took her arm and led her to the cafeteria.

"Any idea who did this or why?" He ordered two coffees.

She shook her head. "I can only think of one possible explanation and I don't like it at all."

"But you said Alves is dead."

"There's one more man. Félix, the lucky one."

"A common enough name. I know a Félix who worked with Tony."

She sighed. "I know. It's near impossible to find him with nothing but the first name. And I don't want to hunt him. I want to stop, Jango. I really do. But if he's now coming after the people I care about..."

Jango held her gaze for a long time then nodded. "I'll talk to Costa Branca and tell him there's more to this shooting than meets the eye. Maybe he'll have a word with the detectives investigating the case. They might be able to catch this Félix. When foreign business men get shot, it's bad publicity for the city. I'm sure the mayor will take an interest as well."

"You really trust Costa Branca?"

"Hope dies last. The *capitão* is an honest cop and he's got the support of his superiors."

Chapter Sixty-Two

Félix cranked up the car radio when the anchorman started babbling about the police's recent attempts to clean up the streets of Rio. Sounded like someone with a different attitude would take over after Rocha, Cortez, and Alves died. Félix chuckled. The voice rambled on about the battle against drug gangs and police corruption.

Félix stopped listening when Lisa stepped through the large glass doors of the hospital, wiping at her eyes. She scanned her surroundings then sprinted to her van.

Oh Lisa, how different you look. So much tougher. You couldn't stay away from Tony, could you? Well, everyone's got a weak spot. He is yours and you are mine. He blew her a kiss and started the engine.

Euphoria surged through him. He'd picked up her scent and taken out her lover. The hunt was on.

* * * *

Lisa drove on autopilot back to Copacabana. Rio looked dull. A gray sky drained the color from the city and the sea. She felt lonely, abandoned, guilty. Was that love? Why did it have to hurt? Lisa wiped her eyes. He'd survive. She needed sleep. And she had to keep a promise. Her promise to Max.

A red Mazda sports car pulled in front of her, horn honking. Her heart raced. The playboy drove the same model. Could that be Félix? The car turned into Avenida Presidente Vargas. Lisa followed.

Of course, it wasn't him. Too much of a coincidence. Ahead, the famous church Igreja de Nossa Senhora da Candelária towered, reminding her of the infamous massacre of street children years ago.

What if Félix toyed with her? The car turned into the lane leading up to the São Bento monastery. Lisa knew it ended at the small parking lot right in front of the church. If Félix lured her up there, he'd see her. Lisa turned the opposite direction. This was silly. Couldn't be him.

Then why didn't she make sure? Why did her hands tremble, her heart race? Lisa turned right and right again, then left and up the small street to the monastery. A monk waved at her at the entrance to the parking lot. Lisa spotted the Mazda parked close to the church's main gate. No sign of the man.

She abandoned her van on the opposite side of the small lot and strode toward the huge doors. Nervous because there was the slightest possibility that the driver of the Mazda had gray-green eyes, Lisa stepped into the gloomy interior.

The smell of incense hit her. The elaborate gold-coated carvings attracted many tourists, but fortunately not today. One man knelt in the front pew. A couple strode down the side aisle admiring the decorations. Lisa stopped halfway down the center aisle and scanned every niche and dark spot. From the corner of her eye, she saw something red flash past the main door. The red Mazda pulled away. He couldn't have sneaked out without her seeing him. Shivering, Lisa hurried back and stepped outside into the light. Her gaze swept over the public restrooms to the right of the church. He might have been in there when she arrived.

Okay, enough of this paranoia. She climbed back into the van, drove down the small hill, and headed toward Copacabana, cursing herself for driving into the clogged-up *centro* instead of by-passing it.

* * * *

In the bookstore Lisa found Luiz browsing the shelves. "Hey, what are you up to?"

"I'm trying to find that *Peter Pan* book you told me about."

"I didn't know you could read." She looked around. "Where's Rejane?"

"In the back room. Doing paperwork, she said. Can you help me?"

"With what?"

"Find the book. I want to read it to the kids."

"Great idea." She took *Peter Pan* from the shelf and handed it to him. "And I've got an even better idea."

Luiz tilted his head and gave her a skeptical look. "What's that?"

"School."

"Oh, c'mon, we're too old."

"You promised Max."

He put the book down. "It's not fair."

"I know."

"School's expensive."

"No, it isn't. I know just the place for you guys. All of you."

Luiz scowled. "You're mean."

"Your long vacation will end tomorrow."

* * * *

By six in the evening, Lisa sat at Tony's bed again. The nurse had told her he'd woken once and asked for her. She cursed herself for not being by his side.

His hand felt warmer. He looked less pale too. "Tony?"

No reaction. She leaned over and kissed him, stroked his stubbly cheek.

A moan escaped his lips. His eyes blinked open. "Lisa?"

"Yes. I'm here."

His fingers twitched, and she grabbed his hand again. He squeezed. "What happened?"

"I'm not sure, but you might have caught a bullet meant for me. Close to the heart."

He shut his eyes. "Shit."

"You said you wanted to help me."

A smile spread over his face. He peered at her through half-closed lids. "Glad to be of service."

Lisa kissed him. "I'm sorry."

He grunted. "A bit lame."

She smiled. "I love you." A tear rolled down her cheek. "Promise me you'll pull through."

Chapter Sixty-Three

Lisa woke in her own bed to the annoying sound of her alarm clock. She'd slept a full eight hours. The ghosts of her past hadn't dared to trouble her. She snuggled into her blanket and smiled. Then she remembered Tony, badly wounded because of her. Her heart sank. And there was still a murdering son of a bitch out there.

Why did she set the alarm so early? Oh, right. She needed to send the kids off to school. Lisa struggled out of bed. In the mirror she caught a glimpse of her greenish brown arm. Her bruises were fading.

She slipped into yesterday's clothes, dashed to the bakery, and hurried into the backyard. Her gaze swept up to the unoccupied lookout post on the roof. She should alert the kids that the danger wasn't over yet. After school, or they'd refuse to go.

Lisa set bread, butter and jam on the table and walked over to Luiz. He lay on his stomach, one arm twisted under him. She slipped out of her flip-flop and pushed the toes of her right foot into his side. He groaned and rolled onto his back. "What?" He opened his eyes. "No. Please?"

"Time for school. Rise and shine."

Breakfast turned out to be an unusually sullen event. Nobody seemed hungry. Tatu scowled, Rena pouted. Only Ubaldo grinned and couldn't sit still. "I like school."

Tatu elbowed him. "Course you would, Professor."

Lisa marched them over to the community school in the *favela*. Maria awaited them, hugged Lisa, and smiled at each of the kids. "I'm glad you want to learn something. Follow me." She took Rena by her hand and walked ahead.

Grumbling, Luiz trailed after them without a glance at Lisa.

* * * *

At one o'clock school ended and Luiz relaxed. The oldest in class, he felt like the stupidest. He'd last gone to school five or six years before when he was still living with his aunt. And he'd stuck with it for the major part of two years until the cops caught him breaking into a car and stealing whatever he could find.

Max didn't have a lawyer then. He was still a simple car thief. Now, Luiz was a simple car thief—and where would he end up? Of course, he knew that was exactly why Max wanted them to go to school and get proper jobs. Maybe he'd become a bus driver. If someone tried to rob the bus, he'd draw his gun. His stomach grumbled.

They ambled outside toward the main road. Tatu nudged him. "Hey, we should get one of those pocket calculators."

Luiz grinned. "Great idea."

"You should learn to do the dividing and subtracting yourself," Rena said.

Tatu shrugged. "What for, when a machine can do the job for us?"

Rena huffed and pulled Ubaldo away. "Let's go to the beach."

The boy slipped his arm around her waist. Sweet.

Then Luiz noticed a man staring at them. The suit looked familiar. Where had he seen him before?

Tatu slapped his back. "Let's take the bus to the *centro* and find those calculators."

Luiz looked at his friend then back to where Rena and Ubaldo had rounded a corner. No sign of the man.

"Right, let's go."

* * * *

Félix slipped into a side street before the boy might recognize him. Lisa's young friend had thwarted his plans twice already. He hurried around the next corner and spotted the girl and the boy ambling down the street. He slowed and followed at a distance, feeling for the bottle in his jacket. Good old chloroform.

When the kids reached the beach, Félix approached. "Hey, you're Lisa's friends, right?"

They turned. The girl gave him a calculating once over. "And who are you?"

"One of the neighbors. I'm sorry your friend got killed. That was horrible and I want you to know that I despise people who do such things." Félix wasn't even lying. He smiled. "Can I buy you an ice cream?"

They grinned. "Okay."

Félix pulled out his wallet. Her gaze fixed on his hands. He pulled the wallet wide open, revealing a wad of money. Enough bait. He gave the boy twenty *reais*. "Why don't you run and buy us three cones?"

He snatched the money and dashed away. Transfixed by the money, the girl made no move to follow.

"What's your name?"

"Rena."

He stowed his wallet. "I'm Félix. I sell perfume. Would you mind testing our latest creation? I'm collecting feedback from young ladies."

She raised an eye brow. "Perfume?"

He pulled out the flask and a handkerchief and poured some of the chloroform on it. "Smell this."

She stepped within his reach. Her nose wrinkled. He grabbed her by the neck and pressed the cloth over her mouth and nose.

"Hey, leave Rena alone!" the boy cried.

* * * *

Luiz and Tatu slouched on a low stone wall, playing with the cheap calculators they'd stolen at a department store.

"School isn't that bad, actually," Tatu said.

"Yeah, but I won't tell Lisa that." Luiz was still mad at her, confused about who she'd become. He sighed and looked around at the business suits carrying briefcases and lattes. Where were the times when he kept watch all night and lives depended on him, when nobody cared if he had anything to eat or got enough sleep? The glorious days seemed to be over.

"Let's go see Max," Tatu said, pocketing his new toy.

Luiz smiled. "Great idea." Maybe they'd get some action in the *favela*. They took a bus to Leme and walked the rest of the way, joking about the teacher and the other kids who knew so much more school stuff when his cellphone rang. What could Lisa want?

"Hello?"

"Luiz, is Rena with you?"

"No, she went to the beach with Ubaldo? Why?"

"Oh, nothing, just wanted to ask her something."

That was strange. "Really?"

"Yeah, don't worry, Luiz." Her voice sounded flat. Why did she want to talk to Rena? He'd ask her later.

Luiz looked up at Max's guys on the rooftops watching out, protecting the border against police and rival gangs. They didn't talk; their eyes scanned their surroundings continuously. Luiz turned his head. Three squad cars were parked on the street. Nothing unusual. The same stalemate as always. Luiz and Tatu jumped up the stairs two at a time when a girl stepped from a doorway. Luiz bumped into her. She yelped and dropped a bag of groceries. Luiz cringed as he watched oranges bounce down the hill. The girl gave him a miserable look.

"Sorry." He dashed down the steps and stopped as many as possible. Squatting, he picked up her purchases while she did the same. His cheeks burned with embarrassment. When she held out the bag, he dropped his catch into it.

"Hey, you're going to school?" She gazed at his T-shirt with the school logo.

"Yeah, why not?"

"I thought you're with the drug gang."

"No, I'm not."

Grinning, Tatu nudged him. "I'll go ahead, okay?"

"Sure." He watched his friend hop up the stairs, then focused on the pretty girl again.

"I've seen you around," she said.

He gazed into her sparkling brown eyes. "I'm Luiz."

"Pamela."

"Pretty name."

"Thanks."

"You're pretty, too."

She picked up a coconut.

"You live here?" he asked.

"Up the hill a bit."

"Want me to help you carry the bags? In case another fool comes running?"

She smiled. "That would be nice."

Chapter Sixty-Four

Max listened to his brother's excited babbling about school. Tatu might lead a different life from now on. Maybe even a long life. For a moment he imagined Tatu at the age of seventy with a bunch of grandchildren around him, telling stories about their granduncle Max. He smiled.

Fireworks cracked. The shooting started seconds later. A police raid. "Costa Branca. Get the hell out of here, Tatu."

"I can shoot. I'm staying with you."

"Stay close," Max ordered. If he sent Tatu into the streets now, he might catch a stray bullet or take it up with the police alone. He cursed himself for teaching him to shoot, grabbed his assault rifle, and ran up the inside stairs to the roof, Tatu right behind him. Two of his guards on opposite sides of the roof knelt behind the short wall and scanned the area.

"Military police?" Max barked.

"Yeah, the bastards are moving in," one guard yelled.

"BOPE troops are coming down the hill," the other yelled and opened fire.

"Fuck! Costa Branca called for the skulls. These guys shoot to kill. Don't pull any punches." Over the walkie-talkie Max checked in with the other posts and gave orders to use the full arsenal—mortars, machine guns, whatever it took.

He turned to the guards. "They've got tanks, two *caveirãos* at the bottom of the hill. You stay. We'll try to reach post two and get an overview. Watch out for helicopters." Max hopped onto the neighboring roof and made his way uphill climbing and jumping from roof to roof, Tatu just one leap behind. Max's walkie-talkie crackled. "What?"

"They've got snipers in the *favela*, plucking our soldiers."

"Shit. Take them out."

They stopped on top of a building cascading down the hill in layers and took up positions on opposite sides. This was the real thing. A full-fledged fucking war with the police. How many people were dead or injured already? And all that for Nassar, the cockroach. Costa Branca had lost his fucking mind.

Max spotted a police troop sneaking up the lane below. He counted eight cops. Further up, his men headed down a parallel alley. He gave them the position of the attackers and watched the ambush unfold.

Single gunshots behind. He swung around. Tatu was shooting. Max darted across the roof and squatted beside him. He couldn't see anyone.

Tatu whispered, "I saw Capone with two cops, one of them an officer."

"Capone? The fucking rat. Maybe Costa Branca is leading the raid himself. Wouldn't surprise me. Stubborn *filho da puta*. Watch out, now they know where we are."

The staccato bark of automatic fire sent Max running back to his position to see if any of his own men lay among the scattered bodies. He spotted Tito, a new boy no older than Tatu. Then he heard the chopper's rotor blades. He grabbed the walkie-talkie. "Grenade launchers in place?"

"Yo. Let'em come."

The roar grew loader and drowned out the gunfire. Max scanned the sky. The black helicopter flew low. Within reach of their grenades. Yes! A hit. Smoke trailed behind the descending chopper.

"Hey Max."

Max froze. He knew the voice. He forced himself to turn. Capone had wrapped one arm around Tatu's neck, pointing a gun at his head, using him as a human shield. Max's worst ever fucking nightmare.

"Drop your toy." Capone ordered.

Max stared into the man's eyes and saw determination.

Capone sneered. "You know I'll kill him. Never liked the little cunt."

Max bent and laid the assault rifle down. He closed his eyes. Capone would shoot them both unless he killed him first. He straightened and stared at the traitor.

"I've been looking forward to this moment. I wanted to see your face before I kill you. And then I'll kill your little brother. Too bad I can't do it the other way round."

Max's heart pounded in his throat. He had one chance.

Capone's gun hand moved, the muzzle turning toward him. Tatu screamed, but the arm tightened around his throat. Tatu clutched Capone's gun hand.

Now or never. Max drew his pistol, dropped to one knee, aimed, and fired. Holding his breath he stared at Tatu's blood-spattered face. The boy's eyes widened. He looked at the body slumped behind him. Max roared. He'd missed his little brother.

"You did it!" Tatu cried. "You shot the bastard."

"Drop the gun!" barked a deep voice.

Merda. Max swung around.

Shots exploded. A kick against his chest. Max fell back. Searing pain cut through his body. Someone screamed his name. Tatu? Don't shoot him. Blue sky above. He waited for a second salvo that didn't come. Max called Tatu's name, but only coughed up warm blood.

Fingers grabbed his hand.

"Max," Tatu cried. The boy leaned over him. Tears in his eyes. "Don't die, Max. Don't!"

He saw the baby among the shrubs again, his crazy mother at the window. "I…" He coughed up more blood. A shadow moved across. Costa Branca. No, don't kill Tatu. He tried to shake his head. Cold eyes stared at him before the face blurred.

Max squeezed the small fingers in his hand.

Chapter Sixty-Five

Lisa walked along Ipanema beach, wearing the short red skirt and cowboy boots, the same outfit as on the day she killed Cortez. Just like Félix had requested when he called her. She could only think of one reason how he knew what she'd been wearing then. He'd been watching her. A shiver ran through her. She pulled the light jacket that concealed her Firestar tighter around her.

Muscular men played volleyball. Teenagers flirted. Kids kicked a soccer ball. *Cariocas* chatted up tourists. Life in Rio could be beautiful.

She reached Posto 7 an hour early and searched for the Alexis Bar. She didn't expect him to bring Rena to such a public place. And where was Ubaldo?

Fear clutched her heart. Nausea wrenched her stomach. Lisa had to pull herself together and check out the bar. When she'd demanded to talk to Rena, he'd snorted and told her she was out. Since then her imagination tortured Lisa. Tortured her enough to make a call to the police and ask for the *capitão*. But the man was personally leading a raid against a drug gang and she couldn't trust anyone else.

Lisa headed toward the busy street lined with bars, shops, and *churrascarias*. She spotted the neon sign of the Alexis and entered. At the bar she ordered a gin and tonic and took it to a corner table. After a few sips, she went to check out the restrooms. No back entrance and no window to climb through. He'd take her somewhere else for sure. Abandoning her drink, she left the bar, crossed the street, and sat on the steps down to the beach.

No way could she prepare for their encounter. She had no clue what to expect. Someone sat down next to her. "Good disguise." He rested his hand on her naked thigh.

Lisa stared into gray-green eyes. "Where's Rena?"

He stood and grabbed her arm. "Let's go for a walk. I wonder how often I actually saw but didn't recognize you."

She put up no resistance. "What do you want?"

He looked straight ahead. "The big showdown, Lisa. Just the two of us."

She stopped walking. "Sure, except you've got a hostage."

He frowned at her. "I'll set her free if you come with me."

"How do I know you won't bring in an army again?"

He sneered. "Because I want to have you to myself."

"What if I shoot you right here?"

"That's not how it works, Lisa. I'll fuck you and then I'll kill you. And maybe I'll fuck you again. Of course, you'll try to kill me first."

Lisa ignored the tremble running through her body. "You bet. And where would we have this ultimate sex?"

"In a cozy place. Very inconspicuous." He grinned.

"Let Rena go first."

Félix laughed. "And lose my only bargaining chip? Nice try, Lisa."

"Now?" she asked.

"Why not?"

Of course, it was a trap. Her mind raced. Convinced that he really wanted her alone, she decided she might not get a better chance. "Where's the boy?"

"I left him. And the girl's fine. Still. You don't want to frustrate me, though. I might take it out on her. Wouldn't be the first time someone else had to take your place."

Lisa's stomach cramped. Félix led her to his Mazda. The same registration number. What an idiot she'd been to think she could put it all behind her. "So it was you at São Bento? How long have you been watching me?"

"A while."

"How flattering."

"And you kept ignoring me. Not very flattering. I even visited your quaint little bookstore when I lost your trace. Drove me nuts. After I'd let you go and all."

"I'm so sorry," she said, throwing all the sarcasm she could muster into the few words.

She climbed into the passenger seat and smelled the grassy aroma of marijuana. He eased the car into the traffic and followed the arterial road to Barra da Tijuca at the outskirts of Rio.

Félix left the main road and headed up a narrow street into the mountains. "I've been waiting for this moment for a long time."

A long time? Had she met him before her kidnapping? "How long?"

"Weeks."

Weeks? Before they burned Gordinho? She needed more clues. "Why me?"

He cackled. "Your gringo lover told me about your gun. You made quite an impression on him. And me too."

"You know Tony?" Her mind spun. This didn't make sense.

"Just doing business with him."

Realization hit her. The twisted security adviser Tony had mentioned. *Merda!* He simply needed to follow Tony to find her. She swallowed. Tears burned in her eyes. She blinked. "Did you shoot him?"

He smirked. "Maybe. I'm a jealous man."

Get a grip, Lisa. No crying in front of his bastard. "So, it's my gun that fascinates you?" She drew her Firestar from the belt holster on her denim skirt.

He smiled. "Not only the gun."

She shoved the pistol between his legs. "Does that turn you on?"

His fingers clutched the stick shift, knuckles turning white. He could easily push her hand away, but didn't. She ran the muzzle of the gun up along his zipper, his stomach, his chest, and pointed it to his head, like he'd done with her. "I should shoot you right now."

"You'll never find the girl."

"Maybe you've already killed her."

"No, I thought I'd let her watch." He didn't smile. His face looked waxen, nothing moved. He didn't even blink. His expression chilled her more than his words. She took down the gun and held it in her lap. Silence spread, grew dense between them. If she understood what drove him, she'd be able to anticipate his moves and counteract them.

He turned onto a dirt road. "We are getting close."

If she shot him now, could she find Rena on her own? Wait a little longer. A wooden shed appeared between the trees. She lifted the gun. He slammed his elbow into her face. Lisa screamed with pain. He wrenched the gun out of her grip. Her nose throbbed. Blood streamed down her mouth, throat, and chest. She fought to clear her mind. He killed the engine. "Get out."

Chapter Sixty-Six

Luiz crouched in a dark corner in a dead-end lane, waiting for the shoot-out to end. He listened to the rapid automatic fire and the sharper explosions from hand-guns. Hell broke loose when they'd reached Pamela's house. She'd tried to make him stay, but he'd needed to find Tatu. Now he knew it had been a stupid idea. He'd never seen so many cops at one go ever before.

When the gunfire ceased, Luiz waited a while longer. The occasional single shot echoed through the *favela*. Luiz stood up and peered down the short lane. No other people around. He sneaked to the corner. First he glanced uphill, where Tatu must be. All was quiet. But he didn't dare go to Max's headquarters. The police might have overrun the gang.

Luiz scanned the stairs downhill. Two dead soldiers sprawled next to the body of a cop. Luiz walked toward them. At times like these only losers had a reason to run. The first victim's chest gaped with a gunshot wound. The boy looked younger than him. Blood pooled around the corpse.

Luiz picked up a gun from the ground and shoved it in the back of his shorts. He stopped at each crossing, looked up and down the alleys and only continued on his way when he didn't see anyone moving. He counted eight more corpses, three of them in police uniform and one an older woman. He imagined there were a lot more bodies scattered around Max's *boca*.

Luiz reached the foot of the hill. In the road, the police had assembled and medics tended to their wounds. He crossed the street and walked away from the cops. His eyes scanned the hill crowded with houses that seemed to mushroom out of each other. He could just make out the one corner of Max's roof terrace where a guard usually stood. He wasn't there now. Luiz didn't want to leave. He waited for a sign of life from Tatu or Max. Deep in thought, he jumped when a large hand fell on his right shoulder.

"Hey, kid, what are you up to?"

Luiz half-turned and stared at a man in a gray uniform. Two squashed bullets stuck in his vest. The cop stepped back. His right hand rested on the gun in his belt holster. Luiz's heart skipped a beat. The pistol he'd picked up burned against his skin. Why had he taken the stupid thing? The cop still hadn't drawn his pistol. Maybe he hadn't seen the outline of the weapon under his T-shirt? "I can't go home yet," Luiz replied, his voice trembling.

"You live up there?"

No way could the cop know he was armed. "Yes, with my mother and grandma." Surprised by how easily lies slipped from his mouth, he grew bolder. "Did you get the gang?"

"Sure did. Max won't kill any more cops."

Luiz wanted to hit the man, draw the gun, and shoot him. He wanted to yell at him that Nassar was a killer himself. Fighting back the tears, he looked into the cop's grinning face. "Someone else will take over."

An angry frown crossed the man's forehead. "What the..."

"Hey, da Silva," a high-ranking officer shouted. "Get your ass over here and help with the injured civilians."

The cop spun around and marched back. Luiz studied the commander. Was that Costa Branca? The man Max had refused to kill? Their eyes met. Luiz quickly averted his gaze and walked away.

Trying to look casual, he strolled along the border street. Did they arrest or kill Max? What about Tatu? Sick with worry, he decided to find out. He crossed the street and carefully moved up the stairs and alleys toward Max's headquarters. He didn't see a living soul out on the small lanes, only a few dead bodies, and timid but curious faces behind windows. He turned into the alley to Max's *boca* and spotted BOPE officers standing around outside. He jumped back.

The unreal sound of a whistle caught his attention. Mussolini looked down at him from a roof and waved. Luiz climbed up and ran after him. When he caught up, Mussolini stopped and pointed. "He's in Fernando's house."

Luiz saw the tiny shack squeezed between two bigger houses. "Is Max okay?"

Mussolini shook his head and pressed his lips together. Tatu? Luiz couldn't ask. He ran and burst through the door.

Several figures raised their guns, but Luiz didn't care. Max lay on the table, motionless. Tatu sat by his side crying. Tears sprang to Luiz's eyes. He turned away, unable to accept what he'd known already.

Chapter Sixty-Seven

Lisa heaved herself out of the low car. The damp forest air chilled her. Félix slammed his door shut and walked around the car, her Firestar in his right hand. She thought of the knife in her boot, but she'd never get it out fast enough. He shoved her toward the shed. "Don't you want to see your little friend?" He handed her a key.

With trembling fingers, Lisa fumbled with the lock then pushed the door open. Darkness enveloped her. She couldn't see Rena, only the outline of a table and chair. She stepped over the threshold. Slowly her eyes adjusted to the gloom. To her right, Rena sat on a cot with her legs tied, her hands behind her back, a rag in her mouth, her left eye swollen. Lisa sprinted across the room, dropped to her knees and worked on the rope around Rena's wrists. "It's okay. I'll get you out of here."

"Don't you touch her."

Rena's eyes sparkled with tears. Maybe Lisa had loosened her bonds enough. She sat back on her haunches and stared at Félix over her shoulder. He just stood there, gun pointing to the ground. How would he play this? Careful not to hurt her broken nose, she wiped her mouth with the back of her hand, leaving a trail of blood on it. Perhaps he hadn't made up his mind yet. Lisa winked at Rena before she rose.

She walked up to him. One corner of his mouth pulled into a crooked smile. "Take off the jacket."

She shrugged out of it.

"Now the top."

Lisa pulled the tank top over her head, wiped her face and neck, and flung it away. "Cuts heal." She turned her back on him. "You can't break me."

Félix ran the muzzle of her Firestar along the scars on her back. Her skin crawled. Unable to bear it a moment longer, she swung around to face him. He brought up the gun and touched it to her lips. Still on safety. He pushed the barrel against her teeth. She opened her mouth, tasted oil and metal.

She knew he wanted to see fear, but death had never scared her, only life. With a flick of his thumb he might push down the safety catch and blow the back of her head off. No quicker way to die. But there was Rena.

His lips tightened. His left hand curled around her neck almost like a gentle caress. Just what she'd been waiting for. She slipped her hand under his jacket, but found no holster. Damn!

He laughed. "Nice try." He pushed her away and ejected the magazine from the Firestar. "Let's see if there's a bullet in the chamber." He aimed at Rena, his right arm stretched out. Lisa's heart skipped a beat. If she jumped him, he'd still be faster. His sneering face turned to her, while he held his arm in a steady line pointing at Rena.

"What do you think, Lisa? Is your little friend going to die?"

"You promised you'd let her go."

"And you trusted me?" He pulled the trigger.

Lisa screamed. She didn't even hear the hollow click. Breathing hard, she reined in her fear and rage.

Félix tossed the useless gun at Lisa and put the magazine in the pocket of his pants. "Pick it up."

Lisa glanced at Rena. The girl wriggled, trying to free her hands.

"Now," Félix barked.

Lisa squatted, one hand reaching for the gun, the other for the knife in her boot.

He stepped closer. "When I'm done with you, Rena will dig your grave. I think I'll keep her around until she's developed a bit more. A year or two."

The bastard wanted to provoke her, get her to attack. Why not do him the favor? Lisa jumped up, lashing out with the knife. He kicked her hand and sent the blade flying. He lunged at her. His weight hit her full force, knocking her over. His right hand closed around her throat. She tried to pry his fingers away.

"Oh, Lisa. Maybe I expected too much of you. You're turning into a disappointment."

Right, it was the stupidest thing she could do. Forcing herself to let go of the hand strangling her, she pressed her thumbs into his eyes until he released his grip and pushed back, crying out.

Lisa punched him on the chin, tried to push him off her, but he caught her arms and pinned her. She whispered, "Stalemate."

Félix's face contorted with anger. He released one of her arms but she saw the fist too late. For a moment all she felt was pain, with her broken nose at the center. The agony ebbed. Her eyes burned with tears as she looked at his blurred face.

He sat on her stomach and ripped her bra at the middle. Lisa lashed out, but he caught her arm. She hit him with her left. Félix laughed, gripped her other wrist, and pulled her arms down, lowering himself on her, forcing her legs apart. His erection pressed against her. No, not again.

"It's a shame I've got to kill you, Lisa. But that's the beauty of it. You'll die in my loving arms." He snorted.

Lisa believed him. Captain Hook's arms clutched her. She sobbed.

Félix let go of her left hand and stroked her hair out of her face. "Poor little girl."

She pressed her palm against his nose and pushed up. He grunted, bent back, whacked her hand away, and struck several blows at her face. Her head seemed to explode.

He rolled her over onto her stomach. She was too numb to resist. He pushed up her skirt. No! She bucked. He grabbed her neck and crushed her face into the wood floor. His full weight on top of her now, she couldn't move, but felt his hand wrestle with the fly of his pants. Despair gripped her.

"You're mine, Lisa, and you know it." He placed the Firestar in her right hand then shoved the magazine back in and flipped the safety catch. The little red dot told her it was ready to kill. Only she couldn't point the barrel at him.

He snickered. "You're armed and dangerous, Lisa, but you can't keep me from doing whatever I want."

Fool. She aimed the gun at her own face. She'd never be his.

Chapter Sixty-Eight

Luiz and Tatu sat in the gloomy boca with Max's body. It felt wrong to switch on the light. But most of all Luiz didn't want to see Max's lifeless face too clearly. He knew Max was dead, but he still couldn't accept the fact. He'd watched Gordinho burn. These things happened to street kids. But Max had always seemed invincible, immortal, the one person they could always rely on when things got bad.

Tatu broke the silence. "It's all my fault."

His best friend's self-blame brought Luiz close to tears again. "Don't…"

"It's true. I shouldn't have come with him. Shouldn't have let Capone catch me."

"At least you're still alive."

Tatu sniffed. "I don't know why Costa Branca didn't shoot me too. I yelled at him, pounded my fists into his chest, and told him Max should have killed him. He fought me off but didn't even hit me once."

Luiz couldn't help himself. More tears rolled down his cheeks. "Max said he was a good guy."

The door flew open and banged against the wall. Mussolini marched in, followed by two soldiers. "We need to bury him and get back to business. They took out half the gang, but that won't stop us."

One of the men took Max's legs, the other his arms. Silent tears ran down Tatu's face. Luiz wiped his eyes. He couldn't cry anymore. He looked at Mussolini. "You the new boss?"

"We'll see. But I promise you I'll fucking kill Costa Branca."

Átila placed his big hand on Tatu's shoulder and held out a wad of money in the other. "Max gave me this for you."

Mussolini added, "Of course you can have a job with us any time. Both of you. We're a bit short on soldiers right now."

Tatu looked at Átila, his tears drying up. "I don't want the money."

"Don't be stupid," Max's friend barked. "You'll need it."

Tatu took the roll and thumbed through it. "Two thousand *reais*? That's what his life is worth?" Tatu threw the money onto the table. "I don't want your blood money." He stormed out of the house.

Luiz grabbed the wad of bills. Átila noded. They'd need it eventually. A final gift from Max. He dashed after his friend. Tatu ran out of steam quickly. Luiz caught up with him and wrapped his arm around Tatu's shoulders.

They walked down the hill in silence. Luiz knew no words to console his friend. Everything had changed. He could only imagine how lonely Tatu felt. But they still had the kids, and Lisa. "Let's go home."

Tatu nodded without looking up. "Yeah."

A police car burned at the border street. Gunshots still rang out every so often. The streets appeared to stretch further with every step they took. The police still patrolled close to the *favela*. When they finally reached the bookstore, Ubaldo jumped from the doorway. "Have you seen Rena?"

"No, wasn't she with you?" Luiz asked, remembering Lisa's odd call.

"A man took her. The bastard hit me with a small metal club."

Tatu screamed all his rage and hurt at the world. Luiz grew cold. No. Not Rena.

Tears ran down Ubaldo's face. "I couldn't do anything."

Luiz had no strength left to tell him it wasn't his fault. He sank down on the sidewalk and rested his back against the wall. "Where's Lisa?"

"I don't know," Ubaldo sobbed.

* * * *

Lisa looked into the muzzle of her gun, remembering what she'd told Tony up on Cristo Redentor. She carried the gun to either save her life or end it. She closed her eyes. Félix couldn't hurt her. She gently squeezed the trigger.

"No," Rena yelled. Oh God, the girl! She couldn't abandon her.

Félix slammed his fist down on Lisa's hand and pried the gun out of her fingers. "Bitch. You can't do that."

Lisa's heart pounded. If Rena wasn't gagged anymore...

A bare foot appeared at the edge of her vision. A shattering noise. Pieces of wood dropped beside her. Félix grunted. Lisa pushed herself up and threw him off her. Rena held the back of the smashed chair in her hands. Félix, down on all fours, pulled himself up to his knees. Lisa grabbed a chair leg, hit him across the face, then snatched the gun he'd dropped.

Adrenaline flushed out the last of her fear and despair. "You shouldn't have tried that, asshole."

He stared at her incredulously then the crooked smile returned. His lips moved.

Lisa shot him in the groin. Shock rippled across his face. Then he collapsed onto his stomach. She holstered the gun. His screams sounded far away.

Rena took her hand. She was trembling. Lisa hugged her and held her tight. "You saved us both." The girl sobbed against her bare chest. Lisa stroked her hair. "It's over, Rena. He can't hurt you anymore."

After a while her shaking stopped. Lisa dropped down on one knee and smiled up at her. "As long as we're together, nothing bad can happen."

Rena gazed at her through teary eyes. "What?"

"That's what we told each other when we slept on the streets, scared of what could happen at night."

Rena slung her arms around Lisa's neck and hugged her tight. "Right."

"Let's go, kiddo." Lisa rose and draped an arm over her shoulders.

"What about him?" Rena tilted her head toward Félix. He lay curled up, bleeding like the pig he was, and sobbing. It wouldn't take long for him to bleed to death. Anyone could have killed him out here and stolen his car. "We'll leave him to die alone. Gives him time to think and maybe regret. Who knows?" Lisa found her knife near the door and slipped it into her boot. She pulled on her bloody tank top and slipped into her jacket. Then she took Rena's hand. "Let's get out of here."

Outside, she took a deep breath. Last rays of the sun filtered through the trees, illuminating patches of green. A blue sparkle caught her eye. Lisa stepped closer. A high-heeled blue shoe lay in the grass. She walked further into the woods, Rena following close behind her. A mound of overturned earth between trees, another, smaller heap already overgrown with plants. Her gaze wandered to a depression. The grave of a murdered and decayed body?

Lisa fought back her nausea and pulled Rena toward the car. The keys stuck in the ignition. She backed away from the shed and gunned the engine.

* * * *

Night had fallen when they reached the used car dealer where she and Luiz had hidden the stolen Mercedes. Lisa threw the keys at Renato. The man whistled as his eyes caressed the sports car. "How much do you want for it?"

"Just make sure it'll never be found."

He nodded and smiled. "No problem."

Lisa crossed the street with Rena in tow and walked up to a public phone. Searching through the crumpled phone book, she found the number of *O Globo*. Better to call a newspaper than the police, who might want to cover everything up. A tired male voice piped up.

Lisa cleared her throat. "I shot a man who tried to rape and kill me. His body is in a shed in the Tijuca Forest. If you look around, you'll find the graves of his previous victims."

The newspaper man tried to lure more information out of her, but Lisa only described the route and hung up.

Rena looked at her with big fearful eyes. "Why did you tell them?"

"So the parents will know what happened to their daughters."

Rena nodded slowly. "The police won't come and get you?"

"I don't know, honey. Let's go home."

* * * *

Luiz sat between Tatu and Ubaldo, leaning against the shop window of the bookstore. Nobody bothered them. Some people darted them a fleeting glance, others just stared ahead. Was this all they had now? The streets of Rio and people ignoring or loathing them? He swallowed and closed his eyes. His world was crumbling. Nothing to hold on to.

Tatu rested his head on Luiz's shoulder. "What are we going to do?"

"We might as well die too."

"I don't want to die," Ubaldo whispered.

Cars and feet passed. Voices and engines blurred into a monotonous drone. Close by, a door slammed.

"Rena!" Tatu cried.

Luiz's eyes flung open. A cab. A hallucination? Lisa and Rena walked toward them. Tatu jumped up and hugged Rena. Luiz stared into Lisa's bruised and bloody face. Maybe they *were* real. He couldn't move.

Lisa held out her hand to him. He grasped it, and she pulled him to his feet.

"Everything's fine, Luiz. It's over."

He shook his head. "Max is dead."

Lisa swayed, her lips moving, but no words came. For seconds she stood motionless. Then she placed her hand on his shoulder and slowly drew him into her arms. The warmth of her body enveloped him, the metallic smell of blood a reminder of what she'd done for them.

Epilogue

"Where are we going?" Lisa asked.

Tony grinned. "São Conrado."

She frowned. "Okay."

"I like obedient women."

Lisa couldn't help laughing. She turned right and headed toward São Conrado, wondering what he was up to. Tony bent forward to scan the mountain range or sky. Then it hit her. "You're raving mad if you think—"

"What?" He gave her an innocent look.

"You think I'll value my life more after I've jumped off a cliff?"

Tony laughed. "No, I want you to feel pure euphoria."

"You've done this before?"

He smiled. "Every time you told me to go away."

"You're insane."

"When you're up there in the sky, it's like, I don't know. Nothing else exists."

"I don't believe you."

"You'll see."

When they reached the spot where adrenaline junkies ran downhill and soared out over the cliff, her heart beat faster.

Tony took her hand. "Nervous?"

She attempted a smile. "A little."

"You'll love it. It's better than..."

"What?"

"Nothing."

"C'mon, better than?"

He sighed. "Almost said sex, but I guess for you that's easy to top."

Shocked and amused at the same time, Lisa swallowed. Maybe someday. Climbing out of the van, her knees turned to jelly as she gazed down the slope.

He took her arm and pulled her along. "Let's go."

A pretty *mulatta* in coveralls waved and marched toward them. "Hey, Tony, you're back for more?" Lisa felt a sting of jealousy and chided herself for it.

"*Olá* Sal. You look great. This is Lisa."

She smiled at him then glanced at Lisa. "Hi, I'm Salete. You want to jump, too?"

"She'll jump with me. Can you get us a tandem wing?"

Her face locked up. "You know you need a license for that."

Lisa watched him throw a puppy-dog look at her. "You know I can do it."

Salete smiled reluctantly. "All right."

"Come on, let's get ready." He dragged Lisa toward the starting point where Salete and a young man spread out the wing for them. With the easy moves of an expert, Tony slipped into the harness then pulled her close, pushed a helmet over her head and strapped her in. "Hey, where's your gun?"

She smiled. "I don't need a crutch anymore."

"Wow. Now I feel scared. Have you learned to kill with a bat of your eyelids?"

She laughed. "Maybe."

He grinned. "You better do the bottom straps yourself."

Lisa pulled them up between her legs. "You really know how to do this?" Fear crawled up on her. Simple fear of falling and dying. Nothing complicated like being abducted, tortured, raped, and killed. Fear that she'd never start living. She stared at the runway while Tony worked on the clips and ropes. "I've been doing this for ten years. I just don't have an international license for tandem flights."

Lisa took a deep breath.

"Ready?" he asked.

"No."

"Okay, let's do it."

Lisa twisted her neck to gaze into his eyes. He smiled. "Trust me."

She nodded.

"Go."

Lisa ran as fast as she could, trying to stay in sync with Tony, down the wooden deck toward the cliff, her heart beating fast, adrenaline coursing through her body. This was crazy. She'd balk, she knew it.

"Faster," Tony yelled.

"Fuck," she screamed as she kicked air. They sank. Her stomach contracted. Behind her Tony laughed.

"Get us down!"

Tony maneuvered the wing in a circle. Lisa stared at the world below. The rain forest looked like a soft cushion, but she knew it wasn't. Nothing below her feet but a miniature world. The wind picked them up and roared in her ears.

Lisa laughed. "Take me to Neverland, Peter Pan."

"What?"

She shook her head. Tony steered them out over the sea. An up-current rose from the ocean carrying them higher and higher. Lisa relaxed into the new element. Below, the vast ocean reached to the horizon. To her right, the beaches of Rio arched, lined by dwarfed high-rises. The mountains were mere bumps in the landscape. She had never felt so free. Lisa laughed, spread her arms out wide, and felt Tony's hold around her waist. He shouted, but the wind whisked his words away.

Nothing mattered. She screamed with joy. Definitely better than sex. Pleasure turned to fear again as they approached the landing spot on the beach. Tony slowed the wing, but it still seemed too fast.

"Keep running when we touch ground," Tony yelled against the wind.

"We're going to die," Lisa screamed. She thought she could hear his throaty laugh. The sandy ground came closer. They slowed.

"Now," Tony shouted.

Her feet touched the ground. She ran, stumbled, fell. Tony landed on top of her. She giggled and got sand in her mouth. "Would you mind getting off me?"

"I can't. I'm tied to you."

"What a lame excuse."

"All right, pardon me then." He reached under her and fumbled with the straps.

"I have the feeling you're enjoying this more than necessary. Let me help you." She pushed herself up. Tony held her tight and rolled onto his back. She lay on top of him, feeling like an overturned tortoise. "You did that on purpose."

"Much easier that way." He freed her from the harness.

With a few seconds delay she rolled off him and knelt beside his spread-eagled form. "That was fun."

He pulled her toward him and kissed her, their helmets clanking against each other. She lowered herself onto him, easing into the kiss. His left hand reached under her T-shirt. As he touched her skin, heat spread through her body. She wanted him. And *not* to prove something. Time to start living. Goodbye, Tinker Bell.

About the Author

Edith Parzefall studied literature and linguistics in Germany and the United States. She worked as a technical writer, documentation manager, and engineer tamer. Now a full-time writer, she strives to combine her two passions: writing and traveling.

Edith supports a street kids project in Recife, Brazil. When she visited Grupo Ruas e Praças, she took part in a music and crafts workshop with the children. During her stay in Rio de Janeiro, the idea for *Strays of Rio* sparked.

MuseItUp Publishing
Where Muse authors entertain readers!
https://museituppublishing.com
Visit our website for more books for your reading pleasure.

Meet our authors and staff,
have a chance to win a FREE ebook,
and get special discounts on upcoming releases
by joining our Readers Club:
http://ca.groups.yahoo.com/group/MusePub_Readers/

You can also find us on Facebook:
http://www.facebook.com/MuseItUp
and on Twitter:
http://twitter.com/MusePublishing

CPSIA information can be obtained at www.ICGtesting.com
Printed in the USA
BVOW081436060513

320010BV00001B/236/P